Raffles
of the
M.C.C.

by the same author
RAFFLES OF THE ALBANY

Raffles of the M.C.C.

by Barry Perowne

ST. MARTIN'S PRESS / NEW YORK

Library of Congress Cataloging in Publication Data

Perowne, Barry.
  Raffles of the M. C. C.

  I. Title.
PZ3.P426Rafp   1979   [PR6031.E54]   823'.9'12   78-3999
ISBN 0-312-66222-X

Grateful acknowledgment is made to the following magazines for permission
to reprint the stories in this volume:

Ellery Queen's Mystery Magazine for: "Lord's and the Dangerous Game"
(originally titled "Raffles and the Dangerous Game"); "Madame Blavatsky's
Teacups" (originally titled "Raffles and the Shere Khan Pouch"); "The
Graves of Academe" (originally titled "Raffles and the Death Date"); "The
Ordeal of Dinah Raffles" (originally titled "Raffles on the Riviera"); "A
Venus at Lord's" (originally titled "Raffles and the Venus Touch").

Saint Magazine for: "The Hermit of Fleet Street" (originally titled "Raffles and the Weekend Banker"); "Bevercombe's Benefit Match" (originally
titled "Raffles and the Husbands' Boat"); "The Roskelly Injunction" (originally titled "Raffles and the Sherry Bowl Derby"); "The Tongues of Deceit"
(originally titled "Raffles and Shipmate Sadie"); "'Detectives Operate in
This Store'" (originally titled "Raffles and the Seaside Hotel"); "Black
Mask and the Firefly" (originally titled "Raffles and the Firefly").

To
Eleanor Sullivan
In memory of Raffles's creator, E. W. Hornung, cricketer

CONTENTS

(From the Private Documents, Recently Found, of
Raffles's Confederate, Manders)

Raffles
of the
M.C.C.

1

LORD'S AND THE DANGEROUS GAME

All of a sudden, in the fog that blanketed London one midwinter evening, the tall figure of a policeman loomed up at a street corner and, waving a red lantern, brought a hansom jingling to a standstill.

"Sorry, gentlemen," he told the passengers, who happened to be A. J. Raffles and myself, Bunny Manders, "this street is closed."

I had spent the past couple of hours watching Raffles win his match in a tennis tournament in progress at Lord's Cricket Ground, where the building which houses the court for the gentlemanly game of "real" tennis, or *jeu-de-paume,* is for a spectator about the chilliest place in town.

So, being anxious to thaw myself out with a rum toddy or two at my flat, where Raffles would drop me off on the way to his own chambers in The Albany, I remonstrated with the bobby.

"But look here," I said to him, "this is Mount Street. I live in this street."

"Well, sir," he replied, "there's been a gas explosion in a house along there on the left."

"You describe, more or less," I said, startled, "the area where *I* live! Raffles, if you'll excuse me—"

Leaving him to pay off the cabbie, I sprang out of the hansom and, breaking into a run along Mount Street, saw above the roof of some house ahead there a dull red glow pulsating in the fog.

The glow faded out as I arrived upon the scene, but the gabled roof from which clouds of smoke and steam were now billowing up was that of the very house in which I had my domicile.

1

I stopped dead, incredulous.

The windows of the flat on the top floor, the fourth, and of my own flat on the third floor, were shattered, and a brass-helmeted, thigh-booted fireman, dragging a hose, was in the act of clambering from a ladder into my living-room.

"Mr. Manders!" a voice called to me.

I looked round. A tanker tumbril and two scarlet fire-engines with fine great Percheron horses in the shafts blocked the street. The lamps of the vehicles, and the lanterns of fire-men moving around busily, mitigated the fog, and I saw that the man who had called to me was Hobday, the hall porter of the house. He was talking to three of the residents.

"Whoever would have thought it, sir?" said Hobday, as I walked over to him. "A gas explosion in *Mount* Street! In the top flat, it was—Major Torrington's, just above yours, Mr. Manders. The Major was out at the time—still is."

"Luckily for him," said Charles Chastayne, who occupied the other flat on my floor.

A typical man-about-town, who played cards in the best card clubs and probably, I suspected, derived his income from it, he was in evening dress, his cape and silk hat blotched with some sort of white stuff.

"I'd only just come in, Manders," he told me, "when the big bang shook the whole house."

"Anyone hurt?" asked Raffles, who had joined us.

"No, sir," said Hobday. "I had my hands full getting Lady Davencourt and her marmosets out of her first-floor flat. Very disturbed, the creatures were, jumping around and hissing, their fur all bristly. But I bundled them into a cab and off they went to stay with milady's sister in Cadogan Gardens. My word, though, I was worried about Miss Van Heysst here, who's unfamiliar with the premises as yet. It was just as well a few lights stayed on for a minute or two, or she mightn't have found her way out, if plunged in the dark, an' come over panicky, bein' foreign."

"I do not at all panic in the least, Mr. Hobday—*though foreign*," said Miss Margaretha Van Heysst, whose accent was asarming as her person and who had moved recently into the flat below mine. "Only, see now how it is with us! We have run out safely, yes, but the firemen say we cannot go back in. We say, for how long? They only shake their heads, with mournful looks. So we are become refugees in the fog, and your London fog is so *cooold*!"

She drew more closely about her a cloak like Red Riding Hood's—though Miss Van Heysst's cloak, its hood framing her enchanting young face and flaxen hair, was as blue as her forlorn, appealing eyes.

"You make a sensible point, Miss Van Heysst," agreed the man who occupied the other flat on her floor.

A handsome naval officer with a staff job at the Admiralty, he was in uniform, his cap and greatcoat marred here and there with white smears.

"Since we're not allowed back in the house," he went on, "there's no point in our standing here in the cold. Miss Van Heysst, may I suggest that I take you in search of a cab and escort you to a hotel I can personally recommend?"

"Oh, Commander Rigby, that would be kind, for if I am lost in the fog alone and meet with your Jack the Ripper, then yes, I panic very much in myself—being foreign," said Miss Van Heysst, with a flash of her lovely eyes at Hobday.

Accepting Clifford Rigby's proffered arm, she went off with him into the fog.

"You can trust our gallant Navy with a pretty young woman," said Chastayne, the cardplayer. "Or can you?" He shrugged cynically. "Oh, well, no business of mine. I must go and find somewhere to pig it temporarily myself. Good night, Manders."

Only then, as Chastayne left us, did it dawn on me that the white smears on his evening cape and on Rigby's greatcoat must have been caused by ceiling plaster falling when the explosion shook the house—and a sudden thought threw my mind into a cerebral commotion.

"Raffles," I blurted, "I'll just pop up to my flat—see the damage."

He gripped my arm, restraining me.

"Nonsense, Bunny," he said. "You won't be allowed in.

You can have my spare room in The Albany. I take it your goods and chattels are insured, so you've nothing to worry about.''

But I knew otherwise—knew it so damnably well that I did not sleep a wink in his spare room. And while still the lamps were but dim yellow blurs in the murk of what passed for dawn, I inserted my key into the front-door lock of the now silent house in Mount Street.

In the dark hall, I stood listening. All was still. I struck a match. The light quivered on the walls of the water-drenched, chaotic hall. On a coffer stood a candelabrum with three un-used candles in it. Their wicks spluttered wetly but finally lit and, my heart thumping, I stole up the stairs.

The sodden stair carpet was blotched with plaster-white bootprints all the way up to the second floor, where my candles showed the landing littered with chunks, now drenched, of lath-and-plaster.

The ceiling must have come down at the moment of the explosion, and down with the ceiling must have come a pack-age of mine—a package so private that, under a sawed section of floorboard in the corner of my living-room immediately above this landing, I had kept the package hidden on the laths between the floor beams.

I peered up, holding my candles higher, and their light showed me the exposed floor beams. So my package must have fallen, with the lath-and-plaster, on to this second-floor land-ing. I searched vainly through the debris lying here, then crept on up to my living-room, which was a shambles, and checked the hole from above.

There was no possible doubt about it. My package was gone.

I slunk out of the house.

I would rather have blown out my brains than tell Raffles what I had now to tell him, but I forced myself to walk back to The Albany, where I found him at breakfast in his chambers.

The lights were on, a coal fire burned cheerfully in the grate, and Raffles, immaculate in tweeds, a pearl in his cravat, his keen face tanned, his dark hair crisp, looked up from the

Times newspaper propped against the coffee-pot.

"'Morning, Bunny," he said. "Chafing-dishes on the whatnot there. Ring for more toast."

"I don't want any," I said, sinking into one of his saddlebag chairs. "I don't feel up to breakfast this morning. I've had a shock. Raffles, due to that damned explosion last night, some private papers of mine have—gone astray somehow. They were wrapped in a yellow silk muffler with red *fleur-de-lys* on it, the package tied with cord, the knot sealed with red wax."

"A colourful package, Bunny—valuable-looking. I expect some fireman at work in your flat spotted the package and has taken charge of it for you. What *are* these papers—or are they so private you'd rather not tell me?"

"Frankly," I said, "I'd rather not tell you. But I'm afraid I must. Raffles, you know that ever since we were at school together I've had a sort of—compulsion to write?"

"We all have our eccentricities, Bunny."

"Yes, well, if one has this compulsion to write, one naturally writes about things that have made a strong impression on one's mind. Somehow, writing them down seems to be the only way one can get them *off* one's mind—especially if they're things it'd be suicide to talk at large about. So these private writings of mine are accounts, no names or details changed or omitted, of some—recent experiences of ours."

"*Ours*, Bunny?"

"Raffles," I muttered, unable to meet his eyes, "that package contains full accounts of six of our—criminal adventures."

Silence. Only the rustle of the fire in the grate, the quiet ticking of the clock above it. Staring at the carpet, I heard him stand up and cross to the fireplace.

I thought it was to get the poker, and my scalp tingled in anticipation of a terminal impact upon it. But he was only lighting a cigarette with a spill. He turned, standing there on the hearthrug, and I sensed his grey eyes looking down at me, studying me with a clinical detachment.

At last he spoke, his tone even.

"I now know, Bunny," he said, "why it's remarked, of people with the strange compulsion to write, that they've been—*bitten by the tarantula.*"

He made me no reproaches. He merely asked me for further details, and I explained that the package, which did not have my name on the outside, must have been found on the second-floor landing.

"Raffles," I said, "your cricket's made your name very well known. If whoever's found that package opens it to see who it belongs to, and discovers your name in a criminal context on every page of those confounded manuscripts, the finder may hand them to the police!"

"Who, if they once start making inquiries about us," Raffles said, "could certainly be a bit awkward."

"Raffles, we must get out of the country—immediately!"

"And, not knowing whether the police have or have not got that package, have to spend the rest of our lives in Callao?"

"Why Callao, Raffles?"

"Because, as the famous rhyme says, Bunny: 'Under no condition is extradition allowed from Callao'!"

"Ah, I see your point."

"So it's evident, Bunny, that we must try to trace your package. For all we know, it may be unopened. If we bolted, it could be a case of 'the wicked flee, though no man pursueth.' We must go canny here. We'd better not make overt inquiries about your lost package. I'll get Ivor Kern, our invaluable 'fence,' to put some of his snoops on to this. Take a room at your club, Bunny. A red light glows for us in this damned fog. If the light should glow redder still, I'll get word to you. Meantime, keep a valise packed handy for instant travel—just in case."

All the things in my flat had been ruined by water from firehoses. I had to buy a valise and new togs. And toward the end of a week that, for sheer torturing suspense, aged me considerably, I returned to my club one morning, after a fitting at my tailor's, and was told that Mr. Raffles was waiting for me in the Hastings Room.

I hared up the handsome marble staircase and found Raffles, alone except for a whisky-and-soda, sitting in an armchair under a dismal great painting, *The Impeachment of Warren Hastings*.

"Well, Bunny," Raffles greeted me, "we've had a communication."

My heart sank. "From the police?"

"No," said Raffles. "From the Tarantula."

He handed me a large envelope, which had been opened. With shaking hands I drew out the contents—and found myself staring at about forty sheets of sermon paper covered with my own handwriting and held together with a paper clip.

"One of your six manuscripts," Raffles said. "It came in my mail this morning. No message with it. None needed. The sender holds five more of your writings. This one, obviously, is to serve notice on us."

"Notice?" I said, bewildered.

Raffles gave me a grim look.

"Of the Bite To Come," he said.

It came three agonizing days later. It was another of my misbegotten manuscripts. Raffles showed it to me in the Hastings Room. Attached to the manuscript was a typewritten message, which I read with starting eyes:

To A. J. Raffles, Esq.:

There now remain in the hands of the present writer four further confessions from the pen of your confederate, the ineffable Manders.

To hand these manuscripts to Scotland Yard, and so end the career of an individual who, little suspected of being a criminal, frequents high social and sporting circles, would be less to the purpose of the present writer than to exchange the incriminating documents in return for a service to be rendered.

Here, Mr. Raffles, is the service requested and required of you:

Sir Roderick Naismith, a pillar of the British Treasury, frequently has with him, when he leaves his office in the evening, a small dispatch-case. Invariably is this so on Friday evenings, when no doubt his dispatch-case contains matter for study at his Hampstead home over the weekend.

On Fridays in winter, however, Sir Roderick does not go

directly home. He proceeds in a cab to Lord's Cricket Ground, where, every Friday at 6:30 P.M., he exercises himself physically and refreshes himself mentally at the aristocratic game of 'real' tennis.

To you, Mr. Raffles, a familiar of that exclusive haunt of the nobility and squirearchy, the building which houses the 'real' tennis court at Lord's, an opportunity to acquire Sir Roderick's dispatch-case should, in view of your uncommon skill, readily present itself.

Next Friday evening, therefore, you will obtain that dispatch-case. You will then return to your chambers in The Albany—where, it has been ascertained, a window of your rooms overlooks Vigo Street. You will place in that window of yours, as a signal that the required service has been duly rendered, a reading lamp with a green shade.

You will then receive, by second post the following day, instructions regarding arrangements for the exchange of Sir Roderick's dispatch-case in return for your confederate's indiscreet effusions.

Failure on your part to carry out the specified service will result in the immediate delivery of your partner's manuscripts to Scotland Yard.

My heart thumped. "Oh, dear God!" I said.

"Sir Roderick Naismith's match at Lord's on Friday evening," said Raffles, "is one in the intermediate stages of the tennis tournament. He'll be playing against a distinguished soldier, General Lord Kitchener—Kitchener of Khartoum." Raffles gave me a strange look. "Bunny, the Tarantula—so to call our unknown correspondent—has made a significant slip in this missive. It's a slip that may well indicate a curious element in this whole situation. The ball's now in my court—and I intend to play it."

"How?"

"By doing, more or less," Raffles said, "as the Tarantula demands. But, Bunny—now, don't take this amiss—I think perhaps you'd do well to keep out of this matter from here on."

"No, damn it," I said hotly, "I got you into this mess,

Raffles, and I insist on seeing it through with you—come what may."

He raised his glass to me.

So the following evening, Friday, found Raffles and my admittedly ineffable self alighting from a hansom at Lord's, headquarters of the ruling body of world cricket, the Marylebone Cricket Club, of which Raffles was a popular member.

The stands and terraces, so vividly stippled in summertime with the confetti hues of ladies' parasols and men's boaters and blazers, loomed now deserted, spectral in the dank, persistent fog. Only from the tennis-court building, in its secluded corner of the famous demesne, did gleams of gaslight faintly mitigate the muffling vapour.

Capped, scarved and ulstered, we entered the building.

Just inside the entrance stood a glass case. In this was housed the token trophy of the tournament—token only, as it was one of the priceless treasures at Lord's and never left the grounds.

Warped, time-blackened, worm-eaten, the long-handled, curved, stringless old racquet in the glass case was a reminder of that long-ago day when, on a French meadow, a monarch of France had presented to a monarch of England, as they met in conclave among pennoned pavilions and the glittering shields and lances of the armoured chivalry of both nations, a gift of tennis balls.

Now, from the unseen court to our left, sounded hollow thuds and wallops, and from the changing-room, to our right, emerged a wiry man in white flannels and sweater, carrying a huge basket loaded to the brim with tennis balls of a type little changed since that far-off day of the two august but sportive monarchs.

"'Evening, Mole," said Raffles.

"Good evening, Mr. Raffles," said Mole, the resident professional. "Come to see the match? Lord Kitchener and Sir Roderick Naismith are in the court now, warming up. I'm just going in to mark for them."

He went off with his heavy basket—and Raffles strolled

over to the door of the changing-room, glanced in casually, then returned to me.

"Just two men in there, Bunny," he murmured. "Let's hope they decide presently to watch the match. Meantime, we'll watch it ourselves."

Gripping my arm, he opened a door to the left, closed it behind us, and in the almost total darkness of the restricted space for spectators steered me to the rearmost of a half-dozen spartan benches.

Through the interstices of a protective net, I saw the reflector-shaded, wire-caged lights which from aloft shed down their brilliance solely on to the court proper, a stylized version of a barnyard of some ancient abbey in Avignon, or Cahors of the turreted bridge, or grey-walled Carcassonne of the many candle-snuffer towers.

But whereas medieval monks, slamming balls at each other across a net slung between the abbey cow byre and the refectory wall, had played this tennis when stripped to their hairshirts, the two gentlemen now in the court here—second only in celebrity to Henry VIII's at Hampton Court—were in white flannels and sweaters.

"In these troubled times, Bunny," Raffles murmured, "when a sabre-rattling European monarch with a Potsdam moustache is keeping half the world nervous by his rapid expansion of his High Seas Fleet, it's good to see Kitchener looking so fit."

I nodded, my gaze on the powerful figure, granite jaw, heavy moustache and challenging steel-blue eyes of England's great soldier, with whom the distinguished senior civil servant—gaunt, grey-haired, shrewd-faced Sir Roderick Naismith of the Treasury—strikingly contrasted.

From the marker's niche to the left of the court, where a section of penthouse roof simulated the eaves of a cow byre, Mole appeared, carrying his basket of tennis balls, which he emptied into a trough that already seemed full of them.

The match now began. But here in the dark I was trying to discern how many shadowy figures were spaced about on the benches in front of Raffles and myself. There were, as far as I could make out, only about half-a-dozen spectators—members here, of course—but presently I became aware of two more, quietly entering. Closing the door behind them, they groped their way to the front bench.

"The two from the changing-room, Bunny," Raffles whispered to me. "Stay here."

Silent as a ghost, he was gone from my side.

I forced myself to keep my eyes on the game. Sir Roderick was serving, sending the ball, struck underhand, spinning along the penthouse eaves. The ball, falling at the far end, was emphatically thumped back across the centre net by Lord Kitchener. Sir Roderick's return went high, the ball banging hollowly against a piece of wood—shaped like a Gothic arch in simulation of a monastery pigeon-cote—on the wall behind Kitchener.

"Fifteen-thirty," chanted Mole, the marker, as the players changed ends. "Thirty-fifteen—chase three."

The game continued, the players changing ends as service was won or lost. Twanging of racquets, thudding of balls, thumping of plimsolled feet echoed hollowly in the court.

"Better than three," rang the voice of Mole. "Deuce!"

Vicariously, I was with Raffles, breaking now into Sir Roderick's locker in the changing-room. Or surprised red-handed at the job? I did not know. Crypt-cold as it was here in the dark, my gloved hands were clammy with perspiration. Because I could not keep a pen out of them, Raffles now risked total ruin—and the grim quatrain by Omar Khayyám resounded dismally in my memory:

> The Moving Finger writes, and having writ,
> Moves on, nor all your piety nor wit
>   Can call it back to cancel half a line,
> Nor all your tears wash out a word of it.

Never had I been more poignantly conscious of the Persian poet's profound insight into the nature of things than now, as Mole the marker chanted:

"'Vantage! Chase one. *Game!* Game and set to Lord Kitchener."

The players met in mid-court to mop their faces with towels proffered to them by Mole from his marker's niche between the netted apertures which represented the window openings through which monastery cows had once thrust their horned heads, chewing their cuds and dribbling as they mooed for the Dairyman Monk to come and milk them.

Sir Roderick's pale face look as cool as ever, but the hero of Khartoum was considerably ruddier as he dried his brow and his formidable moustache.

"Have at you again, Roddy," I heard him growl.

"Good-oh, H. H.," replied Sir Roderick.

With that, they fell to once more, going at it hammer-and-tongs—and, halfway through the second set, I became aware, with a nervous start, of a shadow at my side.

Raffles was back.

Neither of us said a word until the match was over, with victory to the implacable Lord Kitchener, and we made our way out from the tennis-court building into the fog shrouding the cricket ground, with frozen puddles on its sacred turf, when I ventured to ask Raffles how he had got on.

"I'll tell you when I've thought over its implications," he said. "Let's see if we can find a hansom. I'm hoping there may be a message for me at The Albany."

When we reached his chambers and with a match he popped the gas-globe alight, an envelope was lying on the doormat. He tore the envelope open, read the message enclosed, thrust it into his ulster pocket.

"From Ivor Kern, our invaluable 'fence'" he said. "Come on, we've a call to make."

"On Ivor?"

"No, Bunny," Raffles said grimly. "On the Tarantula!"

He turned off the gaslight, hurried me out of the building by the front entrance to Albany Courtyard and Piccadilly, where we were fortunate enough to get a cab, a four-wheeler. Telling the cabbie to drop us at the corner of Church Walk, Kensington, Raffles thrust me into the dark, cold-seated interior of the cab and, as the horse jingled us off westward, gave me a Sullivan from his cigarette-case.

"Now, Bunny," he said. "Consider your lost package. On the night of the explosion in the Mount Street house, just three people passed along the second-floor landing in making their hasty exits from the house. Any one of those three could have spotted and snatched up your valuable-looking package—and, oddly enough, when we had our brief conversation with them in the street each of them was wearing a garment which could have concealed the package. Charles Chastayne was in evening-dress—with cape. Miss Van Heysst had thrown on a hooded cloak—as blue as her eyes. Commander Rigby was in uniform, with a deep-pocketed Navy greatcoat.''

A match flared. We dipped our cigarettes to the flame Raffles held in his cupped hands.

''I had Ivor Kern,'' he went on, ''set his snoops to find out where those three persons had taken up their respective temporary abodes—and keep an eye on them. Then came the Tarantula's missive—with its significant slip, the reference to 'the British Treasury.' No Briton would say that. He'd say, simply, 'the Treasury.' So here was a hint that the writer of the Tarantula missive was a foreigner—and one of our three most likely suspects *is* in fact a foreigner.''

''Miss Van Heysst!''

''Yes, but she couldn't have written that letter, Bunny. Her English is charming, but if she'd written that letter there'd have been more slips, more foreign locutions, than just one in it. No, if it were Miss Van Heysst who snatched up your package, she must have shown it to someone—the person, a foreigner fluent in English and pretty well informed on English ways and social values, who wrote the Tarantula letter. So who—and what—*is* this person with the very sharp bite?''

Our cab was jingling past the muffled gaslamps and flickering fog-flare braziers of Hyde Park Corner.

''And just what,'' Raffles went on, ''is the singularly seductive Miss Van Heysst? A new resident, she moves into a flat adjoining that of Commander Clifford Rigby. A gas explosion puts them on the street. At whom, Bunny, was Miss Van Heysst's forlorn plea of fearing to meet Jack the Ripper in the fog subtly directed? And who takes it up with the dash and gallantry to be expected of the Navy and promptly tucks Little Blue Riding Hood under his starboard wing?''

"Commander Rigby," I breathed.

"Exactly," said Raffles. "And what, in these times when the clang of shipbuilders' hammers is resounding menacingly to us from across the North Sea, is Rigby? He's a naval officer, Bunny—*with a staff job at the Admiralty*."

"Good God!" I said, stunned by the implications.

"What an astute little opportunist," said Raffles, "is Miss Van Heysst with the big blue eyes! But, Bunny, though it seemed to me that a curious element was beginning to creep into this matter of your lost manuscripts, it struck me as odd that the Tarantula was anxious to view the documents in the dispatch-case of a senior civil servant at the *Treasury*. Surely, if the Tarantula is what I was beginning to suspect, it would have been more understandable if the documents he wanted stolen belónged to, say, General Lord Kitchener. Why those of a senior civil servant at the *Treasury*? I decided to have a look at Sir Roderick's documents, in the changing-room at Lord's this evening, and find out."

"And you did?"

"I did indeed, Bunny. Naturally, I left the documents intact and Sir Roderick's dispatch-case and locker relocked. What the Tarantula, as a foreigner, doesn't realise is that a member of the M.C.C. does *not*, however dire his need, rob another member. That's simply not done at Lord's. But a brief skim through Sir Roderick's documents made all plain to me. He's an imposter."

"Sir Roderick Naismith? Raffles, that's incredible!"

"But nevertheless true, Bunny. He's a senior civil servant, but not at the Treasury. That ostensible occupation of Sir Roderick's is a mask for his real one. He's the head of our Secret Security Service."

"I never knew we had such a thing!"

"How could you?" said Raffles. "It's secret."

He peered out into the fog.

"Kensington Gore," he said. "We'll be arriving in a few minutes." And he went on, "I've no doubt whatever now that the Tarantula is a spymaster. He's evidently learned Sir Roderick's real occupation. And what the Tarantula is anxious to find out is whether any of the agents whose activities in this country he directs and controls are under suspicion.''

"Good God!'' I muttered, appalled.

"Significantly enough, Bunny,'' Raffles said, "I found in Sir Roderick's dispatch-case a pencilled list of five names, each with some personal particulars noted against them—the list headed: 'For Expulsion from England Subject to Firm Evidence of Espionage Activity.' Among the names is that of Miss Van Heysst of Mount Street. But *not* the name of the Tarantula.''

"You actually know his name, Raffles?''

"Yes, Bunny, it's in the note I had just now from Ivor Kern. One of his snoops, who'd traced Miss Van Heysst to a respectable hotel—Garland's near the Haymarket Theatre—was keeping an eye on her. It seems that this afternoon she went by a circuitous route to Richmond Park, a place usually deserted on a foggy afternoon. She met a man at the Priory Lane gate, had a brief talk with him. As I'd instructed, any person she met with was to be followed. So Ivor Kern's snoop followed the man. He lives on the first floor of Number Eight, Chuch Walk, Kensington. So we're now about to visit him in his spidery lair,'' Raffles said, "and—let's hope—return his Tarantula bite!''

We were, as always, unarmed—and I was taut with apprehension as Raffles paid off our cabbie at the corner of Church Walk and we proceeded along that silent side street. Here and there, in houses to either side, dim light from curtained windows faintly blurred the fog.

"Here we are, Bunny,'' Raffles said—"that house with the number '8' barely visible on the fanlight over the front door. He's probably in that first-floor room where faint edges of light show around the window curtains. No doubt he's waiting impatiently for word from whatever minion he has skulking in Vigo Street at the back of The Albany that a green-shaded reading-lamp has appeared at a window of my chambers. H'm! Now, how're we to trap this hairy Tarantula?''

Raffles considered the problem for a minute or so.

"Tell you what,'' he said abruptly. "We'll get him worried, Bunny. Got plenty of small change in your pocket?''

"I'm fairly well britched for it, Raffles."

"Good. Now, I'm going to try that front door. It's probably locked, but may not be bolted—in which case the little implement I used on Sir Roderick's locker at Lord's should serve our purpose. If I can get into the house, keep well back in the fog here and toss coins up at that first-floor window. The Tarantula's almost certainly armed, so my prudent course will be to steal in on him from behind when his back's turned as he peers out of the window.''

Instantly grasping Raffles's strategy, I whipped off my gloves, took a handful of small change from my pocket as he moved silently up the two porch steps to the door under the dim fanlight. As I watched his shadowy figure at work on the door, a vertical line of light suddenly appeared there—and vanished instantly as Raffles, entering, soundlessly closed the door.

Drawing further back into the fog, I tossed a coin up at the first-floor window. I heard a tinkle against the glass, a second tinkle as the coin dropped down into the railed basement area.

No movement of the curtains ensued, so I tossed up another coin—another—and another.

Suddenly, the faint lines of light that edged the window curtains vanished. Motionless in the fog, I sensed, my heart thumping, that the curtains had been parted a little and that some evil, spider-like creature, crouching there at the window of the now dark room, was glaring out balefully into the fog.

Listening intently, I heard a muffled thump from within the room. Then I saw the light go on again. For a second, Raffles showed himself to me between the curtains, then drew them closed. I waited, swallowing with a parched throat.

It seemed quite a long time before the front door of the house silently opened and closed—and Raffles rejoined me.

We picked up a cab in Kensington High Street, and Raffles gave the cabbie an address in Hampstead.

"I'm afraid, Bunny," he said, "I was obliged to violate a rule of ours and use a modicum of violence. I bounced the Tarantula's cranium fairly forcefully against his floor, to stun him while I relit the gas he'd turned out. Still, he was beginning to come round as I left. He'll have found by now that he's lost your four manuscripts. They were on his desk. Here they are, still loosely wrapped in your yellow silk muffler.''

"Admirable, Raffles,'' I said, seizing them eagerly.

"I'm glad you're pleased, Bunny,'' said Raffles. "There was a locked drawer in his desk. The lock presented no problem. So we're now richer by about a thousand pounds—spies' wages, I imagine.''

"Better and better, Raffles!'' I exclaimed.

"I also,'' said Raffles, "abstracted from the drawer a batch of the Tarantula's papers—which provide, I fancy from a cursory perusal, all the 'firm evidence' Sir Roderick Naismith needs to justify some deportation orders from this country. I noticed Sir Roderick's Hampstead address on letters in his dispatch-case at Lord's, so we'll drop these papers he'll be glad of through his letter-box, then drive to Piccadilly Circus and see if we can buy a few flowers.''

I was at a loss to divine why Raffles should want flowers at this hour. However, late as it was when we got back from our Hampstead errand and paid off our cab in Piccadilly Circus, we found this hub of London an oasis of activity in the blanketing fog.

The theatres and music-halls were disgorging their second-house audiences and the gin palaces ejecting their inebriates into the blurred glow of gaslights and the naked flicker of naphtha fog-flares.

The harness-jingle of cabs and the plodding hoofbeats of omnibus horses mingled with the cries of the Piccadilly flower women sitting beside their big baskets at their usual receipt of custom on the steps of the recently erected Eros statue.

"Oy, misters—you gents there!''

A cheeky-looking wench, much shawled and petticoated, with a feather boa, a huge hat bedecked with ostrich plumes, and high-heeled button boots, brandished a great bunch of chrysanthemums at Raffles and me.

"Out lyte, you are,'' she said provocatively. "Bin on the spree, you two sports 'ave! You'd best tyke a few flowers 'ome to sweeten yer little bits o' trouble-an-strife! 'Ere you are, look—loverly chrysanths, fresh as a dysy!''

"On behalf of my friend here,'' said Raffles, "I'll give you a sovereign for that bunch of chrysanthemums—and if you'd care to earn an extra half-bar, you can deliver them for him at your leisure. The place is not far. It's just off the Haymarket there—a hotel called Garland's. Hand the flowers in at the desk and say that they're for Miss Van Heysst as a *bon voyage* gift from 'A Gentleman Of Mount Street.' Are you on?''

''Mister, for an extra 'arf-bar, the w'y tryde's bin tonight in this bleedin' fog,'' rejoined the wench, ''I'd walk as far as the Elephant 'n' Castle for yer wiv me whole bloody basket!''

So Raffles gave her the extra half-sovereign and, raising our caps to the outspoken florist, we walked across the misty Circus towards the nearby Albany.

''There are games, Bunny, *and* games,'' Raffles remarked thoughtfully. '''Real' tennis an old one, but espionage is an older one still—and much more dangerous. As far as women are concerned, only a brave woman would play it. It's to be hoped that Miss Van Heysst doesn't continue her activities in the pay of the Wilhelmstrasse, or—in the troubled state of Europe today—she may come to a bad end. That would be a pity, because she's not only an exceptionally seductive young woman, but also a brave one.''

''Absolutely,'' I concurred.

''So I think, Bunny,'' Raffles said, ''although Little Blue Riding Hood was a fellow resident of yours in Mount Street for only a short while, it'd be nice for her to have a small tribute of flowers from you, to take with her when Sir Roderick Naismith has her escorted aboard the Harwich to Hook-of-Holland boat tomorrow. I wish we'd seen more of her. She's a most interesting young person. According to some particulars noted against her name in Sir Roderick's list, her real name is Margaretha Zelle—and she's believed to use other aliases than Van Heysst.''

''Other aliases?'' I said.

He nodded.

''One of them, noted against our Little Blue Riding Hood in Sir Roderick's list, is rather striking,'' Raffles said—''*Mata Hari*.''

2

THE ROSKELLY INJUNCTION

It was mid-morning and blazing hot when the clang of the chukker bell put an end to a polo match on a parched field near the hamlet of Campamento, on the Spanish side of the La Linea-Gibraltar frontier.

A couple of miles from where the Rock itself reared up, massive and leonine, from the glittering waters of Algeciras Bay, this polo field was rented by the Gibraltar garrison from a Spanish landlord.

As the dusk subsided and the eight players and two umpires dismounted from their lathered ponies in the meagre shade of a clump of eucalyptus trees, I walked across the field for a word with A. J. Raffles.

He had come to these parts, myself accompanying him just for the trip, to play cricket for an M.C.C. team invited to Gibraltar to lend a touch of class to a Cricket Festival Week on the Rock.

During one of the matches, H. M. Colonial Secretary, Gibraltar, a Mr. Naughton-Bull, had had the bad luck, while trying to steal a quick single off Raffles's bowling, to tear a muscle. This was the more unfortunate because Mr. Naughton-Bull was the Number Four and mainstay of the Rock's polo team, which had an important match pending, and the muscle he had severely torn happened to be his riding muscle.

With an infantry regiment currently in garrison, the Rock was short of dependable polo players. So Raffles, who was known by Mr. Naughton-Bull to play a creditable game when offered ponies to play on, had been peremptorily co-opted by the maimed Colonial Secretary to stay on after the Cricket Week and pinch-hit for him in this polo match this morning.

That the Rock side had been beaten by its perennial rivals, Los Bodegueros, a team of brilliant young Spaniards from Jerez, was no fault of Raffles's. He had given a respectable account of himself, and I told him so as I joined him now in the speckled shade of the eucalypti.

"It's a pity Tubby Naughton-Bull wasn't playing," Raffles said ruefully, as he hung his borrowed helmet on a tree-branch and unwound the thong which secured his polo-mallet to his wrist. "Los Bodegueros had the edge on us, Bunny. They're too good."

The garrison pony he had just dismounted from, a rangy grey that looked to me a bit over the regulation 14.2 hands, was being led away by a groom. From a line slung between the trees hung the chukker bell, along wth bits, bridles and horse-blankets—and Raffles, his borrowed riding-boots white with dust, plucked a towel from the line and mopped the sweat from his keen, tanned face.

"Actually," I explained to him, "it's the Bodegueros' ponies that were too good. King Alfonso himself, when he skippered the Spanish team in last year's internationals at Ranelagh, wasn't better mounted than these sherry grandees from Jerez."

Los Bodegueos, captained by one of the Domecq family, famous for fine sherries and superb horsemen, all were members of Jerez families renowned the world over for the vinification of Andalusia's inspired contribution to the cause of civilized living.

I looked enviously at their ponies, on which the blue-shirted Spanish grooms were working busily, while artillery troopers from the Rock were similarly engaged on the garrison ponies. Thanks to Mr. Naughton-Bull, who, in the interests of polo, took good care to keep on cordial terms with Don Carlos Tejedor, Commandant of the *Aduana* at La Linea, the British troopers were allowed to wear uniform when they brought the string of Gibraltar ponies over the frontier into Spain every morning for exercising or matches on this field at Campamento.

"By the way, Bunny," Raffles said, "I've heard a rather interesting thing." He threw his towel over the line, drew me a little aside from where the other players were exchanging amiable insults as they towelled off the sweat of equestrian conflict. "You see that little group of people who've been watching the match?"

There had been few spectators, most of whom had now drifted away, leaving a group of a half-dozen or so persons near the goal-posts on the far side of the heat-shimmering field. The group was gathered about a wheelchair in which sat a leathery, aquiline old gentleman wearing a white suit and a straw boater. His sweeping moustache and neat tuft of beard were iron-grey. He was puffing at a cheroot, and his wheelchair was flanked by two most attractive young ladies with raised parasols. One of the young ladies was a brunette, obviously Spanish, and the other was a blonde, evidently English.

Ohey were chatting to the old gentleman in the wheelchair and to Commandant Tejedor of the *Aduana* and burly Colonel Gomez of the Guardia Civil, both of them in uniform. Also in the group were the Port Admiral, Gibraltar, and the Colonial Secretary, both wearing civilian white suits, Mr. Naughton-Bull easing his riding muscle by sitting on a shooting stick as he talked to a tall man in a Norfolk suit and white linen cap.

"The old gentleman in the wheelchair," Raffles told me, "is Bartholomew Gurney. His family, old established wine merchants in London, sent him to Spain as a young man to study the sherry business. He fell in love with a Spanish girl whose family were in the business. Part of that family business came to her as her dowry when she married Bart Gurney. The Spanish call him 'Don Bartolo'—a name you've seen on the label of many a bottle of fine sherry, because Bart Gurney built up that small *solera,* which came to him as his wife Doña Isabel's dowry, into one of the great sherry houses of Jerez."

As Raffles was speaking, four men in white jackets came filing on to the field through a gap in the cactus hedge on the far side. Napkins over their arms, each man bearing a silver tray on which bottles and glasses flashed hotly in the sun-glare, the newcomers approached the group around the old gentleman in the wheelchair.

"Men-servants, Bunny," Raffles said, "from Mr. Gurney's house. He lives now in a big place, the Casa Isabel, just the other side of this hamlet of Campamento. The house is named for his wife. They shared a love for fine horses, and Bart Gurney, riding as an amateur, used to win many races in Spain and on Gibraltar racecourse. He and his wife were very much in love, but they never had any children. So, for love of Spain, they adopted a boy born in Jerez, orphan of a Spanish cavalry trooper. And, for love of England, they adopted a boy born in Gibraltar, orphan of an English cavalry trooper. Both boys, Roberto and Alec, have grown up to be first-rate horsemen. They were playing in this match this morning—Roberto for Los Bodegueros, Alec for Gibraltar."

Raffles offered me a Sullivan from his cigarette-case. On the far side of the field, the four men-servants lined up with their trays in front of the old gentleman in the wheelchair. He examined the bottles on the trays, nodded approval. Two of the men-servants proceeded to proffer refreshments to members of the group there, while the two other men-servants marched across the field to where Raffles and I were standing near the clump of eucalyptus trees.

"When Doña Isabel died," Raffles went on, "old Bart Gurney sponsored a race in memory of her. It's run annually, one year on Cádiz racecourse, the next on Gibraltar racecourse. It's open to amateur riders of Spanish birth or born in Gibraltar or stationed there on military service. The trophy he's presented is a golden bowl, and the race has become a classic in these parts and is known far and wide as the Sherry Bowl Derby."

One of the men-servants paused before us, proffering his tray.

"With the compliments, *señores*," he said, "of Don Bartolo."

We made our respective choices from the range of exquisite sherries submitted to us, and the man-servant joined his colleague who in the tree shade was serving the polo-players and the grooms.

"I gather," Raffles said, sipping his sherry thoughtfully, "that old Bart Gurney has done an unwise thing. His adopted sons both work in the business with him. Roberto works at

Jerez, Alec handles some part of the business that's done through Gibraltar. Old Bart's always passionately hoped that one or the other of them would some day put the name he'd given them, the Gurney name, as a winning rider on the Golden Bowl in memory of the dearly loved Doña Isabel who'd been a mother to them both.''

"Neither of the adopted sons," I said, "has yet won the race?''

"No," said Raffles. "They've both come near it. I'm told that Alec nearly won at Cádiz last year, but was nosed out by a British subaltern on a horse called Lucky Lancer. Old Bart got over-excited. He thinks he may not live to see many more races for the Sherry Bowl. Apparently he'd always intended that Roberto and Alec should inherit the business in equal shares. But in the heat of the moment, there at Cádiz last year, he suddenly threw a challenge at his adopted sons. He told them that if either of them won at Gibraltar this year, he'd get a majority holding in the business, the other a minority.''

"Good God!" I said.

"That's not all," said Raffles. "I'm told that Roberto and Alec both got engaged recently. Roberto's engaged to a Spanish girl, Inez Molina, daughter of Don Luis Molina, a racehorse owner-trainer with a place just up in the hills here. Alec is engaged to an English girl, Joan Roskelly.''

"Are those the girls," I asked, "over there with their parasols?''

"Yes, Bunny. And that hard-faced man in the Norfolk jacket, who's talking to Tubby Naughton-Bull, is Joan's father, Sir George Roskelly, well-known London merchant banker.'' Raffles's grey eyes danced. "With the future of one of the great Jerez sherry *bodegas* possibly depending on it, the Sherry Bowl Derby on Gibraltar racecourse at two-thirty next Saturday should be well worth—''

A shot rang out. The report echoed in the arid hills that swept steeply up from the hamlet, and between cactus clumps that hedged a lane on the far side of the polo field galloped a black horse with a white-robed rider brandishing a long-barrelled, archaic musket.

In the centre of the field, the barbaric rider reined in his horse with a jerk that brought it rearing up on its hind legs in a flurry of dust. The rider was a Moor. I glimpsed his face as, freeing it from a veiling swathe of his head-dress, he emitted a series of brazen whoops.

"I gotta horse!" he shouted. "I gotta horse!"

Veiling himself again to the eyes, he trotted his horse towards the group of notabilities around Mr. Bartholomew Gurney in his wheelchair—and Raffles and I were joined by one of the polo players. A wiry, sandy-haired chap, deeply tanned, he was amused by our perplexity.

"That spectacular rider," he told us, "is one Mallam Juzeed, self-styled 'Emir of Rabat.' The rascal's harmless. He's our local tipster. He has a shack in the hill there. He'll be on Gibraltar racecourse this afternoon. There's a meeting every Saturday through the season. We play our polo matches in the morning, so as to be free for the races in the afternoon."

Our informant was Alec Gurney. Raffles introduced me. "And here comes Roberto," he said.

Old Bartholomew Gurney's other adopted son was slender and dark, with a horseman's steely handclasp. Evidently they referred to their foster-father as Don Bartolo, for Roberto said to Alec, "It looks as though Don Bartolo's investing in Juzeed's five-bob sealed prophecy."

I saw that the self-styled Emir, leaning down from his saddle, was handing a grubby envelope to the old gentleman in the wheelchair.

"No doubt," Alec Gurney said dryly, "that'll be Juzeed's special for—the two-thirty next Saturday."

At this mention of the Sherry Bowl Derby, there passed between the brothers-by-adoption a look so enigmatic that I felt a tingle of premonition. I glanced across the field at the old gentleman in the wheelchair. Watched by the two girls, Inez and Joan, and by the gentlemen in the group, Mr. Gurney opened the envelope, glanced at its contents—and I heard his voice as he looked up at the veiled rider.

"*Anda, hombre,*" said Bartholomew Gurney. "We shall see."

"*Olé!*" yelled the Moor—and, wheeling his horse, went

off at a gallop, brandishing his musket and whooping wildly, down the dust-deep lane to the hamlet.

"Let's join Don Bartolo and the ladies," said Roberto Gurney.

"Yes, let's," said Alec Gurney. "But, Raffles, Manders—just one thing. Don't, in Don Bartolo's hearing, make any remark about next Saturday's two-thirty race. He's so strictly neutral that he forbids all mention of it. I tell you this now, as you'll be coming over on Monday to join his house party at the Casa Isabel."

I was startled. This was the first I had heard about our joining Mr. Gurney's house party, but I had no chance to question Raffles about it until an hour or so later, when we were in one of the rather dilapidated *coches* that plied for hire between Campamento hamlet and the frontier at La Linea.

On the road was a stream of such *coches,* mingled with a variety of carts and of riders on horse or muleback—the crowd headed for the races in Gibraltar. Here and there in the stream walked a blanketed racehorse led by a stable lad.

"Why, yes, Bunny," Raffles said, when I asked him what was all this about our joining Mr. Bartholomew Gurney's house party. "Alec Gurney was telling me, just before the polo match, about this Sherry Bowl Derby matter. He invited us to join the party at Casa Isabel. I accepted for us, as the situation seems fraught with possibilities. Alec's staying at the Casa, with his *fiancée,* Joan, and her father, Sir George—who's brought out from England the horse Alec'll be riding in the fateful race next Saturday."

Raffles laughed.

"One sees Sir George's point, Bunny. He wants his future son-in-law to have the best possible chance of inheriting the *major* holding in the Gurney sherry business. So Sir George, not normally a racing man, has registered his colours and, on sound advice, acquired a promising horse called Master Primrose for Alec to ride. And Roberto, I understand, will be riding a horse call San Roque, owned and trained by his *fiancée* Inez's father, Don Luis Molina."

Our *coche* trundled almost to a standstill. We had reached

the frontier bottleneck. The race-day traffic was creeping along towards the archway through a square, yellowish building, the *Aduana* of La Linea.

We paid off our *cochero* and walked to the head of queue. The robed tipster, self-styled Emir of Rabat, was entering the archway on his fine black horse. Behind him, the British artillery troopers, bringing the polo ponies back from Campamento, were strung out in line, each man mounted on a pony and leading a couple of others. The troopers were pulling the tipster's leg.

"Have a heart, Your Highness!" they were calling. "We're only poor Tommies! Give us your nap for this aft'noon!"

The grinning *carabineros*, in their grey-green uniforms with slung rifles, passed the veiled tipster through, followed by the string of British ponies—and Raffles and I passed through the archway on foot and emerged into the sun-glare over the eight hundred yards of dust-white road that ran straight as an arrow across the treeless, flat expanse of the neutral territory to the British gate.

Ahead of us, Juzeed the tipster was trotting his horse in the stream of race-going traffic.

"A picturesque fellow, Bunny," said Raffles, as we walked on with the perspiring crowd. "I wonder what horse he tipped for the Sherry Bowl Derby in that sealed prophecy he sold old Bart Gurney?"

I wondered, too—especially when, on the following Tuesday morning, we saw Sir George Roskelly's horse, Master Primrose, for the first time.

It was just after dawn on the sands of Campamento beach. I was standing with Raffles, Sir George Roskelly, his fair-haired daughter Joan, and a local trainer, a Mr. Abremis, a Gibraltarian, to whose care Sir George had entrusted Master Primrose.

The tide was out. The firm, wide sands swept in a great arc around the bay to the distant white buildings of Algeciras. Sea and sky, at this hour, had the cool radiance of mother-of-pearl.

The five of us had binoculars glued to our eyes. Framed in

my binoculars was a little group of four horses galloping at the edge of the glassily breaking wavelets. The horses were racing in our direction—and I saw Alec Gurney, on Master Primrose, give the horse his head, and the beautiful lemon roan left the others behind as though they had been standing still.

When we lowered our binoculars, Mr. Abremis was smiling, and Sir George Roskelly was looking as satisfied as was possible for a man of his naturally severe, even grim demeanour. He was not a banker I would lightly have approached for a loan.

"You don't seem entirely pleased, Miss Roskelly," said Raffles.

"Oh, but I am," said Joan Roskelly. "Only—well, it just seems wrong to me that so much should be at stake, between Alec and Roberto, on a *horse* race!"

"Totally wrong," Sir George agreed. "An old man's folly!" He closed his binocular-case with a decisive snap. "However, we shall see what we shall see."

Mr. Bartholomew Gurney's fine old mansion, set among palm and olive groves, overlooked the beach—and at lunchtime Roberto Gurney turned up with his *fiancée*, Inez Molina. Inez lived with her father, Don Luis Molina, the owner-trainer; and Roberto, who normally worked at Jerez, was staying with the Molinas until after the race next Saturday.

At lunch, Mr. Bartholomew Gurney's affection for the two charming girls, his prospective daughters-in-law, was very evident. Yet, though no mention whatever was made of the forthcoming race, awareness of it seemed to me to hang rather heavily over the party—and not least, I fancied, over old Bart Gurney, Don Bartolo, himself.

Roberto invited Raffles and myself to see his mount, San Roque. Next morning, accordingly, we rode up, on a couple of horses from old Bart's stables, to Don Luis Molina's place, in the hills that backed upon the Campamento polo ground.

The Cortijo Molina proved to be a rambling white farmhouse with a good though dusty gallops nearby. We found Inez and her father at the gallops, and Don Luis Molina, a tall man with a haggard, handsome face shaded by a Cordoba hat, pointed to five horses in the distance, galloping towards us.

I raised my binoculars. The horse, San Roque, which Roberto was riding, was a grey, a bit on the small side, but its class was evident—and when Roberto gave the horse its head, San Roque left the other horses in his dust, and swept past us with drumming hooves.

Don Luis clicked his stopwatch. He was smiling, his air one of quiet confidence. But Raffles said, "Señorita Inez, you look worried."

"I am," she said. "I do not like this Sherry Bowl Derby matter. I think it wrong that so much should be at stake between Roberto and Alec."

"*Claro*," said her father. "But we shall see what we shall see."

After taking sherry and *tapas* with the Molinas and Roberto, Raffles and I rode back down the dusty track to Campamento.

To this hamlet, horses were the breath of life. Jockeys who came from all over Spain to ride at the Gibraltar Jockey Club meetings, when the Spanish flat season closed, made Campamento their headquarters. A *café* called Los Tres Hermanos was the hangout of the racing folk—and most evenings, after dinner at the Casa Isabel, Alec Gurney and Raffles and I strolled along to Los Tres Hermanos for a game of billiards.

The place was smoky, noisy, crowded. The self-styled Emir of Rabat usually was there, veiled almost to the eyes, but with his ears cocked for items of stable gossip relevant to his purpose as a turf prophet. Instead of the bullfight posters usual in Spanish *cafés*, photographs of racehorses and jockeys hung on the whitewashed walls. Through a bead-curtained archway, two tiled steps led down into a room that held the scarred and solitary billiard-table—a Spanish one, pocketless. And on the Friday evening before the Sherry Bowl Derby, Raffles and I dropped in at Los Tres Hermanos on our own, Alec having gone off for an eve-of-race conference with Master Primrose's handler, Mr. Abremis.

A Madrid jockey, Jésus Fernandez, had challenged Raffles to a hundred-up. I was marking for them when suddenly the squabbling of hoarse voices in the main room of the *café* fell abruptly silent, as though something extraordinary had occured. Next moment, the bead curtain in the archway was swept aside and I saw that something not only extraordinary but in fact unprecedented had happened.

A woman had ventured into Los Tres Hermanos.

It was Joan Roskelly.

"Mr. Raffles," she said, standing there in the archway, her hair ash-blonde, her blue eyes troubled, "could I please have a word with you?"

"Miss Joan," Raffles said, immediately handing me his billiard cue, "this is no place for you. Let's go outside."

He ushered her out, the beads of the curtain swaying together, clicking. The jockey urged me to take Raffles's place, and I did so, but my mind was not on it and I promptly miscued, in due course lost the game, and was obliged to pay Fernandez fifty pesetas.

I hurried back in the moonlight to the Casa Isabel, where I found Raffles alone in his room. He was pacing up and down restlessly, smoking a cigarette.

"What's happened?" I said.

"A disaster, Bunny. I gather from Joan Roskelly that Inez Molina's father, Don Luis Molina, has had a few bad seasons with his horses. Apparently, he's in debt as a result—mainly to one creditor, a local landowner. Joan has just heard that the creditor has obtained some sort of injunction restraining Don Luis from removing any part of his property from Spanish soil."

Raffles gave me a grim look.

"You see what that means, Bunny? Don Luis's property consists chiefly of his horses. So Roberto's mount, San Roque, will not be permitted to pass through the *Aduana* tomorrow to Gibraltar racecourse, to run in the Sherry Bowl Derby!"

"Oh, dear God!" I said.

"Inez rode down from the Cortijo Molina this evening and told Joan about the service of the injunction. Joan's in an awful state about it. She tells me she's certain it's her father's doing.

You see, Bunny? He must have heard about these debts of Don Luis's, and Joan says that Sir George has been making mysterious visits to a local landowner here. That landowner is the creditor who's now obtained this injunction.''

''Sir George put him up to it?'' I said.

''Undoubtedly,'' said Raffles. ''Joan says that, as a banker, her father deplores old Bart Gurney's impulsive act of putting the future of his sherry business to the hazard of a horse-race. Sir George has been doing everything possible to reduce the hazard in favour of his own future son-in-law, Alec. With this injunction coup, Sir George thinks, of course, that he now has the situation in hand. But Joan—a very nice girl, Bunny—thinks it's horribly unfair on Roberto and Inez. Joan's very upset about it. She feels something should be done, but she's ashamed to tell Alec of her father's action, and she doesn't understand legal matters, so she came to me, a fellow countryman, for advice as to whether this injunction could in some way be—as she put it, in her naïve, girlish way— disinjuncted.''

''You explained, of course,'' I said, ''that that was out of the question?''

''On the contrary, Bunny,'' said Raffles, ''I pointed out to Joan—and to Inez—a legal complexity that arises here. I explained that the Spanish writ doesn't run on the British side of the neutral territory. As far as the Bristish are concerned, San Roque can race in Gibraltar.''

''But the horse won't be allowed through the *Aduana* to Gibraltar!''

''That's the problem, Bunny. Finesse will be needed to cope with it—especially as San Roque has often raced in Gibraltar, so is well known to the *carabineros* at the La Linea *Aduana*. Anyway,'' said Raffles, ''Inez has now gone back home to Cortijo Molina. Roberto, I understand, is going to Gibraltar in the morning to see if he can arrange to ride for some other owner with a Sherry Bowl entry. Inez tells me that Don Luis is so upset that he can't bear to see the race. He's going to Cádiz, where he has two horses running next week. He's instructed Inez to scratch San Roque at Gibraltar, but I've told her not to be in a hurry to do that, as it may not be necessary. Meantime, Bunny, there are a couple of little things *you* can do."

"Me?" I said uneasily.

"First," said Raffles, "keep an eye on Sir George Roskelly tomorrow. Second, here's a hundred quid from our rather meagre capital. When you get to the racecourse tomorrow, you'll probably find that news of the injunction on San Roque is being rumoured around, so you should get good odds."

"I'm to bet this money on San Roque?" I said, incredulous. "Raffles, this is madness!"

"That remains to be seen, Bunny," Raffles said, with a wicked look—and, taking me by the arm, he steered me firmly from his room and shut the door in my face.

I slept hardly a wink. I could not imagine what dangerous plan Raffles had in his mind to subvert the injunction—and I wondered what life would be like in a Spanish prison. As dawn was paling my window, I heard someone on the landing outside my room. Thinking it might be Sir George, on whom I was supposed to keep an eye, I sprang out of bed and opened my door a crack to peer out. I saw Alec Gurney. He was carrying his riding-boots and a primrose silk racing jacket and cap, the newly registered colours of Sir George Roskelly.

"'Morning, Manders," said Alec. "This is the day! Senior partner or junior partner? The die will be cast today."

"May the best man win, Gurney," I said.

I put on a dressing-gown and took a look into Raffles's room. He was not there. Not until eleven-thirty did I set eyes on Sir George Roskelly. There was to be an early lunch before we left for the races. It was a buffet lunch on the sunny terrace of the Casa Isabel. A sumptuous collation was set out on the table, together with the whole remarkable range of "Don Bartolo" sherries. Two white-jacketed menservants hovered attentively as I tried to make up my mind whether to brace myself with a *manzanilla*, soothe myself with an *amontillado*, or do myself a favour and indulge in a rich brown *oloroso*.

Compromising, I had chosen an *amontillado* when Sir George Roskelly, immaculately turned out for racing, complete with grey topper and binoculars, came out on to the terrace. Joan was with him. She looked charming in a summery dress. She carried a parasol.

"Good morning, Mr. Manders," she said. "Where's Mr. Raffles?"

That was what I was wondering myself, so all I could do was reply lightly, "Oh, I expect he'll show up soon, Miss Roskelly."

The creaking of a wheelchair sounded as Mr. Bartholomew Gurney propelled himself out on to the terrace.

"'Morning, all," said the old gentleman cordially. "You look very pretty in that dress, Joan—*muy guapa*, my dear. And where's my other favourite girl? Where's Inez? Is this her coming?"

But the person approaching on a horse up the drive of crushed seashells, dazzlingly white, was a man. Passing the two high-slung, yellow-wheeled carriages which, in the shade of the date-palms, were waiting to convey the Casa Isabel party to Gibraltar, the man on the horse reined in at the foot of the terrace steps. He was Mr. Abremis.

"*Buenos días*, Don Bartolo," he said, raising his bowler. "Good morning, Sir George. I'm on my way over to Gibraltar to join Mr. Alec. He and one of my stable lads walked Master Primrose over there earlier. But I thought I'd look in here for a moment, because I've just heard a strange rumour. It's about this Sherry Bowl race, and I thought—"

He broke off abruptly—for old Mr. Gurney, hurling his cheroot to the ground, spun his wheelchair around and trundled himself straight back into the house.

"Mr. Abremis," said Sir George Roskelly, "Mr. Gurney doesn't allow the Sherry Bowl race to be spoken of in his presence. One must make allowances for the quirks of the elderly. But never mind that. What's this rumour you've heard?"

"I though you'd better know about it at once, Sir George," said Mr. Abremis, who had not dismounted. "I was passing that *café*, Los Tres Hermanos, when Jésus Fernandez, a jockey who hangs around there, ran out and stopped me. He says that Don Luis Molina's horse, San Roque, has been injuncted and won't be allowed through the *Aduana* to race in Gibraltar!''

"Indeed?" said Sir George, his face the impassive mask of a banker.

"But there's mischief going on, Sir George. There's a rumour that San Roque has vanished. According to Fernandez, the loose-box the horse was in at the Cortijo Molina was found empty—about a couple of hours ago.''

My heart lurched. I knew whose hand had been at work.

"I understand from Fernandez," Mr. Abremis went on, ''that the injunction was served on Don Luis Molina last night. He was so upset that he went off to Cádiz early this morning, leaving instructions with Miss Inez to scratch San Roque. But she's just a young girl—inexperienced. The injunction has no validity in Gibraltar. The Sherry Bowl race is very important to her *fiancé*, Mr. Roberto Gurney. Suppose that San Roque should somehow arrive on Gibraltar racecourse—well, Sir George, I must admit I wouldn't myself, speaking personally, blame Miss Inez if she ran the horse.''

"But damnation," shouted Sir George, his face suffused by a mottled flush, ''that horse won't be allowed through the *Aduana*! There's a great fence across that neck of land, the Spanish frontier, and it's patrolled. There's no way across except through the *Aduana*!''

"Sir George," said Mr. Abremis, ''you don't know this corner of the world. The cleverest *contrabandistas* alive hang out around here. A lot of them are *gitanos*—gypsies. If there's a gang of them at work with a big stake in San Roque running in the Sherry Bowl Derby, I wouldn't put it past them to get that horse somehow to Gibraltar.''

"Incredible!" shouted Sir George. "Impossible!"

"Well, Sir George," said Mr. Abremis, "I've been thinking. I understand from that jockey Fernandez that Mallam Juzeed, the tipster rascal who calls himself Emir of Rabat, was running around just now making a great outcry about *his* horse—that good black nag of his—being missing. He lets it graze on the hill behind the polo ground, and apparently the horse had pulled it's tether-stake. *Two* horses missing, Sir George! You can't tell me that that's just a coincidence. I wasn't born yesterday. No, sir, it occurs to me that if there's a *contrabandista* gang at work here, it'd be easy for them to change San Roque's colour for an hour or two, and just as easy for one of them to get hold of the sort of robes that damned tipster veils himself up in. There'll be a lot of traffic through the *Aduana* and—"

"By God!" Sir George shouted. "That's it! You've hit it, Mr. Abremis! We'll catch 'em at it! There's time, there's still time! By heaven, I'll put a stop to this!" He ran down the terrace steps. "You there—coachman! Wake up! Stir yourself! Get me to the *Aduana*!"

So spellbound had I been by Mr. Abremis's revelations that it was only now, in the nick of time, that I recollected Raffles's instructions to me to keep an eye on Sir George. I raced down the terrace steps, sprang after him into the nearest of the two waiting carriages, then gave a hand to Joan as she ran to join us.

The coachman, rudely startled from his snooze in the date-palm shade, cracked his whip, and the horse started off at a great rate down the drive of crushed seashell.

With the canopy swaying, its red tassels dancing crazily, the carriage clattered through Campamento hamlet, passed the Café Tres Hermanos on the right, then the dusty polo ground on the left. With Mr. Abremis cantering alongside us on his horse, I sat facing Joan and Sir George in the carriage, my back to the coachman on his elevated box. He kept his whip cracking. So frequent were the potholes in the road, edged by eucalyptus trees and cactus clumps, that we were bounced about unmercifully on the holland-covered seats in the sweltering shade of the canopy.

There was no chance to speak a word. It was all we could do to hang on to the supports of the canopy. Joan lost her pretty hat overboard. Her hair came down. The bay opened up on our right. A low parapet edged the road. The sea heaved indolently, with a blinding glitter—and as we entered La Linea we got involved with the race-day traffic of carts, carriages, *coches*, mule-riders, bedizened gypsies jingling tambourines.

The crowd was much greater than on the previous Saturday. From all the long, dust-white roads of Andalusia, favoured of the wine-loving gods, race goers were converging upon the frontier, and the great Rock that heaved up beyond, for the Sherry Bowl Derby.

Nearing the *Aduana*, our carriage was forced at last to a standstill, caught in the queue piled up before the bottleneck.

Sir George jumped out of the carriage. I jumped out after him, gave Joan a hand to alight.

Sir George, looking anxiously towards the head of the queue, shouted, "We're in time! There he is, there's the fellow!"

In the very act of entering the tawny shadow of the archway through the *Aduana* was a figure swathed in Moorish robes and head-dress and mounted on a black horse.

Sir George, holding on his grey topper with one hand, his binocular-case bouncing on its strap, ran towards the head of the queue.

"Stop that man!" he shouted. "*Carabineros*, stop that man!"

I followed in haste, my head spinning with surmise and dread, and Joan ran beside me, holding on to my arm.

Startled *carabineros*, with slung rifles, closed around the robed rider and led him off to one side, under the archway.

"The man's an imposter!" Sir George bawled. "Get him off his horse. He's no more Juzeed the tipster than that horse is the tipster's horse. It's Don Luis Molina's grey, San Roque, the injuncted horse! It's been treated with some damned stain or other by a contraband gang. Arrest this gypsy or whatever he is and bring water, turpentine, or whatever's necessary to swab the horse off."

A *carabinero* officer—not Don Carlos Tejedor, the Commandant—pulled the white-robed figure down from his horse. With a sickening premonition, I saw the officer pluck away the swathe of head-dress that veiled the robed man almost to the eyes. To my stupefaction, the face revealed was not that of Raffles. It was the bewildered countenance of the self-styled Emir of Rabat.

"This is Mallam Juzeed," the officer told Sir George. "He's quite harmless."

"Harmless be damned!" Sir George shouted. "He's in the

conspiracy. He must be! I tell you this horse is San Roque. Get the horse swabbed off and you'll see."

The officer gave some orders, two of his men ran off to obey them, and the officer turned on the other *carabineros*, who were clustering round with eager curiosity.

"What are you staring at?" the officer snapped. "Get that crowd moving through—*pronto, pronto*!"

At the head of the queue waiting to pass through the arch were the British troopers with the string of Gibraltar polo ponies, returning from the usual morning exercise at Campamento.

"Pass on, pass on! Keep moving!" shouted the *carabineros*—and their eyes returned instantly to the fascinating operations now taking place on the tipster's horse, which was being unsaddled and sponged down by two men who had come running with buckets.

The clinking of hooves on flagstones echoed back from the arch overhead with a hollow, multifarious clatter as the yellow-blanketed polo ponies filed through at a walk, the cheerful troopers shouting advice to the unfortunate tipster, advising him to run for it.

"Now's your chance, Your Highness!" they yelled. "Never mind their guns! It's ten to one they ain't loaded! Run for it!"

Whether it was the sight of the polo ponies that galvanized my memory, I did not know—but there flashed suddenly into my mind a recollection of the rangy grey pony of rather more than the regulation 14.2 hands which Raffles had played on in the polo match against Los Bodegueros. Unobtrusively, I switched my attention to the polo ponies filing by. There was a grey about midway in the file. Yellow-blanketed, with a led pony to either side of it, the grey ridden by a trooper in khaki tunic with blancoed shoulder-cord. His tanned face was shadowed by a field service cap.

I was looking at A. J. Raffles—on San Roque.

He gave me a wink.

The blood rushed into my head as the string of ponies passed out of the *Aduana* arch into the heat-glare of the neutral territory—while the *carabineros* swabbed away earnestly, the cynosure of all eyes, at the tipster's horse, which obstinately remained as black as a horse very well could be.

The race-going crowd continued to move on through, and it was quite a while before Sir George Roskelly could be convinced of the tipster's innocence and of the integrity of his horse's pigmentation. To his credit, the banker then apologized handsomely, and pressed five sovereigns into the palm of the aggrieved Emir of Rabat.

"I jumped to a mistaken conclusion," Sir George admitted to Joan and myself, as we joined, afoot, the crowd streaming along the straight road across the neutral territory. "However, I can imagine no other way the injuncted horse could be smuggled through the *Aduana*—especially now that I've put the authorities there thoroughly on the alert against the *contrabandista* gang's activities, eh, Manders?"

"I'm confident, Sir George," I replied, giving him my sincerest look, "that, thanks to you, the gang'll find all possible loopholes adequately blocked."

Under the impassive regard of Somerset Light Infantry sentries and the keen scrutiny of Gibraltarian policemen uniformed like London bobbies, we walked with the stream of race-goers through the British gateway and turned to the left on to the Gibraltar Jockey Club racecourse overhung by the precipice of the Rock's towering North Face.

Seldom could this racecourse have presented such a sight as on this day of the Sherry Bowl Derby. It seemed that all Andalusia was here, in the heat-dazzle, to see worked out the enigmatic destiny of the great "Don Bartolo" *bodegas*.

Excusing myself to Sir George and Joan, I left them to find their own way to the grandstand. I had a hundred quid burning a hole in my pocket, and I wanted to get our bet down, as instructed by Raffles. I saw immediately that the rumour of an injunction on Don Luis Molina's San Roque had been noised around, for the bookies' blackboards were offering forty to one against the horse—obviously considered a doubtful runner.

I placed our bet, getting forties, but my innate prudence prompted me to hedge the bet with a tenner of my own as a saver on Sir George Roskelly's horse, Master Primrose.

While two races were run, to the roar of the crowd, I wandered around looking for Raffles. I saw Jésus Fernandez, the jockey with whom we had played billiards at the Campamento *café*, Los Tres Hermanos. He gave me a wink, and I wondered what he meant by it. I also saw Juzeed, the tipster, self-styled Emir of Rabat, wandering around in his robes, shouting that he had a horse, and waving a handful of grubby envelopes to prove it.

I went to take another look at the bookies' blackboards. Clearly, the news was out that San Roque had arrived, for the odds were being rubbed out and re-chalked from minute to minute, shortening rapidly. Then my heart gave a nasty thump, for I spotted Commandant Carlos Tejedor, of the *Aduana*, and Colonel Gomez of the Guardia Civil. On this side of the frontier, they were in civilian clothes. They were conferring together frowningly, clearly unable to account for the arrival of San Roque in spite of the injunction. Thanking heaven that they could do nothing about it on this British side of the frontier, I slunk away and mingled with the crowd.

During the running of the 2.15, the Catalán Bay Handicap, in which I saw that Fernandez was riding, a hand fell suddenly on my shoulder. I spun round. It was Raffles, immaculate in a white suit, a pearl in his cravat, an M.C.C. hatband on his straw boater. He was smiling.

"So far, so good, Bunny," he said. "I nipped over here to Gibraltar very early this morning and hunted up those artillery chaps who take the polo ponies to and fro. I told the chaps the situation and explained that I thought I could arrange for a diversion at the *Aduana* which would cause it not to be noticed if one more trooper came back from Campamento with the ponies than went over with them earlier. The troopers were very tickled, and I arranged with them to bring over, under a horse-blanket, an artilleryman's uniform for me. Then I went back to Campamento, found out where Jésus Fernandez lodges, and had a talk with him."

"Ah!" I exclaimed.

"Ah, indeed!" said Raffles, amused. "I asked him to

watch for Mr. Abremis, waylay him, tell him that San Roque had vanished, and pitch Abremis that fairy-tale about Juzeed the tipster's horse having strayed. I thought I'd probably have to bribe Fernandez, but no, he jumped at the chance to bamboozle Abremis, who never gives him a ride. So all I had to do then was steal San Roque—which was child's play, with Inez and the stable lads turning a blind eye—and lead the horse down to mingle with the ponies exercising on the polo field."

"Abremis came straight to the Casa Isabel with Fernandez's story," I said.

"I thought Abremis would do that," Raffles said, "and I hoped that Sir George would jump to the obvious conclusion—and leg it for the *Aduana*. I was a little anxious about the timing. Believe me, as us chaps with the ponies got near the *Aduana*, I was praying for Sir George to appear. Then he arrived, in the nick of time—and created exactly the uproar and diversion we needed. So all I had to do then was hand over San Roque to Inez and Roberto here at the racecourse and change from uniform into these togs I brought over here with me early this morning. And now, Bunny, it's up to Alec and Roberto, again on equal terms."

The crowd roared.

"Excellent," said Raffles. "I see our friend Jésus Fernandez has won the Catalán Bay Handicap. Let's hope that's a good omen for us, Bunny. Come on, we'll join the Casa Isabel party now, to watch the Sherry Bowl race."

We made our way through the crowd and up into the grandstand, where we found old Mr. Bartholomew Gurney installed in his wheelchair. Sir George was there, with Joan, minus a hat but with a pretty parasol shading her fair hair. At her side was Inez, brunette and beautiful in a lace *mantilla*.

All had binoculars to their eyes, watching the runners going out to the starting-post for the Sherry Bowl race. The post was on the right-hand, the Mediterranean, side of the course. I raised the binoculars I had borrowed at the Casa Isabel. Against the background of date-palms, false-pepper trees and glittering sea, the silks of the gentleman jockeys—eleven of them—shimmered brilliantly in the visible heat currents. And I saw that the official starter for the Gibraltar Jockey Club was none other than H. M. Colonial Secretary, Mr. Naughton-Bull, whose torn riding muscle had involved Raffles and myself in this adventure.

The riders came under starter's orders, there was a certain amount of backing and jostling, one false start, then at last the horses were near enough aligned, the tape flashed up—and with a thunderous roar from the crowd, they were off for the Sherry Bowl Derby, the memorial of an old Englishman's enduring love for his lost lady of Spain.

Left-hand round the far rails poured the vivid blur of silks, a big roan horse making all the running and drawing away.

"Lucky Lancer," I heard old Bart Gurney mutter—"that British subaltern up again, who pipped Alec at Cádiz last year. Come on, Alec—don't leave it too late again!"

"He *is* leaving it too late!" said Sir George. "He's beaten!"

"Beaten be damned, Roskelly! He knows what he's doing. See, now? Here he comes—and by God, here comes Roberto on that good grey of Molina's! *Now* they're riding!" said old Bart. "That's my boys! Look there—Lucky Lancer's jock is going for his whip. He can hear the boys coming up behind him!"

There were only three horses in it as they came sweeping left-hand round the rails into the straight and almost head-on into my binoculars, with Lucky Lancer under the whip and still in the lead by a half-length on the Gurney boys, riding neck-and-neck. They went for their whips simultaneously—and, to the sustained roar of the crowd, the brothers-by-adoption swept past the post with not a whisker between their mounts, as far as I could tell, and the roan Lucky Lancer beaten by a neck.

The roar of the crowd sank to an excited hum, then soared to the greatest thunder yet as the numbers went up.

"By God!" said old Bart. "Dead heat! *Dead heat*—Master Primrose, San Roque!"

Intensely moved, the sherry magnate buried his hawk nose in his handkerchief and blew a blast like a trumpet, and I saw the smiling girls, Joan and Inez, embrace the old man in congratulation, sympathy, and love.

"Aye, my *chicas*," mumbled old Bart, mopping his moustache and his eyes. "What a day! Eh? *Both* my young scamps—the pair of 'em—have put their names on their dear mother's Sherry Bowl! If she were here, if she could have seen this—*ay-de-mi*, she'd be a proud, proud lady this day."

His hands shook as he fumbled a cheroot from his leather case.

"Know what that scoundrel Juzeed tipped in his sealed prophecy? Lucky Lancer! Hah, damfool Emir of Rabat!" said old Bart—and puffed his cheroot alight at the match Raffles struck for him. "When I saw Lucky Lancer's jock go for his whip, I thought, 'That's it, he's beat, Alec's got him!'—and then Roberto come up, and they both come home, *both* of 'em! By God, I don't deserve such luck!"

"With no desire to be unkind, Mr. Gurney," said Sir George Roskelly, closing his binocular-case with a snap, "candour compels me to agree with you. In view of this fortunate result of the race, I now feel free to speak openly of a matter you've hitherto refused to discuss. I tell you frankly that I so strongly disapproved of a horse-race as a way of settling the future of a fine business, and so strongly felt that you yourself regretted the reckless commitment you'd made, that I took such steps as were possible to get the race, at least as far as your adopted sons were concerned, washed out altogether."

We all looked at the grim banker in astonishment.

"Inez," he said, "forgive my saying that I chanced to learn of a certain debt by which your father was temporarily embarrassed. After careful consideration, I went to his creditor and persuaded him to apply for an injunction that would prevent your father's horse leaving Spanish soil. The creditor was exceedingly reluctant to do any such thing, but, when he understood my motives, he finally agreed."

"Your motives, Father?" Joan said. "What *were* they?"

"To ensure," said George Roskelly, "that neither Roberto *nor* Alec should ride in the Sherry Bowl race this year."

I was bewildered. We all were. I glanced at Raffles. Never had I seen on his keen, tanned face so strange an expression.

"It is incumbent upon a banker," said Sir George, "to study human nature, to be a judge of character. Your adopted sons, Mr. Gurney, are a credit to you and your good lady. They are what you have brought them up to be. They are gentlemen. So I had not a shadow of doubt that if, by some misfortune, Roberto were deprived of the ride on San Roque, then Alec, as soon as he heard of it, would immediately withdraw from the ride on Master Primrose."

I stared at the banker. I felt as though I had been sandbagged.

"Thus," said Sir George, "the race would be washed out as far as Roberto and Alec were concerned, and you would be freed, Mr. Gurney, of your ill-advised commitment."

"Oh, *Father*!" Joan exclaimed—and she threw her arms about the tall banker, and kissed him.

"That's all very well, Joan," Sir George said. "Some damnable race gang of *contrabandistas* and raggle-taggle gypsies stole the injuncted horse and somehow—God knows by what chicanery—smuggled the horse out of Spain and so destroyed my carefully considered arrangements. I was dumbfounded when I saw from the bookies' blackboards that the horse had arrived and was running."

He looked sternly at Inez.

"Had your father been here in person today, young lady, and seen his injuncted horse arrive, unauthorised and unexpected, here on the racecourse, he certainly wouldn't have run it. He would have respected the injunction, lest he imperil his license to train on the Spanish Turf, and he'd have taken the horse back into Spain immediately. As your father's representative here, Inez, you've taken a grave risk in letting San Roque run."

"Oh, I know! I was warned of the risk," said Inez, her lovely brown eyes going momentarily to Raffles. "But I was sure—I was *sure*, Sir George—that Roberto could *win* on San Roque. So I *wanted* to take the risk, and I've backed San Roque and won a lot of money for Father. And I know everything will be all right now, because San Roque is a Spanish horse, Spanish owned and trained, and *has* dead-heated in the Sherry Bowl Derby! And our stable lads are already taking San Roque back to Spain, and the horse will get a hero's welcome in La Linea. There'll be a great *fiesta* tonight, and I'm quite sure nothing will be said by the authorities about the horse being a truant for a couple of hours while under an injunction!''

"I fancy, Sir George," Raffles said quietly, "that the Gibraltar authorities would take a similarly lenient view if the situation had been reversed."

"I suppose so," Sir George admitted, "—in the unique circumstances that appertain in these parts. But by God, the fact that the race ended as it did is a damned lucky thing for all concerned!"

"Especially for me," said old Mr. Gurney. "You're sound and right, Roskelly, in everything you've said. You did a fine thing in trying to get the race washed out as far as my boys were concerned. I'm grateful to you. But Roskelly, forgive me if I say I'm even more grateful to the damned scoundrels, whoever they were, who managed to get San Roque across the frontier. *Both* my boys, the Spaniard and the Briton, have put the name I gave 'em on my dear Dōna Isabel's golden bowl. I don't care now if I never see another race. So come on, all of you—my butler Alfredo's down there with the carriages, and he's got the drinks. If someone'll just give me a lift down these steps—"

"Certainly, sir," said Raffles. "Come on, Bunny!"

We heaved up the sherry grandee's wheelchair and, as we carried him down the grandstand steps in the blazing sunshine, he puffed contentedly at his cheroot and raised his hat to the acclamations of the crowd roaring:

"*Viva! Viva*, Don Bartolo!"

"I gotta horse!" cried the Emir of Rabat.

3

THE HERMIT OF FLEET STREET

One hot Saturday, on returning from Shrewsbury, where he had been playing cricket for an M.C.C. team against Shropshire Gentlemen, Raffles dropped in unexpectedly at my Mount Street flat.

"Well, Bunny," he said, looking very tanned and fit as he accepted a whisky-and-soda from me, "what have you been up to while I was away?"

I explained that I had succumbed to my recurrent urge for literary expression, to take me out of myself, and now was wondering what to do, if anything, with a piece I had been moved to pen.

"What kind of a piece is it?" Raffles asked.

"It's intended," I confessed, "to be of a humorous nature."

"Splendid," said Raffles. "You must try it with *Punch*."

"Isn't that aiming rather high, Raffles? I had *Ally Sloper's Half-Holiday* more in mind."

"Nonsense, Bunny! Aim at the top. Give *Punch* first look at your piece. You don't want to sit here reading it over and over. That's not healthy. It'll only make it seem less and less humorous to you. Come on now, pop it in an envelope and we'll drop it in at the *Punch* office before your nerve entirely deserts you."

The *Punch* office was just off Fleet Street and, when I dropped my piece of light literature into the letter-box of the famous periodical, I felt as though a weight had been lifted from my mind.

"And now," said Raffles, "we'll stroll down to the Embankment for a breath of air to give us an appetite for lunch, then we'll catch a train out to Henley and spend the afternoon on the river."

44

Though it was not much past midday, already the pulse of London had slowed to the tempo of a sweltering weekend. Except for an office boy here and there, making for the post office with a batch of letters in his hand and sausage-and-mash on his mind, there were few people about in this maze of old byways off Fleet Street. The premises of newspapers, magazines and publishers were silent and still.

"It reminds one, Bunny," said Raffles, "of Marrakesh in the siesta hour, when the fronds of the palm trees and the lower lips of the camels droop listlessly in the heat." His tone changed. "Hullo, what's this procession approaching?"

Three men had come into sight on the opposite sidewalk of the narrow old street. In the lead was a small man, trim and erect in top-hat, cutaway coat, striped trousers. He had a neat grey beard. His pince-nez, dangling on a cord, flashed in the sunshine.

Walking with a brisk, purposeful air, he was followed by two burly individuals who, towering over him, taking one stride to his two, marched side by side. They, too, wore silk hats, but their frock-coats were bottle-green in colour, with brass buttons. These two men bore between them, each gripping a handle, a leather satchel, evidently heavy.

"Bank messengers," Raffles murmured to me.

Just then, the small man in the lead turned sharply to his right and entered the premises of one of the oldest-established and most influential newspapers in the land. Saluted by the commissionaire at the door, the small man, followed by his laden stalwarts, vanished within.

"H'm," said Raffles. "Wait a minute, Bunny. Let's have a cigarette." He took his case from his blazer pocket, offered me a Sullivan. His grey eyes, shaded by the brim of his boater, held the speculative expression I had come to know only too well. "That was a curious incident. The satchel those bank messengers were carrying undoubtedly contains cash—probably sovereigns."

"No doubt," I said, "it's to pay staff salaries."

"On a Saturday, *after* banking hours," Raffles said, "when most of the employees have gone home and, from the look of it, the building's three parts empty, only a skeleton staff left on duty?''

"It does seem strange," I admitted uneasily.

"Very," said Raffles. He touched the match in his cupped hands, the flame almost invisible in the sun-dazzle, first to my cigarette, then to his own. "The two messengers are coming out again," he murmured.

Sure enough, the two stalwarts in the bottle-green frock-coats had reappeared. They no longer were accompanied by the brisk, small man in the cutaway coat, nor did they now carry the heavy satchel. They had an off-duty-at-last air. Filling their pipes, they lingered for an amiable word with the commissionaire, and then, tossing pipe-smoke over their shoulders, strolled off, large men visibly at ease, towards the large leisure of a hot weekend.

"Curious," said Raffles. "Tell you what, Bunny. See that sign—'The Rasselas Coffee House'—dangling over the door of that old building on the corner ahead there? Journalist chaps from the newspaper probably frequent that place. Let's drop in for a coffee. We might be able to find out something about that banking incident."

Ahead, the two bank messengers were passing straight on along the street as Raffles and I turned in under the Coffee House sign, which depicted that old-time denizen of Fleet Street Dr. Samuel Johnson, the great lexicographer and author of *Rasselas*.

"There's a good omen for the piece you've submitted to *Punch*, Bunny," Raffles remarked. "Wasn't it Sam Johnson who said that only a blockhead writes for anything but money?"

Before I could reply, as I followed Raffles out of the sun-glare into the dimness of the Coffee House, a voice exclaimed, "Raffles and Manders! I *thought* it looked like you two I saw out there!"

From a settle near the bow window, which proffered to the passer-by the invitation of a rotating brassbound coffee-roaster redolently smoking, the only customer in the shadowy little place, with its sanded floor, rose to his feet. He was a wiry, brown-haired, brown-eyed chap in his middle twenties and a well-cut but rather threadbare tweed suit.

Despite the spontaneity of his greeting, a hint of uncertainty came into his expression; his extended hand half fell, as though in response to some sudden dubiety of mind. But Raffles gripped the hand hard.

"Well, well!" he said. "Hugh Tollard!" And he cut straight to the heart of Tollard's momentary diffidence: "Bunny Manders and I were damned sorry to hear about your coming a cropper, Hugh. How long have you been back in circulation?"

"About six months," said Hugh Tollard. "I got a bit of remission."

He laughed, with a shakiness of relief, as we all sat down and a venerable waiter came to take our order.

"You know," Hugh went on, as the waiter hobbled away, "you two are the first friends I've run into since I got out. If you've been in jail—well, you're not sure how people may receive you."

"My dear chap," Raffles siad, "if there were any justice in the world, half the people walking about on the outside would be safely locked up inside. It's all a matter of luck. You were just unlucky, Hugh."

"No, I deserved what I got," Hugh said. "It was my own fault. The judge had the truth of it. As he wisely told me, 'A young solicitor should devote his time to building up his practice, not to playing cricket all through the season. If you'd devoted yourself to your practice, instead of to your wicketkeeping, you'd have observed what your clever partner was up to behind your back, and you wouldn't be standing here before me today. Cricket is no excuse for ignorance. You must go to prison for two years.'"

"The damned old hypocrite!" Raffles said. "Why, you can see that judge watching the cricket at Lord's pretty well any day in the week. He's notorious for hurrying through his calendar so that he can get to the cricket. Anyway, Hugh, now that you're out, why haven't we seen you at Lord's this season?"

"I'm no longer a member of the M.C.C.," Hugh said. "I resigned, of course. And what other club would have me now? Believe me, Raffles, if you've once been on the inside, it's hard to live down. I've discovered that. I've a job of sorts—pretty much a dead end, but I'm lucky to have a job at all."

The waiter brought our coffee.

"Actually," Hugh said, as the waiter left us, "when I inherited that mess my partner left when he bolted to South America, the worst part of it, for me, was that I'd just got engaged. Susan! I can't tell you how wonderful she's been through it all. She stood by me. She was as staunch as a rock when the whole world seemed to be falling to pieces around me. Look, I want you chaps to meet her. She'll be here any minute. We meet for coffee in the Rasselas here every Saturday afternoon."

"Not only would we like to meet her, Hugh," Raffles said, "but we hope we'll be invited to the wedding—eh, Bunny?"

"Absolutely, Raffles," I warmly concurred.

"Wedding?" said Hugh Tollard, his expression strange as he looked out through the bow window at the somnolent street. "There may never be any wedding. It's because of her father. When my disaster happened, Susan's father turned dead against me. I'd been sent to prison—and over a money matter. That finished me with him. You can understand it, I suppose, because he works for a bank—and money has a sort of mystique for bank people. They're peculiarly sensitive about it."

"I've noticed that myself," said Raffles—and I nodded rueful agreement.

Hugh gestured toward the street outside, deserted now except for the commissionaire before the newspaper premises about a hundred yards away.

"Did you happen," said Hugh, "to see a trim little grey-bearded man with pince-nez go into the premises of that newspaper just now, with two bank messengers carrying a satchel?"

"As a matter of fact," Raffles admitted, "we did."

"Well, that satchel," Hugh told us, "contains a thousand pounds—gold sovereigns. And the small man with the beard is Susan's father, Mr. Nelson Pell—the Weekend Banker."

"A curious soubriquet, Hugh," said Raffles, taking out his cigarette-case.

My lips had gone dry. I took a sip of my coffee.

"It's a curious matter," said Hugh Tollard. "Mr. Pell will sit there in those premises until ten o'clock on Monday morning, and not a soul will go near him—except Susan, very briefly—until the two bank messengers arrive to escort him back to the bank with the thousand sovereigns in the satchel untouched."

"How extremely odd!" said Raffles.

"There he'll sit, in those newspaper premises," Hugh said, "all over the weekend, in a building almost empty. He'll sit in a little room tucked away at the back of the building—a room, Susan tells me, with a half-obliterated old label marked 'Cliché' on the door. Nothing in the room, Susan says, except a safe, a camp-bed, a table, a chair. And there Mr. Pell will sit, hour after hour, as he's sat through innumerable weekends and national holidays for many years now—waiting for something that's never likely to happen."

"And what's that?" Raffles asked.

"Why, the newspaper running out of ready cash," Hugh said. "Apparently, by some mischance, it *did* happen, just once, many years ago. Some cataclysm occurred in the Balkans or somewhere. The newspaper wanted to rush correspondents to the scene—hire a special train and a fast steam-launch and so on. It turned out there was no cash on hand. It was the weekend, the banks were shut. The upshot of it was, the newspaper's correspondents were beaten to the scene by those of a rival paper."

"So what happened?" said Raffles.

"I gather," Hugh told us, "that there was a row about it. Feelings ran high, and the then Editor of the newspaper demanded a special weekend service from the bank. The bank assigned their Mr. Pell to be Weekend Banker on the premises. But, of course, the original incident was just a freak mischance. It's never recurred and is never likely to. Susan's convinced that the newspaper has simply forgotten the arrangement was ever made, and the bank—in the conservative way banks have—has just gone on, never having received a cancellation, automatically providing the service."

"Good God!" Raffles exclaimed. "Have you ever heard of such a thing, Bunny?"

"Absolutely not, Raffles," I sincerely replied.

"Naturally," said Hugh, "Mr. Pell would much rather spend his weekends at his home, out near Barnes Common, tending his roses. But his sense of duty to the bank and its client keeps him sitting alone there, with the thousand sovereigns, in the little room at the back of that almost-empty newspaper building—a forgotten man, the loneliest man in London."

"A strange story," said Raffles, "even for Fleet Street, with its uniquely rich folklore. But tell me, Hugh—does Mr. Pell go out for his meals?"

"No," said Hugh, nodding towards the window. "Here are his meals just arriving."

Through the leaded panes of the window I saw that into the Saturday drowse of this Fleet Street backwater a hansom had turned. The jogging hoofbeats of the horse were audible as the hansom came on towards us, then pulled up, a hundred yards off, in front of the newspaper premises.

The commissionaire stepped forward to relieve the passenger of a wicker basket covered with a snow-white napkin; and the passenger, putting a small foot on the step, descended lightly to the kerb and, turning, opened her purse.

"Susan," said Hugh.

The girl made a pretty figure out there, in her summery white dress patterned over with tiny pink roses, and her shady, wide picture hat of a straw colour, as she held up the fare to the cabbie, then glanced fleetingly towards the dangling sign of the Rasselas Coffee House.

"She always looks this way," Hugh said—wondering if I'm here yet."

The horse plodded round in a half-circle, the hansom jingled off, and Susan turned to the commissionaire. He hooked the handle of her basket over her arm and stood smiling after her as she passed into the newspaper premises.

"She brings Mr. Pell's week-end provisions every Saturday at this time," Hugh told us. "She's been doing it ever since she was twelve years old, when her Saturday trip in from Barnes in a hansom was a great adventure to her. She's an only child—and a little girl, you know, an only child, whose mother dies, is apt to develop an extraordinary sense of responsibility where her father's concerned. I know how deep that goes in Susan. She's twenty-two now and could, of course, do as she pleased, but—"

"But?" said Raffles.

"Well, to break irrevocably with her father," Hugh said, "which is what marrying me would mean, I'm afraid, is a frightful thing for her to contemplate. Oh, she won't give me up! Her father knows perfectly well she meets me here every Saturday and that we spend the rest of the day together. She makes no secret of it. She's told her father that she longs for the day when he'll change his attitude towards me."

"But, damn it, Hugh," Raffles said, "you were really guilty of nothing but—too much cricket!"

Hugh smiled ruefully. "Mr. Pell sees it as gross dereliction in a money matter. To him, there's no worse crime, and—once a jailbird, always a jailbird. Susan and I despair of changing him. She'll come along here soon, when she's made his bed and seen that he's all fixed up for his lonely weekend."

Raffles, looking thoughtful, ordered more coffee, which we drank while we were waiting.

"Here comes Susan now," said Hugh.

Through the window, I saw the girl and the trim little banker, half a head shorter than his daughter, emerge from the newspaper premises into the sunshine. Mr. Pell now was bareheaded, his hair parted meticulously in the middle, and he carried the basket. He handed it to Susan and, kissing his bearded cheek affectionately, she turned from him.

He raised his pince-nez, shot one inimical glance through them at the Rasselas Coffee House, then turned and strode back briskly into his weekend prison.

Susan came walking on towards the Coffee House. Her

footsteps quickened. She took off her pretty hat. Her hair had the sheen of amber, her eyes searched eagerly the bow window in which we were sitting with Hugh, and she began to smile, she began to run—with the basket on her arm.

Then she was in the doorway, and then in Hugh's arms—not seeing Raffles and me at all, in the dimness here after the sun.

Hugh took her basket and her hat from her. An arm about her, he brought her to the settle and, as we rose, began to introduce us.

But she smiled and said, "Raffles and Bunny? I've heard Hugh speak of you so often that I feel I've known you for ages!"

And, warmly, she held out a hand to each of us—this girl, Susan.

We were very taken with her, and Raffles invited the attractive but star-crossed young lovers to lunch. It was evident, however, that they wanted to be alone, so Raffles did not press the point. We left them holding hands in the Rasselas, and ourselves walked up to Piccadilly Circus for lunch at Appenrodt's, where one of our favourite waiters, genial old Fritz Niederkel, recommended the Bismarck herrings with potato salad and a lightly chilled Rhenich as just the fare for a hot day.

Raffles seemed thoughtful and, as we left the restaurant, he said, "If you don't mind, Bunny, we'll cut out the trip to Henley. There's something I want to look up in the encyclopaedia. Pop round and see me on Wednesday evening."

His chambers in The Albany were nearby, so I left him there and strolled on round to my flat in Mount Street, wondering what it was that he wanted to look up in the encyclopaedia.

On the Wednesday evening, when I called on him at his chambers, I asked him.

"Oh, that?" he said. "I wanted to look up how to convert troy weight into avoirdupois weight."

"For what purpose?" I asked, rather uneasily.

"For the purpose," said Raffles, "of finding out if two brawny bank messengers were necessary merely to carry a satchel containing a thousand sovereigns, or whether the presence of two messengers was a matter of bank security practise. The answer, you'll be glad to hear, is the latter. The avoirdupois weight is easily portable in, if occasion should arise, a quite ordinary basket.''

He added, ''Now, if you've nothing better to do, we'll go round and see our invaluable 'fence,' Ivor Kern, who's been making a few arrangements for us.''

It was with some reservation of mind that I accompanied Raffles, in a hansom through streets tranquil in the lingering dusk of summer, to King's Road, Chelsea, where Ivor Kern carried on his clandestine activities under the cover of an antiques shop.

Personally, I had been giving a good deal of thought to the very human predicament in which Hugh Tollard and his charming Susan found themselves, so it was rather a shock to me to find that what Raffles had been thinking about, on the other hand, was the thousand pounds in gold.

My attitude, accordingly, was somewhat standoffish as we joined Kern in the cluttered, gaslit living-room over his shop.

''Well, Ivor?'' Raffles said.

''Everything's arranged as you asked,'' Kern replied, with his cynical smile. ''I've found just the woman to meet the physical specifications you described. She's a skilled hand, pretty as a picture but hard as nails. She won't try any tricks with us; I know too much about her. She wants a cool hundred quid to do what's required.''

''Never grudge a woman,'' said Raffles. ''Pay her in advance, Ivor, and put it on my personal account with you. Have you arranged about an unidentifiable four-wheeler and reliable cabbie for her?''

''All fixed,'' Kern said.

''Good,'' said Raffles. ''Bunny here and I'll use your brougham and your chap Stoker. He'll be needed, at the denouement, to provide a quick means of retreat from the scene.''

My heart sank.

''Meantime,'' Raffles went on, taking an envelope from his pocket, ''here are my written instructions—the operation order for the sequence of events. I cased the newspaper building yesterday. Their cricket correspondent has been criticising the Ground Committee at Lord's about their plans for new seating arrangements at the Nursery end, so I made that a pretext for calling on him. I carefully 'lost' myself in the building and had a good look round. I found the inconspicuous little room with the old label marked 'Cliché' on the door. By the way, Bunny, you've had journalistic experience—what's the significance of that word 'Cliché'?"

"The cliché department," I explained, "is where the clipping dossiers, the obituaries and so on are stored till called for. Some newspapers, I believe, refer to it as 'the Morgue.'"

"Well, that little room is now the one," Raffles said, "where Mr. Nelson Pell, the forgotten man, the hermit banker, keeps his weekend vigils. Ivor, I've marked the position of the room, and the corridors leading to it, on the operational plan in this envelope. Now, any questions?"

"Just one," Kern said. "What about our lady confederate's wardrobe?"

"Bunny and I'll be handling that matter," Raffles said. "The lady will do her costume change in the four-wheeler on her way back from Barnes Common. Make sure, of course, that the four-wheeler has window-blinds. But you'll find all details covered in my operation order. Now, what about a spot of that excellent whisky you acquired illicitly from the Bonded Warehouse?"

There was a dancing vivacity in Raffles's eyes, as always when he had a coup developing. But, for my part, I could not get the emotional quandary of Susan and Hugh out of my mind, and somehow, for once, I found Raffles's concentration on acquiring the loot, the thousand sovereigns, not wholly to my taste.

Nevertheless, due to my innate weakness of character, I was at Raffles's side when, on the morning of the following Saturday, we jingled over Hammersmith Bridge in Ivor Kern's brougham, driven by his henchman, Jem Stoker.

The heat-wave had remained unbroken, and I rather envied the Leander Rowing Club eight whose boat, with the cox shouting the stroking rate through a megaphone, was passing fleetly under the bridge. Our own more blameworthy mission took us along the main road across the heat-shimmering undulations of Barnes Common, and soon we entered a tree-lined street of pleasant villa residences, each in its own attractive garden. Here the brougham pulled up, at Raffles's call to Stoker, in the shade of a sidewalk tree.

"We've a few minutes to wait, Bunny," Raffles said, taking out his half-hunter for a glance at it. "Let's have a cigarette."

A suburban peace reigned here, accentuated rather than broken by the summer sound of an unseen lawnmower. Here and there a busy housemaid shook out her duster from an upstairs window. A butcher's boy swept by, whistling, on a bicycle, using no hands, his enamel tray cleverly balanced on his head. A straw-hatted milkman trundled his three-wheeled trolley up and down the garden paths, and from somewhere rose the soprano cry of a rag-and-bone man with his donkey-shay.

We almost had finished our cigarettes when I heard, from somewhere behind us, the clip-clop of approaching hoofbeats.

"Right, Bunny," Raffles said, glancing back through the round rear window of the brougham. "We can go now."

As I followed him out of the brougham and across the street, I saw that, about a hundred yards behind our brougham, another four-wheeler had pulled up under the kerb-side trees. Nobody alighted from the newly arrived four-wheeler.

We turned a corner to the right, into a very similar street, and Raffles said, "Mr. Pell's house is just along here. He himself will be at the bank now, counting the thousand sovereigns into his satchel. Here we are, this is his house— 'Rosy Acre.'"

The front garden was shielded by a beautifully trimmed macrocarpa hedge.

"I reconnoitered the house yesterday," Raffles told me. "Susan keeps house single-handed—no servants. She's almost certainly in the kitchen at this hour. I caught a glimpse of her there yesterday. She was roasting a sirloin—probably to be carved cold today for Mr. Pell's weekend basket." He glanced each way along the street. "The coast's clear. Come on, in we go!"

He opened the white-painted gate and we moved up a Y-shaped path of red and blue tiles. Each side of the path, edged by carefully pruned standard roses, was a small, well-kept lawn. A gay sun-curtain hung before the front doorway of the attractive little house, and all the windows, upper and lower, were wide open. Bees and butterflies abounded, and I could well understand why Mr. Pell would rather have spent his weekends at home than immured in that cliché room off Fleet Street.

The left branch of the tiled path passed between the side of the house and a neat little greenhouse ablaze with blossoms and ripe tomatoes, and it was by this way that Raffles stealthily led me, round to the back.

Here the ground-floor windows stood open to a small patio, and a rose-covered pergola led down, between gooseberry and currant bushes, to a well-kept kitchen garden.

On the patio, we stood with our backs pressed to the wall of the house, and Raffles peered obliquely to his right into a window that stood wide open. From the sound of a drawer jerked open with a slight rattle of cutlery, I guessed that the room there was the kitchen.

"We've timed it perfectly," Raffles whispered, glancing round at me. "Mr. Pell's basket is on the table. Susan's just beginning to pack it."

I craned forward a little, to peer round him into the kitchen.

Susan was standing at the kitchen table. She was in profile to us. She was sharpening a carving-knife briskly on a steel. The blade flashed in the sunshine. She tested the blade lightly with her thumb. Satisfied, she laid the knife and steel down on the table.

She crossed to a white-painted door that had a key in its lock. Opening the door, she stepped into what I saw was a larder with a small ventilation grille high up. A ray of sunshine slanting down from the grille brought out the amber lights in Susan's pretty hair as she lifted a domed wire meat-cover from a dish on a shelf. Her back was half-turned to us.

Before I realized what was happening, Raffles ducked in over the window-sill, took three swift, silent steps across the kitchen floor, closed the larder door on Susan, turned the key in the lock.

I heard a dish crash to the tiled floor of the larder—and Raffles gave me a wicked look.

"Papa's sirloin," he whispered, and he beckoned me in.

From sheer habit, I obeyed—though the thought of poor Susan standing rigid in the larder, her heart pounding, her eyes wide, the broken dish at her feet, made me detest Raffles at that moment.

He took up the basket and starched napkin from the table and, beckoning me to follow, left the kitchen. We found ourselves in a little hall. The floor was of beeswaxed parquet. Japanese wind-chimes tinkled their faint music.

Reluctantly, I followed Raffles up a carpeted staircase to a landing, where he opened a door and looked in.

"Obviously Mr. Pell's room," he said—"military hairbrushes." He closed the door, moved along the landing, opened another door. "Ah, here we are, Bunny—this is Susan's room."

Without a moment's hesitation, he went in. I did not follow him. It seemed hardly a done thing to enter a girl's bedroom behind her back. Compunction rooted me to the threshold. Yet some base fascination prevented me from averting my eyes.

Sunshine from the open window flooded the airy room, redolent of roses. On the dressing-table, with its dainty feminine appurtenances, were photographs of Mr. Pell and a gracious lady who, I assumed, was the late Mrs. Pell. There was also a photograph of Hugh Tollard that must have been taken before he fell foul of the Law, for he was shown standing on the pavilion steps at Lord's, wearing wicket-keeping gear and an M.C.C. cap.

On the crisp white counterpane of Susan's bed, with its polished brass knobs, lay her shady wide picture hat and her summery rose-patterned white dress.

"That's what I want," said Raffles. "All laid out ready—

she was going to wear it in to town today."

Folding the dress carefully, he placed it in the basket, laid the hat on top of the dress and, shaking out the folds of the starched table-napkin, covered the contents of the basket with it.

"Right," he said. "Off we go, Bunny!"

We stole out by the sun-curtained front door.

"Raffles," I said, "what about Susan?"

"She'll come to no harm in the larder, Bunny. She won't know whether the marauders are still in the house, so it'll probably be quite a while before she starts calling out for help."

Less and less did I like this business as we walked round the corner to where Stoker waited with the brougham. He jumped down from his box, and Raffles handed him the basket. Stoker walked off with it to where the other four-wheeler waited, further down the street.

I saw a woman's fashionable leg-of-mutton sleeve reach out from the four-wheeler. Her hand took the basket, drew it into the four-wheeler, then the blind was pulled down.

Stoker returned to us, mounted to the box of the brougham, and Raffles and I got in, and we jingled off again. Looking back through the rear window, I saw that the four-wheeler was following, but falling behind, for our nag was the livelier.

"So far, Bunny," said Raffles, "all's gone according to plan. Now for the thousand sovereigns—and let's hope our timing's right."

It was twenty minutes to one by the Law Courts clock when our brougham passed by into Fleet Street. Already, as on the previous Saturday, there were few people about, as our brougham turned off into the maze of adjacent side-streets and, threading its way through them, arrived at the entrance to the street where the Rasselas Coffee House and, further on, the famous newspaper office were situated.

Calling to our driver to stop, Raffles said to him, "Now, Stoker, your job is to wait here and be ready to whip away fast when the time comes."

"You can count on me, guv'," said Stoker confidently.

Leaving him, Raffles and I walked on along to the Coffee House. The roaster was still rotating and aromatically smoking in the bow window. We went in, and there, in the same settle-seat near the window, sat Hugh Tollard, the only customer in the place, lighting his pipe.

"Why, *hello* there!" he exlaimed. "I didn't expect to see you chaps today."

"We know now where to find you at this time on Saturday," Raffles said, as we sat down. "We thought we'd stroll round and hear your news."

"*I've* no news, worse luck," said Hugh. "I just live for Saturdays, when I can see Susan. She'll be along at her usual time."

But I knew better—and, thinking of Susan locked in the larder of her home away out there at Barnes Common, I could not bring myself to look at Hugh. I busied myself with stirring my coffee. It was beginning to become clear to me how extraordinary was the situation which Raffles had contrived. It seemed that we were to sit here at this window and watch, almost as from a theatre-box, the commission of a crime which he had prepared in masterly detail.

The narrow, sunstruck street, seen through the leaded panes of the Coffee House window, seemed to me to have indeed almost the look of a stage—set, as it were, for a light opera with an Old London theme. I seemed to see it filled suddenly with mobcapped girls selling lavender to sauntering gentlemen in beaver hats, while pickpocketing urchins darted to and fro through the throng, and gruff old Dr. Johnson of Bolt Court made his entrance, stumping on shortsightedly, the volumes of his *Lives of the Poets* under his arm as he sang "Sweet Thames, Run Softly" in a resonant baritone.

"There he is!" said Hugh Tollard's voice suddenly.

My fanciful vision dissolved in an instant, and I saw that, on the opposite side of the street, Mr. Nelson Pell, trim and erect, his silk hat flashing, was striding past the Coffee House. Carrying between them the satchel of sovereigns, the two tall bank messengers in their bottle-green frock coats followed the small banker to the newspaper premises, a hundred yards or so from us. Mr. Pell wheeled to his left and, to an amiable salute from the commissionaire and followed by the messengers, entered the building.

I hardly heard what Raffles and Hugh were talking about. I could not take my gaze from the street outside. I saw the two messengers reappear. Relieved of the satchel, they lighted their pipes, exchanged a word or two with the commissionaire, then came sauntering back our way, and passed by on the opposite sidewalk.

Raffles called to the venerable waiter for more coffee. I drank mine without really tasting it—and I put down my cup abruptly as I saw a four-wheeler cab come into view. I recognised it instantly as the cab I last had seen at Barnes Common.

"I wonder," Hugh Tollard said, "if this can be Susan? This is just about the time she normally arrives, but she doesn't like four-wheelers. She always comes in a hansom."

I felt a sudden misgiving. It seemed that Raffles, for all his meticulous planning, had made a tactical error in arranging for his bogus Susan to change into Susan's dress in a four-wheeler. The bogus Susan should have arrived here as Susan herself had arrived last Saturday—in a hansom, not a four-wheeler.

I saw the horse reined in now in front of the newspaper premises. The commissionaire stepped forward, opened the cab door, and received from feminine hands, reaching out, the basket with the snow-white napkin.

"Yes, it's Susan," said Hugh happily.

But now, as a slender figure in a shady picture hat, and a summery white dress patterned over with tiny pink roses, stepped lightly from the cab and, keeping her head a little bowed, took the basket from the commissionaire and hurried into the building, again Hugh spoke in a tone that betrayed puzzlement.

"Curious," he said. "She hasn't paid her cab off, as she usually does."

A *second* error in Raffles's planning! I felt a sudden moisture in my palms. I dared not look at him.

"I wonder why she's kept her cab?" Hugh said. "I wonder if something's happened and she's got to go straight off somewhere?"

His expression was increasingly troubled as he gazed from the window.

"She doesn't seem quite herself today," he said. "She always looks towards the Coffee House here, wondering if I've arrived yet, when she gets out of the cab. She didn't even glance this way this morning."

My mind was in a tumult. A *third* error of detail in Raffles's written instructions to his hirelings? I simply could not credit such carelessness; it was totally unlike him. There must, I felt, be some other explanation—and it suddenly occurred to me to wonder if his seeming carelessness could possibly be deliberate and that he had, in fact, so stage-managed events as to be just sufficiently right to get the bogus Susan past the commissionaire, but just sufficiently wrong to create a doubt in the mind of the man who best knew Susan and her ways: namely, Hugh.

Excited by my theory, I stole a glance at Raffles. He was sipping his coffee. His keen face was expressionless, but I sensed his tension.

"I've got a feeling," said Hugh Tollard, staring anxiously through the window at the waiting cab a hundred yards along the street, "that something's upset Susan. But I'm sure she'll look in here and tell me about it, whatever it is."

"Here she comes now," Raffles said.

"Strange," said Hugh. "It usually takes her longer than this to make up Mr. Pell's bed and so on."

Not only had the bogus Susan emerged from the newspaper premises, but the small banker as well. As last week, Mr. Pell was now bareheaded; as last week, he carried the basket. The commissionaire opened the door of the four-wheeler, and Mr. Pell, using both hands, lifted the napkin-covered basket into the cab. The bogus Susan stepped into the cab, the commissionaire closed the door on her, the cabbie whipped up his horse. The small banker stood motionless, gazing after the cab as it came on towards the Coffee House.

Hugh Tollard sprang to his feet. His face was deeply flushed.

"Did you see?" he said. "She didn't kiss her father good-bye! And did you see the way he lifted that basket? The damned thing should be empty, but it was obviously *heavy*! And look at the way that cabbie's whipping up his horse! Something's wrong! *I don't believe it's Susan in that cab!*"

He lunged for the door. Raffles followed him. I followed Raffles.

The cab almost had reached the Coffee House.

"*Stop!*" Hugh yelled.

He threw himself in front of the horse, seizing it by the reins and wrenching its head round as the horse dragged him along for a yard or two, then came to a standstill. The driver made a flying leap from his box and raced off up the street. With him went a flutter of summery white dress patterned with tiny pink roses. It was the bogus Susan, who must have leaped from the cab on the blind side.

Unencumbered by the heavy basket, the pair were running like hares to where, at the street corner, Jem Stoker waited with the brougham to whip them away to safety.

"After 'em!" Hugh yelled.

Raffles seized him by the arm. "Wait! Steady, Hugh! Mr. Pell's shouting urgently to us!"

The small banker came running up, hatless, his face pale.

"Never mind *them*, Tollard," he panted. "It's Susan that matters. The thieves' confederates are holding her at Rosy Acre under threat of death. We must get out there at once, calling at the police station on the way—"

"To hell with the police station!" Hugh shouted. He leaped up on to the box of the four-wheeler, seized the whip from its socket. "*Giddap!*"

Mr. Pell, Raffles and myself just managed to scramble inside, stumbling over the napkin-covered basket on the coir floormat, as the cab lurched into motion.

"I don't know who you gentlemen are," said the small banker, feeling for his pince-nez with a shaking hand, "but this has been the most appalling experience of all my banking life. I never thought to see the day when I would surrender the bank's money to robbers. But, on my oath, I had no option. My daughter's life was at stake. That horrible woman who impersonated Susan and came to my room at the back of the newspaper building ordered me to open the safe, put the thousand sovereigns in my charge into the basket, carry the basket out to the cab under the nose of the commissionaire, and wait two clear hours before I raised the alarm. The alternative—death to Susan!"

"Good God, sir!" Raffles exclaimed.

"It was no idle threat," Mr. Pell said shakily. "I knew that my daughter was indeed in criminal hands—for the woman who impersonated her was *wearing Susan's own dress*!"

"Incredible!" said Raffles, astonished.

"I am a banking man," said Mr. Pell, "dedicated all my life to the sanctity of property. Yet, gentlemen, confronted with a choice between my duty as a banker and my instinct as a parent—"

"It would have been unnatural in you, sir," Raffles said, "if, in such a moment of starkly compared values, you hadn't placed the worth of your daughter above that of the contents of this basket."

"A thousand pounds," said Mr. Pell.

"Just so," said Raffles, lifting a corner of the napkin for a look at the sovereigns neatly packed in rolls of blue paper, each roll sealed with red wax. "No mean sum, Mr. Pell. But, thanks to our mutual friend, Hugh Tollard, you have it safe and sound."

Not without, I fancied, some iota of regret, Raffles dropped the napkin back over the swag.

"If I may say so, sir," he went on, "it was fortunate that Hugh was in the habit of meeting your daughter at the Coffee House on Saturdays. He penetrated the disguise of the summer dress, put two and two together, and took instant action. I've never seen quicker thinking, have you, Bunny?"

"Absolutely not," I fervently concurred.

"Indeed yes," said the small banker. "This outrage was obviously planned with great adroitness—and, but for Tollard, would certainly have succeeded. I shall so inform the bank—which, I'm sure, will materially indicate its appreciation. As for myself, my personal debt to him is beyond computation, if only—if *only* we find Susan none the worse for her rough handling!"

His fears on this score were dispelled when we arrived at

Rosy Acre, where we all dashed in—Hugh Tollard in the lead, and Raffles and myself ostensibly as anxious as our companions.

From the larder, a small voice was audible, calling forlornly, "Help! Let me out!"

Naturally, with all the details which Susan and her father had excitedly to recount to us, over the dish of tea which Susan said she was simply dying for, it was some time before Raffles and I were able decently to take our leave.

Susan and Hugh walked down to the gate with us. Though Susan, unfortunately, had lost her summer dress and her hat, the radical change which Raffles had so subtly brought about in Mr. Pell's attitude to Hugh more than made up for the trifling loss. Never, in fact, had I seen two people so happy as Susan and Hugh.

We stood talking for a little at the gate, and Raffles, in his courteous way, commented on the neatness of Mr. Pell's garden and the beauty of his roses.

"Perhaps he'll able to do some gardening at weekends now," Susan said. "After what's happened today, I should think the newspaper will wake up to my father's existence. I'm sure they've quite forgotten him, but they'll realise now how unnecessary and—and *dangerous* the weekend banking service is." She smiled. "Are you fond of roses?" she asked us.

"Excessively so, Susan," said Raffles.

She turned and, from a nearby bush, plucked two roses. She gave me one, but the other she reached over the gate—for we were standing outside it—and with her own pretty hands tucked the rose into Raffles's lapel.

With this as his reward for what personally I felt to be the most selfless of his crimes, Raffles and I raised our hats and walked away, smiling, leaving her in the summer sunshine with Hugh at the gate—that girl, Susan.

4

THE GRAVES OF ACADEME

"Talking of rugger," said Raffles, "I was discussing the season's prospects recently with that chap Wodehouse, who used to play for Dulwich College when he was at school there three or four years ago."

It was a Saturday evening in November, raw and misty, and, in a cab that smelt of damp stables and trundled along as though drawn by a hearse-horse, Raffles and I were on our way back to civilization with a couple of fellows we had run into while watching a rugger match at our own old school, which reared its spartan pile on the western outskirts of London.

"'Plum' Wodehouse?" said Norris Peters. "He went into journalism afterwards."

"Writing squibs," said Henry Saulsby, somewhat patronizingly, "for the 'By The Way' column of the *Globe* newspaper."

"Ah, but he told me he's now tapping a richer vein," Raffles said. "He has a theory that the average healthy Englishman, looking back, realises that his schooldays were, as is so often said, the best days of his life. He likes to be reminded of them. So Wodehouse, shrewdly enough, has taken to writing novels of school life while it's still quite fresh in his mind, and he seems to be on velvet with them. In fact, he calls the one he's just published *The Gold Bat*—a significant title, as I told Bunny Manders here, eh, Bunny?"

"You did indeed," I said grimly—for although, like the others, I had loyally put on a school scarf to go to the rugger match, it was years since I had been anywhere near the school and I was vexed with Raffles for dragging me there today and causing me to get my feet wet, standing about on the muddy touchline.

But he seemed impervious to my discomfort.

"Wodehouse," he said, "keeps a keen eye on London schools rugger, for those lucrative novels of his, and he tells me his own old school will mop the floor with ours this season."

"Nonsense," said Saulsby. "We usually beat Dulwich."

"You're only just back from abroad," Peters said sardonically. "You know nothing about current form, Saulsby."

"Anyway," said Raffles, "rugger's a serious matter to Wodehouse and, if one's making any bets, his considered opinion's worth bearing in mind. 'Raffles,' he said to me, 'the word flies round London rugger circles this season—"*Watch Dulwich*!"'"

Huddled morosely in my ulster, I took no part in the argument. It left me cold, and I was cold enough already. I never had liked rugger, or my schooldays, excessively. I just wanted to get home to my snug flat in Mount Street.

The horse clopped along interminably, the cab springs creaked, and I lapsed into a comfortless doze—from which I was abruptly roused by Raffles.

"Come on, Bunny! We get out here."

I stumbled out, my joints gone stiff—and as the cab rumbled off with the other fellows, I looked about with dismay in the mist.

"This isn't Mount Street, Raffles!"

"No, it's Knightsbridge, Bunny. We're going to dine here at Demaria's Restaurant."

"But I thought you'd drop me off at my flat! I can't possibly dine till I've had a hot mustard bath. My feet are numb. I think they're frostbitten."

"Don't worry, Bunny—you've nothing to lose but your toes."

Taking me firmly by the arm, Raffles steered me into the restaurant. Fortunately, a good fire was burning in the wide brick fireplace. Blazing logs cast a pulsing glow on the old oak beams of the ceiling. And when a waiter had relieved us of our outdoor things, and we were seated at one of the tables, which were in leather-padded booths sparsely occupied this early in the evening, Raffles ordered two hot toddies to warm us up. All the same, my mood remained querulous.

"Why have we come here?" I said sullenly.

"For a purpose, Bunny. You know, I thought that Wodehouse's example might kindle your own rather fitful literary ambitions. I hoped that seeing our own old school again might prompt you to try your hand at a novel of school life yourself—particularly as there's just a possibility that I may be able to put you on to the track of a plot. D'you remember a chap called Tarran, at school?"

I nodded, sipping my steaming hot toddy. My feet were beginning to tingle and probably steam, too, as they thawed out under the table.

"Tarran got an army commission," I said, "but fell into debt and had to send in his papers."

"That's the chap," said Raffles. "I'm afraid he's gone downhill a lot. He called on me last week, at The Albany, and asked if I could lend him two hundred pounds. I was low in funds myself. The best I could do for him was a tenner, so he said he'd have to fall back on his last hope—our old classics master at school."

"Mr. Digby Lavelle?" I said. "Good God!"

Raffles said that Tarran may well have stood a chance of touching Mr. Lavelle for a loan, as he was well connected and had considerable private means. Unlike most of the masters, he did not live at the school. He had a house in Knightsbridge, where he lived with a widowed sister and her daughter, and he went to and from the school daily in a hansom.

"I understand that his sister's now deceased," said Raffles. "Anyway, Tarran told me that he'd already dropped Mr. Lavelle a line, asking if he could consult him on a personal matter, and had had a reply inviting him to come and drink a glass of wine at Mr. Lavelle's house at ten o'clock on Monday evening. That was last Monday."

"I wonder how Tarran got on?" I said, intrigued in spite of myself. "Have you seen him since?"

Raffles gave me a strange look. "Bunny," he said, "*nobody* seems to have seen him since. At midweek, a Hunt Cup horse I had a tip on did me proud, romped home at long odds, so I sent you fifty quid and thought I'd see if Tarran was still in need of a modest transfusion. He was renting a room in Pimlico, so I went there. His landlord told me that Tarran went out about nine o'clock last Monday evening and hadn't come back. All his things are in the room, but his habits are irregular and the landlord told me that he intends to wait a day or two longer before he notifies the police.''

''Mr. Lavelle probably turned him down when he asked for a loan,'' I said. ''Tarran was being dunned, so I expect he's made a moonlight flit. I did it myself, more than once, when I was failing as a journalist.''

''Did you leave all your suits and things behind, Bunny?''

''Oh, God, no! One has to keep oneself presentable.''

''Exactly,'' said Raffles. ''So I'm puzzled, Bunny. What happened to Tarran last Monday night? I thought that if we went to that rugger match this afternoon, we might find Mr. Lavelle there.''

''He wasn't.''

''No, but I had a chat with one of the masters who was there. He told me nobody knows what Mr. Lavelle does with himself on Saturdays. He's rather odd and secretive about it, but apparently he goes out of London somewhere in a hansom. I was told that he lives quite alone since his sister died, and he always dines at this restaurant, Demaria's, which is not far from his house.''

Sure enough, we had scarcely started our dinner with a game soup, piping hot, and a quite decent burgundy, when I heard a voice that in my green years had been all too familiar to me—a clear, precise voice that many a time had penetrated tartly to me as I sprawled, dreaming of future fame, on a rearmost bench in the form-room.

''Place my coat on a hanger, Guglielmo,'' the plangent voice was now commanding. ''Venerable as you no doubt consider the garment, I expect it, with due care, to last my time.''

I laid down my spoon. There he was—Mr. Digby Lavelle, whom so often I had seen come sweeping into the form-room, gown billowing about his tall, slender, erect figure, to impart to such minds as we had the marvels of Greek and Latin literature. Gownless now, he was handing to a waiter a distinctive kind of basket and a broad-brimmed black felt hat. Unwinding from his neck a long black woollen scarf, Mr. Lavelle handed that, too, to the waiter, who helped him off with his black overcoat, which seemed hardly to derserve the aspersions he had cast upon it, while the frock-coat he wore under it, with a wing-collar and black stock, had in fact a fastidious elegance. So upright that he seemed to incline slightly backward, Mr. Lavelle glanced around the restaurant.

"Raffles," I murmured, "that basket—it's a creel. *That's* how he spends his Saturdays. He goes out of London to fish somewhere."

"Then where's his rod?" said Raffles, exposing the flaw in my theory—for Mr. Lavelle, though equipped with a creel, was visibly rodless.

Excusing himself to me, Raffles rose. His dark hair crisp, his tweeds immaculate, a pearl in his cravat, he walked across the restaurant and, with that ease of manner I always had envied him, approached Mr. Lavelle. I saw them shaking hands. They they were coming to the table where I sat. I stood up hastily.

"And this is—now, don't tell me," said Mr. Lavelle. "Ah, yes—*Manders*, I fancy. How do you do, Manders?"

He gave me three delicate fingers to shake. His close-clipped moustache, and thin hair brushed straight back from a high, shining forehead, were grey; but his face, faintly pink from the cold air outside, was as unlined as a boy's, though it seemed to me that, as he said he would be delighted to join us, his pale blue eyes gave us an oddly suspicious look.

"I regularly frequent this restaurant," he said, when he had made his selections from the menu, "but I have never seen you here before. I should have thought that young men-about-town would prefer the more animated dining places of Piccadilly and Leicester Square."

Raffles said that we had been watching a rugger match at the school and, this restaurant being on the way back to our respective domiciles, we had dropped in here on impulse. He went on in his easy way to speak of various chaps who had been at the school in our day. He insinuated Tarran's name very smoothly into the list—too smoothly, perhaps, for Mr. Lavelle did not rise to the bait; he did not remark that he had had an appointment with Tarran as recently as last Monday.

"I happened, not long ago," said Raffles, jiggling the bait temptingly, "to run into Tarran."

"So many boys," said Mr. Lavelle. "One sees so *many* boys' faces, receding down the vista of the years. One quite loses track."

I sensed his evasiveness. Two small patches of heightened colour burned in his smooth cheeks. Clearly, he did not want to talk about the school. Instead, as we dined, he explained to us the regret he felt at observing the proliferation of Circulating Libraries in London.

"They encourage light-mindedness," he said. "It is mere self-indulgence to read any work of fiction subsequent to *Vanity Fair*, all so-called modern novels being quarried, of course, out of Mr. Thackeray's great work."

He enlarged on the subject, yet I had a feeling that his mind was not wholly on it. He was making conversation, and he kept darting at us glances that seemed furtive and probing. And suddenly, when we had been served with coffee, he seemed to reach a decision. He set down his cup.

Addressing it, he said in a strained tone, "Has it *always* been known at the school how I spend my Saturdays?"

I felt myself flush, but Raffles said coolly, "I don't quite know what you mean, sir."

"Do you not?" said Mr. Lavelle. He went on looking at his cup; he seemed to be forcing himself to speak. "Since it seems to be a matter of some curiosity at the school, I may say that I go out of London every Saturday. I seek out a certain sylvan solitude in the vicinity of Kew. I take with me a creel containing horticultural implements—trowel, hand-fork, secateurs and so on—for my Saturday outing is in the nature of a pilgrimage, undertaken for the purpose of tending three graves."

Tense with embarrassment, I stared down at my plate.

"One grave," said Mr. Lavelle, "is that of my parents. In a second grave my beloved sister sleeps. The third grave is reserved for myself."

"May its occupancy, sir," Raffles said, very quietly, "be long deferred."

"As to that," said Mr. Lavelle, "the memorial stone which marks my family plot is engraved, as is customary, with relevant dates—except, necessarily, just one. My Saturday pilgrimage, I considered, is my own concern, nobody else's. Today, I found evidence that a vandal had visited my family plot. It saddened me, but in my calling there is light and shade, reward and regret. I obliterated the vandalism, dismissed it from my mind, and in the silence and solitude there, on this misty November day, I proceeded with the labour of love I had come to do, and solaced myself with memories dear to me. "

I dared not look at him.

"*Yet*," said Mr. Lavelle, "I come here this evening to Demaria's, as is my habit, and I notice, when Guglielmo opens the coat closet, that hanging on the hooks there, among other garments, are two woollen scarves checkered black-and-white—the school colours."

"We wore them, sir," Raffles said, "to go to the rugger match."

"Hard by my family plot," said Mr. Lavelle, as though Raffles had not spoken, "there grows, very beautiful in its time of blossom, a thicket of broom, bramble and moss roses—and accidentally, on a thorn of the rose brier, the vandal who had been there left *this* behind him."

Mr. Lavelle took from his pocket and laid on the tablecloth before us a mist-damp tassel, pied black-and-white in wool, from a school scarf.

"Waiter!" Raffles called sharply—and the waiter, Guglielmo, came to the table. "My friend and I deposited with you two black-and-white scarves. Please bring them to us. Just the scarves."

Mr. Lavelle sat rigidly erect, his sensitive lips tightly compressed, his eyes fixed on us with a blue glitter. The waiter returned, Raffles motioned him to hand the scarves to Mr. Lavelle, who began carefully to examine each end of each scarf. I felt hollow inside. It was years since Raffles and I had worn those damned scarves. Tassels might well be missing. It was the sheer fortune of heaven that none were.

"I beg your pardon," Mr. Lavelle said. He laid the scarves aside on the table. "I do most sincerely beg your pardon." The two patches of colour on his pale cheeks burned brighter; he was embarrassed. "Gardening," he said. "Such a mistake to come to it only late in life, as I do. One misses so much. I often think, as I delve with my trowel and muse on seedtime and harvest, the procession of the equinoxes and the survival of the soul, that there may be something more than mere poetic license in Mr. Swinburne's beautiful lines: 'As a god self-slain on his own red altar, Death lies dead.' So protean a reflection, is it not? Oh, *most*!" He called to the waiter, "Guglielmo, bring me my remains now, if you please."

Guglielmo came to the table and deferentially handed to Mr. Lavelle a small brown paper bag.

"The residue," Mr. Lavelle explained to us, "of the excellent halibut on which I dined. I have a *cat*, don't you know." He rose, his manner now fussily cordial, and presented us in turn with three of his fingers to shake. "So nice to have seen you," he said. "Delightful, quite delightful!"

He left us. We remained standing, watching him helped on with his overcoat. He wound his black woollen scarf several times about his throat, tossed the end of the scarf back over his shoulder, donned his wide-brimmed black felt hat, accepted his creel from the hand of Guglielmo, and departed. We sat down again. We looked at each other.

"I think, Bunny," Raffles said slowly, " we need a couple of brandies." His keen face was thoughtful. He frowned. "And we'll take this," he said.

Mr. Lavelle had left behind on the tablecloth the mist-damp pied tassel. Raffles pocketed it. And I knew what that meant. It meant that Raffles intended to go further into the matter of a vandal at Kew—and the question of what had become of Tarran since his ten P.M. appointment at Mr. Digby Lavelle's house almost a week ago.

Uneasy but curious, I went round on the following evening, Sunday, to Raffles's chambers in the Albany. I found him in.

He was in evening dress, as I was myself, and he was in the act of putting on his hat. He told me not to take mine off, as I was just in time to accompany him to a club he wanted to look in at.

"I haven't been there lately," he said, "but the Honourable Secretary was at our old school, though a bit before our day, and I seem to remember that Tarran's a member of that club, or used to be. Come on, it's not far off—just behind the Comedy Theatre. We'll walk it."

"I had a feeling," I said, as we left The Albany by the front steps to the courtyard and Piccadilly, "that you wouldn't let this school matter rest."

"I'm thinking of *you*, Bunny," Raffles explained. "Living as I do, I may find myself in handcuffs any day. I'd hate to see you in the same fix. You're wasting that writing itch of yours. It's no good writing about your experiences with me. You can only hide your output away somewhere and hope to God nobody finds it."

"You fascinate me somehow," I said.

"That's what worries me at times, Bunny. Odd! You'd be so much safer if you could turn your mind to other subjects. There's a Pegasus *in* you somewhere, champing at the bit, and if you'd only mount the beast decisively you could go more or less straight. Look at Plum Wodehouse—on velvet with his school yarns. Don't you sense such a story in this strange business of Tarran and Mr. Lavelle?"

"I must admit I'm curious about it, Raffles."

"Then we progress, Bunny. As a matter of fact, I've dug up a little more material for you today. I've been out to Kew, poking around churchyards in that vicinity, and I found the one where the Lavelles have their plot. Evidently our Mr. Lavelle has a green finger, because the plot's meticulously kept, even now in November. The family memorial stone is in the form of a marble lectern with a marble book on it."

"An open book, Raffles?"

"Necessarily so, Bunny, to reveal the names recorded on the marble page: the Reverend Desmond St. John Lavelle and his wife Amanda Jane Lavelle (*née* Awnsham); their daughter,

Ursula Rose Debaran (*née* Lavelle); and their son, Digby St. John Lavelle—*our* Mr. Lavelle," said Raffles. "The relevant birth and death dates are recorded."

"Except, of course," I said "*our* Mr. Lavelle's death date."

"I'm afraid you're wrong," Raffles said. "What 'saddened' Mr. Lavelle when he arrived at his family plot yesterday was that a vandal had visited it. The one missing date on the page of the marble book had been painted in—with red paint. Mr. Lavelle tried to scrape if off, probably with his trowel. But he didn't *entirely* 'obliterate' it, Bunny. Faint traces remain."

I swallowed with a dry throat. "You could make them out, Raffles?"

"Yes, I could just make out the date specified by the vandal," Raffles said. He gave me a hard look. "When would you expect Mr. Lavelle to make his next pilgrimage to Kew?"

"Next Saturday," I said.

"That's the date," said Raffles, "painted in on the open book."

A chill fled up my spine.

At the club behind the Comedy Theatre, the Honourable Secretary told us that Harry Tarran was no longer a member.

"*Entre nous*," confided the Hon. Sec., "he was chronically in default with his subscription. I had to 'post' him—and, by God, he turned damned nasty!"

"Did he now," said Raffles softly. "H'm! Bunny, let's go up to the writing-room."

It being Sunday evening, we had the writing-room to ourselves, except for the melancholy faces of Wilkie Bard, Little Tich, and other great comedians gazing mournfully down at us from their portraits.

"Sit down, Bunny," said Raffles, offering me a Sullivan from his cigarette case. "Now, then—here's pen and paper. Take down this letter: 'Dear Mr. Lavelle—' Don't look so surprised, Bunny. Go ahead—write."

Sitting on the edge of the writing-table, he drew thoughtfully at his cigarette.

"'Dear Mr. Lavelle,'" he dictated, as I began resign-

edly to write, "'What a happy surprise it was to see you at
Demaria's Restaurant last night! More and more, as the years
fleet by, and I struggle to establish myself in the literary world,
I realise how brilliantly you imparted to me your insights into
the classics. Indeed, I wonder if I might seek your advice on a
small personal problem that is somewhat impeding my own full
absorption in creative endeavour? If you could spare me ten
minutes of your time, my debt to your teaching would be, were
that possible, even greater than at present. Yours, etc.,'" said
Raffles. "If you think that more or less hits off your style,
Bunny, sign it with your name."

"But what's the point of this letter?" I said uneasily, as I
affixed my signature to it.

"The point is, Bunny, that the letter may get you a private
interview with Mr. Lavelle. In that case, you'll ask him to lend
you some money—and we shall then know exactly how Mr.
Lavelle, who's known to have considerable private means,
reacts when an old boy of the school tries to tap him for a loan."
Raffles glanced up at the writing-room clock. "We've missed
tonight's post. If he replies at all, you should hear by Wednesday."

I had put my Mount Street address at the head of the letter,
and the reply came, actually, on Thursday. The reply was in a
sensitive handwriting, full of Greek e's and punctuated with an
emphasis once all too familiar on the margins of my exam
papers:

> My dear Manders: I have received your *note*. Perhaps you
> would care to take a *glass of wine* with me at my HOUSE on
> *Friday* evening at TEN OF THE CLOCK???? We shall be
> QUITE alone!!!!   Yrs., D. St. J. L.

I took the letter straight round to Raffles at The Albany.

"Candidly, Raffles," I said, "I'm not looking forward to
this private interview."

"Don't worry, Bunny," Raffles advised me. "It won't be
altogether private. I shall have broken into the house and
concealed myself before you arrive. So I shall be there, lying
low, with a watching brief, when you ring Mr. Lavelle's door-

bell tomorrow evening—at ten of the clock.''

Accordingly, on the following evening, at the hour so precisely specified by Mr. Lavelle, I found myself in the position Harry Tarran must have been in if, in his desperate straits for money, he had indeed, a week ago, kept his appointment with Mr. Lavelle. I was standing in the dark porch of Mr. Lavelle's house. A thin drizzle of rain was falling. Here and there, in this quiet square in the Knightsbridge neighbourhood, street-lamps gleamed wanly. I could hear the melancholy drip-drip-drip of the rain from the bare boughs of the trees in the railed central garden of the square. Nobody was to be seen.

With a sinking heart, I plucked apologetically at Mr. Lavelle's bellpull. Somewhere in the brooding silence of the premises, the bell faintly tolled. All was still. Only the drip-drip-drip of the rain, which must likewise be grieving down on the gnarled yews and marble angels in the churchyard near Kew, and on the Lavelle family plot marked by the marmoreal book that awaited, irrevocably open, one mortal detail. Had Harry Tarran, refused a loan by Mr. Lavelle, with his abundant private means, gone away embittered and, with God alone knew what morbid intent, committed that tormenting vandalism on the Book of the Lavelles? What did it mean? Where *was* Tarran?

Waiting here in the dark porch, I was a prey to disturbing conjectures and flights of uneasy fancy. I could hear no sound from within the house. Hope stirred in me. Had Mr. Lavelle forgotten our appointment? Perhaps he was from home— dining at Demaria's—and I could go away, relieved of my mission, and not ring the bell again. But if Raffles had kept his promise and was lurking somewhere in the house, maintaining a watching brief, he would know I had rung but once. He would think the less of me for it. Had I better give the bell just one more tinkle, very faint, and hope nobody answered?

As I stood there, irresolute, a pallid luminance bloomed in the fanlight over the door. I was caught. Bolts rattled, the door opened, and there, silhouetted against the meagre gaslight of the hall, stood Mr. Lavelle's tall, slender figure, frock coated.

''Ah, Manders,'' he said, giving me three refined fingers to shake, "I hope I have not kept you waiting. I heard the bell, but I dined on mullet at Demaria's this evening, and I was belowstairs, feeding my remains to my cat. Come in, come in! You will find the house a little dusty, I fear, but when I lost my dear sister I really preferred to live quite alone, so I dismissed the servants and encouraged my young niece to occupy herself in a work of social welfare in the East End of London. A female person comes in to skivvy here daily while I am absent at the school, but I'm afraid she neglects her duties. My young niece, when she visits me, spends most of her time tut-tutting in disapproval and bustling about with dustpans and brushes. *Women*, don't you know. You may put your hat on the hall table there."

On a fine but dusty marquetry table stood his fishing-creel, open, with an earth-stained trowel and hand-fork in it. There was also on the table an exquisite Waterford glass bowl filled to overflowing with yellowed visiting-cards among which, as I placed my silk hat beside it, I glimpsed the cards of the eminent author, Mr. Walter Pater, and the distinguished wit, Mr. Max Beerbohm.

"Nowadays," said Mr. Lavelle, as he ushered me into a room to the left of the hall, "I seldom receive, neither do I go out into society at all. My contact with life is through the school. It is to my association with youth that I owe what some people have been pleased to call my 'well preserved' appearance—though I may, of course, be of the kind that goes to pieces quite suddenly. At all events, one must be prepared, must one not? However, I have learned from school, Manders, far more than I have taught. There is in boys, whether rich or poor, charming or sulky, something of original sin, of course, yet at the same time an essential innocence. It is when they grow into young men, and the disciplines of school life are cast off, that their very eagerness for worldly experience tempts them all too easily into dissolute courses. How often have I been pained to observe that unhappy waste of promise! You will take a glass of port wine with me, Manders."

"Thank you, sir."

As Mr. Lavelle poured the wine from a cut-glass decanter,

I glanced surreptitiously around the room. It was a drawing-room of faded elegance, fireless and cold, lighted by a pendent gasolier with three frosted globes. The wallpaper was white with a thin silver stripe, the Chinese carpet was of an ivory colour, the closely drawn curtains were of crimson velvet, the spindle-legged chairs had candy-striped seats. There were several cabinets filled with Dresden china, and on the walls many gilt-framed watercolours of, to my surprise, seascapes and tall ships under full sail. Above the marble mantelpiece was a portrait, in an oval frame, of a fair, frail young woman with something touchingly gallant in her expression and in the gaze of her fine blue eyes.

"I see," said Mr. Lavelle, "that you are looking at the portrait of my sister Ursula. It was painted by my gifted friend Mr. James McNeill Whistler. My sister, too, painted with spirit—always sea subjects, as no doubt you notice. As a young bride, my sister made, with her husband, a gentleman of New Zealand, an adventurous voyage to his antipodean home. After the poor fellow's death, she returned to England with her child, but her health, I'm sorry to say, was never again robust, and her two sea voyages remained the most treasured experiences of her life."

In the cold room, he still wore his long black scarf, and his forehead shone high and pale in the gaslight as, tossing his scarf end back over his shoulder, he held out a glass to me.

It was excellent port. We sipped it standing. I felt awkward, embarrassed, out of my element, and the house seemed strange, icy and silent about me. I met Mr. Lavelle's eyes. They were fixed intently upon me, with again in them that blue glitter I had noticed at Demaria's.

"Well?" he said abruptly. "What is it, Manders, that you want of me?"

Shamefaced, I began to stammer. He cut me short.

"My experience," he said, "of such missives as that which you addressed to me is that they usually presage an application for *money*. You are in straits, are you not?"

Though I had come here to play a role, it was with a feeling of the sincerest misery that I nodded my hanging head.

Mr. Lavelle took my glass from me, turned to the table.

"So!" he said. "You petition me for money, Manders. You will hardly, then, boggle if I ask you some personal questions." He turned back to me, handing me my glass refilled. "You smoke, of course? You frequently over-indulge in ardent spirits? You are an *habitué* of racecourses, of the card-rooms and billiard tables of Pall Mall clubs? The ladies of the Gaiety Theatre find you often lurking at the stage-door, bearing bouquets and jewelled baubles in anticipation of expensive favours? You need not answer. Your abject demeanour is quite sufficient admission. You were never, at the school, an *exemplary* boy, I'm sorry to say. The seeds of pleasure were all too evident in you. How often have I said to you, in the past, *Obsta principiis*—resist the first beginnings.' Have you made an effort to do so? *Not* the slightest! Manders, I read you like an open book."

Blindly, I stared down at the carpet. My ears burned. If Harry Tarran, subjected likewise to this devastating indictment as prelude to rejection of a plea for a loan, had gone away empty-handed to commit an act of venomous reprisal, it was no longer incomprehensible to me. Yet the resentment I personally felt at the position in which I found myself was levelled against A. J. Raffles, who had exposed me to this humiliation and probably, with his watching brief, was listening from some concealment to every word that lashed my wincing ego. I ground my teeth.

"Look at you!" exclaimed Mr. Lavelle. "You are a reproach to my failure as your preceptor. But I shall not shrug you off, Manders. I decline to saddle myself with the knowledge that I abandoned you to decadence and degradation without giving you at least a chance—*a last chance, Manders*—to amend your ways. Draw a chair to the table and write me out a list of your debts."

Surprised as I was, for his reading the Riot Act at me had led me to expect total and scornful rejection, I had no choice but to drink up my port and obey Mr. Lavelle's order. For once, as it happened, I had few current debts, thanks to Raffles, so I had to invent some. This was not difficult, but when I started to tot up the column, the figures seemed blurred. I could hardly read my own writing. I lowered my head, peering myopically at the figures, and was trying again to tot them up when Mr. Lavelle seized my notebook from me and ripped out the page.

"This will do well enough," he said. "Your usurers and Turf Commission agents I propose to ignore, but your respectable tradespeople shall be reimbursed for their misplaced trust in you."

He handed me back my notebook and I thrust it into what I took to be my breast-pocket but which proved to be my armpit, for the notebook fell to the carpet. With a mumbled apology, I rose to retrieve the notebook, but a curious weakness in my knees caused me to lurch clumsily and knock my chair flying. Mortified, I stooped to set the chair upright, and instead fell over it.

I sat on the floor, feeling all at sea.

The gaslight seemed to shine with a sinister dazzle, and the walls with their maritime watercolours undulated around me. I was dimly aware that the door, which seemed drunkenly tilted, had opened to admit a fair-haired young woman with her hands in a muff. Her blue eyes beheld me with a look of wonder as she came slowly, seemed indeed to levitate, to the side of Mr. Lavelle.

Taking a hand from her muff, she linked her arm in Mr. Lavelle's. The two of them, looking down at me, seemed uncannily tall. I endeavoured to spring to my feet, to make my bow to the lady, but I was betrayed by the floor, which suddenly tilted and struck me so sharp a blow on the back of my head that I lost touch with events—until I became conscious of a speck of light like a star shining in a black void above me. The star grew steadily larger, descending upon me and swaying from side to side with a slight pendulum motion, and it gradually was borne in upon me that what I was peering up at with dazzled eyes was a twin-wick hurricane lantern suspended from what appeared, unaccountably, to be a deck.

Thoughts began to stir sluggishly in my head, which was

throbbing inordinately. Among my thoughts was one that suggested to me that my present debilitated condition must be due to something in the port wine which Mr. Lavelle had given me. I had had only a couple of glasses of it, but I felt now very much as I had done on coming to myself after many a night of convivial indulgence. I made to put a hand to my aching brow, but the hand remained immovable. Dear God, my wrists were bound together behind me! With the realization came an awareness of conversation in my vicinity. Cautiously, I rolled my head sideways.

I was lying in a bunk in what appeared, unbelievably, to be quite a spacious cabin in a seagoing vessel.

At a table covered with red baize on which were glasses and a bottle of grog, a fair-haired young woman with her hands in a muff was sitting in the company of two men. I instantly recognised the young woman as the one who had witnessed my undignified collapse in Mr. Lavelle's house, and it dawned on me now that she rather resembled the Whistler portrait of Mr. Lavelle's sister, Ursula Rose Debaran (*née* Lavelle). In all probability, then, the young woman with the muff was a Miss Debaran, Mr. Lavelle's niece, who occupied herself with a work of social welfare in the East End of London. With wide-open blue eyes and clean-cut features, she had almost the air of an eager, adventurous boy as she listened to what the man beside her at the table was saying.

A barrel-chested man with a leathery, square face and wiry white hair, he wore a pea jacket without insignia, and he spoke between meditative puffs at a pipe.

"Why would I stop at nothing to oblige Mr. Lavelle?" he said. "I'll tell ye, Cap'n Hurn. Mr. Digby St. John Lavelle has given much of his life to the education of boys—*fortunate* boys. Now, me—I'm Royal Navy, retired—*I've* given a good many years to the education of boys, *un*fortunate boys, neglected boys of the East End streets. The training ship I command is philanthropically financed. Twelve years ago we came to a crisis. We were at our last gasp for money. Mr. Lavelle saw in the newspapers our appeal for funds. His sister, who had inherited a tidy fortune from her husband, had recently died.

She left half her fortune to Mr. Lavelle and half to her daughter, Miss Anne Debaran here.

"Mr. Lavelle declined to benefit by his sister's death. It's not in him to do it. His share of her fortune he handed over intact to us. He did what he thought would have pleased his sister. He saved our training ship. We renamed it for her— *Ursula*. And Miss Anne here put *her* money at our disposal— and not only her money, but her time, too. She runs the administration side for us, and finds the boys that most need what we can give 'em—a chance in life. Aye, she's well known east of Aldgate Pump, is our Miss Anne!"

My temples throbbing, I lay still, intently listening. The other man at the table refilled two of the grog-glasses. He was a huge, rawboned man with a square-cut black beard but not a hair on his bullet head.

"As an old friend," said this formidable individual, "I'd like to help ye, Commander Jackson—and you and your uncle, Miss Anne. I've let you talk me into bringing the man-about-town johnnie in the bunk there aboard my ship. But, damme, what you're asking me to do is plain shanghai-ing, old style, right here off Wapping Old Stairs. All right, so he's up to his neck in debt and the police'll write him as a case of moonlight flit, but he could jump ship one day and lodge an abduction charge against me with a British Consul."

"Not a chance," said Commander Jackson. "A court case would make him an object of contempt. He's hamstrung, Cap'n Hurn. Now, look—you weigh anchor on the next tide and you're bound round the Horn for San Francisco. Log this johnnie in the bunk as a stowaway and put him to work. Make a man of him! I tell ye straight, he's not the first black sheep who's tried to touch Mr. Lavelle for easy money—and woke up to find himself in a windjammer's fo'c'sle outward bound for Cape Stiff. I've arranged these matters for Mr. Lavelle. Just last week, we shipped out a waster, name of Tarran. 'If he *has* a better self,' Mr. Lavelle said to me, 'he shall be given a chance to discover it through drastic re-education.'"

"Hard physical work," Miss Anne said eagerly, "is morally bracing for young men, Captain Hurn. One or two of my uncle's black sheep have found their way back to England ultimately as *changed men*. They have gone personally to my uncle and thanked him for bringing them to their senses. Others have made creditable lives for themselves in new, fresh surroundings, and he treasures the letters he's had from them. *Please*, Captain Hurn—won't you give this wretched young man in the bunk just this one last chance to pull himself together?''

Captain Hurn struck the table a resounding blow.

''I'll do it!'' he said. ''Damndest thing I ever heard tell of, but I'll chance the odds. Leave him to me. I'll take him in hand. By God, *I'll* re-educate him so it sticks!''

''Now you're talking,'' said Commander Jackson. He glanced towards the porthole. ''Daylight! Miss Anne, I must see you to your lodgings and get back to the *Ursula*.''

They rose from the table. Captain Hurn opened the cabin door.

''Good morning, all,'' said a voice familiar to me—a voice that sent thrilling through me, in my plight, such a tingle of relief as I never before had experienced.

I could hardly believe my eyes as, without hat or overcoat, his tweeds immaculate, a pearl in his cravat, his promise to me kept, his watching brief maintained, into the cabin stepped A. J. Raffles.

''My apologies, Miss Anne, and gentlemen,'' he said, ''for eavesdropping on your conversation. I'm afraid, Captain Hurn, the anchor watch you keep is not as alert to clandestine incursions as it might me. Still, no harm done, because I'm in sympathy with what I've learned of your activities. You may count on me as an ally.''

''Who *are* you?'' Miss Anne demanded.

''Just one of many,'' said Raffles, ''who've had the privilege of studying, Miss Anne, under the guidance of your uncle—so very rightly considered, in London scholastic circles, the greatest classics master of his time. But I've reason to believe, in connection with his extramural project, Miss Anne, that this day now dawning could be a bad day for Mr. Lavelle. To avert a possible danger to your uncle, I need the help of my friend in the bunk there, so I shall now release him."

He proceeded to do so. Neither Commander Jackson nor Captain Hurn attempted to prevent him. Inhibited by the family complication which had now arisen, they were looking at Anne for instruction. And she was looking, tensely, at Raffles.

"Why?" she said. "*Why* could this be a dangerous day for my uncle?"

"Because it's Saturday," said Raffles. "Are you all right, Bunny?"

I nodded, my head throbbing as I clambered down from the bunk.

"At Number Four Berth, North Quay, Wapping," Raffles said, "I have a brougham waiting. Miss Anne, your uncle is a man of high principles. Confronted by an act of morbid vandalism, he dismissed it, as beneath contempt, from his mind. There's a distinct possibility that Bunny Manders and I can show you a compelling reason why you must see to it that Mr. Lavelle discontinues his re-education experiment, however admirable. Would you care to come with us?"

"Nothing could stop me," said Anne Debaran.

Waiting for us by the warehouses at Number Four Berth, North Quay, when we mounted the seaweedy steps there from the dinghy put at our disposal by Captain Hurn, was a neat brougham. I instantly recognised the coachman as a trusted minion of Ivor Kern, the "fence" and occasional confederate with whom Raffles and I had dealings. In the brougham were Raffles's ulster and tweed hat.

"I left them here," he told Anne and me, as the brougham clattered off over the dockland cobbles, "so that I'd not be discommoded in climbing aboard Captain Hurn's ship from the dinghy of the waterman I'd bribed. You see, Miss Anne, I've been keeping a watching brief on the general situation. I was clandestinely present in your uncle's house, and I heard the conversation he had with you and Commander Jackson shortly before Bunny Manders here rang the bell. I learned, from your conversation, that he was to be harmlessly drugged. I didn't intervene, because your further plans for him were not clear to me. I wanted to know exactly what you were up to. So in this brougham, which I had waiting handily on the far side of the square where your uncle lives, I followed the cab in which you and Commander Jackson took Manders to Wapping.''

"But why,'' Anne said, puzzled, "should you have done these things? *Why?*''

"My dear Miss Anne,'' said Raffles, "we could hardly let Harry Tarran's disappearance, which had come to our notice, go uninvestigated. After all, you know, Manders and I *were* at school with the chap.''

"I see,'' Anne said slowly. "There really *is* a kind of bond, isn't there, between Englishmen who've been at school together?''

"Indeed yes,'' said Raffles. "there are few stronger bonds, Miss Anne. So I feel I should assure you, in order to clear up any misconceptions you may have, that Bunny Manders here has very ably played the role of an impecunious profligate, but is *not*, of course, anything of the kind.''

"Oh, I'm *so* glad, Mr. Manders!'' Anne exclaimed, laying a hand on my knee. "I thought, the moment I saw you, that you have quite a decent face, really.''

"Thank you,'' I muttered, embarrassed.

"Tell me, Miss Anne,'' said Raffles, "d'you think your uncle will go to Kew today?''

"Oh, I'm quite sure he will,'' Anne said. "He always does on Saturdays, so I go and tidy up his house properly while he's absent, as he doesn't like women bustling about him with dustpans and brushes.''

"Yet where should we be without them?'' Raffles said consciously.

He glanced out at the buildings we were rapidly bowling past, then he removed the stopper from the speaking-tube mouthpiece affixed beside his seat, facing Anne's and mine in the brougham. He blew into the mouthpiece, then enunciated clearly into it.

"Coachman,'' he said, "when we reach the square in the Knightsbridge area, drive slowly along the *nearer* side of the square's central garden—the side where you waited for me last night. Is that quite clear?''

On the roof of the brougham sounded two acknowledging knocks. Raffles stoppered the mouthpiece. Anne was looking at him with wide eyes.

"Please, she begged, "won't you tell me what all this means?"

"We may be able to do better," Raffles said—"we may be able to *show* you what it means."

In accordance with his instructions, our coachman, when presently we reached the square where Mr. Lavelle's house was on the farther side of the central garden, reined in his horse to a walk. Letting down the window on its strap, Raffles scanned the garden, where railings enclosed the bare trees, puddled lawns, and shrubberies of evergreens still dripping from the night's rainfall.

I swallowed with a dry throat. I could feel Anne tense beside me.

Suddenly, softly, Raffles said, "Yes— I *thought* he might be here—and *there* he is! There's the man who committed a vandalism with the object of destroying your uncle's peace of mind, Miss Anne. *There's* the vandal! He calculated, knowing your uncle's character, that Mr. Lavelle would scorn allowing a vandal act to deter him from making his usual Saturday pilgrimage. But the vandal's not *quite* sure of that, so *there* he is—can you spot him, Anne? He's standing in that shrubbery to the left of the gate on the far side of the garden. He's watching your uncle's house to see if he comes out today—*carrying a fishing-creel*. D'you see him, Bunny?"

In the grey morning light, under the drab sky lowering over London, I discerned a figure standing motionless among the jigsaw of boughs and wet leaves of the evergreen shrubbery— and, even as I spotted the lurking vandal, I saw the front door of the house he was watching suddenly open.

Raffles said harshly into the speaking-tube, "Whip up! Drive round the end of the garden and come up on the other side—*fast*!"

Two thumps sounded on the roof of the brougham, reins slapped the horse's back, harness jingled, the brougham lurched into rapid movement. Through the flicker of the railings I could see Mr. Lavelle, in his porch on the far side of the garden, locking his door. He turned, tall and slender in his overcoat, wide-brimmed black felt hat, black woolen scarf. Shouldering his fishing-creel, he descended his porch steps and, with his brisk, fussy walk, turned to his left, tossing his scarf end back over his shoulder.

The vandal in the shrubbery made no move—and Raffles spoke again into the speaking-tube.

"Slow down a bit," he said. "If a man comes out of the garden gate over there, you're a cab for hire. Understand?"

Two knocks sounded on the roof of the brougham. Raffles stoppered the speaking-tube mouthpiece. With the nag reined down to a clip-clopping trot, the brougham rounded the end of the garden and started up the other side of it. A whip-crack quickened the horse's pace again, the garden railings flickered by the brougham window, then came to a standstill as the horse was reined in.

"Keb, sir? Lookin' for a keb?"

"Right. Drop me at the Main Gate, Kew Gardens."

"'Op in, guv'!"

The fare opened the brougham door. He was wearing a woollen scarf checkered black-and-white in the school colours. Seeing that the brougham was occupied, he checked sharply in the act of ducking in—and he would have ducked out again if Raffles had not seized him by his scarf ends. Detained, struggling against the stranglehold on his scarf, the fare clutched at his pocket, but Raffles struck first—a lightning uppercut that connected with an audible impact and turned the fare suddenly limp, so that Raffles had to heave the fellow in bodily to the one vacant seat in the brougham.

In her own corner, Anne was shrinking back, eyes wide, her hands in her muff.

"So!" said Raffles. "Main Gate, Kew Gardens, eh? Handy for your uncle's churchyard, Anne—and, incidentally, not more than a brisk half-hour's walk from the school. That's why he's wearing that scarf. When he'd dealt with your uncle in that lonely churchyard, he'd have gone on to the school. He'd have mingled with the boys, masters, and loyally bescarved Old Boys who'll certainly be thronging the rugger ground touchlines this afternoon to cheer on the First Fifteen against whatever school—St. Paul's or Merchant Taylors or even Dulwich College—happens to be on the Fixture List for this Saturday. But tell me, Anne—am I right in thinking that you may have seen this fellow before?"

"Yes, just once," Anne said, her voice a little breathless—"more than two years ago, in my uncle's house, when—when—"

"When your uncle invited him to take a glass of port?" said Raffles. "Quite so. You remember, Bunny? Norris Peters remarked, as we were coming back from last Saturday's rugger match, that this wretched fellow Saulsby had been travelling abroad, so wasn't up-to-date on the current form of London school rugger teams. Well, well, let's see what it is that Saulsby was trying to yank out of his pocket a minute ago."

Groping in the coat pocket of the insensible vandal, Raffles drew out a kind of metal implement of a design unfamiliar to me.

"What *is* it?" Anne gasped.

"It's what's known in nautical circles, I believe," Raffles said, "as a marlinspike. I'm afraid, Anne, that this wretch Saulsby hasn't appreciated the re-education Mr. Lavelle tried to arrange for him. A voyage before the mast, in a windjammer with a hard-case bucko mate, has not so much re-educated Saulsby as merely brutalized him. This marlinspike, used to strike an elderly scholar from behind as he stooped at his gardening in a lonely churchyard, would crack his skull like an eggshell. So do you *see* now, Anne, why you must persuade your uncle to abandon his theory for adult re-education—before a day comes when his theory may recoil on him?"

She nodded. She was very pale. And so, I knew, was I.

"Anyway, Anne," Raffles said, "don't worry about this fellow Saulsby. Here, take his scarf, and this loose tassel from it, and give them to Mr. Lavelle when you tell him what's happened. Meantime, Manders and I will see to it that Saulsby ships out with Captain Hurn, who no doubt will be glad to have him aboard as a substitute for Manders—and if Saulsby ultimately finds his way back to London, his quarrel will be with *us*, and we're perfectly capable of looking after ourselves, eh, Bunny?"

I nodded reassuringly at Anne.

"And now," Raffles said to her, "you probably want to dust round your uncle's house while he's occupied with his gardening at Kew."

Stepping out of the brougham, Raffles gave Anne a hand to alight. She stood looking at him. And she asked, almost in a whisper. "What *can* I say to you?"

"As to that, Anne," Raffles said, smiling, "I was about to inquire if Bunny Manders and I might have the pleasure of calling for you here this evening to take you and Mr. Lavelle out to dinner. So you might, perhaps, consider the possibility of saying—"

"Yes," said Anne. "Yes. Oh, *yes*," she said again—and she turned suddenly and ran up the porch steps of Mr. Lavelle's house.

Taking a key from a pocket in her muff, she unlocked the door and, without looking back, she went in.

The door closed.

For a moment, Raffles stood looking at it, then he turned and glanced up at Ivor Kern's henchman on the box of the brougham.

"Number Four Berth, North Quay, London Docks," he said—and as he rejoined me and the still insensible Saulsby, and the brougham jingled off with us, he asked, "Well, Bunny? D'you think you can develop this raw material of real life into something worth your while?"

"I'm afraid," I said reluctantly, "that there's a faint aura about it of—well—*decadence*, almost, that the average healthy Briton might consider objectionable in a novel of school life."

Raffles nodded, his grey eyes thoughtful as he offered me a Sullivan from his cigarette-case.

"I see what you mean, Bunny. You may be right. What a pity! Look at that chap Plum Wodehouse—on velvet with his school life novels. But, then, of course, he throws into them," Raffles said meditatively, "the things that most appeal to the average healthy Briton—like plenty of rugger. And cricket."

5

BEVERCOMBE'S BENEFIT MATCH

That grand old cricket professional, Frank Bevercombe, long the batting mainstay of one of the southern county teams, was on the eve of retirement, and Raffles, who had known Frank for years, had brought down from London a strong M.C.C. team to play the county in a gala three-day match in aid of Frank's benefit fund.

Hopes had run high for a bumper gate. Instead, not a ball had been bowled. Both teams had been obliged to kick their heels in the pavilion while rain drummed down steadily on the roof, the stands remained deserted, and seagulls paddled in the pools that formed on the turf.

Such, however, is the fickle nature of our famous climate that when Raffles and I, on the morning after the ruined game, strolled out to smoke a post-breakfast cigarette on the terrace of the hotel at which we were staying, a tantalizingly changed scene met our eyes.

The sun was shining, not a cloud marred the blue of the sky, and before us the English Channel spread, serene and sparkling, to the horizon.

"Perfect cricket weather, Bunny," Raffles said to me wryly. "Just too late to do old Frank Bevercombe any good. His benefit fund'll be nowhere near enough to set him up in that little pub he so well deserves."

"It's very bad luck," I agreed—and, to get Raffles's mind off the fiasco, I suggested that, as we had plenty of time before our train back to London, we take an amble along the pier across the way. "We might see an angler catch something," I said. "I've often wondered if they ever do."

But as we paid our twopences and clicked through the turnstiles on to the boards of the pier, the first thing we came to was a row of amusement machines—and, ironically enough, the one that caught Raffles's eye happened to be a cricket game, with the puppet batsmen, fielders and wicket-keeper, all of whom were wearing tiny Kent County XI caps, enclosed in a large glass case.

"It's a pity, Bunny," Raffles said ruefully, "that Frank Bevercombe's benefit match couldn't have been played under glass. Still, come on—I'll give you a game."

He inserted pennies in the slot, a pea-sized ball suddenly appeared in the hand of the puppet bowler, and Raffles and I began to crank the two handles of the machine. My handle caused the bowler to bowl rather jerkily, while Raffles's handle inspired the diminutive batsmen to somewhat St. Vitus-like strokes.

Footling as the pastime was, especially for Raffles, an All-England cricketer, yet it called, as I was quick to see, for a degree of skill in handle-turning. There was a knack to it. Unless the handles were turned in a curiously cunning way, the ball promptly disappeared into one or other of the holes at the feet of the cleverly placed fielders. On this occurring, a wicket was deemed to have fallen, the puppet players froze to immobility, and only by the insertion of further pennies in the slot could the ball be brought back into play and the miniature contestants restored to action.

The game tended to grow on one. I felt a desire, admittedly absurd, to master the knack of it—but as I was feeling for more pennies in the pocket of my well-pressed trousers, I noticed that Raffles's attention had wandered. He was looking back towards the turnstiles at the pier entrance.

Coming through the turnstiles were two attractive young ladies in summery dresses. The young ladies were escorted by two young men, each of whom was carrying a blue ticket, and I fancied that what had caught Raffles's attention was the complaining tone in which one of the young men was holding forth.

"This is simply wasting a day, Dilys," the young man was protesting. "Can't you girls take a joke? What Bill and I were saying at dinner last night was only teasing."

"That's what you say *now*, Steve," replied one of the

young ladies, evidently Dilys. "It didn't sound like teasing last night, did it, Kate?"

"Not in the least, Dilys," said Kate. "It sounded to me very much like—what's that saying?—*in vino veritas*."

"Oh, what nonsense, Kate!" exclaimed Bill, the other young man. "Look, this is our first holiday since our weddings. Let's all spend the day together. It's a glorious day—the first we've had, after all that rain. Why waste the day, then, by insisting that Steve and I go off on this ridiculous—"

"Ridiculous?" said Kate. "Really, Bill, what strange, moody creatures men are! Only last night, you and Steve were talking about the things men miss when they get married—"

"Like the freedom," said Dilys, "to travel light, go where adventure calls, live lean and hard occasionally, a man among men. Kate and I quite understand that husbands get restless sometimes. It's only natural. And we aren't *really* possessive wives, are we, Kate? We should hate you to feel that you were tied to our apron strings. No, no, honestly, we don't in the least grudge you this wonderful opportunity to go off on an adventure without us."

"That's the whole point of it," said Kate. "It's for men only, and we *want* you to go. After what was said last night, we absolutely *insist* that you go. And, anyway, you've bought your tickets now, so—"

The voices of the quartette faded as the young couples passed on by along the boards of the pier, and I became aware that I still was absently cranking the handle of the cricket machine, though the ball had gone down a hole and the puppet players become again immobile.

"Have you ever in your life, Bunny," Raffles said, "seen two young women so demurely pleased with themselves or two chaps so obviously reluctant? What *is* this adventure they were arguing about? Look, there are more people coming through the turnstiles. Quite an influx all of a sudden. And *only* the men seem to have blue tickets. Let's tag along and see what's happening."

Deserting the cricket game, we followed the throng of seaside vacationers, mostly men with blue tickets, along the pier. Right at the end of it an iron staircase crusted with barnacles led down to the lower level of the pier-head. Here the single funnel of a side-paddle steamer, tied up, breathed forth against the blue of sea and sky a transparent shimmer of heat. Over the gangway which led to the deck of the steamer was stretched a banner bearing the legend:

THE HUSBANDS' BOAT

No women! No children! Husbands only!
Blow away your holiday irritations!
Return to your loved ones a giant refreshed!
Day Trip - 7/6d.
Four hours ashore in France. See the casino!
Sailing every Thursday.

THE HUSBANDS' BOAT

I stopped dead. I really had to laugh.

"So *that's* it!" I said. "You see, Raffles? Those two chaps, Steve and Bill, frustrated and restless because of a few days of rain, had a drink or two too many last night and got to wishing for some big adventure, like rounding the Horn in a windjammer, or enlisting in the French Foreign Legion, or lying in ambush for lions by a waterhole in the Great Rift Valley. So what do those two wicked young wives of theirs do? Why, pack the poor idiots off on a day trip on the Husbands' Boat! The sublime to the ridiculous. Sheer feminine mischief! What voyage could be more banal than a day trip on the Husbands' Boat?"

To my surprise, Raffles did not share my hilarity. He was looking thoughtful.

"'See the Casino,'" he said. "H'm! Bunny, if we were to touch lucky at roulette or boule, we could kick in handsomely to old Frank Bevercombe's fund. Who knows? We might be able to make this a replay, as it were, of his washed-out benefit match. Come on, we've nothing better to do—and it looks as though we can get tickets from that steward at the foot of the gangway."

"But we aren't eligible for this trip," I protested, taken aback. "It's for husbands only!"

"I doubt if we'll be required to produce our marriage

lines," said Raffles. Already, gripping me by my elbow, he was steering me towards the foot of the gangway. "Ah, what a treat it is, Bunny," he said, "to play truant for a few hours from debilitating domesticity! Family holidays make a man old before his time. Fifteen bobs' worth of free air will be a tonic for us. Good morning, steward. Two tickets, please."

The steward was a chunky, hard-faced fellow with ginger hair cut short at the back and sides and bunched up in stylish waves on top of his head. I was embarrassed by the way he looked us over. I feared he might ask us for credentials, but he merely separated the counterfoils from two tickets, handed over the tickets and change for Raffles's sovereign, and secured the counterfoils to a clipboard.

"Enjoy yourselves, gents," he said.

Though his tone was civil, I had an impression that he was staring after us as Raffles and I walked up the gangway and, bachelors though we were, stepped on to the deck of the Husbands' Boat.

I felt self-conscious, uneasy, half fearing the indignity of our being tapped on the shoulder and asked to leave the ship. But it was on the point of sailing. Its siren was emitting valedictory blasts. The great paddle-wheels began to rumble and splash in their housings. Bells rang from the bridge and engine-room. Hawsers were cast off. Bunting fluttered in the rigging. The pier-head, gay with the parasols and waving handkerchiefs of deserted women and children, receded across the churning water.

"Fair stands the wind for France," said Raffles.

As the tumult of sailing diminished, and all about us the holiday husbands, obviously in a mood of emancipation and bonhomie, began to get acquainted and form themselves into convivial groups, I noticed Steve and Bill staring back morosely at the dwindling pier and the wholesome English beaches.

"Hey!" I heard someone shout. "The bar's opening!"

The word sped round like wildfire, and I noticed that Steve and Bill were in the forefront of the exodus which left the deck shining white and vacant in the sunshine.

"You see what you've let us in for, Raffles?" I said irritably. "This trite excursion will rapidly degenerate into a mere orgy."

"Par'n me, gentlemen," said a voice.

We turned. It was the hard-faced steward with the ginger hair.

"Could I fetch you any refreshment?" he asked.

"The sun's far from over the yardarm, steward," said Raffles, "but you make a capital suggestion. Whisky-and-soda would do us well."

"Coming up, sir," said the steward. "Lovely day for a trip, Mr. Raffles."

Seeing our surprise, the steward smiled.

"I had a feeling I'd seen you before, sir," he told Raffles, "and it suddenly struck me—cigarette cards! You're in that set, *Famous Cricketers,* issued with Gold Flake. An excellent likeness of you, sir—an' if I may say so, it's a pleasure to 'ave you on board."

With a bow, he left us.

"An ephemeral fame, Bunny," Raffles said dryly, offering me a Sullivan from his cigarette-case—"writ in smoke, so to say—but at least it brings prompt service. With all those married chaps clamouring at the bar, we'd never have got near it."

This was confirmed by the observant steward when he returned, bearing our drinks on a salver.

"Bit of a hugger-mugger down there," he reported. "Warming up early, the gents are, this trip, but it's nothing to what they'll be by the time we starts 'ome. My word, what a shambles it is at times! But there you are—with married gentlemen on the loose for once, what else can you expect? Some of 'em comes just bound and determined to make a moist passage of it. I can always spot that kind. But, to tell the truth—if you'll par'n me the confidence—I was hoping we might have one or two gents of a different kind with us this trip."

"Indeed?" said Raffles. "What kind had you in mind?"

"The kind, sir," said the steward, glancing up rather furtively at the bridge, where the bearded captain was pacing to and fro, "that's come on the trip on a sudden impulse, bein' a bit bored, with a few hours to kill—the kind of gent who wouldn't stand back from a *real* little adventure, if such should be available."

"Steward," said Raffles, "you interest us."

"I knew it!" said the steward. "Sir, when I recognised you, my 'eart leapt up! 'By gum,' I thought, 'Mr. A. J. Raffles, the gentleman cricketer! If anybody'll take it on, 'e will!' Sir, let me just say this." Glancing up again furtively at the bridge, he lowered his voice. "If you gentlemen'll go below presently to the foyer and kind of sidle along aft, you'll come to a few passenger cabins. They ain't in use. Just knock on the door of Cabin Four, like this"—he knocked in a peculiar way on the salver he held—"and say Arthur Crudd sent you."

With a nod and a wink, he stepped back, clapped the salver under his arm.

"Luncheon served in the saloon from eleven o'clock on, gentlemen," he said loudly—and he walked off along the deck.

I felt inclined to pinch myself. I glanced about me. The sea sparkled. The steamer's bunting fluttered gaily in the light airs. The starboard paddle-wheel rumbled and surged, spattering the deck with silvery drops. I looked at Raffles. In his grey eyes was a vivacity I knew only too well.

"This trip may not be as trite as you feared, Bunny," he said. "I think we must look further into Mr. Crudd's matter—with due precautions. Drink up!"

We finished our drinks, tossed our cigarettes overboard and, leaving our glasses on a lifebelt locker, sauntered along the deck and down the companion stairs to the foyer. On the port side was the bar, crammed with men who, to judge from the roar of voices, already were succumbing to the heady elixir of freedom. On the starboard side was the dining-saloon, where stewards were setting the long tables for luncheon.

The din from the bar faded as we made our way along an alleyway leading aft. It was dimly lighted, vibrating to the rumble of the great paddle-wheels.

"There they are, Bunny," Raffles murmured—"the passenger cabins."

There were eight doors, four on each side of the alleyway, with brass numerals on them. We moved forward to Cabin 4.

Raffles put an ear to it, listened for a moment, gave me a wicked look, then rapped on the door in the peculiar way indicated by the problematic steward. Tense, ready for anything, I heard a movement within the cabin. The door opened slightly.

"Arthur Crudd sent us," said Raffles.

The door opened wider, disclosing sunshine streaming in through the cabin porthole—and I was astonished to see, on this of all ships, the shapely figure of a young woman.

"Come in," she said.

Raffles's hand closed on my arm. He drew me into the cabin. I saw at once that it was not officially in use, for on the double-decker bunk lay coverless pillows and folded blankets. I looked incredulously at the cabin's occupant. Though tastefully dressed and, with dark, soft hair and blue eyes, by no means lacking in allure, she seemed to be in the grip of some emotion.

"Oh, thank you—thank you for coming," she said, a little breathlessly. "I hardly dared hope! It seems so dreadful to have to appeal to total strangers—but as you're passengers on the Husbands' Boat, I know at least that you're married and responsible men."

"Quite so," said Raffles coolly—though I myself hardly knew where to look.

"I, too," said the young woman, "am married." She showed us the plain gold ring on the appropriate finger of her hand. "My husband is a Frenchman. I first met him at a time when my father, a master mariner, was captain of one of the regular cross-Channel steamers and I used sometimes to take trips back and forth with him, for the outing. That was how I happened to meet Henri—in the town for which we're now bound. But when he asked me to marry him, I felt obliged to tell him that my father was in poor health and about to swallow the anchor, and I felt I could only marry Henri if he would agree to make his home with us in England, in the town from which we've just sailed. There was nobody but me to care for my father and he would never agree to spend his declining years in a foreign country. I—I'm sorry to have to go into such personal details, but if I'm to make my position clear to you—"

She looked at us appealingly.

"Please go on," Raffles said.

"Henri," the young woman continued, "accepted my condition, but he never really felt at home in England. He's very French. When our little girl was born—she's two years old now—Henri insisted that she be given a French name: Germaine. He wanted her to be brought up in France, where he still owns a house, the Villa Gabriel, on the cliffs just outside the town where we shall be arriving presently. Well, I'm partly to blame, I suppose. A wife's place is with her husband. Yet—how could I desert my poor father? He had, as I kept telling Henri, only a few years to live, so would not Henri please be patient? But no! He was insistent—selfish and unreasonable—and we quarrelled. Yesterday he made the worst scene of all. But I never dreamed that he'd do what he's now done to me!"

Her voice broke. She touched a wisp of handkerchief to her eyes.

"He's left me," she said. "When I woke up this morning, he was gone—and Germaine's cot was empty. *He's taken my child!*" She gave us a distraught look. "Gentlemen, can you wonder that I was frantic?"

"No indeed," said Raffles, and I nodded heartfelt concurrence.

"I had no idea," said the young mother, "at what time in the night Henri had so vilely stolen away with Germaine. But I knew that he had many yachting friends, and I felt sure he'd get one of them to sail him over to France, where he'd go first to his own house, the Villa Gabriel. Of course, he'd guess that I'd follow him—to the very ends of the earth, if need be! He'd think that I'd take the regular steamer from Folkestone, and I knew he'd make sure to be gone from the villa, into hiding somewhere with Germaine, before I could arrive. But then, suddenly," she said, with a flash of triumph, "I remembered Arthur Crudd!"

"The steward," said Raffles.

"Yes," said the young mother, "he used to be a steward on my father's ship and was devoted to him. I knew that Arthur was working now on this excursion steamer, and I suddenly realised that if I could get him to smuggle me on board, I could reach France much earlier than if I crossed by the regular steamer, and so I might be in time to catch Henri before he left his wretched Villa Gabriel.''

''Sound thinking, madam,'' Raffles said, ''but may I ask in what way my friend and I can serve you?''

''To regain custody of Germaine by process of law,'' said the young mother, ''from a *Frenchman*, in *French* courts, could take months and months—even years and years. Every obstacle would be thrown in my way. It would be hopeless! No, no, if I'm in time to confront Henri at the Villa Gabriel, I intend to *appeal* to him to return Germaine to me.''

''And,'' Raffles said softly, ''if he refuses?''

Her eyes flashed.

''Why, then,'' she said, ''my dearest hope is that I may have, waiting outside the house, two fellow countrymen, two understanding and responsible Englishmen, willing to come in at my call and simply *take* Germaine for me!''

My heart gave a great thump. Of all the things I had known Raffles to take, with or without permission, this surely was the most unusual, but I had no doubt that he would offer the young mother our full support, and this he did without a moment's hesitation, while I myself nodded reassuringly at her. Her relief was obvious.

''Oh, *thank* you,'' she said. ''Now, as I've no right to be on board, I mustn't be seen leaving the ship, or I shall be delayed for questioning. My friend the steward will make some opportunity to smuggle me ashore, but it may take a little time. Could I beg you gentlemen to go straight to the Villa Gabriel, on the Impasse Rocher, and sort of prospect it to see if Henri and Germaine are there?''

''And if they are?'' Raffles asked.

''Then keep watch—and if Henri should try to leave with the child, find some pretext to delay him—until I can arrive.'' She looked at us anxiously. ''Do you think you could do that?''

''I feel sure,'' said Raffles, ''that ways and means can be found—eh, Bunny?''

''Absolutely, Raffles,'' I said.

Leaving the clandestine passenger much happier than we had found her, we walked back along the alleyway. The uproar of the husbands roistering at the bar had grown louder. Crudd, the steward, was hovering in the foyer. He gave us a look of suspense. We nodded. His expression lightened.

"I knew it'd be a bit of luck for her that we had Mr. Raffles on board," he muttered to us. And he raised his voice to its loud, official note: "Care to lunch now, par'n me?"

We went into the dining-saloon. At the long tables, flooded with sunshine from the portholes, there was only a scattering of lunchers, husbands of the more sober kind.

"Raffles," I said, as a steward set plates of ham and tongue before us, "I've often read in the newspapers of cases of this kind—one parent or the other bolting off abroad with the child of the union. What are our chances, d'you think, of recovering little Germaine?"

"Not too good, I'm afraid," said Raffles—"because I gravely doubt, Bunny, if the infant Germaine exists."

Thunderstruck, I laid down my knife and fork.

"Consider," said Raffles, helping himself to mustard. "If the clandestine passenger in Cabin Four is what she claims to be—the daughter of the ex-captain of a regular Channel steamer—why should she have got herself smuggled aboard this ship by a steward? There's a fraternity between master mariners. A note from her father to the captain of this ship, explaining the domestic crisis and requesting a passage for the lady, as a matter of courtesy, would have been all that was necessary. No, Bunny, I'm afraid that the young lady's story, though touchingly rendered, fails on several grounds to carry conviction."

"But then," I said, bewildered, "what's the point of it?"

"The point sticks out a mile, Bunny. The young lady and the ingratiating steward are hand-in-glove. For some reason, they're anxious to bamboozle a couple of passengers from this day excursion into poking and prying about a house called the Villa Gabriel—and the steward Crudd's selected *us* for the purpose."

"Naturally," I said "—because he recognised you and immediately thought you'd be the kind of man who'd consider it—"

"Not quite cricket to ignore an appeal from a lady?"

Raffles said. "He's right, of course. That *wouldn't* be cricket. But there's a distinct whiff of conspiracy in the air here, Bunny—and what's usually the motive of conspiracies?"

"Money," I said.

"Which brings up another aspect of cricket, Bunny," Raffles said. "We must bear in mind old Frank Bevercombe's benefit fund. With that in view, we must certainly do our best to see that the wishes of the lady in Cabin Four are carried out—by proxy."

"Proxy?" I said, mystified.

"Have you forgotten two of our fellow passengers on this trip? It occurs to me," said Raffles, "that if Steve and Bill should have an adventure to tell of, when they return from this much derided Husbands' Boat excursion those mischievous young wives of theirs will be properly taken aback and the fellows' self-respect will be restored. Lend me your notebook and pencil."

Puzzled, I handed over the notebook and pencil, which from old journalistic habit I invariably carried in case any valuable thoughts should strike me, and Raffles wrote rapidly in the notebook.

Tearing out the page, he showed me what he had written. It was in capitals:

GAME FOR AN ADVENTURE? SCOUT ROUND
THE VILLA GABRIEL, IMPASSE ROCHER.
A WELL-WISHER.

"There's evidently some joker about that villa," Raffles said, taking back the paper from me, "so it'd be prudent on our part, and at the same time unselfish, if we give Steve and Bill a chance to feel out the ground for us." Folding the paper, he stood up. "Finish your lunch, Bunny, and I'll see you on deck presently."

He walked out of the saloon.

Uneasily, I finished my lunch. A blast sounded from the steamer's siren. I went on deck. The breeze blew salty, gulls swooped and cried about the fluttering bunting and, drawing near, the bright little French resort, in a hollow between chalk cliffs, basked in the heat shimmer.

Eager husbands jostled at the rail for a first glimpse of the magnet of the day's excursion, the large white building of the Casino, high on the westward cliff top. And now, to starboard, the wall of the breakwater was gliding by. The harbour was opening out, and the paddle-wheels were surging slowly in reverse, when I felt a light touch on my arm.

"So far, so good," Raffles murmured to me. "I got behind Steve at the bar. His blue ticket is in the left-hand pocket of his jacket. When he feels for the ticket presently, he'll find the note I've slipped into his pocket. Come on, we mustn't miss the reaction."

We found ourselves a vantage point from which we could conveniently watch the ship being tied up to the wharf and the gangway hoisted into place by blue-smocked French stevedores. Evidently the arrival of the excursion ship was of interest to the local residents, for many of them were gathering on the balconies of the tall old houses round the harbour to witness the disembarkation of English husbands on the spree.

Gendarmes, probably themselves married men, watched the process tolerantly, and at the foot of the gangway the steward Crudd, with his clipboard, glanced cursorily at the blue tickets displayed to him by the disembarking passengers.

"And *there* they are, Bunny," said Raffles, "—our proxies."

As Steve and Bill showed their blue tickets to Crudd, and started walking away along the wharf, I saw that Steve was unfolding a piece of paper. He stopped dead. Bill stopped, too. Steve showed him the piece of paper. They did not seem to know what to make of it. They turned and looked back at the ship. The stream of passengers flowed on around them. After a moment, the two chaps turned and walked on in the stream. They kept on passing the piece of paper to and fro between them for re-examination, as though trying to wring further information from it.

"Right, Bunny," said Raffles. "We must now see if Steve and Bill are mere armchair-adventurers or—faced with a challenge—prove themselves men of mettle. Come on, let's get ashore."

We were almost the last to descend the gangway. Crudd,

obviously relieved to see us, raised his brows at us interrogatively—to which Raffles returned a confirmatory nod.

We walked on along the wharf. At its shore end, cabs laden with husbands were jingling off to the day's diversions, but Steve and Bill were in consultation with a gendarme.

"To judge from his gestures, Bunny," Raffles murmured, "he's giving them directions. Let's hope it's to the Impasse Rocher."

The two fellows walked off in the direction indicated by the gendarme.

"Excellent," said Raffles. "It looks as though they've taken the bait—as they were practically bound to, of course, or how could they face those mischievous young wives of theirs again? All we have to do now is follow these gallant chaps and draw our conclusions from whatever eventuates."

I felt a little uncomfortable as we followed the two young husbands through the sunstruck streets of the old town. Traffic was light. At sidewalk tables under *café* awnings, citizens were whiling away the afternoon at card games or chess, or were unashamedly asleep. Here and there, passengers from the Husbands' Boat were window-shopping.

As the more populated streets began to fall behind, and Steve and Bill continued walking on steadily up the slope of a tree-lined, dusty avenue, I was increasingly troubled by a sense of compunction.

"Raffles," I said, "it's all very well using these chaps as proxies. I can see the merit of your manoeuvre, but we don't know just what risk these chaps may be walking into."

"They wanted adventure, Bunny. There's no adventure without risk," Raffles said. "Hullo, they've stopped!"

He put a hand on my arm, checking me. A small tram was clanging down the avenue. About a hundred yards up the slope, Steve and Bill seemed to be arguing with each other. Abruptly, Bill turned and walked across the avenue. After a momentary hesitation, Steve hurried after him. Together, they vanished from view.

"A side street," said Raffles—"no doubt the Impasse Rocher."

The die was cast. We walked on quickly to the corner of

what proved to be a *cul-de-sac*, a suburban backwater, tree-shaded, with on either side three or four rambling old houses with gardens almost buried in foliage. Across a gateway, in railings at the dead end of the backwater, was a wrought-iron arch that incorporated the name: VILLA GABRIEL. The rusty gate was standing half-open, and we were just in time to see Steve and Bill slip through the gateway into the overgrown, neglected garden.

"Good chaps, Bunny," said Raffles. "They're taking a scout—"

A shout, half-stifled, interrupted him. It came from the garden of the villa. Raffles raced forward along the *cul-de-sac*. When I caught up with him, he was peering in through the railings.

"Our proxies are in trouble, Bunny," he whispered. "I caught just a glimpse of them. They had sacks jammed down over their heads and were being marched in through the door of the house by a couple of men who must have been lying in wait."

"Oh, dear God!" I breathed.

"If we hadn't taken precautions, Bunny, it's you and me who'd be trapped," Raffles pointed out. "Come on, let's see what's happening."

But just then there sounded from the house, which from its neglected appearance seemed to have been long unoccupied, the bang of a door slammed shut. I heard men's voices, speaking in French.

Raffles drew me into the deep shade of a laburnum tree that, shedding its dried pods, overhung the rusty railings of the villa garden. In the speckled shade we stood motionless, listening, as footsteps approached along the garden path.

"They'll come to no harm in that cellar," a man's voice was saying. "They've food enough for a month, if they haven't the gumption to dig their way out sooner."

Two men emerged from the gateway. They were well-dressed. One was a very big man, broad-shouldered, full-bearded, wearing a frock-coat and white waistcoat. He was polishing a ribboned pince-nez. His hat was a white Homburg.

The other man was thickset and wore what looked like a coachman's livery.

"Crudd and Lillian chose a very suitable couple," the big, bearded man continued. "Come sailing time of the Husbands' Boat this evening, Crudd'll report to his captain that two passengers are missing. The captain will have to notify the police here, with descriptions furnished by Crudd. With what they'll have on their minds by then, the police will jump to the conclusion that the smoke-pot job was pulled by two English crooks who came over with the daytrippers. The police will waste days pulling in Englishmen and questioning them. *Et voilà!* A red herring across our track! And nobody hurt—no violence. The two Englishmen, responding predictably to my manipulation, have served their purpose as puppets in the game. So *allons, mon vieux*—forward to the winning stroke!"

As he spoke these grandiloquent words, the big, bulky man in the white Homburg hat was walking away along the Impasse Rocher with his coachman companion. Turning to the left, they passed from view.

"Well, well," Raffles said softly. "So we're puppets, are we, Bunny—like those in that cricket game in the glass case on the pier? H'm! There were *two* handles to that game, and I rather think there are two to this larger game. With that bearded genius turning one handle, we must see if we can turn the other—and in this old seaside town, with a shipload of trippers just in, it's not hard to guess where play's in progress."

"The Casino!" I exclaimed.

"Where else? said Raffles. "Come on!"

"But—what about Steve and Bill?"

"I'm afraid they must be patient," said Raffles. "They're probably used to waiting, anyway. They're husbands. Let's keep our eye on the ball."

Turning to the left out of the *cul-de-sac*, we saw the two Frenchmen walking briskly ahead of us up the slope of the avenue—and, as Raffles had surmised, they went directly to the Casino on the west cliff.

An elaborate building, evidently of recent construction, it had an opulent glass rotunda and was surrounded on three sides by spacious gardens. The building fronted on the avenue. People were passing up and down the broad steps, on which a gendarme was strolling to and fro, and under sun-umbrellas on the terrace other people were enjoying drinks.

"Our two are separating, Bunny," Raffles murmured. "The bearded chap's going into the Casino. I'll follow him. You see where the other chap goes, then come back and sit at one of those tables on the terrace."

He left me. I walked on, following the man who looked like a coachman. I kept to the right-hand side of the road, where there were trees. The coachman, on the other side of the road, was strolling along unhurriedly beside the tall railings that enclosed the Casino gardens.

Where the railings made a right-angle turn, about a hundred yards or so ahead, the road and its tramline ended at the rolling grassland of the open cliff top. The coachman paused. Instinctively, I knew that he would look back. I stepped behind a tree-trunk, counted slowly to twenty, then ventured to peer round the tree.

My quarry had vanished. I crossed the road, walked on to the angle of the railings, took a cautious look round them. They continued straight on towards the cliff edge, a couple of hundred yards distant. The coachman was walking along beside the railings, but he stopped halfway. He took a key from his pocket, unlocked a gate in the railings. He did not enter the Casino gardens. He turned his back on them, walked away towards one of the many gorse-clumps which dotted the cliff-top grassland. The gorse-clump hid him from my observation.

I could faintly hear the small waves breaking at the foot of the cliff. Just as I was wondering how the devil I could reach some point from which I could see what the man was up to behind that gorse-clump, he reappeared. He was wheeling two bicycles. He leaned them against the railings of the Casino gardens. He went back to the gorse-clump, vanished behind it, then reappeared wheeling two more bicycles. These also he leaned, conveniently close to the gate he had unlocked, against the railings. He did not return to the gorse-clump. Like a man whose job was done, he lighted a cigarette. I sensed that he was about to come back my way, so I retreated quickly to the shelter of a tree trunk.

I was well advised—for when he came again into my purview, he was walking back towards the Casino. He went right on past it and continued on down the avenue to the town. I had seen enough. I went up the Casino steps to the terrace. There was no sign of Raffles there, but I found a vacant table and, seeing a waiter approaching, ordered myself a double brandy-and-soda. I needed it. My hands were none too steady as I dabbed at my brow with my handkerchief and tucked it back into my cuff.

I finished my brandy and was about to call for another when Raffles sat down opposite me.

"Well?" he said. And when I had made my report, he was clearly pleased with my effort. "Excellent, Bunny," he said. "Now, I'll join you in a drink, Then it'll be *our* turn to bat."

The afternoon was by now far advanced and the declining sun was beginning to cast long shadows from the cliff-top gorse-clumps when I showed Raffles the unlocked gate to the Casino gardens and the four bicylces that had been placed so conveniently against the railings.

"The bicycles had been hidden originally," I explained, "in that gorse-clump over there."

"Bicycles of the racing type," said Raffles. "I doubt if our bearded friend will be riding one—he's of too imposing a build. But he had a quiet word, in the Casino just now, with four chaps among the crowd around the gaming-tables. The chaps had a nimble, wiry look. They're probably professional bicycle-racers. It's becoming a popular continental sport. The bearded genius obviously manages the team, plans its tactics—and, as we see, he leaves nothing to chance."

Raffles opened the gate in the garden railings. Inside the gateway was a path that led through a laurel shrubbery to the wide-spread ornamental gardens.

"This shubbery will suit us very well, Bunny," said Raffles. "We'll lurk here in it. The fact that the gate's been un-locked and the bicycles placed in readiness for a racing start suggests that we shouldn't have long to wait."

Yet time seemed to me to pass very slowly. My palms were moist, the pulse drummed in my ears. Peering out from the shrubbery where we lurked, I could see, across the flower beds, paths, and fountains of the garden, the coloured glass dome of the Casino rotunda and, below it, tall windows and a spacious balcony overlooking a balustraded terrace. Nobody was in sight, but the thought of the crowds inside and the gold sovereigns and stacks of bank notes sliding to and fro over the gaming-tables filled me with anxiety.

"Raffles," I whispered, "there's certainly going to be a hold-up. Innocent people could get hurt—or even killed."

"No fear of that, Bunny," Raffles said. "The bearded thinker told us himself what kind of a job this is." His hand tightened on my arm. "The lights are being turned on in the Casino. This may be the moment they're waiting for."

The western sky and the tranquil sea were flushed now with sunset. From the windows and rotunda of the Casino, lights shone out—only to become at once strangely dim. Simultaneously, a confused hubbub of shouting and screaming within the building stirred the hair on my head. I heard a crash of glass. From a shattered window that gave onto the first-floor balcony a dense black cloud of smoke poured forth.

"Oh, my God!" I said, appalled. "Fire! They've set the place on fire!"

"Nonsense, Bunny," Raffles said. "The bearded genius stated quite clearly that his operation here is a 'smoke-pot job.' A mere matter of elementary chemistry. Somehow, probably with the connivance of a Casino employee, they've managed to plant smoke-pots here and there in the building. They've now knocked the tops off the pots and are seizing the swag from the tables and making a bolt for it. Yes, here comes one of 'em now!"

Through the smashed window, a man had appeared on the balcony. He hung by his hands from the rail, dropped down to the terrace, vaulted the balustrade and came racing towards us across the garden. As he tore past us along the path to the gate, Raffles reached out from the laurels and grabbed the man by the ankle. He fell flat on his face. Instantly Raffles was on him, seizing him by the back of his jacket-collar and ripping the jacket off, the sleeves of the jacket turning inside out.

The man staggered to his feet, looked about him wildly,

ran out through the gateway, saw the waiting bicycles. He
seized one, ran along beside it, sprang into the saddle and, head
low over the handlebars, his legs pumping the pedals, receded
rapidly along a rutted chalk track across the cliff-top grassland.

Raffles tossed me the man's jacket.

"Fill your pockets from his, Bunny. There are two more of
the chaps coming. We'll let 'em go—and wait for Number
Four."

Peering from the laurel thicket as I feverishly transferred
the bank-notes from Number One's jacket pockets to my own,
I saw clouds of smoke pouring from the Casino. Two more of
the criminals were tearing across the garden towards us. They
ran past us, out through the gateway, seized bicycles, rode
away at high speed along the cliff-top track through the gorse
bushes. I had barely cast aside Number One's now valueless
jacket than Number Four arrived—only to have Raffles seize
him by the ankle and, as he went down with a stifled cry, tear
the jacket from his back. Reacting precisely as Number One
had reacted, the man tottered to his feet with a wild look and
fled in panic, barely retaining enough presence of mind to seize
the last of the bicycles on his way.

"Right, Bunny," said Raffles, transferring to his own
pockets the contents of Number Four's jacket pockets, "we'd
better get round to the front now and see what's happening.
Tidy yourself up a bit and preserve a calm appearance."

Though I did my best to steady myself, my heart was still
thumping uncomfortably as we made our way round to the
front of the Casino, where we found a considerable crowd,
mostly with smudged faces, excitedly watching the smoke that
was billowing out blackly from the doors and hastily opened
windows of the building.

The backs of the crowd were turned to us. Nobody paid us
any attention as we walked on past and continued on down the
avenue towards the town.

"And now, Bunny," Raffles said, "as the Impasse Rocher
is just ahead, we'd better do something about our proxies.
Lend me your notebook and pencil."

He wrote something in my notebook, tore out the page,
returned the notebook to me.

We walked along the *cul-de-sac*, entered the overgrown grounds of the Villa Gabriel. The door of the house, unlocked, opened onto an unfurnished hall, dim in the twilight.

"Anybody here?" Raffles called loudly.

An urgent shouting and thumping broke out from somewhere below. We found the cellar steps and, at the foot of them, a door that was bolted at top and bottom. While I struck matches, Raffles shot the bolts and drew open the door with a creak of rusty hinges. The young husbands, Steve and Bill, much dishevelled, stood blinking in the match-light.

"Good heavens!" said Raffles, amazed. "Didn't we see you chaps on the Husbands' Boat?" They both began to talk at once, but he interrupted them. "Found a *note* in your pocket?" he said. "Why, so did I!"

He produced the page which he had torn from my notebook a few minutes before. In the light of the matches I was striking, he compared it with the page which Steve produced.

"Good God!" Raffles exclaimed. "Look at that! Identical messages, absolutely identical! My friend here and I decided that the note I found in my pocket must be some kind of practical joke. We don't go much on that kind of thing. We like a quiet life. We just ignored the note. We fooled away the afternoon, but then my friend here suggested that, before we returned to the ship, it'd be interesting to find out if there really *was* a Villa Gabriel."

"We're very much obliged to you," Steve said. "We've been locked up in this damned coal hole for hours. Why would anybody do a thing like this?"

"Why indeed?" said Raffles. "Anyway, it's getting on for sailing time. We'd better get back to the ship."

When we reached the steamer, the ginger-haired steward Arthur Crudd was standing at the foot of the gangway, checking against the counterfoils on his clipboard the tickets of returning passengers, many of whom had smudged faces and red-rimmed eyes and were coughing dismally.

At sight of Raffles and myself, Crudd was obviously startled. His hard face paled. We showed him our tickets and, without a word, walked on past him up the gangway. I felt him staring after us.

"He's in shock, Bunny," Raffles murmured to me. "He's wondering what's gone wrong, but he won't dare come anywhere near us."

With all passengers present and accounted for, the steamer sailed on time. Watching the lights of France receding astern, Raffles and I had the deck almost to ourselves. From below, where most of the passengers had foregathered at the bar to discuss their various experiences during the Casino outrage, sounded a roar of excited voices.

We saw nothing of the steward, Crudd. He was giving us a wide berth. But Steve and Bill joined us briefly, and Raffles asked them if they had chanced on any clue to the writer of the mysterious notes.

"Not a thing," said Steve. "Everybody's talking about this business of a robbery at the Casino. For all we know, of course, it may be connected in some way with those notes."

"That's pretty unlikely," said Bill. "But, by Jove, who says a trip on the Husbands' Boat is no adventure! Steve, I just can't wait to see Kate's and Dilys's faces when we tell them what's happened to practically every man jack on this ship today. It'll be an eye-opener to the girls!"

Delighted with themselves, our two proxies went forward along the deck to watch impatiently for a first glimpse of twinkling lights along the English shore.

"Well, Bunny," said Raffles, "I think we can regard this trip as a rewarding substitute for old Frank Bevercombe's washed-out benefit match. From the proceeds of this replay, as it were, we can kick in handsomely to the fund to set him up in a little pub, and there'll still be a trifle left over for ourselves. As to practically everybody else on board, they've all more or less had a part in the game, and have an adventure to tell of—"

"And a wide-eyed woman waiting eagerly to hear all about it," I said, feeling a curious stab of envy.

Raffles laid a friendly hand on my shoulder.

"If you fancy a feminine audience, Bunny," he said, "you might go below and take a look in Cabin Four—though I'm afraid it's doubtful," he added sympathetically, "if you'll find the lovely Lillian still there."

6

MADAME BLAVATSKY'S TEACUPS

Perched on a ridge seven thousand feet up in the rhododendron forests of the Himalayan foothills, the famous resort of Simla was the summer capital of the Viceroy of India.

"It's now about nine o'clock, Bunny," Raffles remarked to me, on the evening of our arrival, "so we're in good time for dinner."

At this season, with the Viceroy in residence at Viceregal Lodge, Simla was a centre of administrative and social importance, so we had taken the precaution of booking rooms in advance at the well-known Peliti's Hotel.

Nevertheless, when we dressed for dinner and sauntered down into the dining-room, with its ornate chandeliers and conspicuous portrait of our widowed Queen-Empress, we were greeted by the turbaned Head Waiter, tall and dignified in white tunic and crimson sash, with the news that no table was at present available for us.

"But surely," Raffles demurred, surveying the spacious room which hummed with the decorous conversation of ladies and gentlemen of obvious consequence, "that's a vacant table I see—over there by that potted palmetto?"

That table, the Head Waiter explained, was reserved.

"For a lady renowned for her deep learning," he said, giving us an important look, "who has come here to the hills to recuperate from the heat of Madras."

Adding that he would see what he could do for us, he moved away—and I noticed that on the table reserved for the lady from Madras, and on that table only, was a fine alabaster bowl in which floated the green leaves and waxen blossoms of the revered water-lily of India, the white lotus.

Raffles and I exchanged speculative glances.

Returning, the Head Waiter told us that he had made an

arrangement on our behalf, and he conducted us to a table at which a man in civilian evening-dress was dining alone. Of short stature and tropically seasoned complexion, with closely trimmed brown hair but rather bushy moustache and eyebrows, and thick-lensed glasses, he set aside a newspaper and rose courteously to greet us.

"But, sir," Raffles protested, "we intrude upon you!"

"On the contrary," replied the diner, "you deliver me from reading at meals, a deplorable practice. Share my table by all means."

He was English and, despite his mature manner, I judged him to be three or four years younger than Raffles and myself and in fact no more than twenty, if that. Glasses notwithstanding, his eyes, bright blue, were observant, for he commented—when Raffles and I had made our selections from the menu—that the fresh air of the hills had given us an appetite, after the jungle heat of Nawanagar.

Seeing our surprise, he smiled.

"I guessed where you'd come from," he said, "because I saw you arrive this evening and I noticed a cricket-bag among your luggage. I happened to know that Kumar Shri Ranjitsinjhi, cousin of the Ruler of the Indian princely state of Nawanagar, had brought out a party of cricketers from England."

"You're perfectly right," Raffles said. "I met young Ranji when I played for an M.C.C. side against Cambridge University. He's an undergraduate there, at Trinity College, and is an unusually promising cricketer—for a freshman. He invited my friend here and me to join the party he was bringing to India for the vacation. Ranji and the other chaps are on their way back to England now, for the start of term at Cambridge, but we ourselves were under no such obligation, so we thought we'd come up and have a look at Simla."

"I come up every year myself, on leave from this Lahore sheet, the *Civil and Military Gazette*," said our fellow diner.

He tapped the newspaper he had laid aside.

"The editor," he said, "having only two of us on his staff, stimulates our output by letting us sign our nonroutine efforts with our initials, and he allows us six weeks annual leave. My colleague and I, who're by way of being friendly rivals, take it in turns to come up to Simla at the time when the Viceroy's in residence—and perhaps, with luck, there's a story or two to be picked up.''

"What kind of story?" asked Raffles, interested—for we actually had come to Simla in the hope of picking up an opportunity to replenish our dwindling store of rupees.

"Well, for instance," said the young journalist, "your Rajput friend Ranjitsinjhi may have mentioned the Shere Khan mystery to you? No? Well, it's a strange affair—an affair of state. With the Russian bear to our north keeping a jealous eye on India, this Shere Khan matter is causing considerable disquiet not only at Viceregal Lodge here in Simla but also at the India Office in London."

Shere Khan, the young journalist from Lahore explained to us, was the name by which folk down in jungle country referred to the enemy they most feared—tigers.

"I dare say," continued our informant, "that you've heard of the corps of elite couriers known as Queen's Messengers? No? Well, they travel in civilian clothes, and their insignia, worn under the lapel, is a silver greyhound. Armed with diplomatic immunity, these elite couriers carry across the world the sealed pouches of highly secret documents that pass constantly to and fro between Her Majesty's statesmen in London and her proconsuls overseas."

Recently, according to this young man from Lahore, a train in which a Queen's Messenger on mission had been travelling to Bombay, there to board a P. & O. liner due to sail for England, had chanced to be derailed in jungle country.

The train had been carrying remounts for a cavalry detachment, so the courier, on the authority of his Order of Mission, had requisitioned one of the horses. On this, in the sweltering heat of the noonday sun, he had ridden off posthaste along a trail through the jungle towards a railway junction where he had hoped to connect with another train.

"Unfortunately," said our fellow diner, "at a certain point alongside that jungle trail a tiger lurked in the striped shade of a thicket—and the yellow eyes of Shere Khan are blind to the significance of diplomatic immunity. The outcome of that tragic encounter was discovered later by a police sergeant, a man of unimpeachable integrity. Shere Khan and the Queen's Messenger had died together, the courier with his head clawed half off and the tiger with five bullets in him from the courier's revolver. The horse was also found dead. But someone— someone unknown—must have passed that way *before* the police sergeant. For the diplomatic pouch and the courier's silver greyhound insignia were not found by the police sergeant—and have not been recovered since, in spite of the offer of a reward. Hence the profound disquiet at—''

Our informant broke off abruptly. I followed his glance. A sudden hush had fallen here in the dining-room. Between the curtains of rich red velvet that draped the doorway, a woman had appeared. A small woman, slender and erect, wth the grey hair of one in her late fifties, she wore a white *sari*.

Receiving her with marked deference, the turbaned Head Waiter, towering over her, escorted her to the table by the palmetto. They passed close by us, and I saw her face clearly. Worn and sallow but of a haunting distinction, with light, strange, wide-set eyes, it was not the face of a woman of India.

The Head Waiter holding the chair for her, the small woman in the *sari* seated herself at the table with the alabaster bowl in which floated the flower of meditation, the white lotus.

''The most controversial woman in India,'' the young man from Lahore murmured to us. ''Philosopher, traveller, adept of the occult, clairvoyant—Madame Helena Petrovna Blavatsky, of New York, Madras, and Tibet.''

Behind his thick-lensed glasses, our informant's blue eyes were bright with interest.

Some fifteen or so years ago, he told us, as the hum of conversation resumed in the dining-room, Madame Blavatsky had made what was, for a foreign woman, a unique journey. She had travelled over the high Himalayan passes of perpetual snow into the closed country, Tibet, on the roof of the world. Not only had she been admitted, but she was said to have gained there the confidence of a brotherhood of wise men, who had initiated her into the secrets of a system of practical mysticism handed down through the ages.

''Nowadays,'' said the young man from Lahore,

"Madame Blavatsky divides her time between New York and Madras, where she's founded a phalanstery for the study of the intuitive powers she believes to be latent in all mankind. She herself is said to have achieved feats of divination by means of leaves, especially the leaves of the tea-plant. There's much talk, pro and con, much controversy, about Madame Blavatsky's teacups. By any criterion, she's a remarkable lady. You should read her work of esoteric speculation, *Isis Unveiled*."

He told us that we might find a copy of the book here in Simla at a shop kept by an unusual man called Cyrus Hone, who often visited the China coast in search of valuable curios for his shop and who had the strange gift of being able to cure "sick" pearls.

"You'll find Hone's shop worth a visit," said our informant. "My own interest is in Madame Blavatsky. While she's here in Simla, I'd much like to witness some instance of her power of divination, but I fear that's too much to hope for. Still, who knows?" He took a seasoned briar pipe from his pocket. "I can't very well smoke this in the dining-room. So perhaps, as I've finished dinner before you, you'll excuse me?"

He left us to our dessert.

"Well-informed chap, Bunny," said Raffles. "I see he's discarded his newspaper, this *Civil and Military Gazette*." Taking up the paper, Raffles riffled through its pages. "H'm! Several sets of verse here and two or three short tales. Some are initialled K.R., others have the same initials reversed. Rather odd, that. If we see our friend again, we must ask him which he is. Meantime, we'll have a look round tomorrow for Mr. Cyrus Hone's shop. I like the sound of his valuable curios."

"Shh!" I muttered uncomfortably—and glanced to see if Madame Blavatsky was looking our way. But she seemed lost in thought, gazing at the white lotus in the alabaster bowl.

Somehow, she impressed me, and I was thinking about her when Raffles and I took a look around Simla next morning. On the principal mall, the Ladies' Mile, rickshaw chaps sped to and fro, pulling red-coated Army officers and pith-helmeted *sahibs* who looked like important officials of the Civil Secretariat.

"There's Viceregal Lodge, Bunny," said Raffles, drawing my attention to a fine building with white domes and Mogul-arched doors and windows.

Over the building, which was guarded by magnificent tur-baned sentries, the standard of the Raj proclaimed the presence of the Viceroy.

Several of the streets of Simla, perched here on its ridge between the hot plains far to the south and the remote snow-capped mountain ranges to the north, seemed to end in ravines. And Cyrus Hone's curio shop, when we found it, proved to be a two-floored old building that backed upon just such a ravine at the dead end of a side street.

A bead curtain hung in the doorway. We went in. The shop was cluttered with such things as divans, screens, images, gongs, palanquins—and Mr. Hone, as I immediately guessed him to be, for he was behind the counter, was holding forth in a dogmatic, lecturing voice at a seated lady elegantly dressed and a handsome Army officer impeccable in scarlet tunic, well-cut breeches, glossy riding-boots with glittering spurs.

Oddly enough, Mr. Hone, a tall, gaunt man, parchment-coloured and hairless, was talking, as we entered, about "sick" pearls.

"'Sick' pearls," he was saying, "as they are commonly called—" He broke off, holding up a ribboned pince-nez for a look at us as he demanded impatiently, "Yes?"

"Books?" said Raffles.

"Up those stairs," said Mr. Hone—and, as we went up a short flight of stairs to a gallery landing lined to the ceiling with shelves crammed untidily with volumes, resumed his inter-rupted discourse.

"Pearls, my dear Major and Mrs. Cambray," he said, "are like the ocean that engenders them—capricious and mutable. The condition termed, with reference to their loss of lustre, their 'sickness,' is mysterious. Some ladies simply cannot wear pearls without this deterioration occurring."

"But, Mr. Hone," said Mrs. Cambray, "my own problem, as I explained to you yesterday, when my husband persuaded me to consult you, is quite different. There's nothing the matter with the lustre of my rope of pearls, which was a gift from my late father, Rear-Admiral Ercutt, Royal Navy. No, no, *my* problem is that just lately, whenever I wear my pearls, they have the effect of causing unsightly blemishes to appear on my neck.''

''Extraordinary!'' said Mr. Hone. ''I've had, as you know, some success in curing 'sick' pearls by a method peculiar to myself. I've subjected your pearls to intense scrutiny, Mrs. Cambray, but frankly, I find myself at a loss. Your problem is unique in my experience.''

On the gallery landing, I stole a sidelong glance at Raffles. His back to the three persons in the shop below, he was pretending to look at books, but I knew that, like myself, he was listening curiously to the conversation.

''My wife,'' Major Cambray was saying, ''has consulted Colonel Jebb, Director of Army Medical Services, Punjab Area.''

''My problem is quite beyond him, Lionel,''said Mrs. Cambray. ''All he did was mumble about women getting queer fancies with the advancing years. 'It's all in the *mind*, Dorothy,' he said. How absurd! The blemishes appear on my *neck*!''

''Well, they're certainly caused by the pearls, Dorothy,'' said Major Cambray, ''so my advice to you is—get rid of that damned necklace.''

''How, pray? Every lady in Simla would once have jumped at the chance of buying my necklace, but now they all cringe away from it.''

''You've talked too much about your problem, Dorothy.''

''What a horrid thing to say, Lionel! Actually, the only person I mentioned my blemishes to, in strict confidence, was Lady Royelme. How was I to know that she—the Judge-Advocate-General's wife, of all people—would blab the matter all over Simla? One lives and learns. In future, I shall keep my own counsel. I've always intended that Ella should have my pearls as an engagement gift. Mr. Hone, I may tell you, in strict confidence, that Major Cambray and I are on the eve of announcing the engagement of our daughter Ellaline to Lieutenant Peter Pemberton, Bengal Lancers, aide-de-camp to the Viceroy.''

"You can't fob off your necklace on Ella, Dorothy," said Major Cambray. "The gel's taken a horror of it."

"Mrs. Cambray," said Mr. Hone, "I've been giving this matter a good deal of thought. I have your necklace here in my safe—"

I heard the jingle of keys on a ring—and with rising tension I saw that Raffles, at the mention of a safe, had started drifting along, apparently absorbed in a book he held, towards a point on this gallery landing from which he might be able to get a quick look down, over the banister rail, at Mr. Cyrus Hone's side of the counter below.

"Your unique problem, Mrs. Cambray," I heard Mr. Hone continuing, as I plucked another book unseeingly from the shelves, "fascinates me. I'd like to devote further study to your pearls—and, at the same time, it would please me if I could relieve you of your dilemma. I may, of course, be faced by an insoluble riddle—in which case I shall be saddling myself with a necklace I could not, in all conscience, offer for sale to some other lady."

"Mr. Hone has his good name to consider, Dorothy," said Major Cambray.

"Quite so," Mr. Hone concurred. "However, the problem posed by these pearls tantalizes—nay, challenges me. It tempts me to take a chance. So here now, Mrs. Cambray, is your necklace. In the case with it you'll find a note of the best price I dare venture, in the circumstances, to offer you for the necklace, in order to relieve you of your dilemma."

"Now, by God, Dorothy," Major Cambray exclaimed, "considering the reputation your pearls have acquired, it's damned sporting of Mr. Hone to risk making an offer at all! You'd better think this over very carefully."

Mrs. Cambray, sounding relieved and appreciative, said that indeed she would do so—and, assuring Mr. Hone that they would be in touch with him on the morrow, the Cambrays departed.

"Well, Bunny," said Raffles, who had drifted back along the gallery landing to my side, "what's that book you've found?"

I looked at the title of the book I held. It gave me a queer feeling. For the volume to which uncanny chance had guided my random hand was the work of esoteric speculation, *Isis Unveiled,* by Helena Petrovna Blavatsky.

It seemed very strange.

However, we bought the book and a couple that Raffles had chosen—and, bidding good day to the gaunt orientalist with the pince-nez, we went out through the bead-curtained doorway into the pleasant sunshine.

"Our journalist friend from Lahore, Bunny," Raffles said, as we walked away from the cluttered old shop that backed upon the ravine, "was quite right when he told us we'd find a visit to Cyrus Hone's shop worth our while. I got a look at Hone's safe. It's under his counter, and it's a pretty good safe. When he opened it to take out Mrs. Cambray's necklace-case, I got a glimpse of other things in the safe, including a tray of gemstones—mostly, as far as I could see, unset rubies."

Raffles offered me a Sullivan from his cigarette-case.

"Our journalist friend told us that Hone often makes trips up the China coast. I rather think he also visits Burma, where the world's best rubies are mined—and where," Raffles added, "I believe there's a clandestine trade in stones secreted by the mine workers."

"You think Hone's an illicit ruby buyer?" I said. "You think he's crooked?"

"Bunny, I've seldom heard a conversation more suggestive of something crooked going on," Raffles said, "than that talk between Cyrus Hone and the ineffable Cambrays."

We were coming out again on the Ladies' Mile, where rickshaws sped to and fro, bearing military and civilian pillars of the Raj to their well-earned tiffin.

"Now, if I remember rightly," Raffles went on, "I noticed in one of the other side streets a jeweller's shop. We've time to drop in there before lunch. I want to see if we can buy a reasonably good ruby—unset."

"*Buy* one?" I said.

I was astonished. True, it was only recently that Raffles had allowed me to associate myself with him in his way of living by crime without sacrificing the interests and pastimes normal to a gentleman. In fact, our trip to India, as guests of K. S.

Ranjitsinjhi of Nawanagar and Trinity College, Cambridge, was the first notable experience I had had of the advantages Raffles derived from his ability as a cricketer.

All the same, I knew enough about Raffles's methods to realise that it was highly unusual for him to acquire a gem by purchase. It seemed unlike him. At the same time, I knew him well enough to be aware that it was futile for me to pester him with questions as to why he wanted a ruby. He would divulge his purpose when it suited him.

So all I knew, when we slipped out of Peliti's Hotel that night by way of a balcony which ran along under the windows on our side of the building, was that Raffles had in the pocket of his immaculate dinner-coat an unset Burmese ruby and six silk scarves which he also had bought.

From the balcony, which was of teak, steps led down to a small terrace from which we were able to make our way round to the street without any busybody in the hotel knowing that we no longer were in our rooms.

From the military cantonments a bugle had long ago sounded the last of the day's calls: "Lights Out." Hatless, in evening-dress, we walked at a saunter in the role of late diners who were taking the air under the stars. Except for a passing policeman, who touched his turban to us, and for a chattering party of ladies in ball gowns and military chaps in mess-jackets, we saw nobody.

At the ravine end of the side street where Cyrus Hone, the orientalist of questionable integrity, had his place of business, we found the queer old building in darkness.

"The door will be bolted, of course," Raffles said, "but let's see where that narrow path at the side leads us."

It led us to Hone's side entrance, but that door, when Raffles gently tried it, proved to be bolted. The path came to a dead end at a wall topped by spikes. Raffles leaped up, gripped the spikes, pulled himself higher, peered over the wall.

"Bunny," he whispered, dropping back down beside me, "there's a sort of ledge between the rear wall of the building and the edge of the ravine. I noticed, this morning, that there's a small window at the rear end of that gallery landing where the books are. I've got a feeling, as the window was cobwebby and looks directly on to the ravine, that it may stand permanently ajar. Let's see if we can get to it."

Tying silk scarves triangularly over our faces, we pulled ourselves up on top of the spiked wall. From this elevation, the ravine fell away so sheer before us that it made my head swim with vertigo.

Following Raffles, I lowered myself with gingerly care on to the ledge of which he had spoken. It was a good deal narrower than I had bargained for. His face to the wall of the building, Raffles started inching along the ledge. I followed his example. There was nothing on the wall to provide handholds, and my heels were so close to the edge of the ravine that I broke out in a prickle of perspiration and I could feel my calf muscles twitching spontaneously in different directions. I was not built to be a human fly.

Out of the corner of my eye, I saw Raffles pause, peering up at a windowsill. It was rather more than a long arm's reach above his head. He crouched slightly, preparatory to springing up to get a grip on the sill. At that very instant, the night was rent by such a wild, uncanny squeal as made me cleave limpet-like to the wall with my heart hammering against it and my eyes clenched shut.

I was paralysed. Suddenly, fingers like manacles clamped on my right wrist.

"Come on," Raffles whispered. "You're all right."

I opened my eyes. His scarf-masked face loomed above me in the star-glimmer. He was in through the window and now, leaning out and down from it, was giving me a hand. I needed it.

"That cry?" I gasped, as I scrambled in somehow over the sill.

"An elephant, Bunny," Raffles whispered "—some old bull gone *musth*, staked and chained in the Army Transport Lines, down there in the ravine. Shh, listen!"

I held my breath, but all I could hear was the surge of my own pulse in my ears. Starlight from the now wide-open window showed me that we were on the gallery landing. At this rear end of it there were bookshelves both sides, but further along and on the right the shelves gave way to the banister-rail, below which was the cluttered shop, all dark. I felt something silken thrust into my hand.

"Scarves," Raffles whispered, "to bind, gag, and blindfold Hone when I give you the signal. Now, I'm going down into the shop. I noticed, this morning, that there's a bell over the street door. I'm going to make that bell jangle as though someone outside had jerked the bellpull. When Hone appears, as I hope he will, from wherever he sleeps—obviously his bedroom's not on this book landing—we'll see if the plan I have in mind works. Keep watch from this landing, and be quick wth those scarves when I signal you."

He stole away, soundless, along the landing. I crouched against the banisters, peering down into the shop. I could see nothing, but I knew that Raffles had a photographic memory. If once he had seen a place in the light, he could find his way about it subsequently in the dark, no matter how cluttered.

Prepared for it as I was, the sudden jangling of the bell made my nerves quiver. It had come quicker than I had expected. Raffles scarcely had had time to feel his way to the street door. Again the bell jangled, a frightful clamour. I heard a sound of thumping.

"Hone?" shouted a muffled voice. "Open up!"

Stunned, I realised that it was not Raffles who was ringing the bell. Someone else was doing it for him. Someone was outside, yanking at the bellpull and pounding on the door.

Light appeared. It came from an oil-lamp carried by Cyrus Hone. I crouched lower against the banisters, peering down between the uprights. Hone put the lamp on the counter, which was just below me. I could see the top of his hairless, parchment-hued head. He crossed the shop. On the back of his red silk robe, an embroidered cobra, poised, with inflated hood, seemed to writhe its coils as Hone moved. Nowhere among the shop's shadowy clutter of oriental curios could I see Raffles. He had gone to ground.

Hone stopped before the bead curtain that hung over the street door. He drew a hand from within his robe. In the hand was a revolver. Above the door, the bell was jumping and jangling, convulsive on its spring.

"Who's there?" screeched Hone.

"Cambray," a voice shouted back—and the bell stopped jangling.

Hone swept aside the bead curtain, unbolted the door, opened it.

Hatless, handsome, a row of silver medals on his scarlet mess-jacket, Major Lionel Cambray lurched in, looking flushed, unsteady on his feet.

"What d'you want here at this hour?" Hone snarled, as he closed the door. "Pah, you're drunk, Major!"

"I've had the honour," said Major Cambray, blowing out a cloud of cigar smoke, "of taking wine with the Visheroy. He dined with the regiment tonight. But that's none of your damned business, Hone. I'm here to get down to brass tacks with you about this offer you've made for Dorothy's pearlsh."

"Is your wife going to accept the offer?"

"Yes, God help her! Your scheme's worked. She'll be bringing the necklace to you tomorrow—which is why I've got to have the matter out with you tonight, man to man. Hone, that offer you've made is nowhere near the real value of Dorothy's bloody heirloom!"

"What else did you expect, Major? The whole point of the scheme is that the difference between the real value of the pearls and the sum I've offered for them approximately equals the total of the money I've lent you from time to time."

"But damn you, Hone, you're treating yourself to an outrageous interest on your money! Outrageous, I say," declared Major Cambray, staggering slightly.

"Major," retorted the orientalist, "I'm a business man. Unlike you, I don't disport myself with expensive courtesans in half the garrison towns of the Indian sub-continent. Solvency, Major, is incompatible with your martial sex virility."

"Sex?" shouted Cambray, incensed. "What does a moulting, bald-headed vulture like you know about sex? I'm not here to bandy words with you about sex. Let's leave sex out of it. I'm here to tell you straight, Hone—man to man—I don't like your necklace offer."

"Very well, I'll withdraw it—and you can pay me in cash."

"Don't talk so idiotic! You know damned well I can't pay

you in cash. The only valuable thing in the family is the necklace Dorothy's pater gave her. Otherwise, would I have let you talk me into your crafty scheme? Would I have crept around my wife's bedroom in my stocking feet at night so that I could get at her bloody heirloom and dip it in that noxious stuff you gave me?"

"Major, I paid the leading professional beggar in the Orient good money for the secret of that stuff. Used lavishly, it produces harmless sores that yet look hideous enough to wring alms from the compassionate—while prudently keeping their distance. Used in the weak solution I supplied you with, it merely induces mild, ephemeral blemishes. As I carefully explained to you, all you have to do, after each occasion your wife's worn her pearls when so treated, is to get at them again, wash them in cold water, dry them, and return them to the necklace-case."

"You glib fakir!" shouted Cambray, with an angry lurch. "You talked me into this with your forked cobra tongue! Let me tell you, the Viceroy made an inspiring speech to us in the Mess tonight, and it made me realise that it's not very nice, when you come to think of it, for an officer and a gentleman to tiptoe around in his sleeping wife's bedroom with a beaker of beggar's brew. Damn it, it's not done, Hone! It comes under 'conduct unbecoming,' in Queen's Regulations. The shame of it has come home to me. I can't stand the dishonour of it. Hone, if you don't improve on your offer, the only decent thing left to me is to blow my brains out."

"Pot-valiant bluster, Major Cambray. I've heard quite enough of your maudlin vapouring at this time of night. I'll expect you and your wife tomorrow—*with* the necklace. Now, come on," said Cyrus Hone, opening the shop door, "out you go, Major. Out with you! Out! *Out!*"

As Hone pushed the insolvent soldier out into the street, I saw a slight movement of the curtains of a gilded howdah conspicuous among the wares in the shop. Raffles stepped out from the howdah, placed something on the floor, stepped back into the howdah, softly drew the curtain closed.

Hone was bolting the shop door. Turning, he started back across the shop. Suddenly, he stopped dead. He was staring down at something on the floor, something that glittered like a fiery ember in the light from the lamp on the counter. Putting his revolver beside the lamp, Hone picked up the fiery ember. It was a ruby. Holding his ribboned pince-nez to his eyes, he examined the stone. It winked hotly as he turned it about in talon-like, nicotine-stained fingers. He was unable to account for it. Then a thought struck him. So visible was its impact that I could divine its purport: Had someone been at his safe?

His pince-nez dropped on its ribbon. He went quickly behind the counter, slid aside a wooden panel. Peering down between the banisters, I saw the safe under the counter. Hone tried the lever. The safe seemed firmly closed, inviolate. Hone snatched up the lamp and the revolver and vanished through the doorway from which he had first appeared.

The shop was dark. The thump of my heart measured the seconds. Before many of them had passed, Cyrus Hone reappeared. Evidently he had gone to get his key-ring from wherever he kept it hidden, for it now was in his hand. Putting the lamp and revolver on the counter, the agitated orientalist selected a key, thrust it into the keyhole of the safe, depressed the lever, pulled open the heavy door.

Raffles ducked out from the howdah. Three quick, light steps brought him behind Hone. Raffles's hand clamped over Hone's mouth. Whirling him round, and out from behind the counter, Raffles thrust him face down on to one of the zenana divans displayed for sale. Holding Hone there with a knee in the small of his back and a hand pressing the orientalist's face well down into the silken cushions, Raffles glanced up at the gallery landing—and nodded.

I knew my cue. Vaulting the banister-rail, I landed on the counter and, nimbly avoiding the lamp, sprang to the floor. With the silk scarves Raffles had bought for the purpose, I bound Hone's wrists and ankles, and gagged and blindfolded him.

Raffles gave me a nod of approbation. We went to the safe, now standing invitingly open for our inspection. Raffles lifted out the tray of gemstones, put it on the counter. The gems, some in rings and brooches, but mostly unset rubies, dazzlingly reflected the lamplight.

Among the gems was an incongruous object. We saw it simultaneously.

It was a silver greyhound.

We stood for an instant thunderstruck—then exchanged with each other, over our scarf-masks, glances of intense surmise.

Abruptly, Raffles took up the lamp, dropped on one knee, peered into the safe. He reached into it, took something out and, straightening up, put it on the counter.

The object was a leather pouch, thick with contents, tightly tied with red tape, and labelled, in bold black letters, *To Her Majesty's Under-Secretary of State, India Office, London*. The tape was prominently sealed in four places. Impressed in the red wax was the cipher *V.R.* surmounted by a crown.

The seals were unbroken.

I could hardly believe what I saw. If the young journalist from Lahore, whose initials were K.R. or vice versa, had not chanced to tell us of the tragic encounter between Shere Khan and the Queen's Messenger, and of the existence of the corps of elite couriers, the silver greyhound insignia would have meant nothing to us. We should have taken what we had come for— the rubies which Cyrus Hone had, almost for certain, acquired illicitly—and we should not have explored further in his safe.

Yet now, on so slender a thread of chance may hang great affairs of state; we had in our hands the diplomatic pouch containing documents of perhaps crucial importance to the safety and future of the Raj.

From the tray of gemstones Raffles was picking out the unset rubies. There were sixteen of them. They seemed to me, now, of minor importance. Nevertheless, he pocketed them. He did not touch the gems that were in settings, but he pocketed also the silver greyhound insignia—which, as I was quick to realise, might at some time expedite our transit over international frontiers, should such need eventuate.

But how, I wondered uneasily, would he deal with the larger issue in which our discovery of the diplomatic pouch had now involved us?

Suddenly, he spoke. For a moment I thought it was someone else, for he was, when he chose, an accomplished mimic, and he addressed me now with the accent peculiar to persons of Anglo-Indian origin.

"So!" he said, giving me a wink over his scarf-mask. "Behold, my friend! We come to steal Hone *sahib*'s rubies—but lo, we find also a bonus! This pouch! For this pouch a reward is offered—oah, yes!"

I realised that Raffles was speaking for the benefit of Cyrus Hone. Bound, gagged, blindfolded, face down on the cushions of the divan, the orientalist was lying very still. The cobra embroidered on the back of his robe had ceased writhing its coils. I sensed that Hone was listening intently.

"Consider!" Raffles said, his tone crafty and exultant. "How comes Hone *sahib* by this pouch? It is clear, my friend, that he is a staging-post for intelligence material gathered in the plains and passed northward by spies. No wonder he makes journeys often to China coast! For curios?"

Raffles cackled evilly.

"Oah, no! He goes there to deliver intelligence harvest to Russian *sahibs* and receive his pay and instructions—oah, yes, that is very sartain now, my friend! So now, I tell you what we do. You take the rubies and hide them. We deny all knowledge of rubies. Me, myself, I go now to the police. I say to them that always I have suspicions of Hone *sahib*—so, as loyal subject of the Raj, I effect an entrance into shop to seek proof of my suspicions. And I say to police: 'Behold, here is proof of treachery within the gates—this pouch!' And I claim for us the reward—our bonus, my friend—oah, yes!"

As he was speaking, Raffles had moved to the divan, where he seemed to be testing the knots of the scarf that bound Hone's wrists.

"Yes, he is helpless," Raffles assured me. "Hone *sahib* will be quite safe here for an hour or so—just till police come to arrest and question him. We have no more to do here. So come, my friend, we go now."

We took off our scarf-masks, Raffles turned out the lamp, unbolted the street door, and we went, closing the door behind us.

"We're now in a curious situation, Bunny," Raffles said, as we lighted cigarettes and walked away along the silent steet. "What I said about Hone is obviously true. The man's a traitor and should be shot. But you and I can't afford to get involved in judicial proceedings, so we've no option but to let Hone escape. For that reason, I didn't tighten the scarf round his wrists, I loosened it. In ten minutes or so he should have freed himself. His fangs are drawn, and I think it's a pretty safe bet that he'll cut his losses on his non-portable stock in trade and be on his way out of Simla—and all India—within the hour he thinks he has before the police come for him."

"That's all very well," I said uneasily. "But, Raffles, what are we to do about the diplomatic pouch?"

"Ah, that's the important question, Bunny," Raffles said. "I have the pouch here under my dinner-coat. We must make good use of this pouch. Clearly, it's of great importance to the Raj. The question of the pouch needs careful thought."

With this I had to be content—and, by way of the rear balcony of Peliti's Hotel, we regained our rooms without anyone in the place knowing that we had been temporarily absent from them. But I could not sleep. I had no doubt what Raffles would do with the sixteen rubies, for I knew that one of the four cricket bats in his cricket-bag had an aperture under the binding on its blade. To unwind the binding, wrap the rubies in a handkerchief or scarf, wad them into the aperture, and replace the binding was a simple operation. I had seen him do it on a previous occasion. I was not too worried about the rubies. What worried me was the diplomatic pouch. Possession of it had undone Cyrus Hone—and it could undo us. What the devil did Raffles intend to do about the pouch?

I determined to ask him in the morning, but dawn was breaking over the hills and chasms of the rhododendron forests before I fell at last into the heavy sleep of nervous debilitation. So I was late down to breakfast.

I found Raffles, immaculate in a white suit, a pearl in his M.C.C. cravat, already at table. I ordered coffee and a lightly boiled egg from the waiter. Just as I was about to tackle Raffles, in a low tone, on the matter of the diplomatic pouch, a diminutive page-boy in a white tunic and red turban came to the table.

"Raffles *sahib*," he said, "an Officer awaits you in the lobby."

"Oh, dear God!" I thought—and my heart sank like a stone.

"I'll be there in a moment," Raffles said.

With a salaam, the page-boy left us. We looked at each other. Raffles's grey eyes were hard.

"I don't know what this portends, Bunny," he murmured, "but keep your head—whatever happens."

He lighted a cigarette. Never had I seen him so tense. He took two puffs, crushed out the cigarette, rose to his feet. I rose, too. I felt it imperative to know the worst immediately, so I accompanied him from the dining-room.

By the desk in the lobby stood a man in a pith helmet, his blue tunic and white jodhpurs impeccable, a revolver holstered on his gleaming leather belt. The page-boy pointed us out to him, and he strode straight at us wth a jingle of his spur-chains.

"Raffles and Manders?" he said. "Welcome to Simla!" He smiled, offering us his hand. "I'm Peter Pemberton, Bengal Lancers. I've had a letter about you from my Rajput friend, Kumar Shri Ranjitsinjhi. He tells me you've been playing cricket with him in Nawanagar, and he asks me to see to it that you meet the right people in Simla. Let me introduce you to one of them." Half turning from us, he called, "Oh, Ella—"

I felt enfeebled by a combination of relief and stupefaction as an extremely pretty girl wearing a summery dress and attractive little hat, and carrying a dainty parasol, came across the lobby to us.

"Ella," said the handsome young Lancer, "may I present Ranji's friends? Mr. Raffles, Mr. Manders—Miss Ellaline Cambray."

I managed to bow without actually falling flat on my face. But Raffles did not turn a hair.

"What a delightful welcome to Simla!" he said. "Won't you join us at coffee?"

"I'm afraid we can't stop now, my dear fellow," said Peter Pemberton. "I'm one of the Viceroy's dogsbodies—his aides-de-camp, don't you know—and he's commanded me to take

Miss Cambray to Viceregal Lodge this morning. The Vicereine wants to meet her—for a rather special reason, eh, Ella?''

"Yes, Peter,'' said Ellaline Cambray, with a faint, enchanting blush.

"What we've dropped in here for,'' Pemberton said to us, "is to tell you that Miss Cambray's parents are giving a dinner-party this evening. We've told them two of Ranji's friends are in Simla, and we're deputed to invite you, aren't we, Ella?''

"Yes, indeed,'' said Ellaline, with a charming smile, "you simply must come. Please do!''

"Nothing, I assure you,'' Raffles said, "could give Manders and myself keener pleasure.''

"Splendid,'' said Pemberton. "Eight o'clock, then, at the Cambrays' place—Sobraon House, just off the Ladies' Mile.''

As the fine-looking young couple, so representative of all that was most admirable in the Raj, left us, Raffles and I looked at each other.

"Well, well,'' he said dryly, "Simla's a small place, Bunny! I'm rather glad this has happened. There's just a chance that it may clear up a question I'm slightly anxious about.''

"What question?'' I said.

"A question,'' Raffles said, lowering his voice, "that concerns the diplomatic pouch.''

He would say no more, though my own anxiety about the pouch was anything but slight. I just wanted the incriminating thing safely off our hands.

To my surprise, among the guests at Sobraon House that evening was Madame Helena Petrovna Blavatsky. She wore a *sari* of dark blue silk.

While dressing for dinner, I had dipped into her volume of esoteric speculation, *Isis Unveiled*. It opened to me vistas of thought quite unfamiliar to a person of my shallow and hedonistic nature. I found the book, as I found Madame Blavatsky herself, impressive and fascinating, yet subtly disturbing.

At dinner, I could hardly keep my eyes off her. Seated next to her was the young Lahore journalist whose eyebrows, moustache and thick-lensed glasses gave him an air of maturity so much in advance of his years. I could see that he was enthralled by the personality of Madame Blavatsky, and, with all that I had on what passed for my conscience, I wondered uneasily what they were talking about.

With the *gateaux*, at the conclusion of dinner, champagne was served.

At the head of the table, our host, Major Lionel Cambray, ruddily handsome in his scarlet mess-jacket, a distinguished hint of grey at his temples, rose to his feet. Swaying slightly on them, he announced that a marriage had been arranged and would shortly take place between his and his dear wife Dorothy's daughter, Ellaline, and Lieutenant Peter Pemberton, Bengal Lancers.

The announcement was received with general rapture. Toasts were drunk to the happy couple. Afther this, the ladies went off to the drawing-room, no doubt to discuss the romance. And over port and cigars so creditable that it was no wonder Major Cambray was insolvent, us men turned to such congenial subjects as pigsticking, polo, and tiger-shooting.

"Talking of tigers," said the young man from Lahore, puffing thoughtfully at his pipe, "I mentioned the Shere Khan mystery to Madame Blavatsky. I asked her if the Viceroy, hearing of her presence in Simla, had taken the opportunity to consult her on the matter. She tells me that he hasn't. Considering that normal investigative methods have failed to trace the missing diplomatic pouch, I wonder if it's occurred to you, Pemberton, as aide-de-camp to the Viceroy, to suggest to him that he may be making a mistake in neglecting to enlist Madame Blavatsky's exceptional gifts?"

"Nonsense!" barked white-whiskered, blue-uniformed Colonel Jebb, Director of Army Medical Services, Punjab Area. "What? The Viceroy of India, pro-consul of the Queen-Empress, dabble in the supernatural—consult a Witch of the White Lotus on a state problem of the Raj? Bah, the day that happens the British'll be finished in India! Pemberton, set this young ink-slinger straight before he comes out with one of his cheeky pieces in the *C. & M. Gazette*."

"As a matter of fact, Colonel," Peter Pemberton said,

"there's been a remarkable development in the matter of the diplomatic pouch."

I sank slightly lower in my chair. I dared not look at Raffles.

"There's no reason," Pemberton went on, "why you shouldn't all know that this morning, very early, a rickshaw coolie presented himself at the police station. He's a scrawny old chap, getting a bit frail for running around pulling a rickshaw. Anyway, it seems he slept last night, curled up in his rickshaw, under a tree near the Indian temple. He woke when the bugle at the cantonments was sounding reveillé. He felt something between his calloused old feet. He looked down—and, by God, there it was—the missing mail-pouch, the seals unbroken!"

Blood rushed into my head. So Raffles had gone out again after we had parted last night!

"The old coolie," said Peter Pemberton, "ran straight to the police station with it. He'll get the reward—and I'm told he intends to buy a bit of land with it at his home village, down near Umbala. He's set up for life."

So Raffles, after careful thought, had indeed made good use of the Raj's mail-pouch—and now was relieved of the slight anxiety he had felt concerning its safe delivery. I met his amused eyes across the table—and, unobtrusively, I raised my glass to him.

After some fruitless speculation as to what vicissitudes might lie behind the unaccountable reappearance of the diplomatic pouch, the discussion was cut short by Major Cambray.

"It's time we joined the *mem-sahibs*," he said, "God bless 'em!"

As we all trooped into the drawing-room, bringing with us a healthy masculine aroma of port and cigars, we found the ladies sitting aound fanning themselves and talking about Dorothy Cambray's pearl necklace.

"Because of its effect on me," she was saying, "and as Ella has a distaste for it, I'd decided to accept an offer which that interesting man Cyrus Hone had made me for it. But when we went to see him about it today, he wasn't at his shop, was he, Lionel?"

"No," said Major Cambray, with a scowl. "Damned strange! I can't make it out."

"His *dhobi wallah*," said Mrs. Cambray, "who also cleans the shop for him, was there. He told us he thought Mr. Hone must have gone off unexpectedly on one of his trips to the China coast, but he hadn't left a note or anything. We thought it most inconsiderate of him. Lionel was distinctly vexed."

Two turbaned servant *wallahs* entered, bearing trays.

"Now, who," said Dorothy Cambray, as the trays were set deftly before her, "would like coffee, and who would prefer tea?"

"Talking of tea, Mrs. Cambray," said the journalist from Lahore, "and of the problem of your necklace, which has been a good deal spoken about, I wonder if it's occurred to you to submit the phenomenon to the attention of Madame Blavatsky?"

At this, there was a general murmur of interest. It was evident that to the cream of Simla society, assembled here now in the Cambray drawing-room, Madame Blavatsky's reputation for arcane knowledge was a subject of great curiosity. All eyes turned to the small, grey-haired, contemplative lady in the dark blue *sari*.

"I am puzzled, Mrs. Cambray," she said, "by what I have heard here this evening about your necklace. I should be interested to see it."

"Certainly," said Dorothy Cambray, and she turned to her husband. "Lionel, would you be a dear and run upstairs and get my necklace for Madame Blavatsky? I keep it hidden under the things in the bottom drawer of my dressing-table."

"Oh, do you? Very well," muttered Major Cambray—and he left the drawing-room with a rather strained look on his face.

I saw the young man from Lahore, having provoked this journalistically promising turn of events, take off his glasses to polish them, his blue eyes keen with interest.

Dorothy Cambray poured the tea and the coffee, Ellaline coped charmingly with the sugar-tongs, and Peter Pemberton, now practically one of the family, passed the cups around.

Raffles and I both chose coffee, and as I stirred mine with my spoon I was conscious of expectation in the air, a growing sense of psychic tension.

Major Cambray returned. A good deal of the ruddiness had drained from his face. The young man from Lahore hooked his glasses back on as Major Cambray, his expression exceedingly odd, handed the necklace case to Madame Blavatsky.

Over the party, all now with cups in their hands—the ladies seated, the gentlemen standing—a stillness had fallen. My palms moistened as I watched the small, grey-haired lady in the blue *sari* open the necklace case. She gazed at the loops of the pearl rope, lustrous against the purple velvet of the case-lining. Putting the case in her lap, she took up the necklace, passed the pearls slowly through her sensitive fingers. She did not look at the pearls. She gazed before her, and her strange, wide-set light eyes were unseeing, introspective.

My heart thumped, sultry. I was conscious of being in the presence of something here beyond the normal ken. There was not a sound in the room. Thinly, from out in the night, sounded the call of a bugle—"Lights Out"—and I seemed to see, far to the north, the enduring snows of the high Himalayas, lonely under the stars.

Madame Blavatsky spoke.

"There is—there has been," she said, her voice a murmur, as from some occult thrall, "something—something wrong—some shadow, inimical—some portent of lost faith and deep sorrow—upon these pearls. And yet—and yet—"

Perception of her whereabouts seem to return to her eyes. She frowned, as though perplexed.

"Mrs. Cambray," she said, "if you are drinking tea, finish it—make three slow circles in the air with your cup— then turn it, the rim *downward,* on the saucer."

Nervously, for she was much affected, our hostess obeyed. Such was the silence here in the drawing-room that a moth was audible, beating frail wings, from some compulsion it could not comprehend, against the fringed shade of a standard-lamp.

"You understand, Mrs. Cambray," said Madame Blavatsky quietly, "that Good or Evil, those adversaries in the eternal conflict which we term the *mysterium magnum,* can sometimes—not always—be divined from the pattern that the tea-leaves assume in the cup?''

''Yes,'' whispered Dorothy Cambray.

The cup, downturned, enigmatic upon its saucer, held her eyes—indeed, all our eyes—with an uncanny fascination.

''And you wish me, Dorothy Cambray,'' said Madame Blavatsky, ''to read this cup?''

Hypnotized, Dorothy Cambray gave a scarcely perceptible nod.

''Very well,'' said Madame Blavatsky, and she took up the cup.

As she studied the pattern of its fragmented tea-leaves, nobody moved. Nobody, it seemed to me, even breathed. Only the moth was audible, fluttering out its brief incarnation against the glass of the lamp-chimney.

With deliberation, Madame Blavatsky replaced the cup on its saucer. She held out the rope of pearls to Mrs. Cambray.

''Put on your pearls, Dorothy Cambray,'' said Madame Blavatsky, with quiet authority. ''There is no harm whatever in them.''

''Now, by God!'' Colonel Jebb exploded. ''Bravo, Madame Blavatsky! Bravo indeed! That's exactly what I told her myself. I said, 'It's all in the *mind,* Dorothy'!''

But Mrs. Cambray, still enslaved to the memory of her disturbing blemishes, winced away from the proffered pearls.

''Oh, come, Dorothy!'' exclaimed a lady with patrician nostrils, whom I understood to be the wife of the Judge-Advocate-General. ''*I* have implicit faith in Madame Blavatsky. See?'' She took the rope of pearls, looped it several times about her neck. ''There now! I've always admired these pearls. If you are so weak as still to wish to be rid of them, I'm perfectly ready to improve on any offer that man Cyrus Hone has made you for them.''

''Oh, but, Dorothy,'' interjected a lady with a peacock-tail fan, ''why should Lady Royelme have your pearls? I've known you far longer than she has! I, too, have absolute faith in Madame Blavatsky, and I'm quite prepared to make you as good an offer as Eustacia Royelme.''

To my astonishment, other ladies began to express their desire to purchase the pearls which previously had been so repugnant to them. And Madame Helena Petrovna Blavatsky, perhaps saddened by the mundane exhibition of human nature now so obviously developing, gathered her *sari* about her and rose to take her leave.

"If you will excuse me, Mrs. Cambray, I feel a little tired," she said—and I did not wonder at it.

"Madame Blavatsky," said the young man from Lahore, clearly enthralled by what he had witnessed, "may I have the honour of escorting you to your hotel?"

His petition being granted, the grey-haired lady and the enterprising journalist went away together.

Their departure seemed scarcely to be noticed by the Cambrays, for the bidding was growing keener. Dorothy Cambray looked totally bemused, Peter Pemberton had whisked Ellaline away into the conservatory, where I could see them giggling together, while Major Lionel Cambray was quite visibly recovering his dashing air at the prospect of a restored solvency.

"A rum experience, Bunny," Raffles said, as we left Sobraon House while the bidding still was in progress. "The lamentable Major certainly doesn't deserve his luck. On the other hand, that old rickshaw runner had well earned a spot of manna. But there you are, that's life," Raffles added wryly. "It cuts both ways, as Madame Blavatsky implies on better authority than you and I can."

What with the sixteen rubies concealed in the hollow bat in his cricket-bag, and with the possibility that inquiries might soon be instigated into the disappearance of Cyrus Hone, Raffles thought it impolitic for us to linger unduly in Simla. So next morning we took a last stroll along the Ladies' Mile in the pleasantly temperate sunshine.

"By the way, Raffles," I said, musing on the events of our visit, "we haven't found out whether that young journalist on the *Civil and Military Gazette* is the one who signs his work K.R. or the one who has those initials reversed."

"We'll ask him his name, Bunny," Raffles said, "—because I think I see him, a little way ahead there."

We were nearing Viceregal Lodge, where the turbaned sentries stood watching the rickshaws speeding to and fro, while the standard of the Raj fluttered in light airs that came from the distant, snowcapped Himalayas.

That it was the journalist, with his mature moustache and thick-lensed glasses, was unmistakable. Smoking his pipe, he stood listening to the lively talk of a barefoot, turbaned boy wearing a tattered Army shirt girdled with rope.

A teak bowl in his hand, the boy was standing at the side of an ancient, wrinkled man in a faded yellow robe who was seated on the ground, his back to the trunk of a magnolia tree. His staff and sandals beside him, his lean legs folded in the lotus position, the ancient of days seemed to be muttering to himself as he fondled with gnarled hands some sort of wooden article.

"Pilgrims, Bunny," Raffles murmured to me, as we approached, "—an old Tibetan lama with his prayer-wheel, and his disciple wth their bowl for alms of rice. Our friend hasn't seen us. Who knows? He may be gathering material for some tale far better than the one that you and I could tell him about the diplomatic pouch. I think we'd better not intrude on him just now."

So, in the circumstances, we failed to learn our journalist friend's name—although, irrelevantly enough, we did learn that of the lama's disciple.

For, as we strolled on past the trio in the shade of the magnolia tree, we heard the journalist asking a question.

"Tell me, boy," the young man from Lahore was saying, as he puffed meditatively at his pipe, "how are you called?"

"They call me, *sahib*," replied the boy with the rice bowl, "Kim."

NOTE: It may be of interest to remark that research into the veracity of this one of Mr. Manders's clandestine records, belatedly come to light in undisclosed circumstances, tends to corroborate his narrative in at least one significant particular.

There were indeed, at the time of which he writes, two rising young journalists on the staff of the Lahore *Civil and Military Gazette* who often signed their contributions with their initials, which were similar, though reversed.

In consequence, the work of K.R., a Mr. Kay Robinson, was occasionally confused with that of his colleague and friendly rival, R.K., who later, however, rose to such literary eminence as to achieve responsible bibliographers, with the fortunate result that early misattributions were duly corrected.

From evidence implicit in Mr. Manders's narrative, there seems little doubt as to which of the two young journalists, K.R. and R.K., is the one to whom he refers.

7

THE TONGUES OF DECEIT

"After your eventful tour of duty on the China Station," remarked A. J. Raffles, "you probably don't much relish this taste of pommie weather, Hubble."

"Too right," Lieutenant-Commander Hubble acquiesced ruefully.

In the wind and rain of a blustery evening in the naval town of Portsmouth, we were descending the gangway of Her Majesty's Australian Ship *Coolibah*, the gunboat which Hubble commanded.

Hubble of the *Coolibah* had been much in the news of late, due to his fine work in evacuating missionaries and diplomats, with their wives and children, from the Treaty Ports endangered by the recent Boxer Rebellion.

H.M.A.S. *Coolibah* was now here at Portsmouth for a refit and for her crew to undergo a gunnery refresher course on Whale Island—and it so happened that, on this inclement weekend, Raffles had come down from London with a team of M.C.C. chaps to play the Navy at racquets.

I myself had come along to provide moral support.

Toby Hubble, a racquets player well known Down Under, had turned out for the Navy. Raffles had played against him in the match this afternoon and, afterwards Hubble had insisted on taking us for a drink on board *Coolibah* before the dockyard shipwrights started stripping her down.

Naturally, Raffles and I had hoped to hear Hubble's own account of the Boxer rampage and, even more, of a subsequent lively action in which the crew of *Coolibah*, laying about them freely with their cutlasses, had liberated a number of persons, notably a Chinese gentleman of high mandarin rank, held to ransom by Yangtse River pirates.

The affray had been well reported in the *Illustrated Lon-*

don News, with vividly evocative sketches by its famous artist, Walter Paget, who had used his imagination to telling effect. Hubble himself, however, to Raffles's and my own disappointment, was not much given to talking about his adventures. All he wanted to talk about was sport, for he was very Australian. He was also very naval, with the consequence that his cabin steward had repeatedly proffered trays of drinks to Raffles and me—and when, with a smile and a headshake, we had indicated the filled glasses in our hands, we had met with an unanswerable rejoinder.

"Captain's orders, sir," the steward had murmured.

So now, as Hubble, Raffles, and I left the quayside to make our way to the nearby Royal Naval Barracks, I was not ungrateful for the wind and rain, as they served somewhat to clear my head of the fumes of my potations.

By the time we reached the Barracks, I was sober enough to notice a queue of obviously damp people shuffling along under the wan gas-globes of a theatre marquee further up the street. But we ourselves turned in at the Barracks gateway, which was set in a high, spike-topped wall and guarded by oilskinned naval ratings who slapped their rifle butts smartly in salute to Toby Hubble. Piloting us across a puddled barrack square, Hubble ushered us into a warm, spacious, well-lighted hall where the time-mellowed portraits of admirals famed in our island story frowned down at us from the walls.

"Now, what about a drink?" said Hubble.

"We'd better not stop now," Raffles demurred. "As our racquets team's invited to dinner and a smoking-concert here, Manders and I'll just round up our chaps and get along to the billets to change."

A Petty Officer Steward stepped forward.

"Beg pardon, sir," he said to Hubble. "The other M.C.C. gentlemen left word to tell Mr. Raffles they've gone on to the billets."

"In that case, Raffles," said Hubble, "you and Manders must have just a quick one for the road. Come on now!"

In all conscience, there was nothing I needed less than another drink, but Raffles and I could hardly do other than allow the steward to relieve us of our caps and ulsters, and Hubble led us into an adjoining room of imposing proportions. Here logs crackled and blazed in an enormous fireplace, paintings of ships-of-the-line thundering forth their broadsides graced the walls, and on a massive sideboard was a remarkable display of silver plate.

A number of officers lounged in a half-circle of saddlebag chairs around the fire.

"'Evening, Hubble," called one of the officers who were toasting their feet by resting them on the club-type fender. "Don't forget the smoker tonight. We've got the great Crichton Hood coming to do his turn for us."

"Gratis, at that," said a bearded officer, puffing at his pipe. "Hood was born here in Pompey. He comes of a naval family. Now he's top-o'-the-bill this week at the theatre up the road."

"Local boy makes good, huh?" said Hubble of the *Coolibah*, as he, Raffles, and I helped ourselves to drinks from a tray proffered to us by a steward.

"I saw Hood's turn at the theatre on Tuesday," said a very young officer, admiring the length of ash on his cigar. "He's a damned clever ventriloquist, but it's just a knack. With a bit of practise, I could throw my own voice."

"Who at?" said the bearded officer dryly.

Raffles, glass in hand, his tweeds immaculate, a pearl in his cravat, strolled over to admire the array of silver on the sideboard.

"By the way, Hubble," he said, "Manders and I read that the mandarin you rescued presented a handsome trophy to your ship, out of gratitude. We hoped you might show it to us while we were on board."

"We couldn't leave it on board while the ship's in dockyard hands," said Hubble. "That's it, there among the Wardroom plate. It's that gold salver thing with the tree design in the middle—supposed to be a coolibah tree."

The tree design in the centre of the exquisite salver was worked in rubies. The hot glitter of the stones dazzled my eyes.

"Superb," said Raffles.

"A bonzer old bloke, the mandarin," said Hubble, embarrassed. "Much too kind, of course. Hell, let's have another drink!"

To my relief, Raffles firmly declined. "We'll see you later, at the smoker, Hubble," he said—and, reclaiming our caps and ulsters, we went out again into the windy, rainy night.

Fortunately, a four-wheeler was decanting a latecomer at the theatre up the street. Hailing the cab, we made a dash for it. The rain-sodden theatre bills were topped with the phrase: "The Great CRICHTON HOOD, Ventriloquist, fresh from European Triumphs."

"Canoe Club annexe," Raffles called to the cabbie, who was wearing by way of headgear a tarred sack that made him look like a rubicund pixie with a walrus moustache.

The Canoe Club annexe, where our R.N. hosts had billeted our racquets team, was away over on the far side of Commercial Road, and what with the Navy gin I had imbibed, the jogging of the horse, and the drumming of the rain on the cab roof, I lapsed into a drowse—from which I was rudely jerked by a sudden shout and a flurry of hoofs. I opened my eyes. Raffles was jumping out. I clambered out after him, to see what was amiss here.

In the gleam of the hansom's candle-lamps, I saw Raffles and the cabbie helping a young woman to her feet.

"Are you all right, miss?" Raffles was saying anxiously.

"Stepped off the kerb, she did," said the cabbie, "like she was in a bleedin' dream! Shaft just caught her."

"I'm so sorry, Mr. Vosper—it was all my own fault," said the young woman, who could not have been more than about nineteen. She was wearing a yellow oilskin, a yellow sou'wester framed her brown-eyed, pretty face, and she smiled shakily. "I'm quite all right, really I am."

"You've had a shaking," said Raffles, concerned. "We'd better take you home."

"This 'ere's Shipmate Sadie," said the cabbie. "She lives at The Sail Loft in Lake Road. Whatever was you thinking of, Sadie, steppin' off the kerb without lookin'? Come on, gents, let's get 'er in the cab an' take 'er 'ome to 'er Shipmates!"

Hastily, I lent a hand to help the young woman into the cab. Raffles got in after her, and I took one of the turn-down seats. The cabbie climbed to his box and, as we jingled off, Raffles suggested that we take the young woman to a doctor first, but she would not hear of it.

"No, no," she insisted. "I was just a bit shaken for a moment, that's all."

"May we introduce ourselves?" Raffles said, no doubt curious about the unusual style by which the cabbie had spoken of her. "This is my friend Manders. My name's Raffles."

"I'm Sadie Renton," she said. "I'm sorry to have caused trouble. I—"

"You were preoccupied, perhaps," Raffles suggested.

"Oh, I *was*—yes. I've been wandering round in the rain, trying to decide—" She broke off. "What *am* I saying? Why should I bother *you* with my troubles?"

"It would be kind if you would," Raffles said. "Who knows? If we could help you in some small way, we might feel a shade less guilty for knocking you down."

"Oh," she said, "I *have* wanted to talk to somebody about this, but I've hated to worry my friends—"

"Sometimes," said Raffles, "it's easier to talk to strangers—just ships that pass in the night."

"How odd," said Sadie Renton, "that you should say that! Oh, I've had an awful week. I—really, I've been out of my mind. I knew how it would be the moment I saw my Uncle Harry's name on the theatre bills here this week. He's a ventriloquist. His real name is Renton, but his stage name is quite famous—Crichton Hood."

"A very striking name, too," said Raffles.

"He's my father's brother," said Sadie. "My father was in the Navy. He warned me many times about Uncle Harry. My father said Uncle Harry's stage career is just a cover for—other things. He's a clever criminal."

"*Is* he now," said Raffles, very softly.

"Unfortunately," Sadie told us, as the cab trundled on through the rain, "my ten-year-old brother, Peter, is absolutely fascinated by Uncle Harry. Peter and I have rooms, rent free, at The Sail Loft, where I look after the premises and play the piano for the Shipmates. Anyway, last year, when Uncle Harry was appearing at the theatre here, Peter ran away from home and went off with him. I had no idea *where*. I was terrified to go to the police, because I didn't know what might be—well, uncovered about Uncle Harry. Luckily, I thought to look in a newspaper called *The Stage*—and, among a lot of notices, there was one saying 'The Great Crichton Hood, now making his Return Visit, by Popular Demand, to the Theatre Royal, Leeds.' So, of course, I rushed up to Leeds—and I brought Peter home. But I just couldn't make him tell me what he'd been up to with Uncle Harry for *ten whole days*!"

"And now," Raffles said thoughtfully, "your Uncle Harry is appearing again in Portsmouth, his own home town?"

"Yes, he's here in Pompey," Sadie said, with passion in her tone, "and the result is that Peter's been playing truant from school all this week—and from home, too. He keeps sneaking off. At this moment, I feel sure, he's in Uncle Harry's dressing-room at the theatre. I'm terrified that Peter might run off with Uncle Harry again—this very night, because it's Saturday and the bill changes weekly, so if Uncle Harry's catching a train after the second house at the theatre tonight, Peter might go with him. And I've been wandering round and round in the rain, trying to decide whether it would be right for me to try to—sort of ransom Peter back from Uncle Harry for good and all."

"*Ransom* him back?" Raffles said.

"Well, you see, I know Uncle Harry's anxious to emigrate to America. If only he had some capital," Sadie explained, "he'd go tomorrow—and I should breathe freely about Peter again, for the first time for over a *year*. I want that more than anything! Well, I have a nest-egg my father left me. It's about five hundred pounds, which I've kept for emergencies. And what I've been trying to decide was whether I'd go to the theatre and offer the money to Uncle Harry on condition that he uses it to emigrate. Only—if I did that—how could I be sure he wouldn't just spend the money on drink and women and horses, and *not go*? Do you see?"

The cab was passing up Commercial Road. The lights of shop windows and pubs flickered by. Raffles took a cigarette from his case.

"Sadie," he said, "—if we may call you so—it so happens

that Bunny Manders and I know that your uncle has an engagement after the second house at the theatre tonight. He's to do his turn at a smoking concert at the Royal Naval Barracks. Now, would you mind if I made a suggestion?"

"Oh, do!" she said eagerly. "*Please* do!"

"Your uncle," Raffles said, "is hardly likely to get away from the junket at the Barracks before twelve-thirty or one o'clock. You seem to know this cabbie, Mr. Vosper, so I suggest that we arrange for him to collect you from where you live at, say, half-past eleven, and drive you to the vicinity of the Barracks gates. Manders and I have been invited to this smoking-concert affair, so we'll slip out after your uncle's turn and join you in the cab. When he himself comes out, you can call to him from the cab. You can then make him your ransom offer, conditional upon his emigration, in the presence of two *impartial witnesses*—Manders and myself. Do you think that that might, perhaps, be helpful to you?"

No doubt of it! Sadie accepted Raffles's suggestion with impulsive gratitude. She seemed to feel that the opportunity to submit herself to our guidance more than made up for being knocked down by us. I could not help warming to her.

The cab was turning to the right, into what Sadie told us was Lake Road—a popular place, she said, with naval ratings on shore liberty in Pompey.

Certainly, in spite of the wind and rain, there seemed to be a lot of sailors, marines, and red-coated soldiers about, most of them with young ladies on their arms. The taverns were doing a roaring trade, as were the small restaurants where, behind gaslit windows, great pans of sausages and chips, pease pudding and faggots, tripe-and-onions with cowheel and mash, and similar homely fare, bubbled and steamed appetisingly.

"Here we are," said Sadie, as the cabbie reined in his horse, "—and there are my friends, the Shipmates, so I'm quite all right now, and I'll ask Mr. Vosper to call for me at The Sail Loft at eleven-thirty."

Raffles stepped out of the cab to hand her down—and Sadie, her arrangement quickly made with the cabbie, Mr. Vosper, hurried across the road to join a group of five women and five men who were standing in a ring near a street lamp.

The gas-jets, flickering in their rain-swept glass lanthorn, glimmered on the black oilskins and sou'westers worn by the men and on the yellow oilskins and sou'westers, like Sadie's, worn by the women. A very tall old fellow with a grizzled beard and tattooed hands was playing a mouth organ, the rest of the group were singing—and, as she joined them, Sadie's voice mingled, clear and pure, with theirs:

> Bobbie Shafto's gone to sea,
> Silver buckles on his knee,
> He'll come home and marry me,
> Pretty Bobbie Shafto—

"Mr. Vosper," Raffles said to the cabbie, who, hooded in his tarred sack, had climbed down from his box, "who *are* these—Shipmates?"

"Salt o' the bleedin' earth, sir," said Mr. Vosper, pulling at his walrus moustache—"like the Salvation Army lads and lasses. Only, the Shipmates—they goes after Navy blokes, more, which is why they're singin' in the rain—to get an audience together, like, then they'll go inside their place, The Sail Loft there."

Behind the little oilskinned singing group, the door of a small, red-brick building with a galvanized iron roof stood open. A wan gas-globe over the doorway faintly illumined a board bearing the legend:

UNIVERSAL ORDER OF SHIPMATES

We are all fellow voyagers on the good ship *Earth*, outward bound under sealed orders. Come into The Sail Loft, sailor, and spin your yarn.

EVERYBODY WELCOME

"You gets free tea an' buns an' stuff inside," Mr. Vosper told us—"yarns an' that, blokes tellin' about experiences they've 'ad sailin' foreign under the old White Ensign all over the perishin' globe. Then they 'as singsongs, too. That Sadie, educated gal, she plays the joanner like a bleedin' Paderooski—'er Dad brought 'er up proper. That there old cove with the chin beard, playin' the 'armonica fit to bust, 'e's in charge, like. They calls 'im the Bos'un. Aye, they've chucked a lifebelt to many a bloke down on 'is luck, 'ave the Pompey Shipmates."

Sailors who seemed to have no girls with them, so probably were attracted by Sadie's charming voice, were beginning to gather round—and the Bos'un, tapping out his mouth-organ on a calloused palm, addressed the lonely celibates with bluff good humour.

"Right, lads, let's get out of the rain," he enjoined them. "Inside now, me hearts-of-oak! Tumble aft, you Sons o' Sinbad! Tea up! All hands to the capstan!"

Striking up "Haul Away, Joe" on his mouth-organ, he played the singing Shipmates and their audience into the hospitable premises of The Sail Loft.

"Mr. Vosper," Raffles said to our cabbie, "Canoe Club annexe, please, then back to the R.N. Barracks."

At the annexe, which overlooked the Canoe Lake at the top end of Granada Road in the residential Southsea area, we found that our racquets team already had left for the Barracks. By the time we had changed hastily into our evening clobber and got back to the Barracks ourselves, dinner in the great dining-room of the Officers' Quarters was pretty well over. Stewards were clearing away the tablecloths, port and brandy decanters were circulating around the mahogany, the room was filled with the din of voices and beginning to haze with the smoke of duty-free tobacco.

Hubble of the *Coolibah*, whose lean Aussie figure and deep tan were enhanced by mess-kit, caught our eye.

"What kept you?" he asked, as we joined him at table.

"A question about a ransom," said Raffles.

"Ransom? What, here in Old Portsmouth?" scoffed Hubble. "Tell that to the marines!"

An obliging steward brought Raffles and myself a bite of dinner, warmed up, and poured wine for us. We fell to with good appetite. Meanwhile, the evening's jollity began to get under way all around us. Drinking choruses were roared out with a will—which inspired one of our M.C.C. racquets players to arise rather unsteadily to his feet and announce that, by way of compliment to the Yangtse River exploit of H.M.A.S. *Coolibah*, he would now render a solo from *The Pirates of Penzance*.

"Jesus Christ!" muttered Hubble, embarrassed.

Though I was myself uncomfortable that one of Raffles's racquets team should make such an exhibition of himself, nevertheless the chap's effort was listened to politely and received with generous applause. Bowing to Hubble, then to right and left, the fellow, blushing hotly, his white tie awry, subsided into his chair, drank four fingers of brandy at a draught and, succumbing to emotional strain, began to sink slowly under the table.

At this juncture, fortunately enough, four stewards carried in a small dais which they placed in a prominent position at one end of the dining-room, under a large painting of the great sea battle between H.M.S. *Serapis* and the Yankee ship *Bon Homme Richard* commanded by John Paul Jones.

The dais, I gathered, was for the convenience of the professional performers—and, soon afterwards, word flew round that the curtain had at last been rung down on the second house at the theatre, and the eagerly awaited *artistes* were now arriving to entertain us.

To let some of the tobacco-smoke out, stewards had opened wide the double doors leading to the hall, so from where I was sitting with Toby Hubble and Raffles I had a good view of the arrival of the group of theatricals. They still were wearing the costumes in which they had appeared before the footlights; and the ladies, with their hour-glass figures and fashionable gowns, their ostrich-plumed hats and feather boas, looked excitingly glamorous, for they had not removed their stage *maquillage*. Neither, for that matter, had the comedians, who were easy to identify by such mirth-provoking appurtenances as baggy and loudly checked trousers, immensely exaggerated bow ties, straw boaters, dapper canes, and preposterously painted eyebrows.

"There he is, Bunny," Raffles murmured to me— "the man in evening-dress—he's almost certainly Crichton Hood."

The Petty Officer Steward was conducting the party across the hall, no doubt to rooms set aside for their use as dressing-rooms. Undoubtedly the top-of-the-bill turn, for he held himself slightly aloof from the rest of the troupe, was a tall man, handsome in a Mephistophelean kind of way. His evening-dress, with cape and silk hat, was immaculate. He had a trim tuft of black beard, was smoking a cigarette in a long holder, and was followed by two stewards carrying a large "prop" hamper.

The opportunity was now taken for a general exodus to the ablutions, which our Navy hosts referred to as "the heads"— and as we were returning from this refreshing interlude I heard the popping of corks in rooms where champagne would certainly have been placed for the *artistes* to re-charge their energies for what would be, counting the *matinée*, their fourth performance this day.

In the event, their respective turns were received with ever warmer acclaim, and the evening reached its climax with the entry of Crichton Hood.

He proved to be a highly effective ventriloquist. Seated on a perfectly ordinary chair on the dais, he engaged in an amusing duologue with a large dummy seated on his knee. The dummy wore evening-dress, had a fright wig of red hair parted in the centre, a white-painted face, slyly rolling eyes, and a huge, quacking mouth. By clever use of his cigarette-holder, the ventriloquist disguised his vocal trickeries; and his many crafty references to Pompey, and to the embarrassing moments that occurred when admirals' wives and daughters visited the fleet, not only brought rapturous applause but betrayed the performer's intimate knowledge of Portsmouth and of naval life.

While the ventriloquist and his dummy were taking their bows, to unstinted acclamations, Raffles and I slipped away unobtrusively and, collecting our outdoor garments, left the Barracks. A couple of hundred yards up the street from the Barracks gate, with its armed and oilskinned sentries, Mr. Vosper's cab was waiting near a street lamp.

We joined Sadie in the cab. The rain was drumming down drearily on the cab roof, but we did our best to divert Sadie with inconsequential small talk during the lengthy wait which ensued before Raffles, who was keeping watch obliquely through the cab window, told us that the ventriloquist was just coming out of the Barracks gateway.

"He's alone, Sadie," Raffles said, letting down the cab window all the way on its strap. "You know what to do."

"Cab." I heard the man with two voices hail us, as he approached. "Cab, there!"

Sadie put her head out of the window.

"Uncle Harry," she called, "may I speak to you, please?"

Caped and silk-hatted, a shadow in the watery glimmer from the street lamp, the elegant thespian looked in at the window.

"Good God!" he said. "My niece Sadie, all the world's little Shipmate! Given up good works, Sadie? Trying your luck as a lady of the night, to pick up an easy quid or two?" He opened the cab door—but, with one foot on the step, checked sharply, peering in at the red dots of Raffles's and my cigarettes. "What's this, Sadie? Who've you got in there with you?"

"Two gentlemen," said Sadie. "I want them to hear what I have to say to you."

"You're getting wet standing there, Mr. Renton," Raffles said. "Why not join us and hear what your niece has to say? As you may know, she has a nest-egg of five hundred pounds—and you might hear something to your advantage."

The ventriloquist hesitated. But avarice overcame his wariness—and, ducking into the cab, he took the turn-down seat beside me.

"Now, what's all this about?" he said.

"Uncle Harry," said Sadie, "where is Peter?"

Renton fitted a cigarette into his long holder. Raffles struck a match for him. Renton's eyes glinted as he dipped his cigarette to the flame, but when he spoke, it was in a tone markedly different from that in which he had addressed his obscene opening remark to his niece.

"Why, Sadie my dear," he said, affecting now, with double-tongued ease, an avuncular concern, "isn't Peter at home? I found him loitering around the stage door—as he's so apt to do, I'm afraid—when I came out after the first-house performance tonight. I'll be leaving Pompey by the first train in the morning, and as I won't be seeing the kid again for a long time, I tipped him a sovereign. Uncles *will* be uncles, you know! I told him to put it in his pocket and not spend it all at once, but cut along home to his sister and be a help to her, instead of hanging around stage doors, ogling the actresses. No good comes of that."

"He hasn't come home," said Sadie. "Do you know where he is?"

"How would *I* know, love? Dammy, he's probably putting up with one of his school friends. Have you tried their houses? Perhaps," he added contritely, "I oughtn't to have given the young rascal a whole quid—liable to get him in mischief, boy of ten."

"Mr. Renton," said Raffles, "when her young brother is again safely in her custody, your niece is prepared to consider the possibility of making you a gift of five hundred pounds to finance a project which, I understand, you have under advisement—namely, emigration to a land famed for its hospitality to exceptional talent. In the light of your niece's intention, would you care to revise your statement at all?"

The rain drummed down on the cab roof as the ventriloquist puffed thoughtfully at his cigarette in its long holder.

"Sadie, my dear," he said, "far be it from me to claim that the unkind things you said to me at Leeds a year ago were wholly unwarranted. But, as I pointed out to you on that occasion, I can't *help* it if young Peter hero-worships me. Boys will be boys. No doubt he'll grow out of it. Meantime, in view of the presence of these gentlemen, whom I take to be your solicitors, I'll go so far as to grant—*without prejudice*—that I have a soft spot in my heart for young Peter; that it's not impossible he begged me to take him away with me again; and that, to avoid the chance of a scene with you at Portsmouth Town Station, Sadie, I sent the lad ahead to a station up the line a bit, where he was to go to an address I gave him, at which I'd collect him on my way to where I shall be going in the morning. All that is, on the face of it, feasible enough, as I now concede—*without prejudice*.'

"In the circumstances, then," said Raffles, "shall we see if we're too late to get a train to the intermediate station and repair to the address you mention? The point is, Mr. Renton, the sooner the boy is back in his sister's custody, the sooner we can discuss the terms on which she will be prepared to hand over to you the sum of five hundred pounds.''

"I'm surprised—and, I must admit, more than a little hurt—that Sadie should have brought solicitors into this purely family matter of a boy's divided loyalties," declared the ventriloquist. Throwing open the cab door, he stepped out into the rain. "Sadie," he said to her through the window, "be on this spot at nine-thirty tomorrow morning, and it's possible that you may find Peter awaiting you. I say that entirely *without prejudice*."

He walked off into the dark and rain and wind.

"Sadie," Raffles said, "we'll take you home now. D'you feel inclined to trust Manders and myself further in this matter?"

"I do," she said, "oh, I *do!*"

"That's what I like to hear," said Raffles. "Very well. Now, you're not to worry. Try to get some sleep—and I promise you, here and now, that Peter shall be back in your charge before dawn."

I barely repressed an exclamation of astonishment at Raffles's unequivocal commitment, and my mind was racing with uneasy surmises when, having seen Sadie safely inside The Sail Loft, Raffles had a word with our cabbie.

"Mr. Vosper," Raffles said, "I don't know about you, but my friend and I had a rather scrappy meal tonight, and I notice there's an eating-house still open in Lake Road here. Would you care to join us at supper?"

Nothing loath, Mr. Vosper drove us to the adjacent eating-house and, adjusting a nose bag on his nag, stumped into the premises with us. At this late hour, we were the only customers—so, without bothering to take off our outdoor things, we sat down to three hearty helpings of sizzling sausages with good dollops of mash.

"Mr. Vosper," said Raffles, as we ate, "would you mind if I asked your first name?"

"Sam's me name, sir, and two-two-four-eight's me 'ackney license number, wiv never a black mark on it."

"How many of us can say the same of our respective

escutcheons?'' said Raffles. "Sam, I'm going to speak to you as man to man. I think you hold the Lake Road Shipmates in high regard, so I tell you frankly that one of them's in trouble—Shipmate Sadie. As you may or may not know, the man we had an interview with in your cab tonight is Sadie's uncle. He's a smooth, glib, clever crook, Sam, and he's recruited an apprentice to crime—Sadie's young brother Peter, a ten-year-old boy.''

"That lad's allus bin a 'andful for Sadie, sir, since their Dad died.''

"I don't doubt it, Sam. But now," Raffles said, "the boy's uncle, Harry Renton, alias Crichton Hood, has put young Peter into a situation of extreme danger.''

The blood rushed into my head. I looked at Raffles in astonishment.

"It's obvious, Bunny," he said. "Renton brought to the R.N. Barracks tonight a large 'prop' hamper, no doubt containing his ventriloquial dummies. When he *left* the Barracks, he didn't have that hamper. So he must have asked permission, on the grounds of there being few cabs about at such a late hour, to leave the hamper in the Officers' Quarters at the Barracks, and pick it up in the morning. Right?''

"Probably," I said.

"There's no 'probably' about it," Raffles said, his grey eyes hard. "It's a certainty—because if Renton, hungry to get his hooks on Sadie's five hundred pounds, could have restored young Peter to her right away, he'd have done it like a shot. Instead, he pitched us that thin story about having sent Peter to a station up the line, and an address to wait at. Now, *why*," said Raffles, "that feeble fabrication? For the simple reason, Bunny, that Renton could *not* produce Peter right away— because the boy, Renton's crime apprentice, is inside that 'prop' hamper in the Officers' Quarters in the Barracks, waiting till all's quiet there, so that he can open a window and let Renton in to steal that highly valuable and much-publicised artifact, the *Coolibah* salver.''

Stunned, I laid down my knife and fork.

"I don't doubt that that hamper has straps the boy's been taught to unbuckle from inside, then readjust to make the hamper appear innocent. Having got away in the night," Raffles said, "with the boy and the swag, Renton'll breeze along in the morning to collect his innocent hamper. There'll be nothing whatever to connect him with the theft. The police'll know it was an inside job, and God help the poor stewards they start questioning."

"Gents," Sam Vosper broke in, "we'd best go to the peelers—on the double."

"And have young Peter caught red-handed where he is? If that happens, nothing on earth will keep him out of Borstal Reformatory for the rest of his boyhood. What d'you want to do, Sam—break Sadie's heart?" Raffles leaned forward. "Or would you rather prevent that happening—by giving us a hand to steal the boy out of the Officers' Quarters before he gets nabbed there?"

"Gawd almighty!" Sam muttered. "Who *are* you gents?"

"Friends of Shipmate Sadie," said Raffles. "Who're you, Vosper?"

Sam Vosper's weather-mottled face, framed by his goblin-peaked coalsack, flushed to a deeper shade of puce. His bloodshot blue eyes glanced furtively round the little eating-house. There was only the shirt-sleeved proprietor scouring pans in the steamy window. Most of the gaslights had been turned out.

Sam said hoarsely, looking hard at Raffles, "Wotcher want me to do?"

"Give us the benefit of your local knowledge," Raffles said. "Renton has an advantage, Sam. He's Pompey born, with a Navy background, so he probably knows the best way to set about getting over that high wall round the Navy Barracks without falling foul of the patrolling sentries. But I put it to you, Sam—d'you reckon Mr. Renton knows more about the ins and outs of Pompey than a Pompey cabman?"

"*Not* on yer bleedin' life," Sam said. "Listen, mister. Many's the time I've picked up a young Navy gent, officer cadet, 'oo's out on the town at two in the mornin' when 'e oughter be in Barracks by midnight, so needs advice from a fatherly cabbie, an' puts 'is 'and in 'is pocket to get it, see?"

"You'll be paid, Sam," Raffles said.

"Not a penny," Sam said, offended, "not one bloody stiver! This 'ere's for Shipmate Sadie, so me advice comes gratis—seein' as I knocked 'er down." He pushed away his plate, brushed a sleeve over his walrus moustache. "Ready, gents?" he said.

He drove us to his nearby jobbing stables, where he picked up a coil of rope and also, at Raffles's suggestion, some strong twine. Then the cab jingled us on through narrow, deserted, rainswept streets in a part of Old Portsmouth unfamiliar to me, and pulled up beside what I saw, in the glimmer from the cab's candle lamps, was a high wall, spike-topped. Leaving our evening capes and silk hats in the cab, Raffles and I ducked out. Sam Vosper climbed down from his box.

"This 'ere's where I've 'elped many a young navy gent over the Barracks wall," he whispered. "The luggage-grid on the roof o' me growler'll take yer weight easy. I'll blow out me lamps an' wait for yer, unless a bleedin' sentry noses round 'ere an' nabs me. Up yer go, gents, an' for Gawd's sake look slippy. I got me license to think of."

Looping the coil of rope round his neck, Raffles climbed up, by way of the driving-seat, on to the roof of the cab. I followed.

"It's against our principles, Bunny," Raffles said, "to rob a place where we've enjoyed hospitality, but circumstances alter cases. So here goes!"

Leaping up, he got a grip on the spikes, hauled himself up, got a firm stance, then reached down to give me a hand to join him. The wind tore at us, the rain drenched us, as Raffles belayed the rope to one of the spikes. We slid down the rope into the Barracks yard. In the black, boisterous night, only one light was to be seen, a dim gas-globe burning over the door of a Barracks block.

"Mark that light," Raffles whispered. "It'll give us a bearing, so that we can find the rope again. We shall need it when it comes to getting the boy out."

It took a bit of prowling round before we found the Officers' block. Here, too, a dim light burned over the handsome entrance. We skirted round the side of the block.

"Here's a likely-looking window," Raffles murmured. "Now, then—there are certainly officers asleep upstairs, but there may be a steward or fire picquet on night duty. Keep your eyes peeled while I work on this window."

Peering about me into the darkness, the rain slashing down into the puddles, I wondered anxiously if we were too late—Renton, the boy, and the *Coolibah* salver already gone.

Raffles touched my arm. "I've got the window open. I can hear water trickling in there. It's the downstairs ablutions. It gives me my bearings. Renton's 'prop' hamper'll be in one of those rooms the theatre folk used. If the kid's still there, which pray God he is, I'll have to gag him quick with my handkerchief before he can cry out. It'll give him a scare, but it can't be helped. If he struggles, I'll have to tie his wrists and ankles with twine, so that I can carry him off and pass him out to you. If Renton comes skulking round looking for a window the kid's opened for him, you know what do do. Right! Stand by!"

Silent as a panther, Raffles was gone—in through the window.

All was black. Here at the side of the block, I was sheltered from the wind, but I could hear its surge and bluster. I kept a keen watch about me. Now and then, I thrust my head in through the open window. I could hear nothing inside there except the trickling of water. As I drew back for the third time from that window, and peered tensely about me, I thought I saw a figure, blacker than the darkness to which my eyes had become accustomed. The figure was moving. It was a man. It could only be Renton. He was approaching. My back pressed to the wall, I edged away from the window and from his approach. I froze, my back flat to the wall. He came on, prowling, soundless. He reached what he was looking for—an open window. He did not see me. He stopped. He peered in through the window into the blackness there. I heard his voice, a half-whisper.

"Peter?" he said.

I moved. I seized him by his cape.

"Renton," I said, "you're under arrest!"

His face a pale blur, he went rigid in my grip.

Shatteringly, I heard a snarl at my back: "*Let him go!*"

Releasing Renton, I spun round to ward off any sudden attack.

There was nobody there.

I spun back to face Renton.

He was no longer here.

I heard his footsteps receding at a rapid run.

For a moment, in the rain and darkness, I stood confounded.

Then understanding struck me like a thunderbolt. I had been duped by the ventriloquist. Harry Renton, alias Crichton Hood, had thrown his voice.

Mortification swept hotly over me. My chagrin at allowing myself to be so grossly deceived was well-nigh insupportable. Fortunately, it never had been my intention actually to detain Renton, but only, as Raffles had instructed me, to act like a plainclothes detective and throw such a scare into the fellow that he would wrench himself from my clutch and, believing his boy apprentice caught and himself blown, immediately start emigrating.

So our purpose, as I realised, listening to Renton's fugitive footfalls die away in the dark, had in fact been achieved. As for my self-disgust at my idiotic credulity, I had no time to dwell on it—for a voice from the window whispered, "Bunny? Take him!"

It was Raffles. He passed out the boy, bound and gagged, and I received him, jackknife fashion, over my shoulder. Raffles joined me and, as he closed the window gently and contrived to relatch it from the outside with a little instrument he always carried, he asked me if I had seen anything of Renton. I whispered that I had had a brief encounter, which had eventuated with the hoped-for result.

Raffles took the boy from me, and without difficulty, despite the darkness and the downpour, we found our rope where we had left it. I shinned up the rope. I saw with relief that Sam's cab, candle lamps out, still was waiting. Anchoring myself among the wall-top spikes, I reached down to pull the boy up as Raffles lifted him as high as he could to me. Raffles shinned up, freed and coiled the rope—and, *via* the roof of the cab, we got the boy to the ground without mishap.

"Stone the crows," said Sam Vosper hoarsely, "got the little bleeder, eh? In the cab wiv 'im, for Gawd's sake, an' let's get movin'!"

"Now, then," said Raffles, as the cab jingled us away from the Barracks area and headed into the byways of Old Portsmouth, "let's get the boy untied. Give us a light, Bunny."

I struck a match—and almost dropped it as its flame illumined the interior of the cab and revealed to me a nightmare apparition. Raffles had slipped up. By some incredible mischance, it was not young Peter he had rescued. Propped there, bound and gagged in a corner seat, was a ventriloquist's large dummy, in evening-dress, a red fright wig on its head, its face painted dead white, except for circles round its eyes, and a huge, clownish grin.

Staring, aghast, I let the match burn my fingers. I dropped it.

"It's all right, Bunny," Raffles said, in the darkness. "This isn't the dummy Renton used in his act. This is Peter. For safety's sake, and as a disguise, Renton had him dressed up like the dummies in his 'prop' hamper. Come on, give us some light!"

Striking another match, I watched Raffles relieve the boy of his gag. His eyes, brown like Sadie's, blinked, dazzled by the light.

"Am I pinched?" he said. "Is Uncle Harry pinched?"

"Never mind your Uncle Harry," said Raffles, taking out his penknife to cut the twine of the boy's bonds. "You won't be seeing him again. He's emigrating. And you can thank your sister Sadie, my lad, that this gentleman and I aren't policemen. If it weren't for Sadie, d'you know where you'd be this minute?"

"In quod," said the boy sullenly.

"I want none of your thieves' argot," snapped Raffles. "And don't loll in your seat. Sit up straight when your elders speak to you. And let's have that hideous fright wig off!"

Raffles snatched off the boy's wig. The match went out. I struck another. The boy was fair-haired, like Sadie, but he was still, with his painted face, a highly unnatural sight. Raffles was holding his handkerchief out of the cab window. Sitting up very straight now, the boy was staring at Raffles fixedly.

"Now, then," said Raffles, handing the boy the rain-drenched handkerchief, "wipe that greasepaint off your face, or you'll frighten your sister out of her wits." His tone changed. He laughed. "Damn it, he nearly frightened us out of ours, didn't he, Bunny?"

"Absolutely, Raffles," I said.

The match went out. I struck another. Wiping the paint from his face, Peter was beginning to look less like something grotesque out of Bedlam and more like a human boy. In fact, he had something of Sadie's clean-cut look.

"You know, Peter," said Raffles, his tone now tolerant, "you're a bit of a chump. Here's you, come of a fine naval family—yet you're mucking about with crime. What a mug! You're getting into a dead end, Peter. But for luck, you'd be under arrest this minute—finished, done for! Whereas you *could* have had a fine career, like your father's—in the Royal Navy. Ever thought about that?"

"Sadie says I've got to stay at school till I'm fourteen," Peter said gloomily. "I'm not old enough for the Navy."

"You speak in ignorance," said Raffles. "D'you know your trouble, Peter? You don't know the right people. Now, suppose—for example—that Mr. Manders and I could pull a string for you. Eh? Suppose we could get you mustered into the crew of a ship run by a man we know? It's a ship called the *Ursula*—a training ship for boys. They have to do *some* book-work, of course, but mostly they learn seamanship—the sextant, the compass, splicing, boat-work. So when they're old enough to go into the Navy proper, they've got a head start on ordinary recruits, and are well on their way to a career like that of Lieutenant-Commander Hubble of H.M.A.S. *Coolibah*, scourge of the Yangtse River pirates. What d'you think, Bunny—is there a reasonable chance we could get Peter accepted by the *Ursula*?"

"A very reasonable chance," I concurred, "—if Peter's interested."

"*Are* you interested, Peter?" Raffles asked.

The boy nodded. His eyes were beginning to shine.

"All right," Raffles said. "Mr. Manders and I'll pop in and talk it over with you and Sadie in the morning. And here we are," he added, as the cab jingled to a standstill outside the closed door of The Sail Loft premises in rainswept, deserted Lake Road. "Out you get, Peter. *No*! Wait a moment. Listen!"

Sadie must have been sitting up, all alone, waiting for news of us—for, through the sound of the rain on the galvanized iron roof of the small building, I could faintly hear her singing to herself, to keep up her courage:

> Bobbie Shafto's gone to sea
> Silver buckles on his knee,
> He'll come home and marry me,
> Pretty Bobbie Shafto—

As the song died away, Raffles said to the boy, "All right, out you get now. We'll see you in the morning. Good night, Peter."

The boy looked back in through the cab window.

"Good night—*sir*," he said, and he ran across the puddled sidewalk and banged on the door of The Sail Loft.

Raffles called to our cabbie, "Canoe Club annexe, Sam," and as the cab rumbled on again in the rain, asked me if we had any matches left.

"Just one," I said.

"Then let's have a cigarette," said Raffles. "Now, tell me—what exactly happened at your encounter with the Great Crichton Hood?"

I told him—with some return of my chagrin as I confessed how the ventriloquist had duped me.

To my astonishment, a mocking laugh sounded from a roof corner of the dark cab—and as I cast a startled glance upward, a strange voice intoned from there above me, "Too bad, Manders! Too bad!"

My momentary stupefaction was succeeded, in a flash, by enlightenment.

"Good God, Raffles," I exclaimed, "I never knew *you* could—"

"It takes pracise, Bunny, I've thought it worthwhile to acquire a trifling amateur skill at ventriloquism, but I don't make a parade of it. I keep it up my sleeve, because it's a skill that might come in handy for *us* some day,'' said Raffles, ''—in a pinch.''

8

THE ORDEAL OF DINAH RAFFLES

The formal opening of the Oceanographic Museum built to house the trophies collected by the Prince of Monaco, famous yachtsman and marine biologist, was a unique social occasion.

Among the beautifully dressed ladies and grey-toppered gentlemen who had the honour of paying their respects to the genial Prince and his gracious Princess, and of inspecting the exhibits, were A. J. Raffles, his young sister Dinah, and myself, Bunny Manders.

With us, as we sauntered under the outrigger canoes, harpoons, strangely shaped nets and monstrous fishes suspended from the lofty ceiling of the museum, was a fellow member of a respected London club to which Raffles belonged.

It was thanks to Raffles's fellow clubman, an influential Riviera resident, that we were present at this notable event, and he identified for us now some of the celebrities in the fashionable throng.

"There, for instance," he said, "is Mr. Joseph Pulitzer, the great American newspaper magnate. And there's Sir Hiram Maxim, inventor of the automatic gun. The dapper gentleman he's talking to is the celebrated Italian physicist, Signor Guglielmo Marconi. All three of them own splendid yachts and are frequent visitors to Monaco."

"No novelist, Dinah," said Raffles, "knows more about the cosmopolitan society of the Riviera coast, or writes with greater authority about its mysteries, intrigues, and hidden passions than our good friend here."

"Oh, I know," said Dinah. "Your books are my favourites," she told the novelist, "because you always set your plots in such beautiful, worldly places."

Our companion smiled at her. Urbane and experienced, he

was well known as an epicure of life's graces, and Dinah, with her fair hair and grey eyes, her lacy dress, becoming little hat, and the pretty parasol and small gold mesh purse she carried, was a creditable young sister for Raffles to have.

"I'm sure your brother takes too good care of you, Dinah," said the novelist, "for *you* ever to figure in the kind of plot I conjure from the air of this delectable Principality. But if you'll excuse me, I must have a word with Sir Hiram Maxim. He's made, in an interview, some interesting remarks on the mathematics of roulette, and there's a point I'd like to take up with him. I'll be on the look out for you at the Casino this evening."

As the novelist left us, Raffles drew the attention of Dinah and myself to the glass-topped specimen case beside which we were standing. In the case was a bed of sand on which curious shells were displayed, together with lumps of amber, branches of coral, starfish, and numerous oysters on the half-shell.

"You see, Dinah?" Raffles said. "Each of these oysters reveals a different stage in the process by which an intrusive grain of sand is gradually transformed into a worthwhile end result."

"What a lovely end result!" Dinah exclaimed. "A beautiful big pearl! D'you think it's a real one?"

"That's a good question," said Raffles.

Immaculate, his keen face tanned, he was subjecting the exhibit to a more searching scrutiny when we were approached by a footman wearing the princely Grimaldi livery.

"Oh, look!" said Dinah, as we accepted glasses of champagne from the footman's proffered tray. "There's a notice over a doorway there that says, 'To the Turtles.' Shall we go and see if they're live ones?"

"Why not?" said Raffles.

Taking our champagne with us, we passed through a low doorway, went down some narow steps cut in rock, and found ourselves in a cavern partly natural and partly hewn.

From dungeon-like, glassless window apertures that faced seaward, sunlight shone in warmly on to a pool, saucer-shaped, in the rock floor of the cavern. Large turtles with scaly heads were swimming around in the pool, some of them scrabbling

with their flippers in vain attempts to climb its shallowly sloping rim.

The splashings of the turtles were drowned by an intermittent surging sound which filled the cavern with hollow echoes.
The surging came from a round hole in a corner of the cavern
floor. A waist-high rail surrounded the hole and when we went
and looked down into it, it was like looking down a well with sea
and sunshine at the bottom of it.

"A natural rock-shaft," said Raffles, "—a sea blowhole."

As he spoke, the sea, impelled by some ground-swell,
quenched the sunshine deep down there, and came seething up,
jade-green and marbled with foam, then sank down to admit
sunshine again into a sea-filled cavern below.

"I'd hate to fall down there," said Dinah.

"Your arrival among the mermaids, mademoiselle," said
a voice from behind us, "would make the Sirens jealous."

We turned. A man was standing there. In tailcoat and grey
topper, a glass of champagne in one hand, the other behind his
back, he was strikingly handsome, in his early thirties—and he
was, quite obviously, drunk.

Swaying slightly on his feet, he totally ignored Raffles and
me.

"Have you not yet missed, mademoiselle," he said, his
dark eyes, heavy-lidded, appraising Dinah, "something you
put down on a specimen case upstairs, the better to accept a
glass of champagne?"

He took his hand from behind his back.

"Oh!" Dinah exclaimed. "My purse! Thank you very
much."

She would have taken the purse, but he did not let go of it.

"Captain Boris Enani," he said, "—at your service."

He still was holding the purse. And Dinah, too, was holding it—and she looked a little startled as Captain Enani, faintly
smiling at her, sipped his champagne, clearly with no intention
of releasing the purse until he got a response to his introduction
of himself.

But, in Raffles's eyes, his young sister Dinah was taboo to
men who approached her when they were drunk—particularly
to men who looked at her as sensuously as this Captain Boris

Enani was looking at her.

"Thank you," Raffles said coldly. "*I* will take the purse for mademoiselle."

He took it, firmly, from both of them. He then handed the purse to Dinah, cupped a hand under her elbow and, turning his back and hers on Captain Enani, moved away with her towards the steps up from the cavern.

"So?" said Enani, thus deprived of introductions. He gulped the rest of his champagne. "*So!*" he said, with an ugly look at me—and he hurled his glass into the turtles' pool.

Ignoring this ill-mannered tantrum, I followed Raffles and Dinah to the steps, where a man who was standing a little way up them moved aside courteously to let us pass on up and re-enter the museum.

Finding that the Prince and Princess had now gone and that the guests also were leaving, we went on out into the blaze of sunshine, where Dinah opened her pretty parasol.

On tall flagstaffs, pink-striped white banners bearing the golden Grimaldi blazon shimmered in the heat-currents, and open carriages drawn by glossy horses were jingling away with the notabilities of Riviera society.

We ourselves had not far to go, for Raffles had wangled, from a rich acquaintance, a fellow member of the M.C.C., the loan of a house, with its resident domestic staff, called the Villa Sappho.

It was one of a number of delightful abodes dotted about, amid date-palms and massed blossoms, on the slope that dropped away steeply before us to the blue water of La Condamine harbour, where many fine yachts lay spotlessly white at their moorings. On its eminence on the far side of the harbour stood the elaborate white Casino.

With Dinah between Raffles and myself, we sauntered down the path towards the Villa Sappho.

"What a strange man," said Dinah, "that Captain Enani!"

Raffles said nothing.

"Didn't *you* think so, Bunny?" Dinah asked me.

"Excessively odd, Dinah," I concurred.

"Dear Bunny, what an agreeable person you are!" said Dinah—and she linked her arm with mine.

But Raffles said nothing.

That evening, as we dined, just the three of us, at a candlelit table on the terrace of the Villa Sappho, I sensed a certain reserve between Raffles and Dinah. This made me slightly uneasy, for really they knew little about each other.

They had grown up separately, due to their parents' early demise, and had quite lost touch with each other—until Dinah suddenly had taken it into her head to leave the shelter of her guardian's roof and join her brother in London.

"What a problem, Bunny!" Raffles had said to me, at the time. "I shall have to do something for her, of course. I'm her only relative. But, good God, I'm a dangerous brother for her to have! I may find Scotland Yard on my track any day. I'm currently England's cricket captain, and if I'm exposed as a criminal, there'll be a howling scandal. It could affect Dinah's chances in life. The best thing I can do for her is take her abroad and amass a dowry for her, so that I can get her safely married into some European family of social and financial consequence—while the going's still good!"

Accordingly, he had borrowed the Villa Sappho—where, as we sat now at dinner, we were waited on by the discreet, white-jacketed houseman, Latouche. He, his wife Cléopatre, who cooked very creditably, and their daughter Fanchon, the skittish parlourmaid, constituted the resident domestic staff of the villa.

Because of the slight strain I sensed in the atmosphere between Raffles and Dinah, I was rather relieved when, Latouche having brought us our coffee and liqueurs and gone back in through the French windows, Dinah announced her intention of not coming with us to the Casino but of having an early night instead.

"Sleep well, my dear Dinah," said Raffles.

It was a warm night, the sky sparkling with stars, as he and I walked together, in evening-dress but hatless, past the harbour where the yacht lights twinkled, towards the brilliantly illuminated Casino.

Abruptly, Raffles broke the silence between us.

"The question is, Bunny," he said, "did Dinah leave her

purse on that specimen case by mere oversight? Or had she noticed that fellow Enani making eyes at her? Was she intrigued by him? Did she leave her purse behind deliberately—to give him an excuse to make her acquaintance?''

"By Jove, Raffles," I said, startled, "that hadn't occurred to me!"

"For the simple reason," Raffles said, "that you know no more about the character of my sister Dinah than I do."

I knew this much—that I was in love with her. But I dared not let Raffles suspect it. If one day he should stand in the dock at the Old Bailey, it was odds on that I should be standing there beside him. So I was far from being the ideal suitor he was seeking for Dinah, and I had to watch my step.

I pointed out to him now that, if he knew little about his own sister, she was not better informed about him.

"In fact, Raffles," I said, "I think she's been wondering about all the nice clothes and things you've bought her. Anyway, she asked me something the other day that I don't think she quite likes to ask you personally."

"What did she ask you, Bunny?"

"She asked me where your money comes from!"

"Did she, by God! What did you tell her?"

"Oh, I fobbed her off, Raffles. I explained to her that it was difficult for a girl to understand a gentleman's financial arrangements—especially if he happens to be England's cricket captain, with its various ramifications—and I advised her not to bother her head about such tedious matters."

"What did she say?"

"She said she wouldn't."

"Well done, Bunny. That must have been an awkward moment for you. You handled it with tact and discretion."

"I had to think pretty quickly," I admitted, pleased by his approbation.

"Girls are flighty creatures." Raffles said. "They often have a weakness for dubious characters. If Dinah feels some sort of attraction to this Captain Boris Enani, I want to find out if he's the obvious cad he struck me as being this morning—and if anybody can give us chapter and verse on Riviera people, it's my novelist fellow clubman, who said he'd be at the Casino this evening."

But the first person we saw when we entered the spacious foyer, all glittering chandeliers, red plush banquettes and gilt-rich walls, was not Raffles's fellow clubman. It was Captain Boris Enani.

"Over there, at the *vestiaire* counter," Raffles murmured to me. "If he sees us, pay no attention to him."

Out of the corner of my eye, as we collected our *cartes d'entrée* from the three starch-shirted functionaries at the high desk, I saw Enani on the far side of the foyer. His back was to us. In evening-dress, hatless, his hair ash-blond, he was collecting a white silk scarf from the *vestiaire*.

People were going to and fro, passing in and out.

Enani turned, looping his scarf carelessly about his neck. He was swaying slightly on his feet, but he saw us. I felt him staring after us as, paying him no attention, we crossed to the arch of the atrium, where a man stood aside courteously to let us pass through to the roulette tables.

Pausing to offer me a Sullivan from his cigarette-case, Raffles glanced back across the foyer.

"Enani's left, Bunny," Raffles murmured.

"He's drunk again," I said.

"Yes, very," Raffles said thoughtfully. He was frowning. "Keep an eye open for our novelist friend."

Throngs four-deep surrounded the roulette tables. Jewels glittered on powdered bosoms, stiff shirt-fronts gleamed. Through the restrained hum of voices sounded the ritual chanting of the croupiers as their ebony rakes slid towers of gold louis and stacks of bank-notes hither and yon across the green baize of the tables, invigilated over by the *chefs-de-partie* on their slightly elevated rostrums at each table. Here and there, against the panelled walls, lurked watchful men in evening-dress, trying not to look like detectives.

"Our novelist friend's stamping-ground," Raffles murmured to me, "—the most discreetly policed Casino in the world."

We wandered from table to table, trying a stake here and there, but it was not our night for auriferous lightning to strike, and I was glad when Raffles's fellow clubman joined us.

We had a drink with him in a small bar off the foyer, and Raffles asked him if he knew anything about a Captain Boris Enani. The novelist nodded.

"I've been watching the baccarat in the *salles privées*," he said, "—the shrine of the Golden Goat. Enani was in there just now, playing against the Greek Syndicate's bank. He left, about an hour ago, with a pocketful of their money."

"Did he now," Raffles said softly. "Tell me, Oppie, is it true that the Casino has a big winner followed to make sure he reaches safely wherever he's going?"

"Yes, that's true of a big winner, Raffles. But Enani's win was only about three thousand pounds, in its franc equivalent—a nice enough packet of bank-notes, but not big enough to warrant the Casino's shadowing service." The novelist, immaculate, his dark hair sleek, kindled a cigar, his light, shrewd eyes, under strongly marked brows, studying Raffles. "What's your interest in Boris Enani?"

"His interest," Raffles said, "in my young sister Dinah. And hers—possibly—in him."

"Ah! Then your question has merit, Raffles. Women are Enani's—avocation. Women, wine, and cards. He's believed to be the by-blow of a Balkan king, and to receive a handsome allowance so long as he stays out of his own country and involves himself in no political plots against his royal sire."

"A character for one of your books, in fact," Raffles said.

"Typical," said the novelist. "I must hatch a plot I can use Enani in, one of these days. 'Lucky at cards,' they say, 'unlucky at love.' Enani seems to be the exception that proves the rule. He wins both ways. Several Riviera ladies of previously unblemished repute are rumoured to have succumbed to Boris Enani's romantic background and slumbrous charm. One wonders if the lucky Lothario has some secret card up his sleeve when he matches wits with the fair sex."

"Oppie," Raffles said, "many thanks for this information."

"As one clubman to another, you're welcome." The novelist finished his drink. "I must get back to the *salles privées*. I have W. J. Locke and his good lady with me. Won't you and Manders come and meet them? W.J.'s a charming chap. He wrote *The Morals of Marcus Ordeyne*."

But Raffles excused us—and, as the novelist left us, gave me a hard look.

"An extra card, Bunny?" Raffles said. "I wonder. If Enani wasn't too drunk to take a quick look into Dinah's purse this morning, he'd have found cards in it—visiting-cards that I had printed for her, with the address of the Villa Sappho. When he saw us here at the Casino—*without* Dinah—can he have thought it, drunk as he was, a good opportunity to pay a private call on her?" Raffles stood up abruptly. "Let's get back to the villa."

As we walked briskly down the sloping road from the Casino, with the lights of the yachts casting reflections in tremulous ribbons across the harbour water on our left, a *fiacre* was coming up the slope towards us. I heard the passenger call to the cabbie to stop. The horse clip-clopped to a standstill level with us—and Dinah, in an evening cloak, the hood thrown back, her hair fair in the light from the white globe of a street lamp, looked at us.

"Oh, thank heavens!" she said. "I was just coming to find you!"

Raffles told the cabbie to take us to the Villa Sappho. We joined Dinah in the *fiacre*, and Raffles asked her if Enani had come to the villa, and she said that he had—about half-an-hour or so after we had left.

"So he lost no time, Bunny, after he saw us in the Casino," Raffles said grimly. "Dinah, did you let Latouche admit him?"

"The Latouches weren't there," Dinah said. "Their other daughter, Fanchon's married sister Simone, is having a birthday party, so I told them they could go to it."

Over the horse's hoofbeats and harness jingle, the cabbie, on his box with his back to us, could not possibly hear Dinah's voice as she told us that, when the Latouches had left for their party, she had gone up to her bedroom, where she had opened the curtains and stepped out on to the balcony.

"It was all so pretty," she said, "—the stars, and the lights in the harbour and over in the Casino. I could hear the crickets in our garden and music in the distance."

After musing upon the scene for a while, she had gone back

into her bedroom, leaving the French windows ajar, but closing the curtains. As she started to get ready for bed, she had heard a sound on the balcony. The curtains had suddenly parted. Captain Enani had stepped in.

"I told him to leave at once," Dinah said, "or my brother would kill him."

I knew that was true, for I knew A. J. Raffles—and though he said not a word, the hair stirred on my scalp.

"But you can't kill him now," Dinah said, and she drew in her breath, deeply, with a tremor in it. "He's dead."

Hoofs clopped and harness jingled as Dinah told us that Enani had seized her hands, covered them with kisses. She had told him that he was mad or drunk or both, and had wrenched her hands free.

"And then?" Raffles said, very softly.

My heart thumped. How could Dinah have killed the man? With what weapon? Pistol? Scissors? Hatpin? But no, she told us that Enani had taken from the pocket of his white waistcoat a small phial of pills. Poison, he had said. One kiss from her lips, he had said—or he would kill himself in her bedroom and the scandal would ruin her.

"And then?" said Raffles.

"I told him he was mad and a coward," Dinah said, "and would never do it. But—he did! He swallowed one of the pills. He had—a sort of seizure. He contorted. He fell back across my bed. I couldn't believe it. I ran out of the room and out of the house—and came to find you."

"I see," Raffles said. "Dinah, my dear, those pills, of course, were about as lethal as sugar candy. If, from fear of scandal, you'd paid that fellow his ransom of a kiss, his embraces wouldn't have stopped at that. You called his bluff. So he went through with his ugly charade, hoping you'd approach him as he lay on your bed, so that he could pull you down with him—and we know what he would have attempted. Thank God, you ran out! Dinah, don't worry. When we get to the villa, we'll find that sensual swine gone—but he'll have to go a long, long way before I fail to settle this reckoning with him."

Raffles laughed, without mirth.

"You see, Bunny?" he said to me. "We're in a Principality where scandal is inadmissible. It means, for those involved, whether innocent or guilty, polite expulsion. If it becomes rumoured that one is *persona non grata* in the Principality of Monaco and Monte Carlo, one is no longer received anywhere in good society. So we now know the extra card up Boris Enani's sleeve in his games with women—the ugly card of scandal. For fear of it, women yield to him—and afterwards, from the same fear, keep silent."

The *fiacre* pulled up at the gate of the Villa Sappho. Raffles paid off the cabbie. In the house, the lights were on. The Latouches were not yet back from their party. All was still.

"To put your mind at rest, Dinah," Raffles said, "I'll just take a look into your bedroom. Wait here in the salon."

He went upstairs to Dinah's room. Instinctively, I followed him. Dinah's bedroom door stood wide open. The lights were on. Raffles stopped dead on the threshold.

Over his shoulder, I saw Enani. He lay sprawled on his back across Dinah's bed.

Raffles moved forward into the room. I followed, staring, unbelieving.

Enani's hands were clamped on the bed coverlet, his face was congested and mottled, his jaw fallen; his bulging eyes gleamed blindly in the light.

Raffles stooped over the bed, slid a hand under the breast of Enani's dinner-coat, sniffed the man's mouth.

"Bunny," said Raffles, "Close those curtains."

The window curtains were slightly parted. I closed the gap, turned. Raffles was picking up from the carpet a small phial of pills, and its cork. He corked the phial, pocketed it.

He went back downstairs. I followed.

Dinah was standing in the salon, an intent question in her eyes.

"Dinah," Raffles said, "Bunny and I have a little job to do before the Latouches get back. We won't be long. Sit down. Don't worry. Bunny, give her a brandy."

While I poured Dinah the drink, Raffles crossed to the *escritoire,* let down the flap. He wrapped his handkerchief round his hand, took from the pigeonholes some sheets of plain notepaper, held them up to the light, then folded and pocketed them.

He took from a pigeonhole a small pot of gum with the brush handle protruding through the cork. He pocketed the pot of gum, tucked his handkerchief back into the breast-pocket of his dinner coat.

"Come on, Bunny."

He strode back upstairs. I followed. He went into his own bedroom, returned in a moment, pocketing a pair of black kid gloves. He handed me a pair, told me to put them in my pocket. He went into Dinah's room. I followed.

"What do you intend?" I said. I could hardly breathe.

"I intend the only thing that can prevent a scandal that would ruin my plans for Dinah's future," Raffles said. "I intend an act of oblivion. Come on, *up* with this carcase!"

We lugged Enani up off the bed and, each taking one of his arms around our shoulders, carried him, facing forward between us, his chin lolling on his shirt front, the ends of his white silk scarf dangling, his feet dragging like a comatose inebriate's, down the stairs and out to the garden gate.

"A warm night, a starry night," Raffles said, "and not much past eleven o'clock. There'll be people strolling by the sea or sitting at the sidewalk tables of the harbour-front *cafés*. So every access to the briny is useless to us, Bunny—except, let's hope, just one."

I knew now where we were going.

Up the sloping path, which we had followed both up and down that very morning, we now bore Captain Boris Enani.

Here and there among the date-palms to either side of the path, shone the white globes of lamp-standards. Crickets chirred tranquilly amid the blossoms. We saw nobody.

We had not far to go before the Oceanographic Museum loomed up before us, its lofty windows unlit, reflecting starshine. The building stood on a slope, so the rear windows were likely to be more accessible than those in the façade, which was raised on piles; and at the rear of the building, we laid Enani down.

"There may or may not be a watchman in the building," Raffles murmured, as we put on our gloves. "We've got to risk it."

He held a sheet of notepaper to the glass of the window before which we stood. He brushed gum over the paper, reversed it, pressed it to the glass. This was by no means the first time I had seen him use the little implement he carried, which had a diamond cutting-edge. It squeaked slightly as he etched it around the paper. He gave a corner of the paper a sharp tap with the implement. A fragment of glass fell inward, scarcely audible. He inserted the implement into the hole and levered the cut square of glass gently outward. It came, adhering to the paper, with a slight cracking sound. He laid the glass on the ground, reached in to the window-latch. The window opened inward—and Raffles went in, soundless, over the sill.

I heaved Enani up and between us we lifted him inside. I followed.

"Hold him," Raffles whispered—and was gone, a shadow in the star glimmer from the skylights of the lofty ceiling whence hung the canoes, nets, harpoons, and great fishes.

Here and there, in the glass-topped specimen cases, gleamed points of phosphorescence, as of glow-worms and crawling things of the seabed. From a dark doorway to my right, as I stood holding Enani's sagging weight, sounded faint splashes and a surging sound, intermittent and cold.

A shadow approached between the specimen cases. Raffles was back.

"When the busted window's found, Bunny," he whispered, "the police'll wonder what the intruder was after. It's advisable to give them a reason, so I've picked the lock of the case with the oysters in it and taken the false pearl. The police'll think, let's hope, that the intruder was gullible enough to think it an exceptionally fine *real* pearl. It should appeal to their Monagésque sense of humour. Now, come on—let's do what we're *really* here for."

Between us, we carried Enani through the dark doorway, down the narrow rock steps, into the cavern of the Grimaldi turtles. In the faint starlight from the iron-barred window apertures facing seaward, the turtles splashed restlessly in their pool. The intermittent surge of the sea in the shaft of the blow hole filled the cavern with hollow echoes.

"Prospero's cell," Raffles said. "Lay our Caliban down

for a minute. There's something I want from him.''

''Of course!'' The realisation flashed upon me belatedly as we laid Enani down on the rock floor and Raffles dropped on one knee beside him. ''His baccarat winnings!'' I said.

''Bunny,'' said Raffles, his hands busy at Enani's collar, ''when I felt for his heartbeat, back there in Dinah's room, I felt also for his bank-notes. He had neither the one nor the other.''

He stood up. I glimpsed in his hand Enani's white silk scarf.

''Right,'' Raffles said. ''Up with his carcase!''

He pocketed the scarf. Together, we lifted Enani over the waist-high rail surrounding the blow hole. For a moment we held him, by his ankles, suspended over eternity. Then we let him take his last dive, head first, and I heard the sea come surging up the dark shaft to receive him—jetsam for the world-wandering currents.

''And this false pearl can follow him,'' Raffles said, ''—full fathom five.''

He tossed the exhibit down the shaft, and we stole back up the rock steps and left the cavern to the restless Grimaldi turtles and the hollow echoes of the resounding sea.

But what had happened to Boris Enani's baccarat winnings? And why had Raffles taken Enani's white silk scarf?.

There were questions in my head, and forebodings, when I went down in the morning to breakfast on the terrace of the Villa Sappho.

Sleek in his white jacket, Latouche was in the act of setting down on the table a tray bearing crisp *croissants* and *brioches* and fragrant coffee.

''Mademoiselle and messieurs are served,'' he said—and, with his discreet smile and a slight bow, went back in through the French windows.

The sky was blue. Monaco, with its opulent building, its harbour clustered with the yachts of the worldly, lay spread before us—a haven of leisure and luxury in the opaline glory of the Mediterranean morning.

I noticed faint shadows under Dinah's grey eyes as she poured the coffee, but Raffles, in a light suit, a pearl in his cravat, seemed his usual easygoing self.

He suggested that we lunch at the Café de Paris, opposite the Casino.

"One sees such interesting people going to and fro past that corner," he said. "It is to Monaco as the corner of the Rue de la Paix is to Paris—everyone passes it sooner or later."

At a tablet under a sun-umbrella on the *café* terrace, thronged with the usual gay, fashionable crowd, we lingered long over lunch, watching the comings and goings of the Principality's citizens and visitors, while two white-uniformed gendarmes sauntered to and fro on the Casino steps, and carriages with tasselled canopies jingled past.

Dinah grew restless.

"Why don't we go somewhere else?" she asked.

"Personally," said Raffles, lighting a cigarette, "I enjoy this corner. It's so rich in human nature. But, Bunny, why don't you take Dinah to see the Jardin Exotique? It's said to display a unique variety of cacti."

To my surprise, Dinah fell in with this suggestion—and I understood why a little later. For as we strolled together, Dinah with her pretty parasol raised, along a path through that high-up prickly garden brilliant with rust-red and yellow blossoms swimming in the heat-currents, she asked me a question.

"Bunny," she said, "what became—last night—of Captain Enani?"

"Dinah," I said, "your brother would like you to put Captain Enani completely out of your mind. He won't be bothering you again."

She was silent for a while as we wandered on, then she said, "I believe my brother thinks I left my purse on that specimen case in the museum *deliberately*. But, Bunny—I didn't."

"I'm glad, Dinah," I said. "Thank you for telling me that."

"It's strange," she said. "Sometimes I think I love my brother. But sometimes—I'm not sure."

"That, Dinah," I explained, "is because you don't yet know him as well as I do."

"Oh, Bunny, what a loyal person you are!" she said, with a

smile—and impulsively she linked her arm with mine.

It was a way she had, but I wished she would not do it to me, for her touch set up a cardiac turbulence in me—and in Raffles's eyes she was no less taboo to me than she had been to the late Boris Enani. In the circumstances, as I did not trust my own carnal nature overmuch when alone with Dinah, I thought it prudent to suggest that it was time we rejoined her brother.

But Raffles was gone from the *café* opposite the Casino. Nor did we find him at the Villa Sappho when we returned there. So I was alone with Dinah all through dinner, which we had at the candlelit table on the villa terrace, waited on by the enigmatic Latouche.

I found it so hard to keep my eyes off Dinah that, as the hour grew late, I was relieved when she decided to retire. I saw her light come on in a window upstairs. She was not now using the bedroom in which Boris Enani had played out his fatal farce.

I watched her window. Once or twice, across the curtains, I saw her shadow pass. *Taboo!*

Her light went out. I was alone with the stars, the motionless candle flames, and the brandy decanter. I reached for the decanter.

Crickets chirred monotonously in the garden. The lights of Monaco twinkled. I must have drowsed. Suddenly a hand fell on my shoulder. I sprang to my feet.

"Easy, Bunny," Raffles said. "It's all right. Come inside. Bring the brandy."

I followed him into the salon. He closed the French windows, drew the curtains together, crossed to the door, opened it, listened for a moment, then shut the door. He poured himself a brandy.

"Bunny," he said, "d'you remember the courteous gentleman who stood aside for us to pass through the arch to the roulette tables in the Casino?"

"Vaguely," I said. "I hardly noticed him."

Raffles dropped into an armchair, lighted a cigarette.

"D'you remember," he said, "that when Oppie told us that Enani had about three thousand pounds of baccarat winnings on him, I asked if the Casino had a big winner followed—

for his own safety?''

"Yes. But Oppie said Enani wasn't a big enough winner for that."

"So," said Raffles, "the courteous gentleman, who gave me a distinct impression that he was following Enani when Enani left the Casino, wasn't a Casino agent. But I had a feeling I'd seen that courteous gentleman before. And I remembered where. He was the same man who stood politely aside for us on the steps up from the turtles' cavern after that little scene in the morning, when Enani returned Dinah's gold-mesh purse."

Raffles drank his brandy.

"You see the point, Bunny?" he said. "If the courteous gentleman was keeping an eye on Enani in the morning, when he had no baccarat winnings on him, then it wasn't for the money that Enani was followed out of the Casino in the evening. So what was the courteous gentleman following Enani around for?"

"I can't imagine!"

"Neither could I, Bunny. But I was certain that the courteous gentleman *did* follow Enani from the Casino. And Enani came straight here to the Villa Sappho. He saw Dinah on her balcony—like Juliet. And the courteous gentleman saw Enani, that rapist Romeo, watching Dinah from the garden. And saw him pull himself up on to the balcony and enter her room. And the courteous gentleman himself climbed to the balcony. Through the slight gap Enani had left in the curtains, the courteous gentleman watched the scene between Enani and Dinah. He saw Enani 'collapse' on the bed—and Dinah run out of the room."

Raffles took a small phial of pills from his pocket.

"Am I giving you a headache, Bunny? Try one of Enani's pills. I've tried one myself. They're aspirin."

"But Enani was *dead* on Dinah's bed!"

"Very dead," Raffles agreed. "But it was pretty evident, from his face, that he hadn't died of poison. Good God, Bunny, there was never the remotest chance that Enani would have swallowed one of those pills if they'd been poison. No, Bunny, when Enani played out his ugly charade and 'collapsed,' and Dinah ran out, Enani started drunkenly to get up off the bed—

but the courteous gentleman came at him from between the curtains. Bunny, Enani died of strangulation.''

Raffles crushed out his cigarette in an ashtray.

''I'm much obliged to the courteous gentleman,'' he said. ''But he left us to clear up after him—and I wanted to see him again. So I watched for him from the terrace of the Café de Paris on that corner everyone in Monaco must pass sooner or later. And he passed by, on foot, just about an hour after you took Dinah to the Jardin Exotique.''

I swallowed with a parched throat. ''You followed him?''

''Yes, to a street near the P.L.M. railway station—a narrow old street called the Rue des Oliviers. The courteous gentleman has a small office there. He stayed in it rather a long time. When he left, no doubt to go to dinner, I went in—with the aid of my little picklock. In the office was a metal filing-cabinet—locked. I got it open. I found a thick portfolio in it—a portfolio containing carbon copies of reports, in French, on Boris Enani, over the past eighteen months.''

''Reports?''

''Reports addressed,'' Raffles said, ''to a postbox number in a Balkan capital. The reports told the story, Bunny. Enani *is*, as our friend Oppie suggested, the by-blow of a royal person—who's had him watched, got good and tired of his doings, the expense of his fat allowance and his constant demands for more, and finally ordered the royal agent, that courteous gentleman, to liquidate the liability. And the courteous gentleman saw his opportunity when he witnessed the scene in Dinah's room.''

Raffles looked at me with a dancing vivacity in his eyes.

''Incidentally, Bunny,'' he said, ''the courteous gentleman awarded himself a bonus for his exertions. It was locked in his metal filing-cabinet. *Catch!*''

He tossed to me a thick sheaf of Banque de France notes held together by a paper band.

''Enani's baccarat winnings,'' he said, ''—a good start, Bunny, toward amassing a worthy dowry for Dinah, after you've taken your half.''

''No,'' I said, twisting the arrow that impaled my own unworthy heart. ''No! All of it—for Dinah's dowry.''

I handed him back the bank-notes.

"All right, Bunny," Raffles said, giving me a strange look. "All right, old boy—I shall remember." His tone changed. "Anyway, I left a receipt in the courteous gentleman's filing-cabinet. It seemed only right that he should have a receipt for this three thousand pounds. So I left him the thing he strangled Enani with. I left him," said Raffles, with a wicked smile, "Enani's white silk scarf."

The door-handle turned. My heart stopped. The bank-notes vanished like magic into Raffles's pocket as the door opened.

Dinah was standing there.

She came in. She was in *negligée*, her fair hair in two braids, her grey eyes, so like his own, on Raffles.

"Enter Lady Macbeth," said Raffles lightly.

"I couldn't sleep properly till I knew you were back," Dinah said to him. "Then I heard you talking in here."

"Did you now," said Raffles suavely. He took a Sullivan from his cigarette-case. "And did you," he asked, "hear what we were talking about?"

"Why, no," said Dinah. "What was it?"

"We were talking," Raffles said, "about the kind of plot of mystery, intrigue, and passion that your favourite novelist conjures from the air of this delectable Principality. I ran into him an hour ago. He was coming out of the Casino, so we had a nightcap together. He's invited you and Bunny and me to a tea-party his wife's giving on their yacht tomorrow—or, rather, today."

"On their yacht? Oh, how exciting!" Dinah exclaimed. "I've never been to a party on a yacht before. What d'you think I should wear?"

Her brother smiled.

"That's a good question, Dinah. Your favourite novelist knows all the best people, so you'll probably meet some of them on board. In the circumstances, and I'm sure Bunny will agree with me, there'll be no danger of your breaking the bank if we take you shopping in the morning for something especially attractive for you to wear," said A. J. Raffles, "—at the tea-party with Mr. Phillips Oppenheim."

9

"DETECTIVES OPERATE IN THIS STORE"

Much to our surprise, when Raffles and I sauntered out of the booking hall at Victoria Station one glorious summer morning and proffered our tickets to the collector at the platform barrier, he made a long face at them.

"Sorry, gentlemen, you can't go on this train," he said, returning our tickets to us unpunched. "Yours'll be the next—the nine-thirty. The train now standing at this platform is a Special."

Civilly enough, he drew our attention to a blackboard on which was chalked: "9 A.M. Special—Staff Annual Outing—Forshaw and Jason, Ltd."

As it happened, Raffles and I each ran charge accounts with the Wines & Spirits Department of Forshaw and Jason, whose famous Piccadilly premises, scarcely a cricket ball's throw from The Albany where Raffles had his domicile, catered to virtually every gastronomic and sartorial requirement of a discriminating *clientèle*.

In fact, one of the sights of Piccadilly pretty well any morning was the parade of butlers in black jackets, striped waistcoats and bowler hats filing into the Pantry Department at Forshaw's with napkin-covered baskets in which to carry judicious purchases of caviar, truffles, quails in aspic, plover's eggs, and reliably matured cheeses.

Later, on most mornings, when the butlers had departed with stately mien to supervise the activities of their underlings, Forshaw's richly carpeted DuBarry Buttery was invariably thronged with the fashionably trimmed hats of ladies of quality as they folded back their veils to sip hot chocolate from dainty cups and exchange with each other the latest gossip, political and amorous, of London drawing-rooms.

Naturally, customers of Forshaw's though we were, the

noted establishment's Staff Annual Outing was no business of ours—and, our tickets rejected, we turned away from the platform barrier to kill half-an-hour browsing at the station bookstall, which was occupied mostly by copies of the latest novel by Miss Marie Corelli and a large photograph of her, unobtrusively driving round Bath in a chaise drawn by her famous eight snow-white Shetland ponies.

But, as we strolled towards the bookstall, a voice hailed us by name:

"Hey, there—Raffles, Manders! Hold on a minute!"

"Good Lord," said Raffles, "it's George Forshaw!"

The managing director of Forshaw and Jason was a big, burly but highly strung chap with a cordial, enthusiastic manner. Like ourselves, he was wearing a summer suit, and his straw boater, like Raffles's own, sported an M.C.C. hatband. He was in his middle thirties.

"Where are you fellows off to?" he demanded, as he wrung our hands in his jovial way.

"We're popping down to Brighton," Raffles said, "for a breath of sea air. It's too good a day to frowst in town—a marvellous day for your firm's Outing, George!"

"I'd have sent you invitations," George said, "but dammit, Raffles, I thought you were playing cricket at Lord's against Gentlemen of Asia?"

"The wily nabobs skittled us out," Raffles explained, "so stumps were drawn just before tea yesterday."

"Great!" said George, his blue eyes sparkling with zest. "So you're free to join us! Our Outing's to Brighton. No, no, I won't hear a word! We've lots of guests with us. I insist! Here, you'll need these."

He thrust a couple of blue cards into our hands.

"As a matter of fact," he said, "this is a very special Outing this year. We're going to do honour to our Night Detective."

"Night Detective?" said Raffles, with a quickened interest that made me vaguely uneasy.

"By an old Forshaw and Jason custom, dating from my father's time," George told us, "the two Security chaps who look after our premises are always known as the Day Detective and the Night Detective. Each of them's a specialist in his own way. In the year or two our Day Detective, Sam Jeffers, has been with us, he's about halved the toll taken by shoplifters and pickpockets, every kind of daylight prowler. On the other hand, Will Gilford, our Night Detective, who's been with us a great many years, knows more than any man in London about the tricks and techniques of burglars, safecrackers, every kind of after-dark marauder.''

George glanced past us, towards the station entrance, as though he were on the watch for some new arrival, as he told us that shortly after becoming managing director of his firm, he had happened to read an American classic called *Letters of a Self-Made Merchant to His Son*.

"It was an eye-opener to me," George said. "It made a deep impression on me. They're a go-ahead people across the Atlantic. They say, over there, 'Time Is Money,' so they move fast. The author of the book calls it 'hustling.' Well, I suppose we English hustle too, but not in public, of course—we're too shy. All the same, I picked up some pretty good wrinkles from the book, but now I wish I'd never read it!"

"Why so, George?" Raffles asked.

"Well, it prompted me to introduce one or two innovations at our Piccadilly place," George said. "Nothing too daring. I preferred to err on the conservative side. It wouldn't do to stick up notices like 'WARNING! Detectives Operate in This Store'! That may be all right in Chicago, but it wouldn't do at Forshaw and Jason's. Our customers—people like yourselves, for example—wouldn't like it. Piccadilly, after all, *is* Piccadilly, don't you agree?"

"I'd be dismayed to find it wasn't," Raffles admitted.

"At all events," said George, "I had a time-recording device—the latest American gadget—installed on each floor of our premises for Mr. Gilford, our Night Detective, to punch when he makes his rounds and so establish their times and frequencies.''

"It sounds eminently practical," said Raffles, "don't you think so, Bunny?"

"Absolutely, Raffles," I concurred, somewhat uncomfortably.

"Oh, it is," George assured us. "It couldn't be more so. Mr. Jeffers, our go-ahead Day Detective, was all for it, but Mr. Gilford, our Night Detective, didn't seem to cotton to it. Not that he *said* anything. In fact, he hasn't spoken a word to me since the device was installed. He just coldly ignores me. And this has put me in a most embarrassing position, because— well—I'm frightfully keen on his daughter Nan. She's head of our Bespoke Modes Department. She's artistic to her fingertips, a marvellous dress designer—her fashion sketches are a delight to the eye, as she is herself. Just wait till you see her! Actually, she and I are secretly engaged, but we haven't dared break the news to Mr. Gilford yet. We've been waiting for this Outing. You see, the firm has good reason to do him honour today, and I'm going to see to it that it's done with real Forshaw's style—and if it thaws him towards me, then I'm going to tell him frankly that I want to take Nan from him. And by Jove, there she is now!" George exclaimed—and hurried off to meet a hansom that was jingling to a halt at the station entrance.

I saw George hand down from the hansom two most attractive young ladies in summer dresses and enchanting hats. Bringing the lovely newcomers to us, George presented Raffles and me to them. The alluring brunette was Miss Priscilla Hallam, who presided over the flower alcove, "Priscilla's Bower," in the Forshaw building, and her delightful, fairhaired companion was George's *inamorata*, the talented Miss Nan Gilford, Head of Modes.

Soon we were all installed in a first-class compartment and, with ponderous reverberations and a shrill whistle from the locomotive, a crack flyer of the London, Brighton & South Coast Railway, the Outing Special steamed out proudly from under the grimy station roof into the full blaze of the sun.

The excursion was of a nature quite unfamiliar to Raffles and myself, and seemed very much a family affair. Besides the two girls, George Forshaw, Raffles, and myself, also in the compartment were Mr. Burnaby, Head of Wines & Spirits, and his pleasant spouse, and Mr. Josiah Durward, Head of the Counting House.

Mr. Durward, a bachelor, was a rather gaunt man with a dry kind of smile that somehow reminded me that my bill at Forshaw's was no longer eligible for the usual discount, not having been paid for almost a year. I fancied that Raffles's bill was in no better case. But this was no time to trouble oneself with such matters—for as the train gathered speed past the Gasworks and entered the area of suburban gardens stippled with tulips and golden with laburnum, Mrs. Burnaby leaned forward to admire the flowers Nan Gilford was carrying.

"Your poor father *will* appreciate them," Mrs. Burnaby said kindly. "How's he getting on, Nan dear, after his dreadful experience?"

"He's much better, Maud, thank you," Nan replied. "I went down to Brighton to visit him last Sunday. He's very comfortable in the hotel. He has a lovely balcony room with a south-west view. He asked for his clothes and things, which I thought was a good sign. I asked his colleague—Mr. Jeffers, the Day Detective—to take down a portmanteau of father's things when he went to visit him on Wednesday." She coloured faintly. "I don't need to say how grateful I feel to the firm, and especially to Mr. Forshaw, for the way—"

"Now, now," said George, embarrassed. "The least we could do for your father was pack him off down to the seaside, in charge of a trained nurse, to convalesce. Raffles, Manders, you must have read in the newspaper about the attempted looting of our premises a few weeks ago?"

"Yes, I remember the matter," Raffles said.

"It was an ugly business," George said grimly. "There was over five thousand pounds—sovereigns—in the safe that night. The attempted robbery was cleverly planned. It was a gang job. They first made a raid on a jewellers in Bond Street—"

"A feint raid," said Mr. Durward.

"Exactly," said George. "They disturbed a gem-cutter who happened to be working late on the premises. He had a revolver. A masked intruder grabbed at it. It went off, the gang bolted, and the gem-cutter raised the alarm."

"It drew practically every policeman in the Piccadilly area," said Mr. Durward, "to Bond Street."

"Thus leaving the coast clear," George told us, "for the gang to raid our place—their real objective. It was damned clever. But they reckoned without our Night Detective. He'd just punched the time-recorder on the second floor, where our Counting House is, and they ran right into him. Shots were exchanged, Mr. Gilford was wounded, but he winged at least one of the raiders, and that scared the whole gang off—empty-handed. It was a great show by Mr. Gilford. And today we're going to hold our Outing Luncheon at the hotel where he's convalescing. We can't have him feeling that he's left out of all the fun of our annual junket."

From the wink which George gave Raffles and myself, I guessed that the conspicuous honour he planned to pay Mr. Gilford was to come as a surprise also to Nan, and must not yet be mentioned—though I sensed that Mr. Durward and Mr. and Mrs. Burnaby also were in the secret.

The Brighton Flyer roared along, non-stop, the telegraph poles flashing by, the basking meadows gilded with buttercups, the hedges pink with the wild rose—and it was mid-morning when we steamed into the freshly painted, green-and-gold precincts of the famous seaside station.

"I rather think, Bunny," Raffles murmured to me, as, with the rest of the managing director's party, we alighted from the train, "that the honour to be paid to Mr. Gilford is of a material kind. D'you notice that small Gladstone bag Mr. Durward, Head of the Counting House, is carrying? It's secured to his wrist by a chain." Raffles's eyes danced. "Don't look now! It's nothing to do with us. We're on a day off."

George Forshaw, rubicund with high spirits and hospitality, was making announcements to his staff members and their families, and extraneous guests, mostly favourite customers, as they all streamed along the platform, the little girls in voile frocks and carrying buckets and spades, the small boys wearing sailor suits and armed with shrimping-nets, fishing-rods, and water-wings.

"Remarkable, Bunny," Raffles said to me. "Who would have thought that behind the dignified efficiency and grave courtesy one meets with in the great establishments of Piccadilly lurks this effervescent human element?"

"Now, don't forget!" George was bawling, beaming on everybody. "You're free as air until the Luncheon, which is at one o'clock at the hotel. It's printed on your cards."

Rubbing his hands together with enthusiasm, he turned to us of his managing director's group.

"A great day, a great day!" he boomed! "I can smell the briny already. Now, look here—Durward, Burnaby, you and I have things to see to at the hotel. I expect Mrs. Burnaby would like to come along with us? Ah, good, splendid! In that case—" he took Nan's bouquet from her "—perhaps you wouldn't mind, Mrs. Burnaby, putting Miss Gilford's flowers in water at the hotel, so that they'll keep fresh for her father."

"But, Mr. Forshaw," Nan objected, "I was going to take them straight to my father now!"

"Please, Miss Gilford," George begged, perspiring with earnestness, "leave it till the Luncheon, will you? Um? Do me the favour? Ah, great! Bless you! Capital! Right, then—Raffles, Manders, I'm trusting you two to keep the young ladies entertained. See you at the hotel—one o'clock—eh—what? Tophole! Stupendous!"

The big, cordial chap bustled Durward and the Burnabys off along the platform, leaving Nan looking after him with a rather puzzled air.

"Shall we," Raffles suggested tactfully, "see if we can find a cab?"

We found, with no difficulty, an open victoria, and in this, with jingling harness-bells, we rode in and out among the yellow tramcars, down to the sail-dotted heat-shimmer of the wide blue sea.

We had some discussion as to whether first to take a stroll along the promenade to Hove or to start our explorations with the Aquarium. Nan and Priscilla rather fancied the latter. So down we plunged into a subterranean labyrinth of lurking shadows, hollow echoes, and the subdued effulgence of tanks where chains of silver bubbles gurgled endlessly upwards, dainty seahorses floated vertically, and peculiar fish mouthed mutely at us through the glass.

Presently we reached the large octopus's tank. As the girls were commenting excitedly on the complex physiology of this insidious creature, Raffles offered me a Sullivan from his cigarette-case.

"Bunny," he whispered, "there's a man standing a bit to your left. Ever since we came in here, he's been keeping closer on our heels than is quite natural. There's a faint whiff of perfume coming from him. Try to get a look at his face."

As I took a cigarette, I slid a cautious glance to my left.

Such air-current as there was blew lightly from that direction through the darkened ways of the aquarium. And Raffles was right. A subtle scent, as of some intriguing lotion or, possibly, after-shave unguent, seemed to emanate from a man who stood a little back from a tank in which fringed jellyfish with red spots on them wavered eerily up and down. In the watery gleam from the tank, the lurking man was no more than a motionless shadow in a dark suit and a black felt hat.

The girls were moving on, chattering, to the next tank past that of the octopus—and, as we followed them, Raffles murmured, "The chap's sheered off. Did you get a look at his face?"

"It was too dark, Raffles."

"A pity—because it's odd about that scent, Bunny. The girls, I'm sure, were unaware of it—for a curious reason."

"What reason?"

"They're wearing," said Raffles, "exactly the same scent themselves!"

This was indeed puzzling. I hardly knew what to make of it. All the rest of the morning, I kept my eyes and nostrils open for some trace of the perfumed man, but I came upon no further evidence, either visual or olfactory, of this enigmatic person.

The hotel, to which in due course we made our leisurely way, turned out to be a huge old rambling place with turrets and curlicues. A first-floor balcony, enclosed by diamond-paned windows of stained-glass and copiously festooned with wisteria, ran round three sides of the building.

Parting from Nan and Priscilla in the foyer, we had a wash and brush-up, and waited for the girls at the arched entrance to the dining-room. Soon, refreshed and sparkling, they rejoined us; and we showed our blue cards to a tall, ramrod-backed man with a waxed moustache who, wearing Afghan War and

Matabele Campaign medals on his frock-coat, was invigilating at the entrance.

"This is a busman's holiday for you, Sergeant Spofforth," Nan said to him.

"A happy one, howsomever, Miss Gilford," replied the veteran, "—and all the more so if we're to see your father rise up from his bed and participate in our jollification."

"Oh, I hope so, Sergeant," said Nan—and as we passed on into the dining-room she explained to us that Sergeant Spofforth was the commissionaire who presided over the main entrance of the Forshaw premises in Piccadilly.

"I thought I recognised him," said Raffles.

The great dining-room, with the sunshine beaming in on to the long tables set with napery, silver, and flowers, already was pretty well filled, but Raffles and I found good places for Nan and Priscilla and ourselves. Scarcely were we seated than a round of applause broke out. This was for George Forshaw, who was ushering to the Speakers' Table, which was raised on a dais, a number of persons of obvious distinction.

Signalling for silence, George announced that at this year's Outing we were privileged to have with us His Honour the Mayor of Brighton, together with Archdeacon Mountmarr, Sir Jasper Hack, M.P. for the constituency, and two famous Sussex sportsmen—Mr. Harry Preston, a pillar of the Turf; and Mr. Hesketh Prichard, the Sussex fast bowler, explorer of Patagonia, and author of the splendid adventure tales, *The Chronicles of Don Q*.

While the Mayor, wearing his chain of office, was speaking a few kind words, welcoming us all to Brighton, Mr. Hesketh Prichard, a bronzed, handsome man and a member of the M.C.C., spotted Raffles, was surprised to see him here, but gave him a cheerful wave.

Archdeacon Mountmarr then arose and pronounced a brief Grace, to which we all responded with a hearty "amen." The waiters then started scurrying around and we all fell to, with appetites sharpened by the good sea air, on food and wines that reflected the greatest credit on Forshaw's of Piccadilly.

Personally, by the time the children, stuffed with good things, were sent out to play on the beach, and the port, brandy, coffee, and cigars came round, I saw a good deal of point to the idea of Annual Outings, though my heart sank a little when Priscilla confided to me, "Now come the speeches, Mr. Manders."

At the Speakers' Table, George was up on his feet again. The buzz of relaxed conversation died away, and George proceeded to announce to us that this year we were inaugurating a custom whereby the various departments of the firm would take turns, year and year about, in making some small surprise offering at the Outing luncheon. Accordingly, said George, we were all now invited to open the prettily wrapped little parcels which no doubt we had noticed and speculated about, before each place.

"You will find," George shouted, as we all started snapping the ribbons and rustling the paper of the parcels, "that this year's Luncheon Surprise is offered by our Bespoke Modes and Fashions Department. In each parcel, as you now see, is a silk scarf and a small bottle of scent. These are new and unique lines. They were discovered by our Miss Gilford, Head of Modes, on a recent exploratory visit to Paris, and the right to market them in this country was acquired by her exclusively for our firm—an excellent stroke of business, I venture to say."

"Hear, hear!" we all shouted, applauding.

"Miss Nan," said Raffles, unstoppering his bottle and passing it to and fro thoughtfully under his nose, "you've stolen a march on us. You and Miss Priscilla are already using this entrancing scent."

"I couldn't resist it, Mr. Raffles," Nan admitted, with a smile. "And I gave Priscilla a bottle, too. We've kept the secret carefully guarded, so that it would be a surprise at the luncheon. Just Priscilla and I had an advance bottle."

Raffles and I exchanged glances. We knew that Nan was mistaken. Someone else must somehow, for reasons best known to himself, have acquired an advance bottle—the man in the Aquarium.

From the Speakers' Table, George was calling again for silence, please. This achieved, he resumed his discourse.

"Now, to strike a graver note," he said. "I refer to the attempted robbery at our Piccadilly premises, which was thwarted by the vigilance and self-sacrifice of our popular Night Detective, Mr. Will Gilford. As you all know, you started spontaneously among yourselves a testimonial fund for Mr. Gilford.''

I felt Nan grow rigid beside me, saw her pretty eyes open wide, in surprise.

''The specie in the Counting House safe on the night of the attempted robbery,'' George was continuing, ''was packed in sovereign-bags each containing two hundred and fifty sovereigns. Accordingly, it's given the management great pleasure to make the sum subscribed for Mr. Gilford up to the round figure of two hundred and fifty pounds.''

We all loudly applauded.

''Mr. Durward, as Treasurer of the Testimonial Fund Committee,'' George went on, ''then passed to me the Committee's truly sensitive suggestion that the award to Mr. Gilford should take the form of two hundred and fifty sovereigns packed into a sovereign-bag, a testimonial purse, specially designed and embroidered by the clever sempstresses of our Modes Department—unbeknownst,'' said George, beaming down in Nan's direction— ''to its talented Directress—so that Mr. Gilford, when he has deposited the sovereigns in his bank account, may then frame the embroidered purse as a memento to sustain him through the many happy days, weeks, months, years, and indeed decades which, let us hope, stretch out before him. Now, Mr. Durward, if you please—''

Amid growing excitement, as George sat down, mopping his brow, the Head of the Counting House, who had a place at the Speakers' Table, arose with his dry smile and held up by its tasselled drawstring—woven of gold thread—the testimonial sovereign-bag for us all to see. Small, but heavy with the weight of two hundred and fifty sovereigns, the bag was fashioned from the finest doeskin intricately embroidered, in red, with a pattern of £ signs and tiny revolvers.

When we all had had a good look at the charming artifact, and with cheers and clapping signified our satisfaction with it, Mr. Durward sat down and George again rose to his feet.

''I'm delighted to tell you all,'' he announced, ''that Mr. Gilford, who is upstairs in the charge of a trained nurse, is making an excellent recovery. Without betraying the surprise we have in store for him, I asked the nurse if Mr. Gilford would be able to join us at luncheon. On consulting him, the nurse reported that, unfortunately, Mr. Gilford didn't feel up to coming down. In the circumstances, the Testimonial Fund Committee and I all feel that, subject to your approval, the most appropriate envoy to convey our tribute to him should be—"

"Our Miss Gilford!" came in one great thunderclap of sound, and we all rose to give Nan a standing ovation as George signalled her to go up to the Speakers' Table on the dais.

"Now, Miss Gilford," said George, when the beaming Mayor had shaken hands with Nan, and the tumult had somewhat subsided, "perhaps, later in the day, when we all foregather here again for the Outing Tea, you may have some small message for us from our Night Detective. Meantime, is there anyone you would care, as additionally representing us all, to accompany you upstairs on this agreeable mission? Priscilla Hallam? Of course! Capital! Miss Hallam—if you please—"

Again Raffles and I sprang to our feet. We drew out Priscilla's chair for her—and, as she made her way to the dais, I was about to sit down again, but Raffles's hand on my arm restrained me.

"Come on, Bunny," he said.

With so much noise going on, and all eyes on the Speakers' Table, we slipped out, unnoticed as far as I could see, to the hotel foyer. It was deserted, the wide front door standing open to the garden, the promenade, the beach where the Outing children were at play, and the calm, sail-dotted sun-shimmer of the sea beyond.

"Raffles," I said, as we went down the hotel steps and turned to the right, under the enclosed first-floor terrace with its wealth of wisteria, "what's on your mind?"

"That aquarium incident, Bunny," he said. "Who *was* that chap? Obviously he must be somebody connected with Forshaw's, or how else could he have got hold of a bottle of that scent? My guess is that he had a bottle of it in his pocket and the bottle must have been leaking a bit round the stopper. But why would some man connected with Forshaw's have somehow provided himself with an advance bottle of that exclusive and carefully guarded scent unless he anticipated a *need* for it?''

"A need?'' I said. "What *need* could he possibly have?''

"One that occurs to me, Bunny, is that possession of the Modes Department's surprise gift—the unique silk scarf and the exclusive scent—constitutes evidence of presence at the luncheon. Now, suppose—just suppose—that that testimonial bag of sovereigns was stolen during the luncheon, and the Brighton police were called in. They'd most certainly ask everyone, as they come into tea later on, to show his or her silk scarf and bottle of scent. If somebody didn't have them, that person would be asked to explain where he or she was during the luncheon. And I know where *I'd* be, at this moment, if I had designs on Mr. Gilford's Testimonial Purse. I'd be in the room of that sick old man who has only a nurse with him—and who's about to have two hundred and fifty golden sovereigns walk in on him!''

"Good God!'' I exclaimed.

"Didn't Nan Gilford mention, in the train,'' Raffles said, "that her father had a balcony room with a south-west view? Well, here we are—his room must be on this side of the hotel. Come on—and not a sound!''

Swiftly, light-footed, he led the way up a narrow spiral staircase of wrought-iron to the enclosed first-floor balcony. It had a board floor on which stood basket-chairs, deck chairs and bamboo tables.

The rooms which gave on to the balcony had French windows. Some stood open, some were closed. On tiptoe, I followed Raffles as he prowled from one window to the next, glancing in cautiously at each. Suddenly he reached back a hand to stop me. His back flat to the wall, he peered sidelong round the edge of the open French window of the fourth room along. Beside him, my own back flat to the wall, I listened intently.

All I could hear was a faint drone, and an occasional burst of applause, from the dining-room below and more towards the front of the hotel.

I craned for a glimpse past Raffles into the room. I could not see much of it directly, but in the mirror of a dressing-table in the room I could see almost the whole of it reflected.

A pale-faced, dapper man of about thirty, wearing a business suit and a black felt hat, was pacing to and fro in the room. In a wheelchair sat a much older man with a grey-stubbled head and a grey moustache.

His wrists and ankles were bound to the wheelchair. Yet he was not, as might have been expected, gagged. On the contrary, he was *placidly smoking a pipe*. The incongruity seemed inexplicable.

Raffles drew me a little away from the window.

"Bunny," he whispered, "there's a heavy chest-of-drawers drawn squarely across what's probably the door of the bathroom. I bet the nurse is shut up in there. The old man's undoubtedly Nan's father, Will Gilford, the Night Detective. The younger, shrewd-looking chap in the black felt hat is almost certainly the man who was watching us in the Aquarium. I think it's a dead cert that he's Sam Jeffers, the Day Detective. Who else could have found out about the Modes Department's carefully guarded 'surprise' gift, and got hold of a bottle of that scent, except one of the two house detectives—and it couldn't have been Gilford! Yet, whatever Jeffers is up to, it's obvious that Gilford must be in it with him! This is a deeper business than I'd imagined."

Soundless, he stepped back to peer again, obliquely, into the room. I joined him—and I saw Jeffers, reflected in the dressing-table mirror, suddenly step to the door of the room and put an ear to it. Turning, he snatched the pipe out of Will Gilford's mouth, put the pipe in an ashtray on the dressing-table, whipped out a handkerchief from his pocket and gagged Gilford with it.

Taking another handkerchief from his pocket, Jeffers tied it triangularly over his own face. His right hand in his jacket pocket, he stepped again to the door. A knock sounded on it. He drew the door open, keeping behind it.

Into the room walked, with radiant smiles, Nan Gilford and Priscilla Hallam. Nan was carrying, cupped in both hands like a chalice, the Testimonial Purse. Priscilla was carrying the bouquet of flowers which Nan had brought from London.

Simultaneously, they saw old Will Gilford, bound, gagged, helpless in the wheelchair. They stopped dead. Behind them, the door-bolt clicked home. They turned quickly—to face the menace of a stubby revolver in the hand of the masked man.

The girls stood frozen as the man snatched the Testimonial Purse from Nan's hands. He shoved aside the chest of drawers, pulled open a door. I saw a buxom woman in an apron, her nurse's starched cap awry on her grey hair, staring with frightened eyes from a bathroom.

"Get in there," the masked man told the girls, in a muffled voice. "Keep your traps shut—or the old man'll get hurt!"

Without a word, the pale girls joined the horrified nurse in the bathroom. The masked man closed the door on them, shoved the heavy chest-of-drawers back across it. He pulled off his handkerchief-mask, crossed to a portmanteau on the floor beside the dressing-table.

Raffles, gripping my arm, made no attempt to intervene as the man with the revolver opened the portmanteau, dropped the revolver and the Testimonial Purse into it, and took from it a pearl-grey suit and a straw hat. Taking off his black felt hat and the jacket of his dark suit, he dropped them into the portmanteau. His trousers followed. He had wiry legs and was wearing natty, knee-length drawers on which I could distinctly see the embroidered initials—S.J.—until he pulled on the pearl-grey trousers over them.

Tucking in his shirt, he snarled at old Gilford, "Night Detective, eh? Thought you'd heard the last of our mob, eh, the night you beat us off from Forshaw's bleedin' safe? You know better now, cully! You winged one of my mates bad that night in Piccadilly, but by God, you ain't goin' to get no award for it. You can say toodle-oo to *that*, me cocko!"

As he donned the pearl-grey jacket, he gave Will Gilford a crafty wink. It was obvious that his ugly ranting was so much humbug, meant to be heard by the girls and the nurse in the bathroom and so draw a red herring across his trail. His dressing completed, he picked up the jacket of his other suit, transferred from its pocket to the pocket of his pearl-grey suit a bottle of scent and a silk scarf. Dropping the discarded jacket back into the portmanteau, he locked it, clapped on his straw hat at a jaunty angle, and tucked the key—with a wink—into Will Gilford's waistcoat-pocket.

"Quick!" Raffles breathed in my ear—and he drew me in through the open French window of the neighbouring room.

Scarcely had we gained its shelter than Jeffers walked quickly past the window, along the balcony, and we heard him running down the wrought-iron spiral staircase.

"Now, of course," said Raffles, "he'll stroll round and mingle with the Outing folk as they come streaming out from the dining-room. Damned neat, Bunny! Remember Nan Gilford saying she asked Jeffers last Wednesday to take her father his clothes in a portmanteau? Jeffers must have popped in that straw hat and grey suit of his own. Wednesday must have been the day he and old Will Gilford planned this coup. And they've hidden the swag in the last place anybody'd think of looking for it—Gilford's portmanteau!"

"But in heaven's name," I said, "why should Will Gilford connive at the theft of *his own award?*"

"It's obvious, Bunny. They think that if old Gilford's award is stolen by the same gang who raided Forshaw's Piccadilly premises, George Forshaw will make it up to him out of his own pocket. So instead of Will Gilford getting two hundred and fifty quid, he and Jeffers'll have *five* hundred to share between them. They're *detectives*, Bunny—and when detectives step off the straight-and-narrow, they know all the bends!"

"Good God, Raffles!"

He laughed quietly.

"I suspect that Jeffers didn't come down from London with the rest of us this morning. He came by an earlier train. He was probably at the station, keeping out of sight, to watch the Brighton Flyer steam in with the Outing party. He spotted you and me, two unaccountable strangers, in the managing director's party. Because of what he was planning, he was probably uneasy about us, wanted to know who we were. He shadowed us into the Aquarium—a good place to eavesdrop—to try to find out. Unluckily for him, that bottle of scent must have leaked a bit in his pocket, and got you and me interested. Now, it's our move!"

He glanced around the room. It was obviously tenanted, though no doubt the tenant was out on the beach enjoying the sunshine. Raffles bolted the door of the room, opened the door of the wardrobe. Various male garments hung in it, including a floppy-brimmed white linen sun-hat. He tried it on.

"Yes, this fits well enough for our purpose," he said, "—with this travelling dust-coat to go with it."

He donned the long, white linen dust-coat, tied his handkerchief triangularly over his face, then noted among the toilet articles on the dressing-table a pair of sun-glasses with big, round, blue-tinted lenses. He donned the glasses.

"Right," he said, his general appearance now eccentric in the extreme. "You keep *cave* on the balcony, Bunny."

I was at a loss to divine his intentions as I followed him on to the balcony.

He stepped straight into the Night Detective's room. My back flat to the wall, I peered in obliquely at the dressing-table mirror. Reflected there, the eyes of Nan Gilford's venal father, bound and gagged in his wheelchair, started from his head at sight of the weird, blue-goggled figure approaching him with sinister deliberation.

Dipping his fingers in the old Night Detective's waistcoat-pocket, Raffles retrieved the key of the portmanteau. Crossing to the portmanteau, he unlocked it, took out the Testimonial Purse. He held it up, by its drawstring, in front of the old schemer's face, and jingled the Purse's contents, then returned the portmanteau key to Gilford's pocket and stepped out silently on to the balcony.

We nipped back into the neighbouring room, where Raffles took off his borrowed garments.

"The Testimonial Purse is a bit heavy," he said, as he put it into his jacket pocket, "but the bulge is hardly noticeable, is it?"

I reassured him.

"Good," he said. He unbolted the door. "Now, everything here is just as we found it. Come on, we'll leave by the balcony way. They'll be out of the dining-room now, and I fancy that Jeffers, like all the others, will be in a deck chair on the beach. He'll be pretending to sleep off the luncheon potations he didn't have."

We went down the wrought-iron spiral staircase, strolled round to the front of the hotel. George Forshaw was there, bareheaded in the sunshine, seeing the Mayor and Archdeacon Mountmarr into the mayoral landau drawn by four spanking horses. Mr. Hesketh Prichard, the famous Sussex fast bowler, explorer of Patagonia, and author of *Don Q*, whom he resembled in appearance, was about to mount into the landau—but, seeing us, he paused.

"Ah, there you are, Raffles," he said. "You're on the Committee at Lord's and I want a word with you. I was at the Royal Geographical Society's place in Kensington the other day, and I had a chat with Harry Stanley. He was telling me about the appalling devastation he saw wrought by locusts when he was in Africa looking for David Livingstone. It occured to me that the groundsmen at Lord's should be put on their guard against these females who're going around shouting 'Votes For Women!' They're perfectly capable of drawing attention to their 'Cause' by letting loose a plague of locusts on the turf at Lord's, and the consequences for English cricket hardly bear thinking about."

"I'll look into the matter, Prichard," Raffles promised, "and see if precautionary steps can be taken at the next Committee meeting."

"There's a good fellow," said the famous explorer-cricketer-author, and he joined the Mayor and Archdeacon Mountmarr in the landau, which rolled away along the promenade road.

"Well," said George Forshaw, mopping his brow, "I thought the Outing Luncheon went off with a swing, by and large, didn't you? Nan's still upstairs with her father. Now that he's got his Testimonial Purse, he may be in a mood to receive me. I'm going up to see."

"We'll come with you, if we may," Raffles said. "We'd like to meet him—just to make his acquaintance, then we'll leave the coast clear. We know you want a private talk with him."

"That nurse mightn't let us in," George warned us, as we

entered the hotel and mounted the stairs. "I'm keeping my fingers crossed!"

On the first floor landing he knocked nervously on a door bearing the numeral 8. A knocking sound, like an echo, came back, but the door did not open. George knocked again, more loudly—eliciting in reply only a series of repeated, echo-like knocks.

"That's odd," said George, giving us a troubled look. He smote firmly on the door. "Nurse?" he called. "Mr. Gilford? *Nan?*"

More knocks and a faint cry answered him. He looked at us aghast.

"That was Nan's voice!" he exclaimed.

"Try the door-handle," Raffles suggested.

"Good idea," said George. He turned the door-handle. He pushed. The door stood firm. He flushed deeply. "The door's bolted!" he said.

"Strange," said Raffles. "Perhaps something's wrong in there."

"By God," George said, "we'll damned soon see! Stand back, you fellows!" He retreated three paces from the door, then rushed forward and hurled himself at it, shoulder first.

His considerable physique tore the bolt from its clasps and the door flew open with a bang.

"What's this?" George roared, recovering his balance. "What the devil's happened here, Mr. Gilford?"

Gagged as he was, the Night Detective was unable to reply. Tied in his wheelchair, he was staring at the French window standing wide open to the balcony. He had the spellbound look of a man whose eyes had beheld phantasms.

An urgent knocking sounded on the bathroom door.

"Mr. Forshaw!" Nan Gilford's voice cried. "Let us out!"

Raffles and George thrust aside the heavy chest-of-drawers. The bathroom door opened, disclosing Nan, Priscilla, and the nurse.

"Is father all right?" Nan said. She ran to him anxiously. "Are you alive, father? Oh, thank heavens, his eyes blinked! He's alive! Never mind, father—" she began to untie his gag, "—we'll soon have you free!"

"But, Miss Gilford—Nan," said George, "what's happened here?"

"Robbery," said Nan. "There was a masked man crouching in here with a revolver. He snatched the Testimonial Purse from me! He was one of the gang that attempted the robbery at our Piccadilly shop. Oh, father, I'm *so* sorry! It was for you—a surprise—a testimonial from everybody at Forshaw's! *Two hundred and fifty sovereigns!*"

"Nan—my dear," George begged, deeply moved, "don't upset yourself about the money. *I'll* make that up to your father. Just don't give the mere money a thought. It's the swine of a man we want! I'll call the police right away!"

Raffles gripped him by the arm.

"Whoa, George! Just a minute," Raffles said. "If I were you, I'd go a bit canny here. If you call the police, there'll be hours of questioning. The Outing Tea will be disrupted. Your special train will lose its place in the timetable. The children will get fractious. The whole Outing will become a disaster, a shambles. George, why bring the police into this when you've got detectives of your own? Obviously, your Night Detective is in no shape to carry out an investigation, but what about your Day Detective? Why not call *him* into conference?"

"By God," George exclaimed, "I never thought of that! You're right, Raffles! We want Sam Jeffers in on this. *He'll* know what to do. He's a smart fellow—an idea man."

"He's probably taking his ease on the beach somewhere, in a deck chair," said Raffles. "Miss Nan, may I suggest that you and Miss Priscilla run out, see if you can find Mr. Jeffers, and send him here on the double? Don't lose a moment!"

The girls hurried off excitedly, and the nurse, who had been taking her patient's pulse and feeling his forehead, told us that he was suffering from emotional shock and must take things quietly. She added that, as her own head was splitting from her ordeal, she was going to her room to lie down for a while.

As she withdrew, closing the door behind her, I looked curiously at the old rascal of a Night Detective. Sitting there in his wheelchair, he was staring in a dazed way at the open French window, as though he still saw coming balefully in at him from the balcony a masked apparition in a long dust-coat, floppy linen hat, and goggling blue glasses.

"Mr. Gilford," said George Forshaw, "do you feel equal to telling us exactly what happened here?"

The aging detective roused himself with an effort. "Mr. Forshaw," he said tremulously, "please pass me my pipe from the ashtray there." With unsteady fingers, he began to fill his pipe. "Sir," he said, "Mr. Durward of the Counting House is my oldest friend in the firm. I wrote him a letter last Wednesday—a confidential letter, Mr. Forshaw. I asked him not to show it to you until I told him to."

I stole an uneasy glance at Raffles. His keen face was intent.

"I've seen no letter, Mr. Gilford," George said, puzzled.

"No, sir," said Will Gilford, "and it's hard for me to tell you this to your face, but I've got no choice. Mr. Forshaw, what's happened in this room here was—well, it was an arrangement, sir—between me and Sam Jeffers."

"An *arrangement*?" said George. "You mean that the Testimonial Purse has *not* been stolen?"

"No, it *has* been stolen, sir," said Will Gilford, "but not according to plan. That's the mystery of it. It's got me confused in my mind, Mr. Forshaw. It was Jeffers who snatched the Testimonial Purse from my daughter. He put it in my portmanteau there, and off he went. Sir, he hadn't been gone two minutes when—a *figure*, the strangest figure I ever saw in my life—walked in through that window, went to my portmanteau, took out the Testimonial Purse and—and glided away with it."

I dared not look at Raffles.

"Surely, Mr. Gilford," said George, "this—this strange figure you mention was a member of the gang that attempted to rob our Piccadilly premises!"

"Impossible! That's impossible," said Will Gilford, "—because there never *was* any gang, there never *was* any raid on our Piccadilly premises!"

Stunned, I stole a glance at Raffles. His expression was unfathomable.

"There," said Will Gilford, "it's out now. Mr. Forshaw, I must have been out of my mind! All the time I was in the

Metropolitan Police, and all the years I've been Night Detective at Forshaw and Jason's, I've never put a foot wrong till just recently—through *your* fault, Mr. Forshaw."

"*My* fault?" shouted George, incredulous.

"You put in those time-recording gadgets, sir," said Gilford reproachfully. "That hurt me, Mr. George—that cut me very deeply. Your father would never have done such a thing! *He* didn't want evidence that I did my rounds properly. He *knew* me! He *trusted* me! As Sam Jeffers said to me, your father would never have dreamed of insulting me by installing those gadgets."

"*Jeffers* said that?" George shouted. "But he told me he was all in favour of them. He gave me a book that was all about up-to-date merchandising!"

"Ah, that man Jeffers, sir! I'm on to him now. But he got me all worked up, Mr. Forshaw, with his hints and insinuations. Kept on, he did—about how you'd shown you didn't trust me, and about how you were exploiting the talent of my daughter Nan, and how you had designs on her."

"Good God!" said George, appalled.

"Kept on, he did," said Will Gilford. "Why didn't I take Nan away, Jeffers said, and set her up, with all her talent for artistic fashions, in a smart shop of her own? It would be easy for me to get the money for it, he said, because I'd learned from long experience every method and trick of burglars, cracksmen, night marauders. Why not use my knowledge the other way round, he said, and pull off a job on my own account—and he, for a share of the swag, would nip back into the Forshaw building, punch the time-recording gadget on each floor, and so give me a perfect alibi?"

The old detective passed a shaky hand over his forehead.

"Sir, he got me so that I was out of my mind. One night he set up a job that he said would be a cakewalk for me—and, God help me, I tried it on! It was at that jeweller's nearby in Bond Street. There was a gem-cutter happened to be working late there. He came at me with a revolver, and it went off. I got away, but I had a bullet in me. I managed to get back, sir, to our Piccadilly premises. Jeffers was waiting for me. He'd been punching the time gadget for me, so I had an alibi. But I had to account for the bullet in me, so we fixed it up to look as if there'd been a gang raid on our place, and off he went. And then I must've come over faint, because I was found unconscious in the morning."

He lighted his pipe with unsteady hands. I could hear the voices of the Outing children at play on the beach, and the peaceful sound of the small waves breaking.

"Mr. Gilford," George said, spreading his hands in a helpless gesture, "I—I really don't know what to say."

"Sir, the whole truth's in the letter I wrote Mr. Durward. I've done a lot of thinking, lying on my back in hospital, and here convalescing," said the old detective. "To keep my daughter from learning how I really came by my wound, I'd have done—almost anything, Mr. Forshaw. But then, last Wednesday, Jeffers came down here to see me. He had another of his bright ideas. He told me that you and the staff had got up a Testimonial Purse for me, and that he had a foolproof scheme to double it. He wouldn't tell me the details. He said all I'd have to do was sit here in my wheelchair and *he'd* do all the active work."

Will Gilford looked at George Forshaw remorsefully.

"I was very much perturbed, sir, to hear that you all at the old firm had got up a Testimonial Purse for me. All I wanted was to make reparation for what I'd done in my folly, and the best reparation I could make, it seemed to me, was to get Sam Jeffers—a very evil influence, Mr. George—kicked out of Forshaw's. But how? I had no proof against him. *Anybody* could have been my confederate on the time-recording dodge. But then, last Wednesday, he came at me with this new idea of his—to double the amount of the Testimonial Purse. I thought I saw my chance then. So I pretended to fall in with his scheme. But then—that strange figure came at me through the window just now and—"

Words seemed to fail the old detective. And Raffles said quietly:

"At this point, George, I think perhaps I'd better put in a word."

He told George Forshaw of the curious incident of the perfumed man in the Aquarium.

"It aroused our suspicions, George," Raffles explained. "Manders and I looked further into the matter, and it became evident to us that Mr. Gilford was involved in some shenanigan. Naturally, in view of the very personal aspirations you confided to us at Victoria Station, we realised that the situation we'd discovered must be dealt with very discreetly—and that, at all costs, you must be stopped, whatever happened, from calling in the police."

"Oh, good God, yes!" said George fervently.

"At the same time," Raffles said, "it seemed advisable—for safety's sake—temporarily to impound this bone of contention."

He took from his pocket the Testimonial Purse, held it up by its tasselled drawstring.

Will Gilford's pipe fell from his mouth.

"*You*, sir?" he said. "*You* were that uncanny figure that glided in through the window at me?"

Seizing the embroidered, doeskin sovereign-bag from Raffles, the old detective trundled his wheelchair over to the bed.

"However crafty Sam Jeffers's plan turned out to be today," he said, loosening the purse-drawstring with trembling fingers, "I was determined he shouldn't get his hooks on the money subscribed by all my kind, good-hearted friends at Forshaw and Jason's. So in my letter to Mr. Durward, of the Counting House, who I guessed would have the packing of the Testimonial Purse, I told him what to pack it with."

He shook from the sovereign-bag, on to the white counterpane of the bed, a jingling cascade of farthings interspersed with thin, makeweight discs of lead.

In the ensuing silence, I heard the peaceful sound of the small waves breaking on the beach, the happy cries of the Outing youngsters at play, and Nan Gilford's clear voice calling, "Has anybody seen Mr. Jeffers?"

I glanced at Raffles. He met my eyes. I could see that he was as astounded as I was myself by the almost worthless swag lying there on the bed. He shook his head.

"Mr. Gilford," he said, with a wry smile, "my sincere congratulations!"

George Forshaw mopped his perspiring forehead.

"At the Outing Tea presently, Mr. Gilford," he said, "I shall announce that you insist on donating your award to found a Staff Club for the benefit of us all at Forshaw's."

"Thank you, Mr. George," the old detective said simply. "That would be a great relief to my conscience."

"Nan must never know what really happened," George said, "that night at our Piccadilly premises. *Nobody* must know. Raffles, thank God your quick wit stopped me from calling in the police! Heaven knows what they might have ferreted out. I'm deeply in your debt."

"Not another word!" said Raffles. "Now, I believe you have a rather personal matter to take up with Mr. Gilford, George. So come on, Bunny, let's go and take a look at the sea."

He opened the door.

A sly-faced man in a dapper pearl-grey suit and a straw hat straightened up with a startled jerk, then turned and bolted away along the landing.

"Ah-hah!" said Raffles. "Mr. Sam Jeffers with an ear to the door again! Well, George, I doubt if you'll be seeing anything more of him—which seems no great loss, all things considered. Come on, Bunny."

As we descended the stairs to the hotel foyer, Raffles offered me a Sullivan from his cigarette-case.

"It's perhaps just as well, Bunny," he said, "that George Forshaw considers himself in our debt, for we're rather deeply in his—especially his Wines and Spirits Department. But, somehow, I doubt if we shall be getting any tactful reminders from the Counting House. On the contrary, I fancy our credit at Forshaw's, Piccadilly, will remain unlimited for a considerable time to come. Incidentally, I must ask George, at the Outing Tea presently, if he'll lend me that book. We might pick up a few useful pointers from it."

"Book?" I said. "What book?"

"Why, that forward-looking American one George mentioned to us," Raffles replied, as, our cigarettes lighted, we sauntered on down the stairs—"*Letters of a Self-Made Merchant to His Son.*"

10

BLACK MASK AND THE FIREFLY

The afternoon of the big match, Aston Villa *v.* Quoins, in the Second Round of the Football Association Cup competition, was bright with sunshine and crisp with a hint of frost.

Paula Gethlin, the attractive young wife of the Quoins' centre-forward, rightly remarked to me, as I escorted her to our reserved seats in the covered stand, that it was ideal soccer weather.

"And what a marvellous great crowd, Bunny!" she exclaimed.

Villa Park, home ground of the great all-professional Aston Villa team, was packed to capacity with their excited, streamer-waving supporters. They tasted victory in advance, for the visiting team, the Quoins, was composed of amateurs. In fact, it was the only such team to have survived the earlier rounds and carry the banner of "Sport for Sport's sake" into this, the Second Round of the competition proper.

The betting was heavily against Quoins, but I was not altogether devoid of hope for them. They had in their side four amateur internationals, though actually two of them, C. B. Fry and A. J. Raffles, were more widely known as M.C.C. cricketers than as soccer players.

Scarcely had Paula and I taken our seats than a ripple of clapping, sufficiently courteous, sounded around the ground and, here and there in the largely cloth-capped crowd, a grey top-hat was brandished aloft.

"Here they come!" said Paula, her eyes sparkling. "Here comes our side!"

Led by their captain, the *beau sabreur* of British sportsmanship, C. B. Fry, who had played soccer for Repton and for Oxford University, the Quoins eleven were booting a

207

ball to one another as they came trotting out on to the emerald turf.

They were playing in black shorts and white shirts—black-and-white being peculiarly appropriate to a team which claimed associations, of one kind and another, with the world of print, and which had on the breasts of its soccer shirts a small crest depicting a printer's quoin and the motto *Ante Omnia Verbum*.

The association of the team's captain with the printing world consisted in his editorship of his own distinguished periodical, *C. B. Fry's Magazine of Sport*. Paula Gethlin's husband, Alan, could fairly enough claim some association with print in that the mystery novels he wrote managed to achieve it. Raffles's own claim to anything of the kind was rather more tenuous, due to the fact that, though he sometimes was invited to contribute to a newspaper an article on sport, he usually imposed on me, as a dilettante journalist, to ghostwrite it for him.

Fortunately, we always had kept this literary chicanery strictly under our hats. So there he was now, booting the ball about down there, as a tremendous roar from the crowd welcomed the Aston Villa players trotting out on to the field in the colours they had made nationally celebrated.

"It doesn't seem fair, Bunny," Paula complained, "that *professionals* should be allowed to play *at home* against amateurs."

"I'm afraid, Paula," I said, "that that's just the luck of the draw."

The referee, standing down there in midfield with the bright new yellow match ball under his arm, blew his whistle to summon the team captains. A sovereign, spun high, flashed golden in the sunshine. The three men stooped to look at the coin as it fell on the grass—and as they straightened up I saw from Fry's beckoning gesture to his team that he had won the toss.

"Excellent, Paula," I said. "Fry's making Villa play the first half with the sun in their eyes."

"Oh, I do hope it dazzles them!" Paula enthused. "It'll make the match *so* much fairer."

Within ten minutes of the kick-off, we had reason to bless the luck of the toss. A Quoins' goal-kick was nimbly trapped by Raffles, at inside-right. He made ground fast with the ball, swerved round Villa's left-half, deceived their left-back by feinting a long pass out to the wing and, instead, slipped the ball inside to Alan Gethlin, who passed it straight on to Fry, who, wary of Villa's off-side trap, slammed in a first-time shot that Villa's goalie would have stopped nine times out of ten—but for the sun in his eyes.

His vexation was plain to see as he retrieved the ball that had beaten him and punted it upfield. The crowd maintained a rather noticeable hush. Next minute, they were roaring again as Villa counterattacked with a movement of clockwork-smooth professionalism—only to have their finishing shot sail yards over the bar. The crowd groaned. And they groaned several more great groans as Villa, stepping up the pressure, missed what looked like certain goals. The luck was with Quoins. Villa should have been four up at half-time, instead of one down.

"Oh, Bunny!" Paula exclaimed. "Are you going to see an upset?"

We saw it, sure enough. Five minutes into the second half, Villa equalized. From then on, the professional cohesion which came from training and playing together regularly began to tell. More and more, Quoins were forced back, steadily and re-lentlessly, into defence.

"How strange, Bunny," Paula said, puzzled, "—Villa seem to have more players on the field than we have."

"An optical illusion, Paula," I explained regretfully. "It often occurs when a team's getting on top."

For now, unmistakably, Villa were on the rampage. Their goalie was beating his hands together to keep them warm. He had half the field to himself. The sun was gone and in the darkening afternoon most of the play was in Quoins' goal area. Fry had pulled his whole team back. It no longer was a question of Quoins winning. With the score level pegging, the question was whether the match would go into extra time—and, if so, whether Quoins could withstand the pressure and get a replay.

Villa now were forcing corner after corner. Yet still they

could not get that ball into Quoins' net. Again and again, Fry or Raffles or another Quoin got a head or foot to the ball. Villa hit the posts, they hit the crossbar, they shot over the top. Fry was everywhere. An Olympic high-jump champion, he sprang up repeatedly above the scrimmage to head the ball clear. Time now was running out fast. The referee was stealing glances at his watch. Paula and I were on our feet, shouting, our puny voices drowned in the roar of the crowd urging Villa on to the kill as Quoins, perforce, yielded another corner.

It probably would be the last. My mouth was dry, my heart throbbed heavily, Paula's slim, gloved hand was clutching my sleeve in the sudden silence that fell as Villa's winger placed the ball quickly for the corner kick. He took it beautifully. The ball curled in towards Quoins' goal. The goalkeeper, partner in a printing firm in Long Acre, lunged up and as he fisted the ball clear over the melée he slipped and went down. A Villa forward, standing a little clear, trapped the ball neatly and for an instant, with Quoins' goalkeeper spread eagled, had the goal wide open before him—and, in that instant, came the upset.

Alan Gethlin swept the Villa man's feet out from under him before he could shoot.

The foul was committed well inside Quoins' penalty area. The crowd erupted with a thunderclap roar of wrath that drowned the shrill of the referee's whistle. Seizing possession of the ball, he waved back all players and implacably dumped the ball down on the penalty spot.

The crowd was frozen, mute, as Villa's skipper, their tall, imperturbable centre half, prepared to take the kick, and Quoins' goalie, irrevocably alone now, braced himself for this moment of truth.

The whistle shrilled, the Villa skipper's boot hit the ball a thump so perfectly judged that it left Quoins' goalkeeper flat-footed—and, even as the crowd roared its relief and exultation, the long final blast of the whistle sounded through the tumult.

The match was over. Aston Villa 2—Quoins 1. The last amateur team left in the F.A. Cup competition was out—beaten because of an ugly foul committed by a member of the eleven captained by C. B. Fry, the Bayard of Brisith sport, *sans peur et sans reproche*.

Paula and I sank back, stunned, into our seats. The spectators, streaming past us out of the stand, were discussing the scandal of that last-minute foul in terms that made me flush. Poor Paula! I could feel her tense beside me, her hand clenched tight on my sleeve. I dared not look at her.

The players were gone from the field. The stand and mounds rapidly emptied. The brief, frosty dusk of this winter day darkened over the post-match desolation of Villa Park. Paula did not move, did not speak. I racked my brains to find some word of comfort for her.

"Paula," I ventured, at last, "it was—just an act of panic."

"Damn him," she said, almost in a whisper, "*damn* him! I *hate* him!"

I was shocked. "Paula, he's your husband—"

"It's not Alan I'm talking about."

"Who, then?" I said, bewildered.

"The man who corrupted him," she said, "—*The Firefly!*"

Her hand tightened on my sleeve.

"Bunny, that foul was *not* an act of panic. With the goalie down and the goal wide open, a shot in that instant was certain to score. So a foul, however despicable, seemed worthwhile to a corrupt man—because the penalty kick that would result would *not* be a certain goal. The goalie, prepared, might stop it. Don't you see? The foul was calculated—deliberate."

"Paula, you can't possibly *know* that!"

"I know the man I married," Paula said bitterly, "—and Alan is no longer the same man. Bunny, when I married Alan four years ago, he would have been incapable of a deliberate foul to gain an advantage. He would no more have done such a thing than Raffles would, or Charles Fry himself. But Alan has changed. I've seen it happening, seen the corruption growing and spreading in him ever since he started writing those tales about a criminal, a masked marauder who leaves behind on the scene of his crimes a dangling insect, luminous—a firefly!"

"Paula," I protested, "aren't you being a bit morbid? I've read several of Alan's tales about the Firefly, but—"

"Several?" Paula said. "Oh, Bunny, Alan's been writing

one of those sly, shady Firefly tales regularly every month for the past three years! Can a man constantly think himself into the skin of a corrupt individual without himself becoming corrupted? The Firefly has become a drug, an addiction, a compulsion to Alan—and I've been helpless to prevent it. Bunny, the fictional Firefly is infinitely more real to Alan now than I am—*I*, his wife!"

"Oh, dear God!" I breathed, appalled.

"For a long time now," Paula said, her face cameo-pale in the dusk deepening here in the covered stand, "I've felt as though I were living with—with a *werewolf*! Alan lives a life apart—a secret life, of gleeful wickedness, in his own corrupted mind. Bunny, I don't know what to do! This ficitional criminal, the Firefly, is insidiously destroying my marriage. I don't think I can stand it any longer. This vile foul this afternoon! Everybody'll be talking about it. The scandalous end of the Aston Villa match with a gross foul committed by, of all people, *one of C. B. Fry's players*, will be in the sports pages of all the newspapers tomorrow. It'll be in the evening papers *tonight*! It's being printed *now*! Oh, Bunny, this is the last straw!"

Light suddenly flickered. We looked round, startled. Raffles was standing there, matchlight glimmering on his keen face and M.C.C. muffler as he dipped his cigarette to the flame in his cupped hands. His tweeds were immaculate.

"You know," he said, shaking out the match, "this is the first Sullivan I've dared smoke since Charles Fry rounded us up to train for this game today. It's a pity we lost. Still, it's only a game. Come on, it's getting cold and dark here, and I've a cab waiting. I'll stand you tea at the hotel—with toasted muffins, lots of butter on them."

I knew very well that the Quoins and such friends and relatives as they had brought with them would be entertained at a post-match tea by the hospitable Aston Villa management and team. So I guessed at once that Raffles, coming to fetch Paula and myself to the tea, had overheard the disturbing marital confidences she had made to me—and he was trying to make things easier for Paula by whisking her off to the hotel in order to give her a chance to calm down a bit and steel herself before she had to face the others.

I did my best to help him maintain a light, soothingly casual conversation over the buttered muffins. But there was no way we could save Paula from the ordeal of dinner on the nine o'clock train back to London that evening.

The whole team was in the restaurant-car, with its red-shaded gas-mantles, its gilt-bobbled velvet window curtains, immaculate napery, sparkling glass and silver, and its deft, deferential stewards. Seating was four to a table, and Raffles made a point, since nobody else seemed anxious to do so, of our sitting with Paula and Alan Gethlin.

Normally, there would have been competition to sit at table with Paula, but tonight was different. The air of depression in the restaurant-car, filled mostly with Quoins players and their supporters, was due not to the mere fact of defeat but to the discreditable manner of it. Everyone was so intensely sorry for Paula that they were afraid even to look at her.

Fortunately, perhaps, Fry was not present; he had had to go on up to Edinburgh on business connected with his magazine. What he may have said to Alan Gethlin in the visitors' changing-room at Villa Park after the match, I dared not imagine. C. B. Fry rather resembled Julius Caesar in appearance—and when he felt himself to have been stabbed in the back, Fry's reproaches could be as humiliating to the assassin as was Caesar's *Et tu, Brute*!

Yet Alan Gethlin seemed quite unaware that he had made himself a pariah, an untouchable, who never again would be invited to play any game whatever for a team captained by C. B. Fry.

Poor Paula, though silent and very pale, held her chin bravely high. She suffered, I knew how she suffered, but Alan Gethlin seemed not to know, let alone care. He looked a normal enough fellow, with normal sensibility. Never particularly talkative, such remarks as he made were casual, unexceptionable, and he ate with appetite. Yet, in the light of what Paula had confided to me, I sensed that Alan Gethlin was not with us. His seeming attentiveness when he was addressed was superficial; the expressions on his quite good-looking face were sufficiently responsive to the conversation, such as it was, but his brown eyes had nothing to do with it. They reflected some fascinated, gleeful, sly preoccupation with a life lived inside his own brown-haired skull—the life of his criminal *alter ego*, The Firefly.

I was troubled for Paula.

I said to Raffles, when I had a drink with him late that night at his chambers in The Albany, "I know you overheard what Paula confided to me. What d'you think about it, Raffles?"

"I'm afraid it's serious, Bunny. Alan Gethlin's obsession with devising and vicariously sharing in the criminal adventures of his Firefly has totally corrupted him. It's breaking up his marriage and it's ruined him now with Charles Fry. And Gethlin doesn't care! He's not only making himself untouchable but he's also *unreachable*—as Paula has found."

"I'm very fond of her," I said. "I once almost proposed to her. But now—to try to help in a husband-and-wife situation—no, by God, I'd have nothing to do with meddling of that kind. It's always fatal."

"Proverbially so," Raffles said. "Join me in a spot more Scotch. I'm not training for the Aston Villa match now. That's all over."

"Not for Paula," I said, "when she sees the sports pages in tomorrow's newspapers." I felt very uneasy. "Raffles—this Firefly thing—doesn't it cut rather near the bone—*our* bone?"

"Oh, come on!" Raffles said wryly. "Luminous insects! Would you and I, Bunny, dream of leaving any signature whatever, let alone luminous insects, on the scenes of our occasional—nocturnal incursions?" He laughed. "We're not quite *that* amateur, I hope! We take pains to *avoid* police attention, not *invite* it. That's mere egotism. Besides, nothing helps the police like repetition. *Our* maxim is: Variety is the spice of crime. My dear Bunny, the Firefly and his luminous insects are the stuff of fiction. Real life is another thing again."

It was also, I reflected grimly as, having refused another drink, I walked on round to my flat in Mount Street, the black-and-white stuff of the newspapers—the sports pages which Paula would be seeing in just an hour or two. Poor Paula! Would the Aston Villa scandal prove indeed the last straw for her? Would she start divorce proceedings?

I did not want to know. I was a moral craven. I was

absolutely on Paula's side, but somehow, when any of my woman friends got into a divorce situation and needed a shoulder to cry on, I was apt to be clumsy. Their tears made me emotional. I had once almost proposed to Paula when she was single—and if now she should be about to become a *divorcée*, and I should find myself in an intimate posture with her, I might actually blurt out the fatal words. Being a criminal myself, I was no fit husband for Paula or any other nice woman. My way of life was precarious, my prospects were obscure, and it was as likely as not that on my wedding night I should find myself locked up in Wormwood Scrubs. It would not be fair to Paula; she had had quite enough marital shocks without getting involved with a man of straw like myself.

I did not trust my own emotional nature. So, to avoid the danger of seeing her, I deemed it prudent to go out of London for the time being. I went to stay with a friend who had a rough shoot in Norfolk, where I met a man who invited me wildfowling and pike-fishing on his fen near King's Lynn. I stayed out of London for several weeks—in fact, until my money ran out and compelled me to return to see if Raffles happened to have any.

As luck would have it, on the morning following my return to my Mount Street flat I was walking across Berkeley Square on my way to The Albany to put the bite on Raffles, when I saw Paula.

I stopped dead.

Snow was falling. The trees in the square were as pretty as a picture. So was Paula. She was wearing a coat and hat of astrakhan, which enhanced her blonde beauty with a Muscovite appeal. My instinct was to dodge from view into a shop doorway, but she had seen me. Her footsteps quickened as she approached. I had no option but to raise my silk hat with an apprehensive smile.

"Oh, Bunny," she exclaimed, giving me a small, gloved hand, "I'm *so* glad to see you—I've *so* much to talk to you about! Where can we go?"

"The Buttery at Forshaw and Jason's is just round in Piccadilly," I said, not daring to take her to my nearby flat, where anything might happen. "They do the best cup of hot chocolate in London."

"You know, of course," she said, "about the police questioning Alan."

"*Police?*" I said.

"Good heavens, Bunny," she said, "don't you read the newspapers?"

I had to explain that I had been away and had paid little attention to other newspapers than *Shooting Times, The Field,* and the *Fishing Gazette.*

"Well, they must be about the only ones," said Paula, "that haven't reported the awful things that have been happening! I'll tell you all about it over our chocolate."

She told me that two burglaries had been perpetrated, in different parts of the West End, that had attracted a good deal of attention because, in each case, the marauder had left behind, dangling from a piece of gut, a tiny metal insect painted with luminous paint.

"Don't you see, Bunny?" Paula said excitedly. "Some real-life criminal has stolen not only the trademark of Alan's fictional Firefly criminal but has actually used, in each robbery, a method invented by Alan!"

There crept over me, chillingly, a singular premonition.

"And, Bunny," Paula went on, "that's only the *start* of it. Two days after the first robbery, Alan got a strange-looking envelope in his mail. When he opened it, he found fifty pounds in it, in ten-pound notes, and a piece of paper on which was written, in pencilled capitals, 'Herewith author's royalties at twenty per cent. Firefly Two.'"

I sat frozen. I knew, beyond doubt, whose hand was at work here.

"Of course," said Paula, "I was horrified. I told Alan he must take the note and the money straight to the police. Bunny, he hesitated! He was *pleased* with himself because a criminal method he'd invented for fiction had proved feasible in fact! He seemed actually to think he was *entitled* to those—'royalties'! I simply seized the note and the money and took them to the police station myself."

"And then?" I said, swallowing hard.

"Two plainclothes detectives," said Paula, "came to our house in St. John's Wood. They told Alan that the money was, in fact, exactly one fifth of a sum that had been stolen. Well, you know how Alan has changed. That secretive, sly look he has now doesn't make a good impression. The detectives questioned him. It was obvious that they suspected he'd had a mental breakdown, due to his obsession with those Firefly stories of his, and actually committed a *real* robbery! They wanted to know what he'd done with the other four-fifths of the money. Bunny, if it hadn't been that Alan had an alibi, I think they'd have taken him away, under arrest, then and there!"

I did not know what to say—though I realised, of course, that Raffles, whatever his motives for this dangerous game he was playing, would have contrived to make sure that Alan Gethlin had an alibi.

"Well, Bunny," Paula said, "it's been a long time since *anything* has really cracked that—that cocoon of preoccupation Alan's woven round himself. But that visit from the detectives did it. *They* got to him all right! They shook him. He had a Firefly story half-finished, but he couldn't get on with it. He seemed to have doubts about it. He was restless. He kept walking to and fro in his study, hour after hour. But the shock he'd had gradually wore off. He got going again. And then—oh, Bunny! The *second* envelope came!"

"'Royalties'?" I said huskily.

"Twenty per cent," said Paula, "of a bearer bond—negotiable bond—robbery. And the detectives came back—*with* another of the luminous insects! Well, the Firefly angle of the first robbery had got into the papers. We'd had reporters at the house. And when the detectives came again, it was obvious, as they interrogated Alan, that they now suspected he was hand-in-glove with some clever criminal—the criminal taking four-fifths of the money and Alan using the other fifth as a means of getting publicity for his Firefly stories. All of a sudden, people are reading them who never even heard of them till all this happened. It does look terribly suspicious!"

"I can see that, Paula," I said, easing a finger round inside my collar.

"Alan had an alibi again," she said, "but the detectives gave him a really terrible time. He can't write. He's in such dread of a third envelope arriving that—well, I'm afraid he'll have a complete nervous breakdown. I'm *so* glad to have seen you, Bunny, because—will you and Raffles come to dinner with us tonight and sort of help take Alan out of himself? I'm really frightened for him! *Do* please come. Promise!''

In the circumstances, I had no option but to promise—and as soon as I had put Paula into a cab, I hurried across Piccadilly to The Albany. I found Raffles in.

"So there you are, Bunny," he said. "You're quite a stranger!"

"Raffles," I said, "I've just seen Paula!"

"Have you now," he said, giving me an interested look. "And how is the Gethlin household reacting to the crimes of Firefly Two?"

I told him.

"So," said Raffles. "We progress. You know, Bunny, I've missed your help in my clandestine manoeuvres to save Paula's marriage."

"Damn you," I said, "you never gave me inkling of your intentions!"

"How could I," said Raffles, "when you'd made it so emphatically clear to me that you'd have nothing whatever to do with meddling in a husband-and-wife situation?"

Hoist with my own dogmatism, I was devoid of a riposte.

"Don't look so worried," Raffles said, pouring me a whiskey-and-soda, "you'll have your share, of course, of eighty per cent of the proceeds of the Firefly Two robberies."

"I hardly feel entitled," I muttered uneasily.

"Nonsense," said Raffles. "A partnership is a partnership. If it'll make you feel less guilty for absenting yourself, Bunny, I'll admit that I *had* no plan in mind when we last discussed the Gethlin situation. It was only afterwards, when curiosity prompted me to make a careful study of the entire canon of Alan Gethlin's tales of the Firefly, that I saw a possibility of taking fruitful action."

Raffles took a drink, his grey eyes thoughtful.

"They're corrupt tales, Bunny. I can understand why devising them *ad infinitum* gradually corrupted Alan Gethlin himself—and, for all he knows, or in his corrupted state cares, may also be corrupting the more naïve and sedulous members of his readership.''

Uncomfortably, I thought of the records I secretly penned of my own clandestine experiences with Raffles. But I kept *my* manuscripts well hidden. They were for my own eyes only, not for publication. Moreover, I had taken the precaution, as a safeguard against their accidental perusal by an immature or unduly corruptible posterity, of adding to my will a codicil that provided for the destruction, unopened, of any sealed packages of mine which might posthumously come to light. I could hardly do more. Or less.

However, I took a rather deep gulp of my whisky-and-soda—as Raffles continued, ''From my close study of the Firefly series, Bunny, I found that, of the wealth of robbery methods Alan Gethlin has so far devised for his fictional criminal, most of them are too complex to be practicable in reality. I found only two that might actually work—as, put to the test, they fortunately did. So Alan Gethlin fully deserves his twenty per cent share of the proceeds—though I'm afraid he won't be able to keep his swag, as the police'll hand it over to the insurance companies whose clients have been mulcted by my experiment.''

''You understand, no doubt,'' I said, ''that you've stultified the rhythm and flow of Alan Gethlin's writing—and brought him to the brink of a nervous breakdown?''

''That was my intention, Bunny.''

''I've promised Paula that we'll dine with the Gethlins tonight, Raffles, and try to help take Alan out of himself.''

Raffles's grey eyes gave me a look I had come to know well.

''That's excellent, Bunny,'' he said. ''You make yourself useful, after all. If we're dining with the Gethlins tonight, we may be able to do better for Paula than help her take Alan temporarily out of himself. We may be able to complete our self-imposed task of taking the Firefly permanently out of Alan.''

Being at a loss to conceive what manoeuvre Raffles might now envisage, I was not in a relaxed mood when, that evening, the hansom conveying us to St. John's Wood jingled past the walls of Lord's Cricket Ground. Though only an occasional flake was now falling, snow was thick underfoot. The hoof-beats of our cab horse sounded muffled, and the familiar de-mesne of Lord's, so rich for Raffles and myself in memories of golden summers, lay now silent and deserted under its mantle of virgin white.

Cricket's greatest slogger, Gilbert Jessup, playing at Lord's on a famous occasion, once had hit a cricket ball for a record distance out of the ground. The ball, which had been bowled by A. J. Raffles, had landed, curiously enough, in the garden of Garamond House, the pleasant residence that Alan Gethlin had inherited from his father, who had been a respected figure in the world of fine printing and distinctive typefaces but mercifully had not lived to see his son's corruption made man-ifest in the Aston Villa *v*. Quoins soccer match.

Now, as our hansom came to a standstill at the gateway of Garamond House, the coach-drive and the lawns to either side of it were thickly carpeted with untrodden snow—and Raffles, pushing up the trap in the cab roof, told our jehu to take us on up the drive to the porch, as we did not want to get our feet wet.

Since we were wearing galoshes over our evening-dress shoes, I thought Raffles's request rather unnecessary, as did our cabbie, who grumbled audibly at having to climb down from his box, open the gate, and climb back up to his perch again merely in order that we might ride dry-shod right to the porch.

Our arrival must have been eagerly awaited—for, even as we alighted on to the porch steps and Raffles mollified our cabbie with a half-sovereign tip, the door of Garamond House was opened to us by Paula herself.

"Oh, I'm *so* glad you've arrived!" she exclaimed.

In the warm, tastefully furnished hall, as we kicked off our galoshes and a parlourmaid in demure black-and-white relieved us of our evening capes and silk hats, I thought that Paula was looking lovely, though evidently worried. She led us into the drawing-room, where we found Alan Gethlin, huddled in an armchair, gazing despondently into the flames of a log-fire.

"Alan," Paula said gently, laying a light hand on his

shoulder, "here they are."

With a convulsive start, Gethlin sprang to his feet, turning upon us a look so flinching and aghast that it betrayed instantly his fear that we were the detectives returned with the dire news that Firefly Two had struck again. Recovering himself with an obvious effort, Gethlin greeted us with a forced cordiality so overdone that it bordered on the neurotic.

"Shall we," said Paula, compassionately interrupting her husband's excessive but hollow expostulations of delight at seeing us, "have a glass of sherry?"

As she crossed the room to give the silken bellcord a tug, she raised her brows eloquently at Raffles and myself and rolled her lovely eyes in a deeply significant manner.

Nevertheless, our efforts to take Alan Gethlin out of himself met with minimal success. His pretence of attentiveness to our conversation was pathetically unconvincing. His thoughts were elsewhere, though it was obvious that the nature of his preoccupation had undergone a fundamental change.

He had aged beyond his twenty-nine years. There were dark circles round his eyes, but the look of secretive, shifty glee which had characterized them in his obsession with vicariously, in the form of his fictional Firefly, outwitting and ridiculing the police of two continents was now quite gone. Just two interviews with real-life, flesh-and-blood Scotland Yard detectives had stripped Gethlin naked of his smug literary illusions. The poor devil's eyes were haunted now with dread that the detectives would come down on him again as a result of some third depredation by the elusive Firefly Two.

With my knowledge that Raffles, alias Firefly Two, was indeed resolved upon some third manoeuvre of the kind, a hot wave of guilt engulfed me. I took a gulp of my sherry. I wanted to get out of here, but dinner seemed inordinately delayed— and suddenly I understood why. Paula's increasingly anxious glances at the drawing-room clock revealed the bitter truth to me. She had planned a gay dinner-party to take Alan out of himself—but the other guests were not going to turn up. Quite simply, Alan Gethlin had put himself outside the pale of decent society by stabbing England's most popular and irreproachable sportsman, C. B. Fry, foully in the back.

Poor Paula! Her dinner party, just the four of us, was not a success. The shadow of the Villa Park scandal brooded grimly over Garamond House, St. John's Wood.

"Paula," Raffles said, after we had risen from table and repaired to the drawing-room for coffee, "I only smoke Sullivans and I've left my cigarette-case in my cape-pocket. Will you excuse me for a moment? No, no, don't ring—I know just where our things were put."

Poor Paula; for her sake we stayed on for a while, but even Raffles was beginning to show the strain of making conversation, and it was a relief to escape at last into the cold, white, midnight silence of the fallen snow.

"In Baker Street, not far off," Raffles said, as we walked away from Garamond House and passed Lord's Cricket Ground, "there's a horse-drawn coffee-stall I know of—a godsend to the flotsam and jetsam, the waifs and strays, of the London night. Tell me, Bunny—what fictional character, much more famous than The Firefly, was domiciled in Baker Street?"

"Sherlock Holmes," I said, puzzled.

"And what, not so very long ago, did his creator do—for reasons best known to himself?"

"He killed Holmes."

"Thereby exercising a right," Raffles said, "exclusive to a character's creator. And now, Bunny, you and I will exercise our own right to kill an hour or so at the Baker Street coffee-stall, then we'll return to Garamond House."

My heart sank into my galoshes.

"You'll have noted, Bunny," said Raffles, as we walked back to the Gethlin residence after an hour spent among the dregs of London night life warming themselves at the naphtha flares of the coffee-stall, "—you'll have noted that, when we arrived at Garamond House tonight, the snow lay untrodden on the lawns and coach-drive?"

"I observed that fact," I admitted. "What of it?"

"Simply this," said Raffles. "I knew we might need to retrace our steps up that drive without leaving prints of them in the virgin snow. I therefore made our cabbie drive us right up to the porch, so that we can now place our feet carefully in the wheel ruts and hoofmarks.''

"Good God, Raffles!'' I said, taken aback by his forethought.

"Firefly Two,'' Raffles went on, "has now to enter and to exit Garamond House without leaving a trace of how it was done. To go in by a window without disturbing the snow that cushions the sills is out of the question. It would call for levitation. On the other hand, the front door is certain now to be bolted. Still, that presents no problem—because when I absented myself briefly from the drawing-room to get my cigarette-case, I found, as I expected, that Paula's housemaids and cook had sat down to their own dinner in the kitchen. I had the hall to myself quite long enough to remove the screws from the bolt-brackets and substitute screws so almost-threadless that they'll yield when the door is pushed from the outside— and I may add that there's a thick coir doormat just on the inside!''

Accordingly, when Raffles exerted a steady pressure on the front door of Garamond House, now dark and silent, the fall of the bolt-brackets on the doormat was virtually inaudible. We stole in. Raffles soundlessly closed the door. We stood tensely listening. All was still.

"Bunny,'' Raffles whispered, "when I was alone briefly in the hall, I glanced into one or two of the rooms that open from it. I found Alan Gethlin's study—and I saw there the object which we're now going to steal. Its dimensions are such that it could not possibly have been unseen in our possession when Paula saw us off at the front door tonight.''

His hand closed on my arm. He steered me forward in the darkness. I heard a faint sound as he turned a doorknob. I felt carpet under my galoshes as he steered me a pace or two further forward.

"We're now in Alan's study,'' he whispered. "What do you see?''

My scalp suddenly tingled. Hovering before my eyes, in the stygian darkness, was a tiny glow of luminosity.

"A firefly,'' Raffles whispered, "—fashioned in metal by our invaluable 'fence' and criminal craftsman, Ivor Kern. Stay where you are.''

I stood rooted, the pulse pounding in my temples, as eerily in the darkness the luminous bug floated away before my starting eyes, then remained motionless, hovering, subtly inimical. "I've hung the firefly on Alan's desk lamp."

"Bunny"—I heard again Raffles's whisper—"I now need both hands free to replace the front-door bolt brackets with the original screws. Here, take this—hold it under your cape."

The object I felt put into my kid-gloved hands was large but quite light, with four awkward corners. And I had to hold it clasped to my side by the pressure of my arm when, Raffles having soundlessly but securely screwed back the front-door bolts, we regained the porch. For he then, in the faint, spectral snowlight from the lawns, placed in each of my hands something almost impalpable.

"Gut," he whispered, "well-greased. It's looped over the bolt-arm of the lower bolt. You're holding the gut-ends. I'm holding the ends of similar gut looped over the bolt-arm of the upper bolt. Now, if we pull gently but firmly on the gut-ends, we shall feel the bolts sliding into place. All right? Good. Now—pull *downward* on the gut and you'll feel the bolt-arms turning down. Right? Good. Now, then—release one end of the gut and pull on the other. The gut will then slide out through the minute crack between the door edge and the door-frame. All right? Well done, Bunny! The door is again bolted. All we have to do now is look for an owl hansom—and we'll probably find a stray cabbie regaling himself with a hot drink at the Baker Street coffee-stall."

This, as it happened, we did. And when presently, in Raffles's comfortable living-room in The Albany, I downed a double whisky, neat, to recover from the shock of seeing for myself the unique object we had stolen from Alan Gethlin's study, Raffles adjured me to keep an eye open for Paula during the next few days.

To this end, and thinking that if she should chance to be stopping in Piccadilly, the continued snowy weather might tempt her to drop in at the Buttery of Forshaw & Jason's for a hot chocolate, I made a point of dropping in there every morning myself.

Sure enough, on the third morning after the nocturnal

events at Garamond House, I was sitting at a table in the Buttery, and in the act of lighting a cigarette, when suddenly a slim, black-gloved hand arrested my arm.

"Oh, Bunny," Paula exclaimed, looking radiantly attractive in her astrakhan coat and hat, "I'm *so* glad to see you! I've *so* much to tell you! You'll never believe it, but d'you know, on the very night you and Raffles came to dinner, Firefly Two, in some absolutely inexplicable way, broke into our *own house!*"

"Good God, Paula!" I said. "Was anything stolen?"

"A picture, Bunny," she said—"a unique picture of a debonair man in evening-dress, with cape and silk hat *and,* Bunny, a *black mask*! Don't you see? It was the framed, original drawing that was used, reduced in size, to illustrate the jacket of Alan's first book. Bunny, it was the drawing, the artist's conception, of that dreadful criminal Alan created and was becoming utterly corrupted by—The Firefly!"

"And now that unique drawing's been stolen?" I said, affecting stupefaction. "Poor Alan, he must be deeply upset."

"Oh, he is, Bunny," said Paula. "It's absolutely the last straw for him. He's too terrified to go on with his Firefly series, in case that appalling real-life criminal, Firefly Two, uses the ideas, pays those awful corrupt royalties for them, and brings Scotland Yard down on Alan again. So he's sat down and finished that story he couldn't get on with—and, Bunny, d'you know what he's done in it? Oh, I'm so happy about it! *He's killed the Firefly!*"

"Well, Paula," I said, "the right to kill the character he created is, I suppose, Alan's—exclusively." I laid my hand on hers. "I'll tell Raffles your news. He'll be interested to hear it."

"Yes, *do* tell him, Bunny," Paula said. "I like him *so* much. I think Raffles is quite the nicest man in London."

A trifle put out by Paula's tactlessness in overlooking present company, I withdrew my hand from hers.

"*Ante Omnia Verbum*," I thought to myself, philosophically, "—'In the Beginning was the Word.'"

But I made no comment. For the last word must be always, by immemorial tradition, the privilege of the fair.

11

A VENUS AT LORD'S

"Sundays in London are seldom exhilarating, Bunny," remarked A. J. Raffles, "but at least they offer this parade of the reigning beauties of society and the stage."

"A pleasing hebdomadaly custom, Raffles," I concurred.

Like a good many other citizens, we were sauntering in Hyde Park and admiring the *toilettes* of the reigning beauties as they rode to and fro in open carriages driven by cockaded coachmen.

The jingling of the high-stepping horses mingled harmoniously with the melodies disseminated from the bandstand by musicians of the Grenadier Guards, and swans floated regally on the sunny waters of the nearby Serpentine.

Immaculate in morning dress, his keen face tanned, a pearl in his cravat, Raffles drew my attention to an approaching carriage.

"Here comes the carriage," he said, "of a lady who once gave me a keepsake."

"How romantic of her!" I said.

"I value it highly," said Raffles, "—even though she gave almost identical keepsakes to eleven gentlemen from Philadelphia, Pennsylvania."

To the lady in the passing carriage, who had with her now only one gentleman, Raffles raised his grey topper courteously, so I likewise raised my own.

The gentleman did not raise his, for he did not see us. But the lady, exquisite in the shade of her parasol, accorded us a graceful inclination, and I seemed to detect in her lovely eyes, as she smiled at Raffles, a glimmer of mischief.

This intrigued me.

"Raffles," I said, as the carriage jingled on by and we continued our promenade, "isn't that lady the celebrated Mrs. Langtry—'The Jersey Lily'?"

"Yes, Bunny," he said, "that's Lillie Langtry—*née* Emily Charlotte Le Breton. She's the daughter of an eminent divine—the Dean of Jersey, Channel Islands—and is the first lady of social consequence to have defied convention and, much to the horror of society circles, appeared as a professional actress on the stage of a London theatre."

The music of the Grenadier Guards was fading behind us. A distant shouting grew audible. It came from the Marble Arch side of the park, where a space was reserved for soapbox oratory, and the fulminations were those of Sunday agitators preaching the overthrow of the established social order.

As it happened, however, we were going the other way, towards the Hyde Park Corner exit.

"I still was in my last year at school," said Raffles, "so I didn't see the theatrical debut of the Dean of Jersey's beautiful, well-bred daughter. Actually, it was at the Haymarket Theatre, Bunny. She appeared there in the role of Kate Hardcastle in a revival by the famous Bancrofts of Oliver Goldsmith's *She Stoops to Conquer*."

"With her beauty," I said, "the eminent Dean's daughter can hardly have failed to conquer!"

"As to that," said Raffles, "she certainly, a few years later, conquered me—and the eleven gentlemen from Philadelphia, who were in England to make a debut of their own."

"As actors, I presume?"

"No, Bunny, they were more unusual than that—for Americans. They were cricketers. They were the only American cricket team to have visited this country, so their arrival created a good deal of interest. In the circumstances, they were invited to make their first London appearance in a match at Lord's."

"Good God!" I exlaimed. "*Americans* actually played at Lord's, home ground of the Marylebone Cricket Club, the legislative panjandrums of the game?"

Raffles assured me that I should find the match—M.C.C. *versus* Gentlemen of Philadelphia—fully recorded in *Wisden's Cricket Almanac*.

"A vivid account of the event," Raffles said, "was also written by the famous American war correspondent, Mr. Richard Harding Davis. And in fact, Bunny, it was a damned good match. The Philadelphians turned out to be as handy performers at cricket as they were at polo, racquets, golf, or any other gentleman's game."

"Did you play in the match, Raffles?"

"I did indeed, Bunny, and thoroughly enjoyed it. And after the match, both teams went to the Haymarket Theatre to see Lillie Langtry, then appearing there in *As You Like It*, in the role of Rosalind. She was the toast of the town—'The Jersey Lily'! The Philadelphia chaps were captivated by her."

Emerging from the park, we turned to our left. In the noonday heat and Sabbath torpor, lower Piccadilly was deserted except for a pedestrian here and there, a hansom or two, and a Piccadilly flowerseller mooching along ahead of us up the slope, her button boots down-at-heel under the hems of her dowdy skirts, petticoats, and apron, a yellowing straw boater on her head, her basket of blossoms on her arm.

"It so chanced," Raffles went on, "that the match against the Philadelphians was an important one for me, as it counted as the last of the qualifying matches I had to play in to be elected a member of the M.C.C. So I felt that the decent thing to do, to show my appreciation, would be to make a gesture for the Philadelphians. I thought it would give them pleasure if I could wangle for them a personal meeting with Lillie Langtry."

"But did you know her yourself, Raffles?"

"No, I hadn't yet had that privilege, Bunny. But after the *matinée* next day at the Haymarket, I presented myself at the stage door and handed in a fine bouquet of lilies and roses, along with my visiting-card on which I'd written a message asking if Mrs. Langtry would consent to receive me on a matter of significance to transatlantic good relations."

"And *did* she receive you, Raffles?" I asked.

Before he could answer, a cry of outrage attracted our attention. The outcry came from the Piccadilly flowerseller up the slope ahead of us. Hawking her wares, she had waylaid a couple of men. One of them I knew slightly. Thickset, frock-coated, silk-hatted, he had a handsome black moustache.

The other man was taller, slim and erect in cycling knick-erbockers, a Norfolk jacket, and a rather small corduroy cap. His hair, beard, and eyebrows were vividly auburn in the sunshine, and he evidently had passed some remark to which the flowerseller took exception.

"*Press?*" she shouted at him. "Wotcher mean, 'Gen'le-men o' the press pass free'? Not wiv me they don't! Them rosebuds is a tanner apiece an' it don't make no odds to me if you're gen'lemen o' the press or gen'lemen o' the royal bleedin' bedchamber!"

"Ah-hah!" said the red-bearded man. "A fellow radical, I take it?"

"Don't answer him, honey, he's teasing you," said the black-moustached man, and he patted the flowerseller's cheek consolingly.

"Tyke yer 'ands off me!" she shrilled.

"Powerful words," said the red-bearded man. "My friend's advances to the fair sex rarely meet with such emphatic rejection. I congratulate you, young woman. Here you are—here, without prejudice to the right of the press to pass freely on its lawful occasions, is half-a-crown for two of your rosebuds."

"Blimey!" exclaimed the flowerseller, appeased. "'Arf-a-crahn! Thanks, mister—ta muchly!"

Spotting a possible customer on the far side of the street, she hastened across to waylay him. The two men she had just transacted business with came on down the slope.

"Red rosebuds, Harris," said the man with the auburn beard to his companion, as they adjusted the blossoms in their buttonholes, "will mark us as sympathizers with the subversive orators we're about to listen to in Hyde Park. They'll be inspired to more eloquent perorations. But you heard that flowerseller, with her '*Blimey, 'arf-a-crahn!*' It's an instance of what I'm driving at, Harris, when I argue that our Board schools should be made to teach a logically simplified English and a uniform enunciation as a primary step to social reform."

As the two men passed Raffles and myself, the black-moustached man tilted his silk hat to me. I uplifted my own topper in response. The red-bearded man, walking with a curi-

ously jaunty step, merely shot us an alert glance, his blue eyes
sparkling with a vivacity that betokened an exceptionally active intellect. His voice receded as he went on talking to his
companion.

"Who's your black-moustached acquaintance, Bunny?"
Raffles asked me.

"He's a chap I met once or twice when I was failing to
make my mark as a journalist," I explained. "He edits a literary review—published every Saturday. He's said to be irresistible to women. As for the red-bearded chap, I believe he's on
the staff of the review—the music and drama critic or something. But you were about to tell me, Raffles—did Mrs. Langtry
receive you when you handed in your flowers and message at
the Haymarket Theatre?"

Raffles nodded, taking out his gold half-hunter for a glance
at it.

"We're a bit early for lunch at that Jermyn Street restaurant," he said. "Let's stroll up Half Moon Street and round
through Berkeley Square."

Scarcely a person was to be seen in the sweltering Sabbath
streets as Raffles went on to tell me that Mrs. Langry had
received him in her dressing-room.

"She was chaperoned, of course, by her dresser and her
personal maid," said Raffles. "Bunny, you've seen Lillie
Langtry this morning in the high summer of her beauty—but
you should have seen her, as I did, in her springtime! She was
quite divine. She called for a vase and arranged my flowers with
her own graceful hands as she listened to what I had to say."

"And what was that, Raffles?"

"I explained to her, Bunny, that I had just become a
member of the M.C.C.—and she said, with sensitive understanding, that no doubt that was socially advantageous for a
young man-about-town. I admitted it. I said that one of the
advantages was that I could now use the Members' Restaurant
at Lord's. I told her that, by way of celebration, I was planning
to give a luncheon party there to eleven gentleman cricketers
from Philadelphia. I explained how deeply they—and I—had
admired her in the role of Rosalind, and what a wonderful
surprise it would be for my eleven guests, and what a lift it

would give to the cause of cricket in the United States, if she would consent to grace the luncheon with her presence."

"Good heavens, Raffles!"

"She hesitated, Bunny."

"And no wonder! You, a stranger to her, Raffles, were asking the gently bred daughter of an eminent divine to lunch with you and eleven other men equally strangers to her!"

"Ah, but the venue of the luncheon was *Lord's*, Bunny," Raffles said. "That weighed with her. I sensed it as she stood toying with a rose and looking at me thoughtfully with those wonderful eyes. And at last—impulsively, Bunny, as when she defied convention and made her first stage appearance in *She Stoops to Conquer*—she reached a decision. She smiled most graciously and said she couldn't possibly decline an invitation that I assured her would be helpful to the cause of transatlantic cricket."

"Adorable woman!" I exclaimed.

"And never more adorable," said Raffles, "than at my luncheon party. She was enchanting—a Venus at Lord's. My Philadelphian friends date time from the occasion. I had a letter from one of them just the other day."

"You mentioned a keepsake, Raffles," I reminded him.

· "Twelve keepsakes, in fact," he said. "To mark the success of my luncheon party, Lillie Langtry allowed a special photograph to be taken of her. She gave each of us a copy, inscribed to us individually, as a keepsake. It's a unique photograph of her, Bunny. For charm and allure, no other photograph of 'The Jersey Lily' can compare with it. And only the eleven gentlemen of Philadelphia—and myself, of course—have copies of it."

As I expressed my envy, we emerged from Berkeley Square and crossed Piccadilly to St. James's Street. Sentries in scarlet tunics and bearskin busbies guarded the modest palace at the far end where the Lord Chamberlain censored plays before allowing them to pollute theatres, and comptrollers, equerries, and other ponderable persons of the royal entourage had their simple lodgings. The stamping of the sentries rang oddly loud in the Sabbath quiet.

We turned to our left, into Jermyn Street. Only a solitary

woman was in sight here. Between the discreetly elegant establishments of hatters, haberdashers and snuff-blenders whose great-grandfathers had catered to the refined tastes of Beau Brummell and Beau Nash, the lone female was slouching along, about a hundred yards ahead, her back to us, a basket on her arm, a yellowing straw boater on her head.

"Raffles," I said, "there's that flowerseller again."

"Yes, Bunny," he said, "and she seems to have spotted something lying on the pavement. It looks like a wallet—probably dropped by some gentleman."

The wench quickened her pace. She bent down to pick up her find. She seemed to have difficulty in doing so. She scrabbled at it with her fingers, but it unaccountably resisted her efforts.

"She stoops," Raffles murmured, "but not to conquer!"

Suddenly he gripped my arm, jerked me into the shop doorway of a famous shirtmaker.

"Bunny, note that open window on the second floor of the house next but one to the Turkish Baths along there. I saw a curtain move at that window," Raffles said. "That wallet's been glued to the pavement, and the young woman's being watched!"

The same suspicion seemed to dawn on the flowerseller. She straightened up, glancing about her. From the open window above her sounded a laugh, half-suppressed. She heard it, looked up quickly. The curtain was swept aside—and three young men of elegant but asinine appearance were grinning down at her. They had glasses in their hands.

I saw the flowerseller flush deeply as she realised that she had been gulled.

"Bastards!" she shouted. "Garn, get aht of it!"

Her anger and embarrassment delighted them. "Miaouw!" they chorussed. "Miaouw, pussycat—scratch, scratch!"

A youth with classical but vapid features and golden hair leaned from the window, calling, "Puss, puss—here, puss—catch!"

He tossed the flowerseller a coin. It flashed golden in the

sunshine and tinkled at her feet. It was a sovereign.

"Too late," Raffles muttered, his grip iron-hard on my arm, "—too late for alms! They've hurt her pride."

Sure enough, the flowerseller kicked the coin into the gutter. They roared with laughter.

"Stinkers!" she shrilled. "Oh, you rotten, stuck-up, big-headed—"

Her voice broke in the passion of her fury and humiliation—and in her down-at-heel button boots, with her basket on her arm, she ran off along the street.

"Well, well," Raffles said grimly. "West End 'bloods,' Bunny—degenerate heirs of the wits of yore—indulging an imbecile sense of humour to wile away the tedium of a sultry Sabbath. How many inoffensive people have they shamed this morning with that cruel practical joke? Come on!"

We emerged from the shop doorway. From that open window on the second floor of the house next but one to the Turkish Baths sounded roars of laughter and the pop of a champagne cork.

Raffles kicked the wallet loose from the pavement, picked the wallet up, pocketed it.

"We'll create an opportunity to return this to its owner at an early date, Bunny," he said. "Meantime, note the brass plate on the door of the house: 'Prince Regent House—Service Chambers for Gentlemen.' H'm, that depends on what you mean by the word 'gentleman.' Mark the place well, Bunny. We'll get Ivor Kern, our invaluable 'fence,' to put one of his snoops on to finding out who occupies the second-floor chambers in that house. Mark it well."

Walking on past the house, we came to the excellent French restaurant where we had planned to lunch.

"You go on in, Bunny," Raffles said. "I have other business. If the flower girl had been going to Piccadilly Circus, where her colleagues foregather, she'd have turned left out of Jermyn Street here. She didn't. She turned right. So she may be going to her home. I'm going to follow her and find out where she lives."

"With what object?" I said uneasily.

"With the object," Raffles said, his grey eyes hard, "of arranging the revenge of the flower girl on the Joker of Jermyn Street."

He walked off and left me.

And he himself, that hot Sunday, lunched on bread-and-cheese at a pub on the corner of a street in Lambeth, south of the river.

"It was the street where the flower girl lives," he told me, three days later.

He had routed me out from my Mount Street flat just as I was sitting down to breakfast. Giving me no time to snatch even a cup of coffee, he hustled me into a four-wheeler cab he had waiting.

"The landlord of the pub," he went on, as the cab rattled us off westward, "knew all about the flower girl. Her name's Elsie Wiggins. She's nineteen and lives with her father, one Bill Wiggins. He's a pugilist—which fits in rather helpfully for us, due to that letter I told you I had the other day from one of the eleven gentlemen in Philadelphia."

"How does the letter fit in?" I asked, puzzled.

"You'll see soon," said Raffles. "Anyway, Bill Wiggins came into the pub while I was there. The landlord pointed him out to me. I got into conversation with him, bought him a drink. I'm afraid that as a boxer he's pretty well over the hill. I gathered that he picks up a quid or two now and then, pinch-hitting as a substitute in bouts at The Ring, Blackfriars, and Hoxton Baths, but mostly he ekes out by doing casual labour."

Raffles took out his watch, glanced at it.

"I've arranged to meet him this morning at Hyde Park Corner. We've got to be circumspect, Bunny. Elsie has her pride—and a temper that matches her hair, which is almost as red as the beard of that drama critic chap who bought her rosebuds on Sunday. To win her confidence, which is necessary to my plans for her, I must get well in first with her father."

The cab pulled up alongside the traffic island at Hyde Park Corner. The sun was just beginning to break through the muggy morning mist. Near the equestrian statue of the Duke of Wellington, a man was standing. Tall and long-armed, with a leathery, somewhat eroded face, he wore a blue serge suit, a bowler hat, and a watch-chain with medals on it. He moved forward as the cab pulled up.

"Ah, there you are, Mr. Wiggins," said Raffles. "Hop in! This is Mr. Manders, a friend of mine." He called to the cabbie, "Take us to the Star-and-Garter at Richmond. Go the short way, through Richmond Park."

"Right you are, guv'," said the cabbie, and gingered up his nag.

As we bowled off at a brisk clip through Knightsbridge, Raffles offered Mr. Wiggins and myself a Sullivan apiece from his cigarette-case.

"Well now, Mr. Wiggins," he said, "I was just telling Mr. Manders here that, when I had the luck to make your acquaintance on Sunday, I mentioned to you a letter I'd had from an American gentleman. Bunny, you remember my telling you about him and his ten friends—all-round sportsmen, true Corinthians?"

"I recall it distinctly," I admitted.

"The letter mentioned," said Raffles, "that they're sponsoring a young boxer they've discovered in Philadelphia. For the time being, they're keeping him out of American rings. When they spring him over there, they want him to make a sensation. Meantime, to get him experience, they've arranged a few good prelims over here for him. They've asked me to have a look at their boy and give them an opinion. But cricket's my game, rather than boxing, so it's lucky I happened to meet Mr. Wiggins on Sunday, Bunny. He's kindly agreed to give us the benefit of his extensive experience in British rings and have a look at this Philadelphia boy for us. I understand from the letter that the boy and his trainer, a Mr. Vincent Hoyt, will have arrived last week and gone to training quarters arranged for them alongside the Star-and-Garter at Richmond."

"Great place for trainin'," said Mr. Wiggins.

He was not a talkative man, Elsie's father. It was Raffles, glancing now and then at his watch, who bore the brunt of the conversation as we jingled through Hammersmith, clip-clopped across Barnes Common, and trundled up Priory Lane to the great wrought-iron gateway to Richmond Park.

"The Star-and-Garter's about a mile ahead, on the far side

of the park," Raffles said, as we clattered through the gateway. "It's pretty historic, this park. It was once a royal hunting preserve."

The sun, which had dispelled the mist, shone down on the road which meandered, dust-white, over the wide, lonely expanse of undulating grassland dotted with gnarled old oak trees. Deer browsed here and there, circled over by jackdaws sounding their harsh cries.

"The man who founded the city of Richmond, Virginia, came from here," said Raffles. "And Miss Fanny Burney records in her famous *Diary* a disconcerting experience she had here. It seems she was taking a peaceful walk here, all by herself, when suddenly poor old mad King George the Third, making strange grimaces, jumped out at her from behind a tree. Naturally, she was alarmed by the royal apparition, and she took to her heels. The King ran after her, outstripping his courtiers—who were really his keepers, of course. He was making wild gestures and screaming 'Miss Burney! Miss Burney!'—and he finally got her cornered against the rails of a deer enclosure."

"What did he do to her?" asked Mr. Wiggins.

"He invited her to tea," said Raffles. "Hullo, look over there! Can that be the boxer chap we're looking for?"

About a couple of hundred yards distant from the road, a brawny fellow wearing numerous sweaters and a cloth cap was jogging away up a rough track that skirted a coppice of trees. He was followed by man in a sweater and a brown bowler hat who was toiling along on a bicycle.

"Yes, sir," said Mr. Wiggins, "that'll be the Yank boy an' 'is trainer doin' their road work."

Raffles called to our cabbie to pull up.

"The boy's got good legs—he moves very sooent," said Mr. Wiggins, as we sat watching the young pugilist and his trainer recede up the slope.

Suddenly, almost as they reached the brow of it, half-a-dozen or more men, brandishing cudgels, burst out from the shade of the trees and hurled the trainer from his bike.

"Nobblers, by God!" Bill Wiggins roared. "Look at 'em—goin' for the pug's kneecaps with them bleedin' cudgels!''

He flung open the cab door, went off at a run up the grassy slope. Raffles and I followed. The trainer, his bicycle, and one of the attackers were locked in a tangle, rolling over and over in the bracken. The young boxer was striking out at the ruffians as they circled him warily, now darting in to aim a blow at his kneecaps, now leaping back, agile as wolves, from his punches.

The slope was steep. I stumbled. Raffles gripped my arm.

"Steady, Bunny," he said.

Bill Wiggins, well ahead of us, both fists swinging, plunged into the fight, roaring, "Garn, get aht of it!"

The reinforcement was too much for the nobblers. They dived back into the coppice, the last of them scrambling, panic-stricken, on all fours into the undergrowth as Raffles and I reached the scene.

"You O.K., Johnnie?" the trainer was anxiously asking his fighter.

"Sure," said Johnnie, "—thanks to this gent." He shook hands cordially with Bill Wiggins. "But, Jesus—what kind of a country *is* this?"

"That's a good question," said Raffles. "It's one of many you're apt to find yourselves asking, concerning the ins and outs of British prizefighting—and, by Jove, nobody's better equipped to answer them for you than Mr. Wiggins here. He knows the game inside out. As a matter of fact, we were on our way to visit you. I know your sponsors—and they wouldn't be at all happy to hear of this thing that's just happened."

"Damn right," said the trainer, licking his bruised knuckles.

"Frankly, gentlemen," Raffles said, "I think you need, as newcomers over here, the help of someone with long experience of British boxing and its parasites. Otherwise, you could run into worse trouble. Look here, I suggest that we repair to the Star-and-Garter and generally review the situation. Our cab's waiting down there, and we can put this bicycle, which seems to have been rather bent in the affray, on the cab roof."

"This gent makes sense, Vinnie," the young Philadelphia pugilist said to his trainer. "Come on, let's go talk it over with him."

The outcome of the subsequent conference was pleasing to Raffles.

"The point is, Bunny," he explained to me later, in private, "Bill Wiggins now has a job after his own heart. Thanks to his vigorous intervention, he's been added to the Philadelphian payroll. He'll be a useful sparring partner for Johnnie Jessop in his training and a damned good second for the boy to have in his corner. And now, with the excuse of inquiring about Johnnie's progress, I can drop in occasionally on Bill Wiggins at his home. That way, I can get to know Elsie and win her confidence."

"What a bit of luck," I said, "that ambush happening!"

"Well, to tell the truth," said Raffles, "I arranged it myself—with the help of Ivor Kern, our invaluable 'fence.' I had him set one of his snoops to study the curriculum of Johnnie and his trainer, Mr. Hoyt. They take that training run in Richmond Park twice a day—you can set your watch by them—and they invariably follow the same route. So I fixed it with Ivor Kern to hire those ruffians to stage their harmless ballet with cudgels."

"Good God, Raffles!" I exclaimed, thunderstruck.

"Meanwhile," he went on, "another of Ivor Kern's hirelings has been investigating the Joker of Jermyn Street for us. His name's Lord Anthony Dauntsey. He inherited the title, a fortune—and a valuable collection of signet rings. They're of the Regency period, Bunny. They're rings that once belonged to famous dandies, Beau Brummell and the like. I gather that those bygone 'bucks' are Dauntsey's heroes. He apes what he imagines was their way of life, their mannerisms and conceits. Ivor Kern's snoop reports that Dauntsey invariably wears one or other of those rings when he dines out. No doubt they make a good subject for table talk. So the chances are that he keeps the collection handy—at his Jermyn Street chambers. You follow me?"

I nodded. And he gave me a wicked look.

"You'll hear from me anon," he said.

Anon turned out to be about a week later, when a note from him arrived at my Mount Street flat. The note asked me to drop round to The Albany, where he had his chambers, at eight o'clock that evening.

When I knocked on his door, it opened immediately. I stepped in—and my heart gave a great lurch as a gag was whipped over my mouth from behind.

"Don't struggle," said Raffles. "This is just an experiment, Bunny."

Tying the gag tightly, he took me by the arm, thrust me down into a saddlebag chair in his comfortable, gaslit living-room.

It being impossible for me to protest verbally against this extraordinary treatment, all I could do was stare at him with unconcealed but mute reproach.

"You must excuse my taking this liberty with you, Bunny," he said. "There's a purpose behind it." He glanced at the clock above his fireplace. "It's now a few seconds to eight. When the clock goes *ping*, start trying to loosen that gag by jaw movements alone. Remember, jaw only!'

Almost as he spoke, the clock went *ping*—and at once, mollified by his apology for his behaviour, I started to manipulate my lower jaw in such wise as might rid me of my oral impediment.

The clock uttered seven more melodious *pings*, then resumed its quiet ticking—scarcely audible to me as the breath began to whistle in my distended nostrils.

"Jaw only," Raffles warned me. "No hands!" Sitting on the arm of a chair facing me, he was watching my exertions with uncommon interest. "Beads are beginning to appear on your brow, Bunny," he told me. "That's what I like to see. Keep trying!"

My jaw-twitchings seemed to communicate themselves to my other muscles, causing me to writhe and contort myself in the saddlebag chair. While I was thus preoccupied, Raffles lighted a cigarette.

"On the pretext," he said, "of getting Bill Wiggins' opinion of the Philadelphian boxer's progress, I called at the Wiggins domicile in Lambeth the other evening. Elsie was there. I was pressed to stay for supper. Elsie whipped up a rather good dish, quite new to me. It's done with batter and is called toad-in-the-hole. One drinks stout with it. We had a jolly evening, and I'm in solid now with the Wigginses, Bunny, so we can proceed to the next step in arranging Elsie's revenge on Beau Dauntsey of Jermyn Street. Meantime, how are you getting along?''

I mewed through my gag.

"That's right," said Raffles. "Persevere. I'll get a drink ready for you."

Taking a decanter from the tantalus on his table, he mixed a couple of whisky-and-sodas. Sipping his own appreciatively, he placed the other within my reach. At this, I redoubled my efforts to ungag myself.

"So far," Raffles said, "you've been at it for twenty minutes. I see that your pores are now well open. You're perspiring freely. The beads are trickling down and beginning to saturate the gag. Are you becoming aware of a kind of sweet flavour?''

I snorted affirmatively.

"Good," said Raffles. "That flavour, Bunny, is the sweet taste of revenge. I've prepared the gag on the poultice principle. It's a lady's silk stocking partly filled with powdered sugar. As your rising temperature and copious perspiration melts the sugar, it trickles away down your chin, causing the poultice-gag to become progressively thinner—and therefore, if my theory proves correct in practice, looser."

His theory was indeed correct—for, just as three mellow *pings* from the clock announced a quarter-to-nine, the gag, wasted by deliquescence, slid down my chin. Intensely relieved, I drew deep, gasping breaths and gulped my waiting whisky-and-soda.

"Forty-five minutes exactly," Raffles said. "Splendid, Bunny! I have an identical poultice-gag, ready prepared, in my pocket—and we now know the time it should give us to do the job I have in mind. Now, you'd better have a wash. Your evening-dress collar looks a bit sticky and wilted, so I'll lend you one of mine. Then I'll stand you dinner at Frascati's in Oxford Street, the Tottenham Court Road end, which is handy for Russell Square, where we have a business appointment to keep—I hope!''

I had thought that our business appointment would be in

Jermyn Street, so I was at a loss to divine Raffles's intentions when, not long after eleven o'clock, we strolled past the Doric columns of the British Museum and turned into Russell Square.

The night was warm and muggy. In the extensive garden which, enclosed by tall iron railings, occupied the centre of the square, trees loomed up darkly against the background of lighted windows here and there in the surrounding residences. From a large hotel on the north side of the square sounded the music of violins.

"This central garden," Raffles said, "is reserved for the use of residents in the square. They have a key to its gates, of which there's one on each side. That hotel also has a key, which people who stay there can borrow if they wish to walk or muse in the garden. I had one of Ivor Kern's snoops spend a night at the hotel and borrow the key. He took an impression of it and had two duplicates made. This is one of them."

Taking a key from his pocket, he took a glance round, then unlocked a gate in the iron railings. We entered the garden, where the lawns, flower beds, shrubberies, and paved paths were dimly discernible in the starlight.

"Ivor Kern's snoop reported," Raffles said, "that there's a social function going on at that hotel tonight. It's a gathering of Headmasters of some of our most distinguished schools. The learned gentlemen are up from the country, with their families, for a conference and beanfeast. Our own appointment is at the sixth seat on the path from the gate that faces the hotel. Yes, I see the seat. Nobody there—as yet. Come on!"

We walked along to the seat in question. A heavy, park-type seat with curlicued iron arms, it was overhung by the branches of a tree that grew behind it. We took up a position in the black shadow of the tree. Raffles told me to tie my handkerchief triangularly over my face. Similarly masking himself, he took something from the pocket of his evening cape.

"Here, Bunny," he said, "is a coil of window-sash cord—of a length suitable for tying persons to seats. When you see me apply the sugar-poultice gag, you yourself make prompt use of the coil of cord. Is that quite clear?"

"Perfectly," I assured him.

The surge of the pulse in my ears mingled with the

melodies issuing from the hotel ballroom. Now and then, footsteps and voices sounded as pedestrians passed by outside the railings. An occasional cab rumbled by, the horse's hoof-beats sounding hollow.

Suddenly, I felt Raffles's grip on my arm.

"At last, Bunny!" he whispered. "There's a cab pulling up outside the north gate. Yes, the cab's dropping a fare—and jingling off again. Listen!"

My breath held, I heard a metallic clang.

"This'll be our man," Raffles murmured. "He possesses the other key I had made for this garden. He's come in, clanged the gate shut behind him."

Footsteps sounded, approaching. Shadowy in the star-glimmer, a tall figure, top-hatted, was coming along the path.

"Sixth seat from the north gate," I heard the newcomer mutter, as he drew closer. "This'll be it."

He stopped in front of the seat. I made ready with the cord. The newcomer was scarcely a couple of strides from us. His starched shirt front gleamed faintly. The lilt of the violins continued from the hotel. He stood looking toward it, and I could make out his profile—the classical profile of Lord Anthony Dauntsey, the witless worldling who aped the pranks and poses of the great·Regency dandies. He took a cigarette-case from his pocket. Tapping a cigarette fastidiously on the case, he sat down on the seat, his back to us.

Raffles, the deceptive silk stocking held dacoit-wise in his hands, moved a pace forward. Light as his step was, a twig cracked under his foot—and Dauntsey, startled, half turned his head.

"Who's there?" he said sharply.

"Beau Brummell," said Raffles—and looped the silk stocking swiftly over Dauntsey's head.

While Raffles secured the gag over the dandy's mouth, I grabbed his hands, pulled them behind him, secured his wrists with the cord. I gave the cord a couple of turns over the back rail of the seat, then dropped on my knees and, reaching under the seat, seized his ankles. Pulling them back, I looped the cord firmly around them, then tied the end of the cord to his bound wrists, thus effectively trussing him.

Raffles, who meanwhile had been exploring Dauntsey's pockets, tested my cord work, found it satisfactory, gave me a nod of approval. We walked away and, removing our handkerchief-masks, left Russell Square garden, pursued only by the diminishing strains of the violin music.

"So far, so good, Bunny," said Raffles. "Dauntsey is now immobilized—glued to his seat, as it were. We know, by experiment, that it'll be approximately forty-five minutes before the perspiration resulting from his struggles to free himself melts the powdered sugar in his gag and enables him to shout for help."

The candle-lamps of a hansom hove in sight. Raffles hailed it, told the cabbie to take us to Piccadilly Circus.

"Forty-five minutes will be ample for our purpose," Raffles went on, as we jingled past the British Museum. "While you were securing Dauntsey to the seat, I put that fallacious wallet of his into his pocket, and at the same time relieved him of his key-ring. Among the keys on it will be, undoubtedly, his key to the street door of Prince Regent House, Jermyn Street, together with the key to his chambers on the second floor, and the key to whatever drawer, bureau, jewel-case or strongbox he keeps his collection of Regency signet rings in. So what remains to be done is so absurdly simple, Bunny, that we'll part at Piccadilly Circus and you can leave the rest to me."

This I was content to do. And I had a note from Raffles next day to tell me that the Regency ring collection was now safely in the hands of our "fence," Ivor Kern, and that he, Raffles, would be in touch with me again when Kern had negotiated the disposal of the collection.

To obtain top price on the clandestine market naturally took time, and autumn was drawing nigh before I received another note from Raffles. It was to tell me that he was giving a small party that evening—just a theatre-and-supper affair—and I was invited to join him at the Theatre Royal, Haymarket.

The social season was now in full swing, and when I reached the famous Haymarket theatre the gaslights of its pillared portico were shining out into the autumnal mist and many cabs and carriages were discharging a brilliant audience. For it was a first night. And I could not help smiling to myself as

I saw from the theatre bills that the play at which Raffles had chosen to entertain his party was a revival, by the celebrated Bancrofts, of Farquhar's classic comedy, *The Beaux' Stratagem*.

In the foyer, thronged with arriving parties, I deposited my outdoor things with the *vestiaire* and looked around for Raffles. Not seeing him, I consulted a white-gloved, liveried usher.

"Are you, Mr. Manders?" he asked. "Very good, sir. Mr. Raffles left word about you. Follow me, please."

He led me, by way of carpeted staircases and corridors, to a box—and as he opened the door for me, music and the hum of voices swelled loud from the lighted auditorium.

"Ah, there you are, Bunny!" said Raffles.

In the box with him were another man in evening-dress— Johnnie Jessop, the young Philadelphian boxer, with a strip of sticking-plaster over his right eyebrow—and two ladies, who sat toying with their programmes and opera-glasses.

One of the ladies, white-haired, was of tall and majestic bearing; the other was young, of radiant beauty, gowned with exquisite taste. Raffles introduced me first to the senior lady.

"Mrs. Constance Benstead," he said. "Mrs. Benstead has long been a friend of mine."

"I've known Mr. Raffles," Mrs. Benstead told me, "ever since I was touring—some years ago now—with Mr. Henry Irving in his production of *The Lyons Mail*. We played the Prince's Theatre, Portsmouth, and dear Mr. Irving took some of us in the cast to a cricket match in which Mr. Raffles was batting for the M.C.C. against the Royal Navy."

"How many valued friends," Raffles said, "I owe to cricket! These days, Bunny, Mrs. Benstead is London's foremost coach in elocution, etiquette, and comportment. And now, my dear chap, let me present you to Miss Elsie Wiggins."

"How *do* you do, Mr. Manders?" said Elsie graciously. "Mr. Raffles tells me that you know my father."

"Yes, indeed," I managed to mumble as, stunned by the transformation in her, I bowed over her hand, white-gloved to the elbow.

"And of course, Bunny," Raffles said, "Mr. Johnnie Jessop, of Philadelphia, you met during that ugly fracas in

Richmond Park."

"It was lucky for me you gentlemen came along," said the young boxer.

"Last night, Bunny," Raffles said, "Johnnie, if I may call him so, knocked out Alf Burkitt of Bermondsey in the eighth round at Hoxton Baths—so this little party is by way of celebration."

"It was a lovely fight," said Elsie, "—though mind you, Mr. Jessop, when Alf Burkitt opened that cut over your eye, I thought you were a goner."

"So I would have been, Miss Wiggins," said the young Philadelphian, "if I hadn't had your Dad in my corner. He's a wonder with the styptic. He patched me up just great."

"I wish I'd seen the fight," I said, looking reproachfully at Raffles.

"Bunny," he said, with obvious remorse, "I clean forgot to tell you about it. I'm so sorry."

"Dad's gone off with Mr. Jessop's trainer to some music hall," Elsie told me. "They don't go much on high-class theatre plays, them two."

I saw Mrs. Benstead wince, murmuring, "*Those* two, Elsie"—a correction which Elsie took in good part. In fact, she gave the old actress a grateful look. I sensed a *rapport* between them, and it seemed to me almost to beggar belief that this poised young woman with the beautiful auburn hair was indeed the down-at-heel flower girl who had stooped to scrabble vainly at a wallet glued to the pavement by the Joker of Jermyn Street.

"A Bancroft first night," remarked Mrs. Benstead, scrutinizing the auditorium through her ivory-handled opera-glasses, "is always a great theatrical occasion, Elsie. I see many eminent persons taking their seats down there in the stalls. The gentleman with the strikingly bald head in the fourth row is Mr. Arthur Wing Pinero, the playwright. That lovely lady just taking her seat is Lady Randolph Churchill, and the distinguished gentleman escorting her is the famous Mr. Frewen, an English aristocrat popular in Wyoming, where he founded the Powder River Cattle Company and is known as the Boss of Outfit Seventy-six. And the gentleman scribbling a note on his shirt-cuff is the gifted theatrical critic, Mr. Clement

Scott, a darling man—he wrote most perceptively of my performance in the role of Portia.''

"He's not at all stuck-up," Elsie agreed. "He always slipped me a tanner when he saw me standing outside theatres with my basket."

"Well, that won't happen again, Elsie dear," said Mrs. Benstead, "now that Mr. Raffles is making other arrangements for you. Ah, I see that Mr. Bram Stoker, the 'vampire' man, is here. I knew him well when he was business manager of dear Mr. Irving's number one touring company. Mr. Stoker's Irish, you know, and the red-bearded gentleman he's talking to is another Irishman—the rather radical dramatic critic of *The Saturday Review*."

"I've seen *him* before, too," said Elsie.

The lights began to dim. The music from the orchestra pit, and the hum of cultured conversation in the auditorium, died away. Smoothly, the curtain swept up to reveal the elegant stage set of *The Beaux' Stratagem*.

Raffles had insisted that Johnnie Jessop sit between the two ladies, at the front of the box. Raffles and I sat behind them, on gilt-backed, plush-seated chairs—and now, in the darkness, Raffles asked me in a whisper if I had been pleasantly surprised by the transformation of Elsie since he had persuaded her to accept a little tutelage from Mrs. Constance Benstead.

"I was dumbfounded," I whispered back. "But, Raffles—what are these 'other arrangements' you've made for Elsie?"

He explained to me, in a whisper, that Lord Anthony Dauntsey's collection of Regency signet rings had fetched a good price.

"I've invested half of it," Raffles murmured to me. "I've acquired the lease on a small shop premises in Knightsbridge. Shh, now—pay attention to the play."

My mind seethed with questions. I found it hard to keep it on the play. But Elsie enjoyed it enormously, applauding with enthusiasm when the final curtain fell, and her brown eyes were sparkling as we collected our outdoor things from the *vestiaire* in the thronged lobby.

Jewelled bosoms and starched shirtfronts jostled around

us, and Elsie could not stop chattering as Raffles helped her on with her cloak, while Johnnie attended gallantly to Mrs. Benstead's evening mantle.

"Are you taking us somewhere else now, Mr. Raffles?" asked Elsie eagerly.

"Certainly," said Raffles. "We're going to Willis's Supper Rooms—when we can get through this crush and find a cab."

"In the meantime, sir," said a man who seemed to be making impatient efforts to reach the *vestiaire* counter, "would you have the goodness to let me pass?"

"Oh, *oh*!" Elsie exclaimed. "It's the gentleman with the red beard who told me gentlemen of the press pass free!"

"*I* told you that?" said the red-bearded man, a striking figure in evening -dress, his hair brushed up in two small horns from his lofty temples. "You must be mistaken, madam."

Elsie smiled mischievously. "You don't know me, do you?" she said—and, suddenly abandoning her new-found refinement, she demanded, "Wotcher mean, 'Gen'lemen o' the press pass free'? Not wiv me they don't. Them rosebuds is a tanner apiece an' it don't make no odds to me if you're gen'lemen o' the press or—"

" 'Gen'lemen o' the royal bleedin' bedchamber,' " said the critic. "Ah-hah, a hot Sunday in lower Piccadilly! I remember the incident perfectly. But—there's some mystery here—something seems to have happened to you—"

"This gentleman happened to me," said Elsie, delighted, indicating Raffles. "No more mooching around with a basket! I'm going to have a proper shop to run—a florist shop, high class, for the carriage tryde—trade. 'Elsie of Knightsbridge,' the shop's going to be called—if you should happen to be needing rosebuds some time."

" 'Elsie of Knightsbridge,' " the drama critic said slowly. "I shall remember that." He looked searchingly, with blue, vivacious eyes, at Elsie, then at Raffles, then back again at Elsie. They seemed to have made a marked impression on him. "Rest assured," he said, "—I shall indeed remember this remarkable meeting."

Excusing himself on the grounds that he had to write a

review of *The Beaux' Stratagem*, the red-bearded critic bowed and, looking deeply thoughtful, left us—and we made our way out to where the lamps of competing cabs glimmered in the mist.

It was very late when we left Willis's Supper Rooms. I gathered that Johnnie Jessop and his trainer were putting up for the night at the Wiggins home in Lambeth, so Elsie and Johnnie went off there in a hanson, while Raffles and I, in a four-wheeler, took Mrs. Constance Benstead to her flat in Earl's Court. She had indulged in a good deal of champagne and, as we took leave of her on her doorstep and got back into our cab, her rich voice rose in benevolent valediction.

"'Night's candles,'" she proclaimed, "'are burned out, and jocund day stands tiptoe—[*hic*]—on the rosy mountaintops—'"

Her resonant declamation died away as our cab jingled off in the dense mist.

"Well, Bunny," Raffles said, offering me a Sullivan from his cigarette-case, "that's that. When we made over the shop to Elsie's ownership, her revenge on Beau Dauntsey of Jermyn Street will be fully achieved—though, of course, she'll never realise it."

"A sweet revenge, nevertheless," I concurred. "But, Raffles—I haven't had an opportunity to ask you before, but how did you know that Dauntsey had an appointment in Russell Square that night?"

"Come into The Albany for a nightcap," said Raffles, "and I'll show you."

When we reached his chambers, he poured a couple of whisky-and-sodas, opened a drawer in his *escritoire*, handed me a small square of stiff, smooth paper.

"I retrieved this from Dauntsey's pocket," Raffles said, "at the same time as I relieved him of his key-ring. Read that message, Bunny."

He went into his other room, leaving me to read the words that were pencilled, in a large naïve handwriting, on the square of paper:

Sir,

Once, when my parents brought me to London, I saw you riding your horse in Hyde Park. How wonderful you looked! I have dreamed of you ever since!! I am in London again with my parents and have found out where you *live*!!!! We are staying at the hotel in Russell Square. My father is Headmaster of a famous school and is very strict. I cannot bear to go back to the mouldy old countryside without knowing you. Tonight at midnight I shall slip out and wait by the sixth seat from the north gate of Russell Square garden. I enclose a key to the garden!!!!—????

Your Unknown Admirer

Astounded, I turned the square of paper over. It was a photograph of a young woman of entrancing beauty, her eyes wide, candid, a rose held lightly to her deliciously smiling lips.

"Well, Bunny," said Raffles, returning, "could any gilded youth who fancies himself the heaven-sent heir of such Regency 'bucks' as Beau Brummell and Beau Nash resist that invitation?"

"Impossible!" I exclaimed.

"Exactly," said Raffles. "Actually, of course, that's a photograph I had made from one—a valued keepsake, Bunny—of which only eleven gentlemen of Philadelphia, Pennsylvania, and myself have copies. The copies are inscribed to us individually. But, naturally, neither the gentlemen of Philadelphia nor myself would dream of compromising a lady's *name*. That's not a thing one does, on either side of the Atlantic. So I explained to the photographer who rephotographed my keepsake that he must do so in such a way as to omit the personal inscription."

He handed me a much larger photograph in a silver frame. It was the same photograph, irresistible in its well-bred allure, and the inscription was written obliquely, in a sensitive feminine hand, across the lower right-hand corner of the photographic mount:

To my gallant host at Lord's Cricket Ground,
A. J. Raffles of the M.C.C.
Most Sincerely,
Lillie Langtry.

*

NOTE: Research into Mr. Manders's narrative, with a view to estimating its authenticity, reveals that, at the time of which Mr. Manders writes, the editor of the London literary weekly, *The Saturday Review*, was indeed black-moustached, virile Mr. Frank Harris, whose autobiography, *My Life and Loves*, later created excitement in erotic circles.

The music and drama critic of *The Saturday Review*, during much of Mr. Harris's editorial regime, turns out (from research) to have been Mr. George Bernard Shaw, whose auburn beard was then becoming a familiar and respected feature of London theatrical life.

Due, however, to the belated discovery of Mr. Manders's narrative among his clandestine records of criminal experience, no sure inference can be drawn from his description of the conversation with Mr. Shaw in the foyer of the Haymarket theatre.

There would appear to be a reasonable possibility, of speculative interest to students of World Drama, that the encounter reported by Mr. Manders *may* perhaps have started a train of thought in Mr. Shaw's creative mind.

But the question, regrettably enough, must needs remain speculative, since it cannot be authoritatively confirmed, at this late date, that it was in fact upon A. J. Raffles and Elsie, the transformed flowerseller, that red-bearded Mr. Shaw subsequently based the characters of Professor Higgins and Eliza Doolittle in his famous play, *Pygmalion*, on which is founded the scintillating musical success of more recent times, *My Fair Lady*.